FALLEN BEAUTY

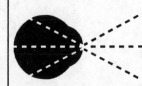

This Large Print Book carries the
Seal of Approval of N.A.V.H.

FALLEN BEAUTY

ERIKA ROBUCK

WHEELER PUBLISHING
A part of Gale, Cengage Learning

GALE
CENGAGE Learning·

Farmington Hills, Mich • San Francisco • New York • Waterville, Maine
Meriden, Conn • Mason, Ohio • Chicago

GALE
CENGAGE Learning

LIBRARY OF CONGRESS CATALOGING-IN-PUBLICATION DATA

Robuck, Erika.
    Fallen beauty / by Erika Robuck. — Large print edition.
      pages ; cm - (Wheeler publishing large print)
    Include bibiliographical references.
    ISBN 978-1-4104-7126-0 (hardcover) — ISBN 1-4104-7126-8 (hardcover)
    1. Millay, Edna St. Vincent, 1892–1950—Fiction. 2. Women poets—Fiction. 3. Female friendship—Fiction. 4. Women dressmakers—Fiction. 5. Unmarried mothers—Fiction. 6. Large type books. I. Title.
    PS3618.O338F35 2014b
    813'.6—dc23   2014014426

Published in 2014 by arrangement with NAL Signet, a member of Penguin Group (USA) LLC, a Penguin Random House Company

Printed in the United States of America
1 2 3 4 5 6 7 18 17 16 15 14

For Kelly McMullen

■ ■ ■ ■

PART ONE:
MARCH 1928

■ ■ ■ ■

FIRST FIG

My candle burns at both ends;
   It will not last the night;
But ah, my foes, and oh, my friends —
   It gives a lovely light!
                    — Edna St. Vincent Millay

ONE

LAURA

Our quick breath encircled our heads in the late-winter air as he pulled me by the hand, through lines of Model Ts and Cadillac Coupes, toward the glow of the Colonial Theatre. My body coursed with elation and guilt, every bit as intoxicating as the rum drinks he'd mixed for us out of the trunk of his car. The frenzy of the Jazz Age had overflowed from the cities into smaller towns like ours in music, film, fashion, and literature, resulting in restlessness and tension between generations and ideals. Fueled by the energy of the new, we had toasted our agreement: That night it was only us in the world, and we would live like it was ours.

He'd lifted a triple-stranded pearl necklace over my head and set it on my skin, kissing the scar on my collarbone, a relic from the first night we'd found each other. He whispered that the necklace was only costume jewelry, but one day he'd buy me the real thing.

As we hurried toward the theater, it occurred to me that time was made of moments like doorways one could never go back through to the way it was after crossing them. That night was a doorway, but I had no power to stop our passage. Distant church bells ignited my doubts like incense, however, and I dug my heels into the grass. When my love turned to see why I'd stopped, his profile stirred me — the sharp jawline, the fine sheen on his skin from his exertion, his pale blue eyes shining from the light of the theater. I often think of him that way, outlined in the lights, with the grin of the waxing crescent moon over us, leading me toward the most exhilarating night of my life.

"It's all right," he said. "We've come this far."

Cold air tickled my neck from my newly bobbed blond hair. I glanced down at my gold evening dress and touched the matching feathered headband I'd sewn in secret, night after night, hiding it from my father and even my sister, losing sleep because I knew they must not know. They wouldn't approve or understand, and my younger sister would have wanted to come. In the eighteen years since her birth, just a year after mine, I'd never kept anything from Marie, but that night I wanted something for myself, alone.

My love had motored us an hour north and east from our Hudson River Valley town of Chatham, New York, to Pittsfield, Massachusetts, to see the Ziegfeld Follies — a daring show featuring the most beautiful girls, talented dancers, and elaborate traveling production in the world. The famous Denishawn Dancers were fresh from the Orient, in company with their well-known leaders, Ruth St. Denis and Ted Shawn and the glamorous Marilyn Miller, preparing to dazzle the sold-out crowd. The car ride had been thrilling and terrifying — a reminder of the first night we'd officially met, when we'd traveled these roads but things had gone very wrong.

I allowed him to continue leading me toward the theater. Competing perfumes hung in the air over the line of theatergoers we joined that bordered the building. Street scalpers hid in the shadows behind the Colonial, trying to sell their tickets. I squeezed my love's hand and leaned into him, relishing the freedom to do so in public, away from the disapproving eyes of our town. He wrapped his arms around me and nuzzled my neck.

I noticed a woman of about thirty in a sagging gray dress and coat, wringing her hands and pacing in what looked like indecision. She stood near a scalper and flicked her gaze between the theater and the man before finally approaching him and offering him something from her threadbare clutch. He looked her up and down and rolled his eyes, shaking his head. I could see only the back of her, her unwashed hair in a flimsy bun, and the soles of her shoes so scuffed and worn, I imagined she could feel the chill of the ground reaching through them.

The scalper shooed her away, and when she turned toward me, she nearly broke my heart. She was crying — crying because she couldn't go in to see a show.

"Laura, why are you so troubled?"

The woman removed a crumpled handkerchief from her purse and wiped her nose.

"She doesn't have enough money to go in," I said, "and she looks as if her life depends upon it."

He followed my gaze and saw her. His eyebrows knitted together.

"Do you have any cash?" I asked. "I have two dollars. The tickets are five, though who knows how much he's charging for them?"

He hesitated a moment, but when he saw

the look in my eyes, he pulled a five from his wallet and said, "Let's give her a night like we've given ourselves."

He walked over to the man and bought the ticket, and brought it back to me. "You give it to her. You saw her. And I don't want her to think I'm some kind of chisel."

She had started to walk away, so I hurried after her. "Ma'am."

She turned, and looked with curiosity over my headband and dress peeking through my open coat. I could see her wondering what a ritzy gal like me wanted with the likes of her. I nearly told her that I was usually dressed as plainly as she, but I didn't want to insult her.

"I have an extra ticket, and noticed that you wanted to go in," I said. "Please take it."

She looked to the left and right and then back at me with a troubled expression, as if she thought I was trying to frame her. This was a woman unused to kindness.

"Please," I said, smiling to reassure her. "The doors are opening. We don't want to miss any of the show."

She hesitated a moment, and then took the ticket. "Thank you. May I give you what I have?" She held out a dollar bill.

"No," I said.

"Laura," he called.

"Enjoy," I said, and hurried to him. When I looked back at the woman, I could see her eyes glistening in the marquee lights.

As white spotlights rolled around the theater, the music of the fifty-piece orchestra began with the brassy majesty of a Hollywood production. I clenched my love's hand, dizzy with excitement and awe. The heavy red velvet curtain rose, revealing a long, curving staircase in front of a shimmering silver curtain. Three chandeliers lifted, and lights embedded in the arches over the fixtures and woven through the silver curtain twinkled in time to the music.

The procession of the famous Ziegfeld girls began down the stairs, women of extraordinary beauty and grace parading like swans in white-feathered headpieces and sequined bodysuits. I was astonished to see their long, bare legs, and covered my mouth while meeting my date's gaze. He smiled and squeezed me close to him before he turned back to face the stage.

They began singing the opening number, while a seemingly endless parade of male dancers crossed in front from either side, pairing up with the women as they reached the bottom of the staircase, and leading them to the four corners of the stage. I could barely stand to move my eyes off the performers, but I wanted to take in the audience around me. I scanned the boxes and rows, and found the woman from outside who almost hadn't made the show. She wore a look of ecstasy that moved me.

I returned my focus to the stage, not moving for the rest of the production. From birds to angels, gods and goddesses, I was transfixed by the transformations of the dancers. As the finale approached, Ruth St. Denis danced "The Gold and Black Saree" in a costume tinkling with gold charms and lined in fringe. Watching the way the lights caught the fabric as it clung to and flung away from her body in response to the movements, seeing this American girl transformed into an Indian woman, noting the near hypnosis of the audience, I knew that I wanted be a part of this world. This symphony of sound, light, fabric, and motion aroused a deep longing inside me.

When the show ended with a crescendo, the audience held its collective breath for a long moment, and finally erupted into an ovation. I gazed around at the eager, happy faces and spotted the woman from earlier. She appeared relaxed, exuberant, lit from within. I caught her eye and her smile warmed me. No matter what the critics said about the bare skin, exorbitant production costs, and provocative dances, the show had transformed her, as it had me, and I was glad to have seen it.

Silence filled the car on the drive home. We traveled along dark winding roads, watching the shiver of the breeze through the shadows of budding branches, feeling the melancholy of reality again burdening us. I removed my headband and ran my fingers over the silken feathers, wondering if I'd ever again get to wear such a beautiful costume. I realized it was the costume that had changed me to act in ways I normally would not. It gave me the courage to take the dare, to see the show, to disobey my father.

My mood was so low by the time we drew close to home that I insisted he take me to Bash Bish Falls. My father had led Marie and me there on frequent weekend hikes, but we would never have attempted such a dangerous climb in the dark. Recklessness still pumped through my body, and I wanted some truth to my excursion so I wouldn't betray myself to my father, and especially to Marie.

"Are you sure?" he said. "You're not too tired?"

I was tired — to my bones — but I couldn't stand the thought of the night ending and of no longer being with him, and having to pretend we didn't love each other.

"I'm sure."

The light from the moon did little to illuminate the deep shadows in the woods. I removed my high heels and slipped on loafers while keeping on the dress. The car crunched to a stop on the gravel, and we got out and started off on the path to the falls. A false spring had tricked us with early budding, until a cold snap sent us reeling back to winter. Frost encased the trees. My teeth chattered, but I stormed ahead, feeling the energy from earlier reassert itself.

"Laura, wait!" he called.

I lunged back and grabbed his hand, pulling him behind me on the path, feeling the wind in my hair, allowing a laugh to rise in my throat. I looked back at him, and his smile had returned.

The forest closed in over us, and it wasn't long before the rushing of the falls grew. He struggled to keep up with me as I ran forward. I slid to a stop in the clearing before the magnificent waterfall as a great slab of ice plummeted over the edge above us and crashed into the pools below. Frozen chunks sat like puzzle pieces on the banks, dislodged and crowded, bobbing in the river's thaw.

I strained to hear the sad ghosts' cries, but heard only the water. According to legend, an Indian woman had been sent over the falls in a canoe to her death for committing adultery, followed by her daughter years later by suicide because she could not have children. Their spirits were said to haunt the shallow pools of the falls, and because people had died by slipping on the rocks or diving into the shallows, many thought this place held a curse.

I felt no curse that night. I felt only my lover's arms around me as I fell into him. He grabbed my waist and pulled me close. Our passion, left smoldering by months of stealth and guilt, had finally ignited from our excursion of drinking, adventure, and abandon. I threw my arms around his neck and gave him my love without reserve. No caution or wariness held me back now. No one was around to judge me, and at that moment, I didn't care for the opinion of another soul in the world. I only knew that this night was a gift we had agreed to give to each other, and by God, we gave it — the fullest expression of our love. We joined ourselves forever in ways we hadn't taken time to consider or weigh. We knew only that we had to consummate our love, no matter what the cost.

VINCENT

Our guests' train arrives late, so we are already tight when they come. My husband, Eugen, holds up a torch he's made of hickory, parading the party up the walk and through the sleet. I carry the gin outside and make each of them take a healthy swig from the bottle before gaining entrance.

Elaine runs her hands up the sides of my costume, grazing my breasts before pulling me into her. She suddenly pushes away and says with fierceness, "How I've missed you."

I do not embrace her back, but instead, give her my cruelest smile. "Tonight, I am an houri, so I'm for the men. Not you."

She pouts, while Floyd, one of my old lovers, pushes around her and lifts me off the ground. I wrap my legs around him as he pretends to ravage my neck. I laugh and allow him to carry me into the house and to the parlor, where he drops me on the settee, and I drop the empty bottle of gin on the rug. He kisses me full on the mouth, and I feel him stir through the thin fabric of my dress.

"I must stay pure," I say, "if I'm to escort you to paradise."

19

He laughs with wickedness as the poet Elinor Wylie pulls him off me and exchanges her body for his between my legs. She nuzzles me and I feel *myself* stir.

"Surely you'll make an exception for me," she whispers.

I look into her eyes from inches away. I want to tell her that I'll always make an exception for her, but my demon returns. "Time shall tell."

Her face hardens and she stands, allowing me up from the couch. I adjust my headdress and climb onto the sofa so I can see all of them. The rest of the group comes singing and tumbling into the room, and once they are in, the small crowd gazes up at me. I know I am impressive in my costume, and I can feel the desire humming in the room as so many of my lovers, current and past, male and female, watch me, wanting to possess me.

Using the flaming bundle of hickory in a daring and dangerous fashion, Eugen, dressed as the Maharaja, lights sticks of incense we brought back from our Oriental travels, and then tosses the bundle into the fireplace. While my guests warm themselves, I jump down from the settee, approach my old lover Margot, and slip my arm through hers.

"Come," I say. "Let us fetch the costumes. Dressing *up* allows inhibitions to fall *down.*"

Margot smiles at me with downcast eyes, and I see a blush creeping up her neck. I reach up to stroke her skin with the back of my right hand, and feel Elinor's gaze fixed on us. I speak just loud enough for Elinor to hear.

"There is nothing as captivating as a woman who still knows how to blush," I say. "You are remembering that night at the Rotunde in Paris, when we were introduced and ended up spending the night with each other."

"How can I forget?" says Margot.

"Why would you want to?" I reply. I look sideways at Elinor and she turns away. Margot and I giggle as we run up the stairs to the trunks of Chinese trousers, Turkish silks, sarongs and slippers, and carry them back down as an offering to the party. My lovers remove their clothing and dance around the fire like devils, telling stories, acting parts, making love and mayhem, and rising to the most delightful level of intoxication, and when the night and our tightness begin to press on us with their weight, Floyd talks of the good old days in Greenwich Village when the war had ended, and we performed plays, and were poor and

21

young and free.

"I'll never forget the day we walked into Vincent's apartment," says Floyd, "and she and her sister Norma sat like two old ladies sewing while the most magnificent swear-words tumbled from their mouths from around the sides of the cigarettes they smoked."

"I had to teach her to curse out loud, and smoke, and walk around without a corset," I say. "It took two days of nonstop debauchery to break her. I was positively ill."

"Such a family," says Margot. "In Paris, Vinny's mother would sit in the corner — a true old lady, smoking and swearing — and watch us drink and fall all over one another without judgment."

"I love my dear mother," I say, "and it's been too long since I've seen her. Uge, we must visit her soon."

"Yes, love," says Eugen. "We shall as soon as the roads clear."

"Now we're so damned conventional," I say, killing the last of my gin and my good spirits. "I'm thirty-six years old. One day bleeds into the next. We are alone up here at Steepletop. Utterly."

"But our friends are here tonight," says Eugen, slurring his words in his thick Dutch accent. "And I'm going to bed because I'm appallingly drunk, so any of you may have your way with my wife."

The group protests his leaving, and Elinor pulls Eugen to her. "No, don't make this night end."

He kisses her on the lips, and she caresses his face.

"It has ended for me," he says, "but you all keep it alive. Don't let the old Maharajah spoil your fun."

He uncoils himself from Elinor's arms and stumbles up the stairs, leaving a subdued group in his wake. I am suddenly overcome with guilt for how long it has been since I've seen or written to my mother or my sisters. Our Greenwich Village and Paris remembrances have depressed me and make me long for that time again. The stark winter weather that refuses to leave us in our isolated mountain estate has seeped into me for so long that I don't know if I will ever again bloom.

And I am drunk — dreadfully inebriated and spewing nonsense and musings on the decline of man and my loss of hope in civilization since the execution of those Italian immigrants, Sacco and Vanzetti, framed for murders they did not commit.

The cry of a bobcat in the distance silences me, and I feel the terrible thrill of dangers lurking outside our doors, and inside too. The cat's cry sounds savage and predatory, and I wonder what she'll kill for herself tonight.

Elinor reaches for me with her elegant fingers and I slap them away and stand, caring not that I've offended her at every turn this evening, from my rejection of her physical advances, to my poetic arguments, to now. Why do I do this to her, when I would like nothing more than to take her upstairs with me? I don't know what evil chills my heart, but I know I have to go before I further poison the room.

As I am about to leave, I catch the eye of the ebony bust of Sappho in the corner, that ancient love poet whose black gaze reflects the light of the fire, and I feel a rekindling. My enchanting power has been stoked, reminded of itself in the company of these old lovers from Vassar, where fifteen years ago my power first pulsed within me. I inhale the energy to feed the dry well of words and love and beauty inside me, and remember that it is fresh, savage love that gives me power. I meet the gaze of the marble bust across the room, and implore her to return my strength after this bitter winter so I may complete this poetry collection whose construction continues to elude me. I'm nearly frantic to know if she'll grant my wish — if she'll lay a new love at my feet and allow me to burst forth again and reclaim the power that I am born to possess.

Two

LAURA

Our home was in a row of redbrick stores and houses that stood, tidy and straight, subject to the frequent blasts of diesel train engines roaring through the center of our small but busy town of Chatham, New York. The front of our house faced Main Street and held the dress shop my mother had started when we were small. My sister and I now worked there. The back looked over the gentle slope of field that ran down toward the forest and its hidden waterways. The curve of the hills lay like an invitation to my feet to race down to the woods, and I continued to heed its call, even though, at nineteen, I was well past the age for such adventures.

I'd waited until the morning of the show to tell Marie that I was going out with my secret love, and wouldn't get back until very late, refusing to tell her where we were going because her jealousy would stop her from helping me. I'd made up a story about hiking the falls along the Housatonic River by moonlight. She'd rolled her eyes and called me crazy because of the cold, but agreed to go along with my feigned illness.

By five o'clock, I had put on quite a show about my aching stomach for my father. Marie insinuated that *the curse* was the cause of my troubles, effectively silencing his questions. I had balled up bedding under my covers to fake my presence there, and waited until my father left with Marie to visit the drugstore soda fountain. Once they were safely away, I'd pulled out my secret bag and the old shoes I'd dyed to match my dress, crept out the back door, and hurried through the field to the forest to meet my love. He had come to me with a flurry of kisses, and drove while I dressed. When I'd emerged from the back of his car at the restaurant near the theater, utterly transformed into a gilded flapper, his face had given me all the approval I'd hoped for.

When I returned home, I used the key to unlock the low doors that led to the cellar around the back of the house, and hid the bag with my dress, shoes, headband, and necklace on the top stair. I would conceal the bundle better in the daylight after my father left the house. For now, I just wanted to crawl into bed to think of all that had happened to me that night. I felt dizzy with love and promise, and I couldn't wait to tell Marie about my dreams of costuming.

I would tell her that he'd surprised me with the tickets, which wasn't entirely untrue. Then I would describe the lighting, the music, and the gorgeous forms of the supple dancers. Finally, I would conjure the image of the exquisite costumes, which enabled the dancers' transformations from nobility in a Baroque ballroom to goddesses in an ancient Oriental palace, to beguiling birds in a dazzling garden. I knew Marie would be as swept up as I was — we had spent endless nights reading aloud to each other from F. Scott Fitzgerald's stories, discussing his wife Zelda's wardrobe, reading about Follies productions in *The Saturday Evening Post.*

I did not yet plan on telling Marie about what had happened after the show. I still couldn't quite believe it, and felt such conflicting emotions that I didn't want known to anyone but myself and my lover. It thrilled me that we had finally given every piece of ourselves to each other, and I fully understood the depth of his love for me. But now that we had taken our passion so far, could we ever turn back, and would we want to? The height of our love seemed to make the circumstances of our separation even more painful.

Marie had left open the back door that led to the kitchen, just as I'd asked. One of the chairs was not pushed under the dining table, and as I thought of my love, I ran into it, cursing as I knocked my knee against its thick wooden legs. I stopped short and listened, swearing that I heard a noise. My heart raced and I began to sweat in spite of the chilled air. I stood there for what felt like hours, though it must have been only a minute or two, and then continued to the staircase.

In the black night, I had trouble finding my way. The only light in the house came from the last chunks of charred embers still smoldering in the fireplace. I was so cold from my walk down the road that I ventured to the fireplace to warm my hands. I shivered, but I thought that might have as much to do with the cold as with my shock over what had transpired earlier that night. It wasn't until I drew near the fire that I saw my father. He sat in the shadows, staring into the embers, with only the dying firelight illuminating his face. I sucked in my breath.

"I never thought I'd be waiting up for you

like this," he said, without looking at me. I felt sick, and thought that he must know what I'd done, the way one senses a change in the weather.

"I don't know who you're sneaking out to in the middle of the night," he continued, "and I don't understand why you cut off your hair, but you live in a small town. You are judged and I am judged by how you behave."

I noticed my parents' oval wedding picture on the mantel, and I shrunk further into myself when I met my mother's gaze. She looked out at me from her proud, unsmiling face, formal as a statue next to my handsome father. She had died in the flu epidemic of 1918, and my father had kept her memory alive by canonizing her with every story and utterance. He'd taken us to church every weekend since her death, despite having no faith himself. It was what she would have wanted.

"Your mother and I never quite fit in around here to begin with, being from out of town. If these people think I'm raising loose girls, no one will patronize the shop, and I won't get handyman work. I would hate to see you ruin your future."

I stared at the fire, wishing with all my heart that I could get as far from my father as possible. It destroyed me that he suspected what I'd been up to, that I might be jeopardizing my family's livelihood by carrying on as I had. How disappointed he would feel if he knew with whom I'd been earlier that night. The tears I'd been holding escaped, but I made no move to brush them away. I wished I could melt into the fire, but all I could do was stand paralyzed by fear and remorse.

"Go to bed," he said.

His firm words gave me the push I needed to start up the staircase. I paused on the bottom step and looked at him with guilt and sorrow in my eyes, but he would only stare into the fire. I climbed the stairs and went into my room.

When I opened the door, Marie stirred in her sleep and turned from her side to her back. Moonlight fell on her sleeping face, casing her like a bas relief on a tomb. I longed to crawl into bed with her like we had when we were children. Instead I climbed into my own bed, under the covers, and willed myself not to think of the possible consequences of this night. I thought of the Follies, and the dresses, and my love filling me with his passion, and making promises with his body, assuring me that we would find a way to be together in spite of the odds against us.

VINCENT

I offend my dear Elinor. My antics leave me cold in bed. I want to reclaim my position as goddess of all people and all words, but my plan has backfired, and I am ill from the alcohol and the wounds I inflict on those around me.

She calls my behavior pathological, and I fear that she is right.

Oh, sweet Elinor, how I wish I could redo the night. I wouldn't be cruel to you or insult your dear love of me or your poetry. I wouldn't argue with you so, or bother your husband while he mourned his dead mother, or bring up the barbaric slaying of those poor men Sacco and Vanzetti to cast a dark shadow over our revelries. I wouldn't torture my old lovers by playing them off one another like fools in a Shakespearean play. I would open my mother arms and bring you all into me to join our light instead of extinguishing each of you with my wet fingertips.

Don't you understand? My cruelty is always a bag of arrows meant for myself but misdirected. I do not deserve any of your love. I deserve to rot and age, like the crone I am becoming.

I hear a door close in the hallway and wonder if Eugen is up early. I wrap myself in my robe and creep downstairs. He has already arisen and sits at the fire, wearing his leather gloves and wrapped in a scarf. How I feel my love swell for him at this moment. How dear to me he is.

He hears me in the hall and turns to me as I stand in the doorway, his face alight with kindness and no surprise to see me at the fireside so early. He knows my deviances yet he never, never judges me for them. He loves me in spite of them and never asks for a thing in return. He is the true immortal. I have no capacity for omnipotence, only a flesh-eating selfishness. I cross the room and crawl into his lap.

"The morning is cruel," he says.

"The cruelest," I reply. "Rejuvenation is saintly hogwash. We are all mortals, and the morning sits white and pure to remind us of our foulness. With the exception of you. You are my patron saint."

His eyes crinkle in the corners.

"Don't beat yourself, Vincie," he says, his voice still deep and thick with sleep and booze. "This little minute by the fire is who we really are, not all that big devilishness we pretend at in the night."

33

I burrow into his chest, and he rubs my hair.

"I hurt everyone I love, and I love everyone," I say.

"Why do you say that?"

"I've offended Elinor. She left on the train and took her hurt with her."

"She is just bruised," he says. "She will heal, and then she will be back, and the two of you can make beautiful love and words together."

I warm at the thought of his prophecy. "How did I ever get so lucky to find the man who understands and accepts me so completely?"

"How did I get so lucky to find the poet star with a universe of love big enough to enfold me and all the others in her pockets?"

"This poet star is flickering," I say. "I feel a darkness that I hope the coming spring will lighten. I must finish my poetry collection and begin anew. I feel as if I'm on the pulse of a new beginning, but I can't find the path to take the first step. April has always been kind to me. Or not kind, but provocative. Stirring. I'll put my faith in April."

"What you need is a new flash of experience. I hoped last night would inspire it, but I think you need something really new.

34

Brand-new."

Eugen, my manufacturer of experience. I know what he suggests. I need a new lover to consume me. Perhaps I will revisit my virgin days when I would burn a candle on the third night of every month, hoping to conjure my perfect love. With April marching in, it will be the perfect time for such a ritual. Then I will have to watch and wait to see who will be laid as an offering at my temple.

I can imagine the candle's light growing in the fire, and I feel a thrill beginning inside me. I know someone new will come, and I can barely contain my excitement at all that lover will bring.

THREE

LAURA

My father's behavior toward me was stiff and formal over the next couple of weeks. I avoided him as much as possible, and spent my free time at the library, sitting in the kaleidoscope of color filtering through the Tiffany stained-glass window, poring over reference books on costuming, and soliciting the help of Mrs. Eleanor Perth, the librarian, for schools of fashion design in the city. She produced a brochure from the New York School of Fine and Applied Arts with information on satellite and weekend classes, and I checked it out, along with a film costuming book.

"I can see the seed of something in you," said Mrs. Perth.

I started at her observation. Everything in me felt changed since that night, but did I look so different?

"Nothing to trouble about," she said, placing her hand on mine. "You just have a sparkle. You may keep that brochure, by the way. I'll send for more tomorrow when the Harlem line comes through."

Mrs. Perth had worked at the library as long as I could remember, though she didn't look as old as she must be. She had a mass of hair the color of cherrywood she kept in a loose chignon, and wore trim suits in bright colors. Marie and I agreed that she had the look of one who could at any moment let down her hair, throw off her jacket, and run off in a field of daisies.

Her husband worked as a farmhand at Steepletop, the seven-hundred-acre Berkshire estate in the nearby tiny village of Austerlitz, owned by the poet Edna St. Vincent Millay and her husband, Eugen Boissevain. Steepletop provided an endless source of mystery and speculation for our town. Some said it was a den of sin where bacchanalian parties raged for days. Others said the woman had gone mad and the place was like an asylum.

When Millay's visitors passed through Chatham, they stirred up the townspeople for days. New cars would arrive with strange passengers — men and women in clothing rich and fashionable enough to grace New York City society pages, or threadbare enough to come from peasants' closets. Their backseats would be piled high with illegal booze, or if Eugen came to meet them at the train, they'd raid the corner store for victuals, leaving empty shelves and a wake of laughter and smoky, disturbed air.

Their familiarity with one another never failed to shock the onlookers — men in full embrace, women kissing on the lips, all the time in a tumble of limbs, curled hair, and coats draped over one another's shoulders. Motion and energy were what united these strange gatherings. It was explosive and seemed to stir the town into a frenzy of secret envy and curiosity.

It was rumored that Mrs. Perth had attended poetry readings at the estate, and she was vague enough about her visits to stoke the flames of the town gossips. She seemed to enjoy what some would consider her double life, that of a steady librarian who sometimes escaped her confines to live loose. I knew I envied her for it.

I leaned over the counter and said: "We must keep this a secret. I'm just exploring ideas for the future. I haven't made any decisions."

"A girl has got to dream," she said, and pretended to lock her lips.

I left her with a wave, and started for

home, noting the train whistle. So many trains came and went each day through Chatham that the whistles were as common as the sound of wind in the trees or the rushing waters of the Stony Kill. I'd often watch the Pullman cars destined for New York City and wonder what it would be like to hop on board, like the wealthy residents in town, and catch a Broadway show. My father feared the trains. With so many switches in Chatham, there was a long history of railway accidents. As a result, Marie and I had never ridden a train. I suspected, however, my father was more afraid of losing us to the world beyond Chatham than to a derailment.

When I stepped onto the sidewalk, I saw the town priest, Father Ash, on the other side of the road, walking parallel to me, holding his journal tightly with both hands. He carried that book with him everywhere, and could often be seen stopping at a bench to scribble notes to himself. He even carried it with him to the podium on Sundays, and referenced it during his homilies. Judging by the depth and immediacy of his talks, one could surmise he was forever preparing, watching those around him, helping us to make meaning of our small lives in poignant ways. He saw me, and looked at me twice before dropping his gaze to my arms and the books I carried.

How strange we must have appeared, each of us moving in the same direction, but separated by a local street and a universe of experience. Each of us holding books with great personal meaning, but on my face, a dreamy expression, and on his, one of intense concentration. His dark hair and black clothes contrasted with my fair hair and pink dress.

As we turned on Main Street, he slowed his step as Agnes Dwyer and her daughter, Darcy, walked toward him. Could it be that he didn't want to speak with them? The church and community respected Agnes and Darcy, who had married a doctor from the hospital, Daniel Dempsey. In many ways, our small society revolved around them.

I wasn't interested in polite conversations while undergoing their silent scrutiny, so I quickened my step and pretended to take great interest in the facades of the houses and storefronts I'd passed thousands of times. The buildings stood in an orderly line of Colonial dwellings with stately chimneys, leaded glass, and flags announcing patriotism, loyalty, and dedication. I inhaled the sweet aroma drifting from the Candy

Kitchen, waved to the firemen outside the station, and waited for a train to pass before I finally arrived home, deposited my acquisitions under my bed, and returned to the store downstairs.

My father had left a note that he was delivering firewood to his friend, the oculist Dr. John Hagerty, and I wondered where Marie had gone. I grew impatient to talk to her, but she was forever in and out of the shop, meeting her new beau, Everette Clark, and talking incessantly about him when she wasn't with him. Everette had moved to Chatham in his teenage years, but was five years older than we were, so we hadn't known him well while growing up. He now served on the town council, and had higher political aspirations, according to Marie, who had no doubt he could be president someday.

The day passed slowly, with only a few new orders — a set of window valances, a new church dress, some mending. My father came and went on errands and handyman jobs. I kept imagining someone new and interesting would come through the door with a unique order, but was only greeted with the usual townspeople. Just as I was about to turn the sign to CLOSED, however, Darcy walked in without her mother.

Her visit was inevitable, I supposed, but I had been dreading it. Agnes had recently commissioned a christening gown for her first grandchild, but the gown would not be needed. By all accounts, Darcy had had a miscarriage, her second. Marie had heard the churchwomen whispering about it at the last bake sale, and reported it to me at once. I couldn't help but flick my gaze to Darcy's stomach, but looked away and mentally chastised myself. She stood stiff as an oak.

"I've come for the order my mother placed." Her voice was icy, and held a challenge. It almost sounded as if she dared me to ask why she still needed it. Her strength in coming to pick it up impressed me. I had planned on eating the cost and putting the little ivory dress away for a future customer. Darcy did not usually evoke my pity, but as someone who had succeeded at everything she'd ever set out to do in life, she must have found her failed pregnancies particularly hard to bear.

"Certainly," I said, hurrying to the storage closet to get the gown.

I brought the small box to the counter and placed it in front of her.

"No charge," I said, quietly.

Something flickered in Darcy's eyes, but then she narrowed them to slits, and her cheeks blazed red. I suddenly felt terrible for acknowledging something I should not have known.

She stared at me until I had to look down, and she reached into her pocketbook. Darcy slammed a five-dollar bill on the counter, picked up the box, and stormed out of the shop, passing Marie on her way in.

"Hello, Darcy," Marie said. She met no response and widened her eyes when the door closed.

"She wanted the christening gown," I said. "I told her there was no charge. It must have made her angry."

"Oh," said Marie. "I don't imagine Darcy wants anyone's pity, though she deserves it. A sad thing to lose a baby."

We watched Darcy as she hurried out of view, and then Marie turned back to me, her face transformed with delight.

"What is it?" I asked.

"I think he wants to marry me!"

I passed the rest of the evening listening to Marie's speculations about why Everette had winked at her when he said he'd be spending the weekend in New York City. I tried to caution her: They hadn't been dating long, and shouldn't rush into anything, but my words fell on deaf ears and made me feel guilty because I knew they came more from the dark jealousy inside me than from my concern for Marie, though that was abundant.

Everette was a politician. His manners and dress were impeccable, his words always perfect but his sincerity somewhat lacking, his handshake too firm. I personally never trusted a man who took that much care with his hair, but Marie had laughed that off as nonsense. I might have sounded silly, but I didn't like the importance he placed on appearances. I could imagine it would be hard to be married to a man like that. But Marie wouldn't hear a dark word against him, so I had stopped uttering them. She had made up her mind, and I would have to accept it.

That night while I finished washing dinner dishes with Marie, my father sat on the front porch smoking his pipe. He came inside and went up to bed earlier than usual, and Marie and I exchanged troubled glances.

"He's really holding on to this grudge," she said.

"I've apologized and haven't been out of his sight since that night. I don't get the impression he wants to talk any more about it, and I wouldn't know what to say even if he did."

"Just give it time," said Marie. "He's upset

because he sees we're growing up, and eventually, he'll be alone. It's a hard thing to have to face."

My thoughts returned to the design school brochures. Marie chattered along as we cleaned our way upstairs and I daydreamed about the Follies. When she finally went to bed and fell asleep, I crept downstairs, lit a candle, and completed the application for the school. My fantasies had included Marie coming with me, but now it seemed that I'd be alone. All of the flutters of excitement I'd felt about my idea became anxiety. I told myself that was normal, and slipped the envelope into my purse to post the next day.

The rest of the week passed slowly and with unease, and even the flurry of graduation dress orders didn't lift my spirits. My father's behavior was still cool; Marie was either gone or preoccupied with Everette. I longed to reach out to my lover, but counseled myself that if he wanted to see me, he'd find a way. Every hour that he did not increased my hurt.

When Sunday arrived, something in my father seemed to shift. After church, he surprised me by looking up over the top of his copy of *National Geographic* and announcing that he wanted to hike Bash Bish

Falls before the big thaw.

"John Hagerty plans on motoring to the area with his wife for a luncheon with his family," said my father. "He said they could give us a lift up and back."

"We should probably wait until after the thaw," I said. "It's dangerous up there, especially this time of year with all of that half-melted ice." Never mind that I would be able to think only of what I'd done there, and the idea of visiting that spot with my father made me ill.

"It will be good for all of us," he continued, never taking his eyes off me. "We should get out for some fresh air."

"I don't want to go," said Marie.

"Why not?"

"Because Everette wants to take me to a picture at the Crandell Theater. *The High School Hero* with Nick Stuart and gorgeous Sally Phipps is playing, and I'd like to say yes. If it's all right with you, that is." She widened her eyes like those of a Kewpie doll.

At the mention of Everette, I stiffened. Marie had no idea what it was like to have to hide love, the way it cast a shadow over every moment of the day, the way one wore its absence like grief. One sometimes forgot, but then would suddenly remember, and the pain and anger would return.

"That's fine," my father said. "I appreciate your asking my permission."

He turned on me a steely gaze that made me want to crawl under the table. Why did he have to torture me? I'd rarely disobeyed him before the night of the Follies, whereas Marie had gone her own way countless times. It wasn't fair that one indiscretion brought my father's anger upon me so harshly.

"We have all of those graduation dresses to make," I said. "We'll never get them done if we don't work through Sunday."

"I'll work later into the night," Marie said.

"Don't give her trouble, Laura," he said.

Marie stood, dropped her sewing on her chair, and climbed the stairs to primp before her date. My father walked to the closet and pulled out his hiking boots, his thick coat and hat, and his walking stick. He tied his snowshoes with a leather strap and flung them over his shoulder. I stood and walked to the kitchen to pack a lunch for him, muttering my frustrations under my breath. When I returned to the front of the shop, Marie had already left to meet Everette. I was glad I didn't have to see her fawn over him, or the way they could waltz out the front door to Main Street, holding hands.

I held out the pouch to my father, and he fastened it to his belt under his jacket.

"There's cold ham and cheese, and carrots," I said, not meeting his eyes.

"Laura," he said, lifting my chin, "I'm harder on you because you're better than your behavior that night."

I looked up at him and felt like crying.

"I think of your mother," he said. "I worry that I'm not doing right by you girls."

I found my voice. "You are."

"I try," he said. "But it's hard."

My father's forehead creased, and I could see his pain and discomfort over being at odds with me. It made me wish I could tell him about my love and get his advice, but that could not be so. He left me with a hug and a wave out of the side of Dr. Hagerty's Ford.

I wish I had begged him not to go. I wish I had apologized for ever sneaking out and placing that rift between us.

That afternoon an unstable rock at the top of the falls sat waiting for him. It crumbled under his weight and sent him plunging sixty feet.

VINCENT

The buck's hot blood seeps into the snow. One moment there exists life; the next, by my gun, there is none. When I look up, the doe in the brush stares me through, and seems unafraid and even a bit triumphant, before she turns her tail to me and bounds off through the woods.

The cold wind of early April and a winter that has overstayed its welcome sting my cheeks. Against the gray-and-white landscape, the only color comes from the dead thing bleeding at my feet, and from my skin and my red hair. I understand, though, the changing of the seasons. I hear it dripping all around me in the thaw. I feel the raw energy of the world stirring beneath the nearly naked trees, and it seems to me that once this deer blood melts the snow beneath it and makes contact with the yellow grass below, it will give new life to the earth.

Try as I might, however, I cannot resurrect the joy of my youth. My last thread of hope in man was executed with those Italian immigrants, peaceful anarchists framed for murder and murdered for it. I wore down my shoes walking the lines, protesting the injustice of our judicial system. I lost sleep, went to jail, and begged politicians for mercy for them, but I was only met with the stony silence of men hardened by power and so-called principles.

Everything reminds me of the execution of those men and the futility of my marching, but instead of encouraging my inner softness, I've become savage. Dark, murderous thoughts blacken my vision and incite incessant headaches, and only the swift violence of hunting, writing, drinking, and copulation gives me escape.

I hear the crunch of Eugen's boots through the shallow snow behind me. "Vincie, you are a natural killer," he says with joviality.

I pass my gun to Eugen in silence. Words are finding one another in my head, and I don't want to scare them off. I know he'll understand. He'll see the fever in my cheeks, the flush of the poetic energy coursing through my nerves, and leave me alone where I can feed off this meat.

My writing shanty seems frozen in the landscape like a jagged shard of ice. Without a stove to heat it, without a morsel of food, it is truly barren and empty, like a hollowed womb, but I will fill it with my words.

I pull a fag out of my pocket and light it with a match. With each inhalation I feel a growing contentment such as I haven't felt in weeks slide over me like hot spring water. This absence of electricity and plumbing, decoration and paint is pure. Fresh paper, simple writing instruments, and holy silence give me freedom to create. Nestled on a small hill, accessed by a crude stone path, framed in trees and grasses, this shanty is my church. It is where I fulfill my vocation. Today's hunt was my sacrifice at the altar, and some goddess was pleased because the words come faster than I can write — insistent, frantic, building in intensity, making my heart pound.

Though I tremble from the cold, I work without ceasing, filling the ashtray to overflowing, losing the light as the hours pass, shaping and working poetry of hunting, of execution, of death without hope, of mortal anguish. I feed on the words and stop only when I run out of cigarettes.

When I close the notebook, I feel the assertion of my physical hungers and rise to go, knocking the table and spilling ashes. I don't stop to clean them. Instead, I pick up my notebook and swing open the door, allowing in a gust of cleansing wind, and start back to the house to find Eugen so he can fill me with another kind of fire.

When I find him in his study that night, I attack him with a new fierceness, and he

51

responds. Fingers in flesh, kisses so deep they nearly smother, raw appetites fed over and over again. When I climb on him for a third time, he closes his eyes and shakes his head back and forth. "Edna, you will kill me. I . . . I can't anymore."

I cover his mouth with my hand and make his body do what he didn't think it could until I am satiated. He is exhausted, so I help him off the rug by the fire and into his bed, where I cover him. He falls asleep before I close his door, and I take a moment to stare at him. The moonlight gives an unearthly glow to the room and Eugen's face, and a chill rises on my arms when I realize he looks like a dead man.

A sudden terror closes like a fist around my heart. What if I do kill him? What if I give him a heart attack? He is so much older than me, and here I am, pushing him beyond what he wishes. Who will take care of me if he dies? How will I live?

I place my own hand over my heart and stagger back to my room. My skin still holds the heat of our lovemaking and of my creation, and I throw open the window to bring in the cold. I stare out into the night with wide eyes, fearful of the darkness and of what ghosts travel at this hour. The moonlight is surely playing tricks on me, but I swear I see the dead walking, slipping in and out among the trees, circling the house.

A movement at the forest's edge catches my eye, and I see a deer emerge, a doe. She walks straight toward the house and stops in the yard beneath my window. I feel the moonlight on my face, and clutch the windowsill, the cold of it chilling my hands, and wonder if she is the doe I saw earlier, whose mate I killed. She looks up and sees me, her large black eye expressionless, haunting, piercing my heart like an arrow.

FOUR

LAURA

Marie and I sat at the hospital, flanking our father like reluctant apostles, gutted that he lay so broken between us, with no real hope of recovering. The fall had shattered his spine and nearly every other bone in his body, rendering him paralyzed from the chest down.

When my father hadn't shown up to meet the Hagertys, John had taken the trail to the falls and found my father where he lay in the shallows. He'd carried my father to the car, where his wife sat helplessly watching, and rushed him to the hospital. My father had lost consciousness and, when he did wake, rambled and cried until he exhausted himself to sleep.

John Hagerty told Marie and me about the accident. His usual calm had been shaken, compassion dripped from his words, and he made incoherent references to the curse of the falls as we sobbed and held each other. My horror had quickly turned to guilt. If I hadn't gone out, I wouldn't have disappointed my father. We would have hiked together. I could have been there to talk him out of the climb to the top, the ascent he'd always wanted to make but never had for the safety of us girls. Without us there, Father had been reckless and now he had paid the price.

Marie fingered the oval diamond ring on her finger, its facets catching the light and sprinkling over the walls. Everette had met with my father to ask his permission weeks before, and had been on his knee proposing as my father fell. Now Marie's engagement would be forever tinged by what had happened that day.

I squeezed my father's cold, limp hand, rubbing warmth into it, willing feeling back into him. His palm still had calluses from chopping wood, and I wondered if he'd ever raise his ax again. I moved to the foot of his bed and massaged his calves and feet through the blanket, imagining the slow atrophy of these fit, muscular legs, wondering if they'd ever lead him one foot in front of the other to walk again, let alone hike, his greatest passion.

"Why do you bother?" said Marie, her

voice low and empty. Since receiving the news, Marie had seemed to collapse into herself. She felt we'd suffered enough with the loss of our mother, and it wasn't fair for this to happen. I agreed, but I could only feel anger at myself. My guilt was never far, and I wondered if Marie blamed me the way I did myself. I didn't have the courage to voice my fears.

"I have to do something. I can't just sit here."

"He's broken, Laura. He can't be fixed."

"He's not a bird I can watch die outside the window." I felt my voice catch but I did not want to cry here, where unfamiliar nurses and doctors and strangers came and went all day. I didn't want my father to feel my anguish, so I steadied myself and continued rubbing his legs.

"You're driving me mad with all your motion," she said, standing and crossing the room to look out the window. "I hate this place. After this, I never want to step into a hospital again."

For us, the hospital marked the terrible times in our lives: my mother's early death, the car accident Marie and I had suffered, and now our father's fall. I shivered at the thought, and almost spoke of it when Nurse Lily Miller, Agnes Dwyer's sister, stepped into the room. Nurse Miller was in her early fifties and childless and, like her sister, widowed at a young age. Lily had tended to my mother before her death, and had always been kind to my sister and me. I could see that my father's condition affected her by the sympathy in her eyes.

Marie returned to the bedside, where Nurse Miller took measurements, administered needles, and checked pulses, and I took my place at the window. Birds twittered and cheeped from the bush outside until one of them flew toward the tree above, followed by the others in her wake. The tree shivered as the bird slipped through its curtain of new leaves.

Marie spoke. "Will he ever get better?"

I felt the heavy pause, as if Nurse Miller didn't want to answer the question. When she spoke, I almost couldn't hear her.

"It is unlikely. Spinal cord injuries are very difficult to rehabilitate."

She spoke what we knew in our hearts. I turned to my father, and was grateful he wasn't conscious to hear his sentence.

"Of course, your father will have the very best care we can offer. He has been such an asset to the town. All of you are."

Her words moved me. We owned a simple dress shop, where my sister and I had taken over the work of my mother. My father kept the books, fixed broken things, hauled wood, shoveled snow. I turned to thank Lily, but she had gone.

"I need to go home," said Marie. She picked up her coat and hat from the chair by the door and put them on. "Are you coming?"

I shook my head.

"Aren't you hungry?"

"No," I said. "I can't eat. I don't feel well."

"I hope you're not getting sick," she said. "You need to rest. You've been at his bedside for weeks. You look terrible."

I knew I looked awful. I hadn't been outside or to the stream, and my skin had paled from lack of sun and wind. As my father had lain in the bed, springtime had arrived, my favorite time of year. I'd nearly forgotten the shop, and I'd need to tend to it, especially since Father could no longer earn money for us.

As for my lover, I'd avoided him as much as possible. I wondered if he'd left me any letters in our secret place, if he ached to hold me as much as I wanted him to. His skill at acting unattached to me while in the presence of others was so convincing, it was unsettling, though I knew it had to be. Any warm thoughts of our night together were swept away by the rush of guilt I felt about every aspect of our relationship, now forever connected with my damaged father.

"I'll leave food for you and finish our orders," said Marie. She kissed me on the cheek and left.

The church bell tolled the half hour. I knew Father Ash would be hearing confessions soon, and I felt I must unburden myself. Perhaps if I sought atonement, I could start over. I knew it was childish to think so, but maybe if I did, my father would get better. As I moved to get my coat, I glanced at my father and was startled to see his eyes open and clear.

VINCENT

I will myself not to cry. I must save my tears to fuel my turbulent anger, not reduce me in sadness, but I have difficulty controlling my emotions at Arthur Ficke's bedside, at the farm he has purchased just miles from Steepletop. He is no longer my Arthur, as he is married to another, but he once was and always will be mine, at least a little bit. Even though we are both married to others, the rope that binds us will hold fast forever, especially now that he is so close.

I think of Arthur often as the young, handsome soldier to whom Floyd Dell introduced me in Greenwich Village all those years ago; who sat on the floor making up silly poems with me and my sister; who made such perfect love to me; whom I almost married but allowed a zephyr to part us and make it so it could not be, though we remained close. So close, in fact, that I now sit here at his bedside while his wife makes soup in the kitchen of his half-fixed house, and we try to distract him from his tuberculosis flare-up, to fight the inflamed infection threatening to destroy his lungs and take his life.

This man before me is reduced, but not reduced. While his body betrays him, his mind and his passion are still as sharp as ever, and he is bitter, so bitter that his health confines him. It is the bitterness to which I will appeal. It will give him the anger to fight.

"Vincie," he says, between gasps, "did you write that poem for me? Did you? Please tell me; I must know if I'm to die."

I don't want to tell him that I did write for him, many times. I don't want to give him this power by admitting that I love him and he hurt me, but if he dies and he has made this one small request of me, perhaps I will regret not telling him. And what does it matter? He knows how he can destroy me with his judgment or stern looks. He knows that I will do anything to turn up the corners of his beautiful mouth.

Then there is another thought, a whisper in my ear in a voice like that of Sappho. If I don't use my words for truth, I will never get new words. I will not be able to write. Perhaps this holding back is what is keeping me from finishing my collection. Maybe if I confess everything to everyone the phrases will breathe, and will give new life to my work. I hesitate no longer.

"Yes, Arthur. You know I wrote for you, my love. You know it without me having to say it."

He begins to weep. No, this is not what I want. The weeping makes him cough harder. Why is he destroyed? I thought admitting it would build and strengthen him, and also me, but naming our mutual regret has given it life and weight instead of freeing it.

I clutch his shoulders and kiss his neck with passion, burying my face in him. He kisses me on the head and runs his hands through my hair, which I've allowed to fall in copper rivers over his bare chest. Such intimacy. I wish we could be fully intimate right now. But I must stop these thoughts. He could be dying. And here, his wife enters, bringing the soup.

She pauses a moment in the doorway, her face a mask of dour frustration. She quickly rearranges it. She *wants* to be progressive, to allow this open love to go on before her where she thinks she may control it, but it kills her. She is not evolved enough to live as we do. Eugen would get aroused if he saw me splayed over this man in this way. Mrs. Ficke wilts. I choose to ignore her. I have no use for weakness in the face of my old love's pain.

"Why do you cry?" I ask, in hushed mother tones, wiping away his tears. I feel him stiffen. He does not want to hurt his wife, and all at once, I realize that if he knew that I wrote love poems for him many years ago, it might have changed something for him. He might never have married her. He might have taken my body, soul, and mind in some kind of spiritual or true matrimony, and he regrets the loss of what could have been our sacred years. I will not tell him that I wouldn't trade my time with Eugen for all the summers left in time. I will pretend I don't know Arthur's true heart.

A sharp wind blows in through the drafty window, and the candle at his bedside flickers, throwing shadows over his face, her face, the walls. I hear the drip of a leaky faucet in the bathroom, and here, inside the brown walls, in this dark and stagnant place of illness, I feel as if I'm in a cave under the earth, and the only thing shining in it is this golden mineral of a man in bed before me. I feel a sudden pressure in my chest as the room closes in on me, making me feel claustrophobic enough that my breathing becomes as labored as his.

"Don't answer," I say, trying to make this feeling go away. "Eat the soup your wife has made. Gain your strength. When I see you next, I want drunken revelries, nudity, photographs."

He smiles weakly at me, but she does not. I peer at her through this flickering atmosphere and command her with my eyes to care of him. Aside from the candle, he is the only light in this place, and I'm not convinced he has much fight in him. She casts down her eyes.

I stand to leave, and they do not speak. Arthur's cough follows me down the stairs, where my dear husband waits for me to escort me home, where I will take him inside of me while imagining Ficke, and will good health to Arthur through our intercourse, strengthening him through the gloom of this dark night.

FIVE

LAURA

My elation at my father's consciousness was followed by despair. Had he heard what Nurse Miller had said? Did he know it was likely he would never recover?

"Father," I said, moving to sit at his bedside, careful not to shift his broken body, though I knew he couldn't feel anything. I kissed his stubbled cheek. "You're awake."

"I'm sorry," he said in a voice thick with emotion and fatigue. A tear escaped his eye.

"No, I'm sorry. You shouldn't have been alone. This never should have happened."

"Don't apologize. Please." His voice faltered, and he began to cough. I could hear the efforts of his shallow, inefficient reflex. I pressed his side the way the night nurse had shown me to assist his body in what it could now barely do. My imaginings slipped to the insides of his chest, where I knew fluid accumulated where it should be moving, infecting his lungs with the poison of a slow death. I pressed harder, and the fit subsided.

"Why didn't I die?" he moaned. "I wish I'd died."

"No. Please don't say that. I can't stand it."

"You must," he said. "You must face it."

I stood in a hot rage. "Damn Marie for asking Nurse Miller in front of you."

"I knew before Marie asked it. You did too."

He spoke the truth, but it didn't make me any less angry. I needed a place to direct my frustration, and Marie was the closest target.

My father's arm twitched at his side and he looked at it. "I guess that's something."

I sat back at his bedside. "See. The doctor said you'll have limited mobility in your arms. With work, you might gain better control. Your spine was injured below the place where everything would have been shut down, had it been any higher."

He didn't respond and, after a few moments, closed his eyes. I'd exhausted him. I put my face in my hands.

Was this our new future? Just weeks ago I'd felt young, in love, passionate, invincible. I'd dreamed of shows and theater and costumes. I'd made a gold flapper dress with a headband, and bobbed my hair. Now I felt old and tired. My quick impulses of passion had transformed to fast tempers I had to suppress so I didn't alienate Marie, my only family. My acceptance from the New York School of Fine and Applied Arts had come, and I'd dropped it into a box in the back of my closet. I couldn't eat. I felt fatigue to my bones. This couldn't be good for any of us. I must be healthy inside and out to help my father. I kissed him, stood to put on my coat, and left the hospital to visit the church.

As I passed under the tree outside my father's window, the birds that had been hiding in its foliage took flight over the top of the building into the evening shadows. My gaze followed them until they were out of sight, and traveled down the side of the hospital to my father's room, where a movement caught my eye in his window. I felt uneasy, and could not understand why. I thought perhaps I should go back up to the room to check on him, and turned to do so when the church bell tolled the new hour. I didn't want to miss a chance for confession. I looked back up at the room and saw nothing, so I smoothed the goose bumps on my arms and continued to Our Lady of Grace.

■ ■ ■ ■

The church was quiet as a tomb. Candles flickered in rows, changing the shadows on the portrait of the Virgin hanging over them, her face unreadable and distant. John Hagerty waited outside the confessional, along with Agnes.

The door to the confessional opened, and Dr. Hagerty's wife, Caroline, wheeled herself out. She wore a black veil over her brown hair, and motioned for him to enter. He stood to his full six feet and removed his hat before opening the confessional door.

My mother had been a patient of Dr. Hagerty's when he was just starting in the field. His wife's bout with polio had left her unable to walk, and prone to melancholia. Though he was not yet forty, he wore the burden on stooped shoulders, and often reached under his glasses to rub his eyes.

Even younger than John, Caroline Hagerty looked years older, with a pale complexion and dark, troubled eyes. She didn't often go out, except to church and confession, but could usually be seen in their front window, watching the motion of a town in which she could not participate. I wanted to thank her and her husband for getting my father to the hospital, but Caroline had already wheeled herself to the altar candles to pray.

Dr. Hagerty finished quickly, and when the door opened and he saw me, his dark eyes filled with pity. It made the wound inside me ache, but I went to him so I could whisper my thanks for his finding my father. He looked at the floor for a moment, turning his hat in his hands.

"How is he?" he asked.

I couldn't answer without crying, so I simply shook my head. He nodded.

"I'll get over to visit him soon. It's just . . . hard." Dr. Hagerty glanced at his wheelchair-bound wife and back at the floor.

I returned to my seat and watched him push Caroline out of the church, thinking that maybe I'd have to do the same for my father, if he should be so lucky.

When they left, I tried to examine my conscience, but Agnes entered the confessional, and my thoughts went with her. What would a woman like her say to a priest? Did she confess to gossip or judgment of others? Or were there darker sins she held in her heart? Was she so haughty and stiff because of past wrongs, or was she merely the product of a spoiled upbringing and vast wealth?

And what about Father Michael Ash? How could he truly separate himself and become a portal, a messenger of God? How could he remove his own human frailty and speak with authority? How could he not look at all of us and imagine the scarlet letters on our breasts? *Oh, there's the adulterer, the thief, the gossip, the murderer?* Did his costume — the collar, the robes — transform him, elevate him above his human status?

When Agnes emerged, I glanced down at my folded hands, reprimanding myself for my doubt and distraction. Once her heels had clicked out the back of the church, I rose to enter the confessional.

I rubbed my sweaty palms against my coat and placed my hat on the floor with my handbag. Incense hung thick in the air, filling me with a strange calm in spite of my unease. I could see Father Ash's outline through the grate separating us, the sharp line of his jaw lit in the light coming through the small high window. He sat still and stoic, and the slump of his shoulders led me to believe he felt burdened himself. I wondered to whom he made his confession.

"Forgive me, Father, for I have sinned," I began. "It has been two months since my last confession."

Did I imagine it, or did he snap to attention on the other side of the partition? He tilted his head a bit, and though it was dark, I saw his eyes dart to the side and then away. He leaned closer to the grate, and if it wasn't between us, I could have reached out and touched his face.

I sensed that he was acutely aware of me, Laura Kelley, and it nearly made me mute. Where was the impersonal moderator, the empty messenger of God? How could I make a good confession when the man Michael Ash sat just inches from my whispering lips? I thought about running away, but I felt trapped. This little box felt like a platform where I was naked, exposed for all to see. I covered my face with my hands.

Courage, Laura. I thought. *You must do this.*

When I looked up, Father Ash tugged at his collar and sat up straight, moving farther away from me, giving me space. Finally, he spoke. "Courage. Do not be afraid."

He gave voice to my thoughts, and his words steeled my spine.

"I lay with a man, and I am not married to him."

There. A simple string of words like footsteps on a path out of a dark wood.

Father Ash did not move. He had become

the statue I needed him to be. I continued.

"Because of circumstances, I can never have him. And being with him has led me to lie to my father. My sister. Myself."

Cotton seemed to be stuck in my throat, every word painful and foreign on my lips, but I had to continue.

"And it has caused a terrible accident. My father is hurt. Critically so. And I think God might be punishing me for what I've done."

"You must not think that way. Sin is its own punishment. Bad things that happen are bad consequences of human choices. God is no puppet master. That is not love, and love is what He is."

"But I love whom I cannot have. And God is not in that love because it is wrong."

"The love is not wrong. The action of thought and body in the context of it is wrong. Tell me: Do you intend to stop your relationship with this man?"

I must have known this question would arise here. I'd been avoiding it in my mind and heart because it hurt too much to face. I knew there was only one answer I could give to set my soul at ease and begin life anew.

"It is finished." Saying it out loud, in combination with my fatigue and my guilt, brought on tears. I reached into my purse

71

for a handkerchief and wiped my eyes, suddenly sure I smelled my lover's aftershave. I realized that I held his handkerchief, and thought I'd be sick.

"Are you sorry?" His voice held an urgency that made me feel more exposed than ever. And what a question. Sorry to have loved another and been loved so fiercely? Sorry to have lived such a night that gave me the heights of earthly happiness, and aroused a longing to create in my heart?

No, I was not sorry for that. It was agony, however, knowing that I'd been a party to my lover's betrayal and sin. I couldn't stand the thought of the guilt he must bear for breaking his vows, and how he would have to carry that with him, always. I was deeply sorry for that.

"I am," I said. "I should never have let it happen."

Father Ash did not speak, and I wanted to flee. How I wished to gulp the clean fresh air by the stream, surrounded by quiet trees and noisy birds with no concern for me or my problems.

"Then you are forgiven. Go forth. Sin no more. And try to put him out of your mind so you are not led to sin again. Pray the rosary and ask Our Lady to make you more like herself."

I couldn't believe that was all. One rosary for an affair, for deep betrayal and a broken father? It made me doubt the authority of Father Ash. An older priest might have had me flogged in the town square. Or maybe that's just what I thought I deserved.

I said an act of contrition and received his absolution, yet when I left the confessional, I did not experience the usual lightening of soul. I still felt the burden of the affair deep inside me, unwilling to leave, tethering me to my lover in a way I did not yet understand.

VINCENT

I dream I am on a stage with a vast audience of angry and shocked faces before me. It seems they all know my dark heart and hate me for it, and when I look down, I see my naked body heaving breathless before them, but my arms and legs feel so weighted, I cannot move to cover myself, or run off the stage.

Former lovers, men and women, fill the front row, wearing faces revealing a range of emotions from pain, to anguish, to bitterness, to spite, until their features blur and I can no longer distinguish one from another. I fear them because their wish to see me suffer is palpable, along with the bitter chill

73

on my naked flesh.

I hear a sound behind me, but my head will not turn. It feels as if I am held in a vise, forcing me to look at the hurt I've caused, and my heart pounds harder because I can't see who has come.

Then my shoulders feel the softness of a cloak in thick scarlet velvet, like a stage curtain. I begin to cry in gratitude for this kindness. Feminine hands fasten the cloak and smooth it over my body, warming me, but I still cannot see my helper. As soon as the calm arrives, however, I am again filled with alarm. I can smell something burning.

I jolt awake to the sound of a shout. The dawn makes its way into the room, where it is cold as a crypt from the open window. I jump out of bed and rush down the stairs and out the front door to find the source of the commotion and the terrible burning odor. I follow the sounds and smells to the swamp pasture, where my husband and three farmhands are fighting a blaze.

"What is this?" I shout to Eugen.

"Vincent! One of the men threw a match into the dead grass. Go and protect the house."

"No, you need me here."

He wants to argue but he sees that we need all the hands we can get. He shouts

74

for one of the farmworkers to take the horse and alert the neighbors. I grab a broom and head to where the jagged line of fire reaches its killing fingers toward the sheep barn. The animals bleat in fear.

With the farm staff and the neighbors who come, we beat and stifle and suffocate the fire for six hours. We work in twos, cursing the fire and the fool who thought the pile where we'd heaped ten years of grass to dry was a good place for a match. He will be fired as soon as the blaze is under control. I hope he dies of smoke inhalation first.

I see my poor Eugen on one knee, clutching his chest, and I run to him.

"You must rest, Gene."

"No," he says. "I will be all right. I just have to take a moment."

He coughs and spits into the dirt. His face is streaked in soot and sweat. My valiant knight.

Once the fire is contained, we all stagger back to our homes. Eugen and I wash each other in the bath and collapse into bed, where sleep does not restore us. Eugen's coughing wakes me through the night, and reminds me of Arthur, who rests in a sanatorium, seeking recovery for his own wasted lungs. When I do sleep, my nightmares take the fire to the house and my writing cabin.

I watch my poems burn, but I can do nothing to save them.

Six

LAURA

I went to sleep that night and tried to banish all thoughts of my lover from my mind, but I could not. Skipping dinner left me nauseous, and I had an actual, physical ache in me. I half-wondered if my heart had truly broken. I pressed my chest, but flinched at the raw pain in my breasts. Why did they hurt so badly?

It took a long moment for the realization to overtake me, and as it did, I felt heat burning up my body.

"No, no, no," I whispered, throwing off the covers and sitting on the side of the bed. I sat up so quickly, my head spun, and I had to close my eyes until the dizzy spell passed.

I'm just hungry, I thought.

I hurried on bare feet down to the kitchen and opened the bread basket. The biscuits Marie had made yesterday remained, and I tore into one with my teeth. Before I finished a bite, I followed with another and chased it with a glass of water. I chewed and chewed, but I couldn't swallow, and the bread seemed to expand in my mouth. Sweat formed on my brow and I began to chew more slowly, but the floury thickness wouldn't move past my throat, and I gagged.

No, no, no.

I gagged again, and lifted the lid of the wastebasket just in time to heave up what little I'd chewed. I slid down the wall and my hands began to shake. Mentally calculating the last date I'd had my cycle, I realized it was long overdue. My father's accident had distracted me from noticing. My stomach still felt flat, but I knew that if I was in fact pregnant, I wasn't far along.

What could I do? It would kill my father to know. And what would happen when word spread? How could I have been so foolish?

I buried my head in my hands and wept.

Soon a new thought grew in me. Maybe all was not hopeless. Perhaps this child could bring us together. Perhaps this was what had to happen, and now he'd be compelled to leave the life he lived to join mine.

I prepared a letter for him, stating that we

had an urgent matter to discuss, and we needed to meet as soon as possible. I didn't want to put the news in writing, especially because I didn't know for sure if it was true.

At the first light of dawn, I pulled on a dress, and wrapped a shawl around my arms. If Marie awoke and discovered I had gone, she would think nothing of it. I took frequent walks along the woods and waterways at all hours of the day and night.

The hem of my blue dress was soaked by the time I reached the cemetery. I'd set out through the field behind our shop, into the forest to stay hidden, and emerged along the stone wall at the back of the cemetery. In the corner of the wall farthest from town, a stone darker than the others marked the spot I sought. With a shimmy it could be removed and replaced, and made an excellent hiding place for love notes. I hadn't been able to check our secret post in so long that I'd imagined a pile of unopened letters there. When I arrived, however, there was just one damp, folded piece of newspaper with a review of the Follies show. Next to it, in the margin, was his small handwriting. "Of all my life, the best night. Now and forever. With love . . ." I turned the page over to see if he'd written more, but that was it. I didn't want to linger, so I slipped my letter in the hole, covered it with the stone, and hurried back the way I'd come, uncomfortable in my wet shoes, chilled from the morning air, and fatigued.

As I moved back to the safety of the forest, I opened the newspaper and reread his short message, unable to ignore my disappointment. That night had meant everything to me, now more than ever. And all I had from him after all these weeks was a hastily scribbled line that could have come from one of the talkies. He'd never been one to write long notes or love letters, but I felt certain that with our lovemaking we'd crossed into new territory, and forged an unspoken bond.

By the time I reached the shop, I had talked myself into a better mood. He had reached out after that night; perhaps he couldn't put into words how the experience had affected him. After all, I couldn't. Maybe he wanted to tell me in person, but couldn't since my father's accident. No, I knew that this must be for the best, and that God surely wanted us to be together.

I prepared eggs and toast for myself and Marie when she awoke, a breakfast for which I was suddenly ravenous. As I put the water to boil on the stove, a knock at the door stopped me. Marie came downstairs in her nightdress, and we looked fearfully at each other, sensing that good news didn't come this early. I walked through the kitchen and out toward the front, and pulled aside the flowered curtain over the glass in the door. Dr. Daniel Dempsey, Darcy's husband, stood there. Marie came up behind me and began to cry.

I swept the curtain closed as if I thought I could keep the tragedy away, as if I could end the act in the terrible play we were living.

Daniel called to us through the door. "Laura, Marie, please, let me in."

Marie and I embraced each other and she buried her head in my shoulder. I used my free hand to let Daniel in.

"He's gone," I said, inspiring even greater sobs in Marie, but somehow in control of my own emotions.

Daniel nodded, his face dark and pained.

Nausea roared up so quickly, I barely had time to push Marie off my chest, and run to the bathroom. Daniel followed and placed his hand on my back. When I stood, I rinsed out my mouth in the sink and turned to face him. He looked terrible.

"When did he go?" I asked.

"I found him this morning during my rounds."

"So he died . . ."

"In his sleep," said Daniel. "Peacefully, by the look of him."

I could hear the blood pumping in my ears and felt so overcome by fatigue that I nearly collapsed. Daniel held me up and led me to the couch, where he helped me to recline. Marie stood, then paced around the room.

"What will we do?" she whispered. "Whatever will we do?"

"He was just saying he wished he'd died," I said, more to myself than anyone.

Marie gasped. "He wanted this."

Daniel couldn't seem to find any words.

"But I don't see how he died so quickly," I said. "Was it his lungs? Were they infected?"

"It is likely," said Daniel. "Once you've dressed and had some time to yourselves, I'll need at least one of you to come to the hospital for paperwork and to see him, if you'd like."

I nodded, but I could not meet anyone's eyes.

"I can't," said Marie. "I never want to go to that place again." She broke into fresh sobs and came to me. My sister's grief compounded my own, and I cried with her, pulling her into my shoulder and rubbing her hair. She clung to me the way she had

after our mother had died. It was the closest I'd felt to her in weeks.

"I'm so sorry for you both. If there's
anything . . ." His voice trailed off. I looked
at him and thought he might break down
himself, but he cleared his throat and stood
taller.

"Thank you," said Marie, lifting her face,
and wiping her tears with the back of her
arm. "Thank you for coming. That was very
kind of you."

He nodded and started out the door. As
he passed us, he laid his hands on our
shoulders, and then left.

Marie and I held each other for a long
while. Our breakfast grew cold, and the
shadows on the floor moved with the passing time. My parents' wedding picture
stared stiffly out at us, offering no solace.
People walked by, glancing in our dark shop
with the sign showing we were closed long
into business hours, and they must have
known through whispers and deduction.

I was seized with an urge to lay eyes on
my father, and helped Marie up to bed so I
could go. I brushed her hair off her forehead
as if she were my daughter. She pulled the
covers up to her chin, and shivered.

"What will we do?" she said. "The books,

the deliveries, the orders. Who will take care of us?"

"We will take care of us, each other."

I left it unsaid that Everette would take care of her, and I would be alone, but not alone.

Marie had doubt all over her face, but she nodded, and turned on her side. I waited until she fell asleep before summoning the strength to go to the hospital.

My walk through town under the pitying glances of the people I'd always known, with the secret I now carried, followed by seeing my father's lifeless body, was a miserable affair. Nurse Miller gave me a hug on her way out of the room. I clung to her a little longer than she must have expected, but I felt so alone that I needed to. She finally pulled away and turned from me, no doubt so I wouldn't see her cry.

On the way home, I sought comfort in the familiar streets and faces of my youth, but the wind had picked up, and the sky threatened rain, so I passed very few people. Lights began burning in windows, illuminating the figures of those inside, and making me feel more separate from them than I ever had. I knew that as my shame grew, I would be further alienated, and that realization threatened to collapse me. I had no one to blame but myself, of course. I'd consummated an affair with a respected member of the town, a man I could never have. If anyone found out, the very fabric of our small society would be irreparably torn.

I passed Agnes Dwyer's impressive Victorian on Kinderhook Street. It was set back from the road, and as with all its neighbors, tall trees protected its whitewashed facade from railroad dust. Twin oaks stood tall on either side of the front door, and flower beds bordered a tidy green lawn. Every window blazed with electric light. She had a staff to serve her alone. Her daughter, Darcy, lived on nearby Hudson Avenue in another charming Victorian that Agnes' late husband had once rented out as part of his real estate investments. The house had been a wedding gift to Darcy and Daniel.

When I reached Dr. Hagerty's row house, its dark windows contrasted it with the warmly lit homes around it. Through the gloom, I caught the figure of his wife at the window. Caroline was separate from the town in a way I would soon be. She was crippled and withdrawn, and I would be shunned — a fallen woman. I had always pitied her, but now I understood we would both be outsiders, and my heart broke anew. I hurried past her and didn't stare, so she couldn't see my anguish.

When I finally reached the church in front of our shop, the voices of the choir women singing "Ave Maria" drifted past the heavy oak doors. Under the shedding white petals of the Bradford pear trees lining Main Street, I stood at the foot of the stone steps, my hat in my hand, unable to go in and light a candle for my soul or my father's, but hoping the sweet music would bring me absolution.

VINCENT

Eugen returns from the post, just before the rain begins, with a pocketful of letters.

"A letter from your editor, Vincie. When will you send the poems?" He waves the thick envelope before me. "Also a letter from your mother, and from your sister Kathleen."

"Did you read all of my mail before I had a chance?" I say in mock anger.

"If you cannot trouble yourself to ride to town with me, this is the price you must pay," he says, not unkindly. He leans down and kisses me on the neck while he places the packages in my lap. "You should have come, Eddie. You're shutting yourself up again. The world is full of things that it wants you to write about."

"I'm writing," I say. "I need silence. I need escape. I can't be expected to dip into the physical world while inhabiting the landscape of my mind. It's too jarring a transition to make."

"I know," he says. "But I saw something today that I wished you had seen so you could transform it with your words."

"What do you mean?"

"I saw a woman standing outside a church, with flower petals falling over her like snow."

"That sounds fresh and light and lovely."

"But it wasn't," says Eugen. "She was the saddest woman I ever saw. She held a leghorn hat in one hand, and the other was open before her. I could feel her anguish."

I stare at Eugen, suddenly seeing the image of this woman in her sadness contrasted with the spring day. "Go on," I urge.

"She stood in front of the church as if she wanted to go in, but she couldn't. And the music of the 'Ave Maria' spilled out the door, and it sounded sad. And a priest came to the door and looked at the woman like he wanted to have her."

I place my hand over my heart. "Have her in the carnal sense?"

"Have her in every sense. It was worship that I saw, true worship. It reminded me of how I feel about you when you are inaccessible to me. And it filled me with great sadness on this spring day."

I reach for his hand. "Poor Eugen. You go to town to escape my darkness, only to find more. We must find light for you, my love."

I pass him my tumbler of Fleischman's Gin and he drains it in a single gulp. Then he stands and smoothes his shirt and then his hair with his large hands. "You are my light, Vincie. Even when your candle burns at both ends."

He turns with a wink, and proceeds to leave the room.

I can't help but think again of the sad woman, and I want to have the vision in its whole before he leaves.

"Eugie," I call. "Eugie, what did she look like?"

"She had blond flapper hair, and she was soft and round with full lips, full breasts. A perfect curve from her waist to her hip. Nearly as tall as I am. I've seen her in town before, but I can't place where."

I run my mind's eye over her lovely form. I imagine she carries some guilt if she stands just outside the church but cannot go in. I feel a poem rising from the image and the feelings that have crept into my heart. I scribble impressions in my notebook, ignoring the spitting clouds and rushing wind, and hurry out to my writing shanty, where I can work without distraction.

My feelings give way to thoughts, which grow into themes through sentences, whose architecture forms a poem. The music of the "Ave Maria" makes a musician of my subject. In the fading, melancholic spirit of the poem, the flower petals change to autumn willow leaves, and the day gives way to evening.

It seems a sudden thing that the light is gone and I cannot see the page, but when I look up with my stiff neck and find the clock, I realize four hours have passed.

I am seized with a sudden longing to see this woman from town. To know her. It flashes through my mind like a revelation from Sappho. I think of how the words have come from Eugen's mere description of her. What would happen if there was true intercourse?

Maybe she is the one, my new experience, the one who is meant for me.

SEVEN

LAURA

The weeks after my father's funeral passed slowly and with a strange amplification of my already heightened senses. His death reminded me of the impermanence of life, and made me wish to breathe life, smell it, experience it with deliberation. I sought comfort on the banks of the Stony Kill, often removing my shoes to place my feet deep in the mud as if trying to grow roots or find solid footing. I walked early in the morning and late at night, trying to accustom myself to solitude, willing myself to prefer it to interaction on the street with people who would look on me with disgust once they knew my secret.

I ached for my lover.

He had taken the letter from our secret place in the stones behind the cemetery, but left nothing in return. I avoided the town to avoid him most of all, because I did not trust that I could hold myself back if I saw him. I'd never wanted to fling myself into his arms as badly as I did while his child formed inside me.

Instead I put everything I had in me into helping Marie with her upcoming wedding, crying with her because our father would not be there to give her away, leaving my feelings of separation from her and from the town unacknowledged and festering inside me, stitching her dress with more care than I'd ever before used in hopes that it would inspire good feelings in me about her nuptials.

I still hadn't told her about the baby.

On the first day I had awoken without getting sick, I sat with Marie in the shop, sewing costume pearls into her veil, when the door bell tinkled and Everette walked in. Marie leapt to her feet and threw herself into his open arms.

"My darling!" she exclaimed. He looked over her shoulder at me with a somber expression. She kissed him, but he pulled back, seemingly embarrassed to be so fussed over in front of me. Marie never would have behaved this way if my father were alive.

I slipped the veil under the counter. Marie noticed and covered his eyes with her hands. "Bad luck!" she said. "You can't see the wedding clothes."

"I think that just means with you in them," he replied. "But I'm just popping in. I have a present for you both."

I narrowed my eyes. What could Everette possibly have for me?

He reached into his suit jacket and pulled out an envelope. Marie tore it open, and read aloud, " '*Romeo and Juliet* in the park.' It's a play!"

It was the first time I had smiled since my father's death. It seemed Everette did have something that could make me happy. I stood and walked over to see the tickets, while Marie squeezed him again.

"Just for the two of you," he said, giving me a knowing glance.

His acknowledgment of my fear of being left alone was a gift — the reassurance that even though he'd marry my sister, I would still have her. I looked away so he would not see my tears.

When the night of the production arrived, mere weeks later, Marie and I walked arm in arm to the field behind the hospital, where a traveling theater company had taken over the town's summer stage. All afternoon I'd planned that I would tell Marie about the baby later that night, after the show. She'd been asking with increasing persistence for me to reveal my lover's identity, and grew more frustrated every time I put her off, but I could not tell her. As a result, the fissure between us that had begun the night of the Follies had widened in small but meaningful ways. When Marie had realized that I no longer shared everything with her, something inside her must have rebelled against me.

We were a pair that night, however, reveling in the evening of warm breezes, summer energy, and lights that began in the grass as fireflies, then rose to the electric lights strung on strands in the trees, and evaporated into stars in the blue-black sky. I'd sewn a new dress for myself to accommodate my swelling abdomen. It was a floral cotton shift, distracting to the eye but comfortable on my skin. My hair had grown a bit since I'd bobbed it, and had a wave from the humidity. Marie had told me how beautiful I looked.

I felt strangely serene as we searched for our seats in the outdoor amphitheater, and I resolved to concentrate on this perfect moment and put off future worry for the duration of the play. Almost as soon as we arrived, however, I saw my lover on the other side of the crowd. When he caught my eye, and I saw on his face how he still loved me, all peace and calm dissolved. The knowledge that I carried his baby but we could not be together made me unsteady on my feet. I leaned on Marie.

"Are you all right?" she asked, helping me into my seat. Her skin felt warm and familiar. "You've seemed so ill, lately."

I nodded and turned my attention to the stage, where the lights flickered the warning that the play was about to begin. I forced myself to concentrate on the production and the costumes, trying not to think of the Follies night.

The actor playing Romeo was fully himself but fully another. Here were men and women in their own bodies living stories someone else had written. The sets were important to creating the scene and igniting the imagination, but the costumes were my fascination — purple wool, black satin, green velvet, red silk that poured from Juliet's knife like blood across the stage. These sumptuous fabrics were what turned the actors into other characters, what removed the men and women from themselves and allowed them to try on other lives and other times. The costumes held power, and I felt that familiar longing to take part in such an act of creation and transformation.

In the final moments of the play, I felt my lover's gaze on me, and dared to look across the audience. Again his face wore open longing. It was murder to be so close to the one I wanted without being able to possess him. I told him that with my gaze, and suddenly, I felt the first quickening in my womb. On the stage, Juliet had done her deed and Romeo had discovered it. I clutched my belly and was unable to stop my tears.

"What is it?" Marie asked, as she put her arm around me.

I should not have looked at my lover, but I couldn't help it. His eyes were still on me, but this time they had dropped to where my hands cradled my abdomen. I could see his realization as his mouth opened and his eyes widened. I felt one of the knots inside me untie itself at the tiny release his knowing gave to me. I willed him to look into my eyes, hoping to see his love and final surrender, but when he met my gaze, there was only horror in his face. As the applause announced the ending of the show, he slunk away from the audience, and disappeared into the night.

I sat like a statue. Marie said my name, and when I finally looked at her, she wore the same look of horror. She couldn't take her eyes from my stomach.

"Oh, no, Laura."

I did not reply. My tears had dried, and I felt their salt stiff on the hollows of my cheeks.

"You're not . . ."

The motion of the crowd around us called Marie to action. She pulled me away, and I made myself start the walk back to the shop at her side. Her arm was laced through mine, and trembled against my hip. As we traveled away from the crowd on the dark path at the stream's edge, she babbled next to me, but I couldn't speak. All I could see was his face before me, a face that had meant warmth and love and adoration for so long, but now was like a stranger's. He'd behaved so cowardly.

"Who is he?" she demanded.

I did not answer. I still could not say it. She would judge me, as I deserved, and I needed her on my side. As long as I could keep him a spectral figure, I could keep my sister.

"He needs to marry you!" she said. "Don't let him get away with it."

"You don't understand."

"Then help me to understand," she said. "You've never kept anything from me. Why this?"

"It's too wrong to speak of. And it's over. I can never have him."

Pity crossed her face, then a flash of determination.

"We'll find someone to marry you," she said. "The Winslow boys love you."

I stopped walking. The Winslow boys were terrible bores with bad complexions — lettermen in high school track whose entire lives were guaranteed to go downhill from the summit they'd reached in school varsity athletics. They seemed content to bag groceries at their father's market.

"Listen to yourself," I said.

"You can't have this child alone. You'll be an outcast," she said. Marie suddenly looked as if another idea had occurred to her. She dropped her voice and leaned into me. "I've heard there are ways to fix this."

"Fix it?" I said. "It isn't a torn fabric; it is a child. My child, with the man I love."

"Don't be foolish, Laura," she said. "You just said you cannot have him."

I wrenched my arm away from her, dizzy with frustration and confusion. She reached for me but I shook her off and folded my arms over my chest, heading for the solace of the forest, leaving her behind as she called my name.

I walked for what felt like hours, though it

couldn't have been long, and my wanderings brought me to the bridge. Watching the car taillights, I wondered if I should run away to make a new life for myself and my child. We'd have no life here. I thought about how I'd heard of young women going away to convents and having their children put up for adoption. Perhaps that would be best for all of us. But then I thought of my lover, and my foolish hope that once we talked, we would find a way to be together. I went over and over it in my head and thought that I'd rather live alone in the world with his child than give up our baby. It was the one piece I had of our love, and I couldn't imagine losing that.

Several cars passed, and without knowing what came over me, I raised my arm to flag one down. Before long, a Lincoln Tourer pulled up alongside me and a middle-aged man looked at me over his glasses. I recognized him as one of the men who worked at the train yard.

"If you were my daughter, I'd lock you in your room for hitchhiking," he said.

I looked at the ground, trying to push away thoughts of my father, when it suddenly occurred to me where I wanted to go.

"Can you take me to Bash Bish Falls?"

He stared at me for a moment, then

looked at his wristwatch. "Park's probably closed this time of night. . . ."

"I need to go," I said. "Please."

He looked at the empty passenger seat, and then back at me. I could see that he was wondering why a young woman like me would want to visit a place like that at night, and he would probably turn me down.

"My father died there," I blurted. "I . . . I need to pay my respects. No one else will take me. Please."

His forehead creased. "I suppose I could run you there. I don't live too far. But you can't take too long, because I'll have to motor you back home, and my wife will be worrying."

I crossed in front of his car and joined him in the front seat. He started forward, but looked sideways at me. I concentrated on the road ahead and the film of memories of my father, my lover, Marie, the Follies. The man tried to make conversation, but I could not speak.

"Do you want me to go with you?" he asked as we pulled up to the path leading to the falls.

I shook my head and opened the door.

"Hurry back, now," he said. "And be careful."

I left the car and started on the path that

had taken me to this place just months ago. Before long, I could hear the rush of the water as I struggled to see the ground under the canopy of leaves. As if in a trance, I chose the trail that climbed to the top of the falls. I thought of my father, who had walked this path, and also of the Indian women, hundreds of years before him, as bereft as I was now.

On the climb, I had to sit several times to catch my breath. When I reached the top, I made my way along the large boulders with trembling hands until I reached the edge of the falls. The wind and rushing of the water reminded me of the danger I was in, and I felt paralyzed with dread. I stared over the edge and thought how many had died by falling or jumping. It seemed I heard a whispering in my ear. I could join them and leave this earthly pain, it seemed to say.

I began to cry deep, aching sobs, and felt that a hundred pairs of eyes were watching me, though I was alone. I glanced around, catching movements of small animals, seeing the shiver of the understory in the great shadow of the trees overhead. I again thought of the woman who had thrown herself over the edge for sins like mine, and I believed in the curse.

Once I'd cried myself into exhaustion, the

forest went strangely still. I noticed only the rushing of the water. I felt as empty as a reed, and seemed to sense the hum of the forest life in vibrations deep within me. To fall here, to become one with this place forever, tempted me, and I felt myself step forward.

Then I felt the quickening again, a fluttering in my belly like moth wings on a window or a breeze rippling over the surface of a stream.

My child.

I stepped back, trembling, horrified at what I'd almost done. I clung to the boulders and dropped to my knees to crawl to safety. When I finally reached the path — wet, dirty, and exhausted — I sat for a moment to collect myself. I didn't take in the walk back to the car or the man's reaction to seeing me in such a state, but I was delivered safely home just before midnight.

On the ride home, I had convinced myself that the episode at the falls was a nightmare. I stole into the house and thought of my father at the fireside the night I'd snuck in from the Follies. The wedding picture on the mantel glowed in the moonlight. Those formal, unsmiling people did not seem like my parents. They were like icons hanging in a church, saints who had no remembrance of what it was to live the seasons and trials on earth. I wished I could pray to them for advice and guidance, but my shame prevented me.

I climbed the stairs as quietly as I could so as not to wake Marie, but there was no need. I peered in and saw that she lay with her eyes open, staring at the ceiling.

"Do you remember the girl Jane who was in the upper school when we were in the eighth grade?" she asked. "Do you remember how Jane became pregnant and wouldn't tell who the father was, and was sent away?"

I walked to my bed, took off my shoes and wet clothing, and crawled under the covers wearing only a slip.

"Jane never came back," said Marie. "And her parents — they owned the feed shop. They went out of business and left. You remember. I know you do."

In truth, I hadn't thought of them until Marie brought them up, but I could hear the fear in her voice.

"You must give up the child — somehow," she said.

"You needn't worry," I said. "Everette will take care of you. I'll manage on my own."

"But what if you don't?" she said. "This town is small. If you don't have their approval, you have nothing. Everette always says that."

"Are you sure it's me you're worried about?" I said, an edge of cruelty I could not hide creeping into my voice. If she hadn't brought up Everette, I might have thought her motives were pure, but now I suspected she was more concerned that her fiancé might be tainted by the scandal of his future wife's sister. "Don't worry, Marie. You don't have to associate with me anymore, if I embarrass you."

I turned my back to her, and within moments, she crawled into my bed and burrowed into me. I kept my arms crossed rigidly in front of myself.

"I'm just so scared," she said. "For both of us. We are orphaned. I'm about to leave you. And now this? How will you support yourself?"

"I'm quite capable," I said. "Just worry about your trousseau and your new duties as a political wife. That will keep you busy."

"That's not fair."

"I'm beginning to see that nothing is," I said, hating myself for my nastiness directed at the only person I had left in the world, but unable to control my tongue. "But all is well for you and has been since you met Everette. You haven't had a care for another since, and you'll be more distracted once you're living under his roof. You won't even have to pretend we're related if you don't want to."

"Stop it," she cried. "How can you say such things? I would never abandon you."

My ugly resolve crumbled and I began to cry. She turned me toward her, and we embraced.

"Did this happen the night you snuck out?" she asked.

"Yes."

"Tell me about it."

I had to tell her something, so I began my story. Speaking about the pain made it hurt less and knit us closer together. While keeping my lover masked, I told her the details of the night at the Follies, even the most intimate. She confessed that she and Everette had almost consummated their relationship, but were able to hold out, knowing the wedding was coming.

After we had exhausted ourselves, we fell asleep together, forehead to forehead, until the front bell rang the next morning. Marie climbed out of bed and pulled on a dress to answer the door. I rolled over and pretended to sleep. Everette's voice rose up the staircase. He'd been up all night waiting to ask us about the play. Marie's voice dropped, and I imagined her telling him about me.

My heart pounded as I realized that the scandal that had been circling like a wolf was about to be unleashed.

VINCENT

I ride to town, reluctantly, but Eugen says I must get out. He has made an appointment with the oculist to see if he can help with my headaches and the spots in my vision. I know there is no specific medical cause, but rather, my acute artistic sensitivity, but I humor the man who so wishes to make me better.

Eugen slows the car as we pass the church. A bride and groom stand on the steps, while a collection of people throw rice at the handsome couple. A large, well-built man, blond hair slick with pomade, and his small, matching blond bride beam like the midday sun. It seems as if the August heat doesn't touch these pure people, these sunny good citizens about to embark upon a life of domestic bliss. I can't help but dislike them.

"I do love a wedding, Vincie," says Eugen. "A party of pretty people in church clothes all thinking about the consummation to come. Do you think he's yet taken her, or will he force open the gates for the first time tonight?"

"No, I can tell by her stiff walk that she's

105

never ridden any way but sidesaddle."

"It gives me a thrill to think of it," says Eugen. "I wish I'd been the first to pluck your cherry."

"But then I wouldn't have been ripe enough for your taste."

Eugen laughs and grabs my hand, kissing up my arm to the elbow before turning his attention back to the street.

"Wait," I say. He stops the car and we continue to watch.

Another woman, who looks like the bride, stands at the top step, though by the glazed look in her eyes, she is far away. She wears a becoming though shapeless dress in pink crepe de chine and a matching cloche hat. She lifts one hand from the pink rose bouquet she holds low in front of her to wipe a tear from her eye.

"Look at that lovely, melancholy woman," I say. "Is she sad that the bride, who must be her sister, is marrying first, or that things will never be the same between them? Does she pine for someone?"

"That's the girl I told you about," says Eugen. "The girl who stood at this very church in agony while the priest looked on."

I touch my neck and feel a heat rising in it. She is exactly as I have imagined her. It is as if I'm watching my creation come to life, conjured by my pencil. I'm breathless.

"Oh, Eugen," I whisper, "we must find out who she is."

"Yes, my darling."

The sad young bridesmaid suddenly notices us. Her glistening eyes catch mine, and I feel the force of the connection. It is broken only when Eugen drives away.

Minutes later, we park in front of the oculist's shop. Eugen crosses the front of the car to open the door, and takes my hand to help me out. I look back down the street and see the wedding party far off, walking around the back of the church to the hall where they will celebrate. The bridesmaid is out of sight.

EIGHT

LAURA

The summer turned to fall, and I was mostly alone now that Marie was married, though she lived just down the street.

Everette didn't want her working, and she agreed. She visited me, but while she was at the shop, she didn't take up mending. Instead she made tea and drank it with gloved fingers. She told me news of Everette's meetings and town gossip. I made her clothes — an endless array of new fashions for luncheons, dinners, awards ceremonies. Creating such a gorgeous new wardrobe for my sister while sinking into a shapeless wardrobe of my own felt like scratching a mosquito bite — momentarily satisfying but ultimately painful. As if to inflict further hurt on myself, I'd taken to using drab colors, cheap fabric, bland patterns. I told myself it was because the wardrobe was temporary, but I knew it reflected my guilt and what I thought I deserved.

Marie didn't speak of my growing stomach. I wondered if she prayed my pregnancy would go away on its own, like Darcy's. I knew it wouldn't. I could feel the insistence of this child rooted deep inside me, this little being who twisted and poked about incessantly. I wondered if in-womb acrobatics had any relevance to disposition after birth. The thought made me cross myself.

I rarely ventured out now, and restricted errands to early morning or late evening and inclement weather. I asked for deliveries instead of picking up groceries. While at home, I listened to the music of the Jazz Age on my father's radio, imagining what it was like to live in New York City and attend Follies shows in flapper dresses, wondering if I'd ever again experience life like that.

I was grateful for the arrival of the cool fall weather, which allowed me to wear a billowing coat to church. But I knew my time for hiding would soon end. I'd never seen a doctor about my pregnancy because I was terrified of word getting out. I'd never spoken to my lover about the child. After his recognition at the theater and the letter I'd left months ago, he'd never come to me. My bitterness grew like a tumor, engulfing my heart and silencing my tongue, and I wondered if my unease was what induced my child's.

One September afternoon, Marie entered the shop flushed and smiling, clutching an envelope in her hand. "Agnes' hospital ball!" she said, thrusting the mail at me.

I pulled the invitation from the heavy envelope and read the script cordially inviting Everette and Marie to a ball to benefit the new maternity ward of the hospital. Envy nearly blinded me, and I forced the invitation back in and shoved it at her.

"Are you trying to torture me?" I asked.

Marie's face fell. "N-no. You'll be invited too. Everyone from this town to Hudson will have an invitation, even the poet Edna St. Vincent Millay."

I widened my eyes. "The bohemian poet? Agnes invited her?"

"Everette says Agnes may be a church-woman, but she has no illusions about what makes the world go around. Millay's husband is some kind of coffee-export heir, and the poet herself pulls in thousands a year. They are enormously wealthy."

I thought of the poet on the mountain. In truth, I'd been thinking of her more and more often. I saw her the day of Marie's wedding, and was arrested by her penetrating gaze. Since that afternoon, I'd had the strangest feeling that she and I shared a secret. I had also begun to envy her — a woman with her own income, living as she wanted, away from society. The idea held greater and greater appeal to me.

"And more good news," said Marie, continuing in a breathless rush of excitement. "At Agnes and Darcy's last ladies' tea, many of the women spoke of how they want you to make their clothes for the ball. You'll see a lot of orders coming in."

I stiffened at Marie's mention of the ladies' tea. Agnes' bimonthly gatherings were for married women only. There they discussed the town's betterment, the latest books and fashions, and the state of the community. I was convinced that the meetings were excuses to gossip.

I gazed around the shop at the displays and racks I'd arranged, a maze of fabric samples, clothing, and patterns behind which I could hide while women came to me for various commissions. Most of them kept their measurements on file, so a simple discussion of material with a rack between us was all we needed. But a ball would require more specific measurements. I would not be able to hide.

In a flash of anger, I stood and leaned back, emphasizing my stomach.

"And just where should I put this while I pin material on the church ladies?" Marie stepped away, her face contorting with a disgust that made me ache. "Have you forgotten what's going on here? I'm growing a bastard."

She covered her mouth with her gloved hand. "I didn't forget. I just thought —"

"What, that I could keep my secret forever?"

"No, it's just that no one knows yet, and you do such a good job of hiding —"

"I can't hide anymore."

She stood there, dumb. My hands shook with frustration.

"Go," I said. "I want to be alone."

"I'm sorry," said Marie. "I'm so sorry." She lifted a handkerchief from her purse and daintily wiped her eyes before turning to leave.

Once she had gone, I locked the door and flipped the sign to CLOSED. I looked out at the busy town. Billy Winslow pushed a cart of groceries across the street for a delivery. Father Ash walked down the church steps, clutching his journal. Mrs. Perth moved along Main Street under a pile of books, her hair slipping from its confinement. Caroline Hagerty's form darkened her front window.

I turned away and exited the back door to walk in the forest, alone.

I pulled my cloak around me and hurried to the woods. I hadn't seen a firefly in weeks, and the evening air had begun to hold the chill of autumn. Even the bugs had quieted, dulled by the change in temperature.

I turned over my anger at Marie, working myself into a state. She had changed since her marriage, and not for the better. Everette had effectively groomed her for a position as a political wife, just as I'd anticipated. Everette was always cordially polite to me, but he never let his eyes fall below my face. Marie invited me to dinner several times a month, and I marveled at the disturbing way both of them ignored my condition. What would they do once my secret was revealed?

My anger inevitably turned to my lover. How could he leave me alone like this? If he would just talk to me, somehow, I could have some peace, but his avoidance was the worst torture.

The shadows deepened around me, and I imagined the blackening of my heart. What kind of mother would this bitterness make me? What poison was I inflicting on my child, even before the baby was born?

I felt the hair on the back of my neck stand, and glanced over my shoulder. I suddenly had the feeling that I was not alone. My gaze darted over the path, and I saw shadows moving. I turned away, and hurried forward, thinking of the shortcut home, just around the bend. The unmistakable sound of a breaking stick came from behind me, and as I turned, I was shocked to see my lover. My heart lifted, and without thinking, I rushed to him, flinging myself into his arms. He felt stiff, and though he lifted his hands to my back, it felt less like passion and more like obligation. I stepped back and burned with embarrassment when I saw the pity on his face. He dropped his gaze to my stomach.

"Laura."

Silence settled between us. It seemed an eternity passed before he finally spoke.

"How are you?" he asked.

"Not well, I'm afraid." I struggled to keep my voice steady.

"I know," he said. "I'm sorry."

"Why have you waited until now to seek me out?"

"Because I am a coward."

"And do you think it pardons you to speak that out loud?"

"No. I deserve your hatred."

"I wish I could hate you," I said. "But I still love you, despite the fact that you are not worthy of my love."

He wiped his face with the back of his sleeve. His shoulders slumped and he looked broken.

"What do you want?" I said. "My forgiveness? I'm not capable of that right now. Do you want me to say I will be all right? I won't. When the town finds out, I will be ruined. Do you want me to demand that you'll support me in secret? I won't. If you can't give me yourself, I want no part of you or your money. Do you want me to hit you? Gouge out your eyes? I wish I could, but I'm tired. I'm so tired."

My voice cracked. I was mortified to show my weakness to him, but I had no choice. As I stood there, I could see that he wanted to come to me. I could feel it burning in the space between us. But he would not, nor would he leave me.

"If you have nothing to say, go. Now. Forever."

He stood immobile, like a man whose feet were submerged in cement blocks. I don't know how long we faced each other like that, but it occurred to me that I didn't want anything else to be on his terms. I also wanted to punish him.

I felt my active baby pushing in my stomach. With two steps I crossed to him, grabbed his hands, and forced them onto my belly. He felt the child, and cried freely. He tried to pull away, but I held his hands in place.

"When you try to sleep at night, don't think of me. Think of this child. This is who you deny."

After another moment, I released his hands and stormed past him, leaving him alone in his misery, shedding him like an old skin.

Later that night, I knocked on Marie's back door, clutching a package. She let me in and embraced me.

"I'm so sorry for earlier," she said. "Truly. I am a monster for not being more sensitive."

Everette was in the parlor smoking and listening to the radio. I met his gaze briefly and turned back to Marie.

"Here." I thrust the bag into her hands. "For the ball."

She carried it over to the dining table, and slid out the golden flapper dress. She gasped. "Oh, Laura, it is exquisite."

I lifted out the feathered headband and matching shoes.

"How did you? When?"

"I've had it for a while," I said, keeping my voice flat. "It's perfect for you. There's just never been a good time to give it to you until now."

She held it up to her body and hurried over to Everette. "Isn't it grand?"

I heard a quiet sound of approval from him in the other room, and she ran back, placed the dress on the table, and hugged me.

VINCENT

I am at the ball to benefit the hospital.

I consented to attend because Eugen begged. He couldn't resist a chance to mingle at a party. The more I thought about it, the more I realized I might actually meet the woman — the sad bridesmaid — of whom I've thought often since the day I first saw her on the church steps. It made me happy to please Eugen, and I thought I'd throw him a bone before the deep winter isolation set in at Steepletop.

When we arrive, I begin looking for the woman I am destined to meet. In my search, my eyes find the most glorious fabric ever made into a dress, a golden feast for the eyes that must have been spun in heaven. When I see who wears it, my breath catches.

It is the bride from the steps, now a full woman, on the arm of her husband, who looks at her the way a wolf eyes a rabbit.

I run my hands over the black velvet gown I picked up the last time we went to New York City, and feel greedy for what that woman wears. Eugen spots the oculist talking with a priest at the punch bowl, and I shoo him away to make conversation with the sad, sterile men. He can't resist wounded animals. I want to be near that couple, who will ultimately lead me to my heart's desire. Before Uge leaves me, I reach into his jacket and take a healthy gulp from his flask. Then I shove it into my handbag, and walk across the room.

Both of them spot me at the same time, and their eyes light. They know who I am. The man speaks first, while the woman looks me up and down. I resist the urge to reach out and stroke her.

"Miss Millay," he says in a voice as slick as maple syrup. "Everette Clark. An honor."

He lifts my hand and places a kiss on it, distracting me from his wife. He holds on a moment longer than etiquette would allow, and I give him the full power of my stare. I finger my hair, and he looks as if he wishes to pet its coppery softness, but instead, he pulls his wife closer to him and introduces her.

"My beautiful wife, Marie."

I smile, enjoying the little adjective he uses to remind himself whom he is with. Honestly, men like him are too easy. I turn my attention to Marie, a golden goddess in this hall of fussy people, ripe as an apple who wants plucking.

I bow my head and give her a demure smile while she takes my hand. Her skin is warm and soft, and a faint blush colors her cheeks.

"A pleasure," I say, leaning into her and inhaling her floral perfume. "I know you both."

Marie's blue eyes widen like a doll's at my cheeky flirtation. I can see she is fascinated by me, though she is no doubt confused by the feelings I surely arouse within her.

"I drove through town on your wedding day, and I said to myself, I must know these pure, lovely people on the church stairs. I wonder if they'll ever come to one of my parties."

Marie giggles and looks down, bashful. The man comes alive.

"I've heard of your readings and parties," he says. "You are quite the talk of the town, you know."

"And aren't you curious as to exactly why?" I ask.

He grins.

"One day, you will find out." I reach into my handbag and take a long drink from my flask, feeling a drop of gin slide from the corner of my mouth. I use my tongue to lick it off, and nearly laugh aloud at the way the two of them stare. I hold the flask up to Marie. "Drink?"

She looks at Everette, a good wife seeking permission. He still stares at my lips, but I see an almost imperceptible shake of his head.

She looks back at me. "Not here," she says. "Maybe sometime, at your house."

He looks at her with surprise, and we share a laugh.

After a moment, Everette is called away by a group of suited men. Before he goes, he says to Marie: "Are you all right if I step away?" Is he afraid what will happen to her if he leaves her with me, or does he not want to miss a thing?

"Of course," she says. He kisses her cheek and nods to me.

"May I touch you?" I ask, as soon as he is out of earshot. She is startled. "I mean, your dress. May I touch your dress?"

"Oh, yes."

I reach out and run my hand along the intricate brocade that frames her hip, feeling the warmth of her body seep through the material.

"I must know where you got this," I say.

"My sister made it. Laura is the best seamstress. In the world," she adds with a laugh.

My ears prick at the mention of her sister. I try to control my eagerness. "I see that. And is your sister here?"

I wait with delicious anticipation, but when Marie doesn't answer, I turn to her and see that she has paled. "I'm afraid not."

My disappointment is acute. To be so close to the woman from my imagination, just a family relation away, and not to meet her feels cruel. It is the whole reason I consented to come. I look around for Eugen and see him talking to the librarian Eleanor Perth, who has been to our estate for poetry readings, and think I'll tell him that I want to go.

"Excuse me," I say to Marie, and leave her.

I suddenly feel a cold hand on my arm. I turn and look up to see a regal woman with a crown of white hair smiling over me. At her side are a young raven-haired woman and a lean man who looks as if he could use a good night's sleep.

"I'm Agnes Dwyer, the host of tonight's event. This is my daughter, Darcy, and her husband, Daniel, a doctor at the hospital that will benefit from our ball. We are so happy you could come. We are all very curious about such a worldly literary sensation living so close to our small town. You do us an honor."

This woman leers at me like a vulture. I mistrust anyone who refers to me as a literary sensation because it means they want something from me. I would have hoped the hefty price of admission would be enough. I stand as tall as my meager height will allow.

"I wouldn't have missed it," I say. "I need material for my new book of poetry, and the characters in this hall are good enough to eat."

She tries to hide her shock at my words, and laughs while reaching up to cup her hair.

"We do have quite a town," she says, "though I'm afraid we're all probably too conventional for your tastes."

I can see she is not afraid of me, and this piques my interest. I take the flask out of my purse and drink from it. She narrows her eyes, but the tight smile on her lips never leaves. I screw the lid back on and put it away.

"Oh, I don't know," I say. I inhale and glance around the room, letting my gaze touch Marie and Everette, the priest, Mrs. Perth, and, finally, Agnes Dwyer's daughter and son-in-law. "I sense a smoldering undercurrent of passion and energy. There's no telling what could happen if it ran unchecked."

The smile leaves Agnes' lips. The couple at her side shifts. I wink at her and walk away to join my husband.

He is not ready to go, so I align myself to him, allowing him to lead me through the room for the rest of the night. I stare openly at Marie, and her dress, and her husband. I learn that he is a rising politician. I hear the townspeople mention Marie's sister, Laura. They wonder why she is not here, and then their voices drop in speculation. I deduce that Agnes is the head of the town because she is its great benefactress, and that moral order is important to her, and that makes the demon in me wish to shake it up.

I mention to many people that someday we will host a party on the mountain with actors and music and drink. I stir up the gossip. I touch my fire to their waiting matches. I end the night by telling Marie

and Everette that I will be personally offended if they aren't in my garden in the
future, and I see they are greedy to come to
me, to see what life is like on the mountain
where there are no rules or naysayers, but
only the pulsing energy of nature where it
may run free.

NINE

LAURA

It was cruel to parade my sister at the ball in that dress where I knew he would be, but I gave in to my cruelty. An hour after she'd left, however, I hated myself and the monster I was becoming.

I thought that severing ties with him and destroying evidence of our love might help my state, so I burned his handkerchief, his letters, and the newspaper from the Follies. The flames bled the ink from his words before consuming them. It was a pity I could not destroy the triple-stranded pearl necklace, or let it go. I hadn't been able to bring myself to give it to Marie to wear, fearing the questions it would inspire. The necklace lay in a velvet box lined in red satin in the back of my closet, and there it would stay.

November arrived and, with it, the inevitable discovery of my condition by the town.

One afternoon, as I put the final touches on the baby's layette, Agnes entered my shop. Instinct caused me to shove the sewing under the counter as I noted the group of community women with her, including her sister, Lily, and her daughter, Darcy. They'd been making these visits regularly since my father's funeral. Agnes had started a meal calendar where church ladies could sign up to make dinner for Marie and me a couple of times a week in the months after my father had died and before Marie's wedding. She had pinned it on the bulletin board in the church lobby, and written across the top: AGNES D., COORDINATOR. I couldn't help but narrow my eyes every time I saw it. The meals had stopped, but the unannounced visits had continued.

It was rumored that in her early years Agnes had acted in plays, but that a religious awakening in her twenties — and being jilted by a handsome leading man — had taught her that vanity was the foundation of acting and that she must give up the stage at once. To Agnes, vanity became the root of all evil, and my father had often said that a family of beautiful girls making beautiful clothes irritated her. Rather than give up the stage, however, it would appear that it had expanded to encompass her entire life in town, with her and Darcy as the stars.

Agnes allowed the door to close behind her group; she was holding a loaf of bread wrapped in a red gingham napkin and made pretty with cinnamon sticks. Marie was supposed to call on me, but she was nowhere in sight, so I would have to stand to accept the bread. I glanced out the window, willing Marie into view, but she did not appear. I reached out my hands but Agnes raised an eyebrow and stood still across the shop, forcing me to rise and meet her.

I'd known this moment was inevitable, and I was glad the revelation would at least take place in my territory. What pained me most was how it would dishonor my father and mother. I placed my sewing on the table and tried to suck in my stomach as much as possible, but when I stood, a stabbing pain in my lower back caused me to reach behind and apply pressure to it, highlighting the outline of my pregnant stomach.

Agnes spoke seemingly before thinking. "My, it seems my effort at keeping you well fed has proven successful." My face burned at her audacity, and turned a deeper shade of red when I saw her eyes reflect her realization. The women behind her set their gazes on my stomach, and then began to back away from Agnes, as if her rising outrage would engulf them. Pride gave me courage, and I straightened my posture, stepped forward, and reached for the bread, which she placed in my waiting hands as one would feed a caged animal. She snatched back her fingers once they were relieved of their offering and cupped the bottom edge of her clean white pile of hair.

That hair was her main source of vanity. The fifty-eight-year-old woman wore it like a crown and often petted its softness while she spoke, drawing attention to it like a preening bird. When her husband had died five years ago, she had risen to the stature she'd always craved: a blessed widow of the church, an elder, the choir director, entirely independent and free to reign however she chose, well cared for because of her late husband's frugality and his investments in transportation and real estate. Her money fed the church, so Father Ash was indebted to her in a way that only Catholic priests could experience — the woman who said she loved you like a mother, ruled you with an iron fist, and no doubt fantasized about you like a prostitute.

And here she stood, unable to take her eyes from my stomach. I marveled at her rudeness. It would seem that with all of her genteel upbringing, someone must have taught her not to stare, but she stood transfixed. I turned away and placed the bread on the counter, and returned to my sewing table, where I sat, and finally found my voice.

"Yes," I said, "your generosity is overwhelming."

Someone sniggered, but stifled it when Agnes' head whipped around. The women began to trickle out of the shop, first her sister, Lily, followed by the others, leaving only Agnes and Darcy, who couldn't seem to tear themselves away. I dared to let my eyes meet Agnes', and her cruel smile hurt me more than any glare could have, withering any courage I might have summoned. She stood leering at me for so long that fear crept into my heart. This woman looked as if she wished to do me violence, and I thought I might not have the strength to protect myself.

I heard the back door to the kitchen open and Marie entered. She stood up straight when she saw Agnes.

"Good day, Mrs. Dwyer," said Marie.

She was greeted with the sound of the door slamming as Agnes and Darcy stormed out of the shop.

It was then that I saw silver flashes in my field of vision, and was overcome with fatigue and nausea. Marie was at my side before I fell, and I could hear her voice in a panic just before everything around me went black.

VINCENT

The moon is full and round — a harvest moon, a time of new beginnings, of birth.

After my reading at the University of Chicago, I stare in the dressing table mirror and see my husband and the student reflected back on either side of me. My Eugen is more than a decade ahead of me, the student more than a decade behind. He introduces himself in a gentle Southern voice.

"George Dillon."

At once, I feel the woes of Cressid unearthed as I see my destiny before me, one that will try to make room for both and will fail. This boy will either destroy my marriage or my heart. This I know, but I also understand, in fidelity to my vocation, that I must accept the experience and all of its consequences. I must lay my undoing as a gift on the altar of poetry, and she will snatch it with her bloody fingernails and leave not a scrap for me.

George's cherubic innocence combined with his ripe curiosity overwhelms me. I reach out my hand and Eugen places the flask in its comfortable resting place before I bring it to my lips and drink, never taking my eyes from George's eyes in the mirror. I counsel myself that he is just one of the procession — like one of Helen's suitors — but the way the air changes between Eugen and me, I know deep in my heart's soul that this will be different. I understand that George is the one whom Sappho intends for me.

It is you who are my compass for the rest of this night. I allow you to lead me, the poet star, clad in black — not of mourning, but of darkness as in a womb, a place of comfort and safety where our love may begin. I look up to your great height and listen to your poetry when they ask you to read. I see your eyes dart to me throughout; you cannot believe how we have switched places, admiring each other from an audience on the same night. You cannot understand how the man who has come with me, my husband, has fallen into the background to allow me the satisfaction of this impulse.

When you finish and I'm so breathless I think I'll faint, I find a little piece of paper and scribble a note telling you where you should meet me the next day for lunch.

That night I do not allow Eugen to come

to me. I shut him out of my body, resurrecting my virgin self. I bathe in lavender soap, and I write sonnets by candlelight in a white dressing gown. I can barely keep up with the words as they color my notebook — words for you and for me. By dawn, I am nearly hysterical with ecstasy. When I see you come into the dining hall, I can barely speak, so I slip you a poem. I run my finger along your wrist. I don't know if we eat or drink at the table, but we feast on each other afterward. I could live on your soft, wet kiss alone, if the rest of my life depended upon it.

As the days pass, you allow Eugen and me to lead you, bewildered, through the city. We torture you by not answering your questions with words, but by showing you that it is all right for you to hold my hand and nuzzle my neck and place your self inside a woman whose lawful man reclines one room away. You can't control your desire, but you hate yourself for it. I want to delight in your torture, but every time I force a smile at your lack of control, my insides want to bleed for you, for the innocence I steal from you, for your blood I can almost see on the sheets after that first consummating fire.

Oh, how I ruined you — how I felled the angel.

And I can foresee my own ruin reflected in you, but I am powerless to stop it.

Ten

Laura

I awakened with my dress soaked, in excruciating pain, and with Marie leaning over me in hysterics, her tears falling on my face.

"Laura, wake up!"

I blinked and felt a deep ache in the back of my head where it must have hit the floor. I had momentary relief from the pain in my abdomen and attempted to sit up. Vertigo forced me to close my eyes and lie back on the floor, just as it felt as if a large rubber band began squeezing my stomach. I gasped from the force of it, struggling to find my breath, as if drowning. When the pain again subsided, I allowed Marie to help me to sit up. I opened my eyes and stared at the floor around me, slick with amniotic fluid and blood.

"I think it's too soon," I said, and began to cry.

"All right," said Marie, wringing her

134

hands. "It will be okay. We have to find someone, though. Tell me who he is. He needs to be here."

I shook my head. "No, he's dead."

"Dead?"

"Dead to me. Nothing. Never again."

"Laura, now is not the time to be stubborn."

"He's dead!"

Marie stared at me and then nodded. "I'll see if I can find Dr. Waters."

"Hurry." A contraction cut off my breath and I leaned over, squeezing my abdomen while it cramped and hardened. Sweat plastered my hair to my face, and I felt panic. I did not want to have this child on the shop floor. Once the pain stopped, I got on all fours, and Marie helped me to stand. I held on to the counter and squeezed my eyes shut until the room stopped spinning. Then I staggered to the stairs and began to climb them with Marie's support. We had to stop midway up while I cried through another contraction. I also had a terrible sensation between my legs that urged me to push, but I knew I could not. The contraction ended, but the burning sensation of the baby poised to get out did not.

"Oh, God, I don't know if there will be time to get anyone," I said.

"Oh," Marie whimpered, beginning to cry herself. She urged me up the stairs and nearly carried me to the bed. I curled on my side and tried to breathe through the pressure, but it would not go away.

"Can I go get the doctor?" said Marie, a note of hysteria in her voice. "Can you hold it?"

Before I could answer, another gush of fluid poured out of me, and an urge to push that I could not resist.

"No," I said, as I turned onto my back. "Help me."

Marie stared at my open legs in horror for a moment, but set her face with determination and came to me at the bed.

As evening bled into night, the pain nearly made me lose my senses. Minutes or hours passed. There was confusion. I seemed to remember a knocking on the door, but no visitor. Each contraction brought the face of my lover to me, and when I pushed, I imagined thrusting him as far away from me as possible until I almost couldn't see him any longer. I didn't know what time it was when the pain gave way to great relief, as Marie placed the screaming infant on my chest, crying and laughing at the monumental thing we had just accomplished together. Marie pulled up a fresh blanket to cover me and my girl, who had started to calm down and blink her swollen eyes. She gave a tiny sneeze, and Marie and I laughed and cried some more.

Shortly after the birth, Marie fetched Dr. Waters, our family physician. He would help finish what we had started, and would check the baby. He was serious but kind, and praised Marie for assisting in a safe delivery. If he was shocked to see me with a child, he did not show it, but once we were clean and attended to, he sat with his heavy girth on the side of my bed and removed his glasses. Marie had gone to my father's old room to sleep, so it was only us. He rubbed his eyes and then his white hair before putting his glasses back on, and he did not look at me when he began to speak.

"What now?"

"What do you mean?" I said.

"Shall I take her away?"

"I don't understand."

He turned to me. "Do you want me to take this baby away? Or did you plan on keeping her?"

I pulled the infant close to my chest and trembled. "I'm keeping her, of course. She's mine."

He stared at me until I had to drop my gaze to the quilt covering me.

"Don't think you are the first woman this has happened to," he said. "You are brave and maybe foolish to try to raise her alone."

I was not able to speak, though my mind raced at the idea that there were others who had gone through what I had, and maybe in this very town.

"I've been a doctor for many years, and I have seen quite a few bastards born." I flinched. "No one without a husband has ever kept those children."

I stared at him again, shocked by what he was saying. I sat up in the bed as straight as I could.

"I'm not like them," I said, defiance in my voice. "Times are changing."

He looked away this time, and rose to get his bag. He zipped it and started for the door, but paused before leaving. "I hope you don't regret your decision, Laura. Good luck."

The baby began to fuss. He looked at her and left.

Once I heard the door downstairs close, I opened my nightgown and attempted to feed her. She latched greedily onto me, but her sucking brought me toe-curling pain. I pulled her off and tried again without better results.

Over and over again, I tried, but I could

not seem to get her in the right place, and no milk came out of me. I wondered if it took time or if the milk should be here now. I wondered if feeding her would ever stop hurting.

Exhausted and terrified, I was finally able to soothe her to sleep with the tip of my knuckle, but I knew this couldn't be a permanent solution. I stared around my room and out the window, feeling so alone. I must have fallen asleep, because when I awoke, the dawn was just reaching in, turning the room a warm shade of pink. The light bathed the baby's face and caused her to open her eyes. I was filled with a rush of love for her and knew she was my grace, and I called her by that name.

I positioned her at my breast while she was calm, and this time, her feeding didn't hurt.

I thought of Dr. Waters' words and knew that no matter how hard it would be, I would never regret keeping my child.

Never.

VINCENT

Since the birth of our love, time has never moved so swiftly.

November 2, our birthday. The genesis of our love, which burst forth that night at the reading, has brought me to throbbing heights of ecstasy in my flesh and with my pen, such as I have never before known. Our love is the well I needed, and I nearly drown in the water, the abundance of life-giving fluid that pours forth from our loving cups.

I am drunk on George. His sweet, merciful philter is the antidote to all the pain from death — Elinor has died! — to all of the pain of life I have ever experienced.

George's presence in my home represents the perfection Eugen and I always knew could come from freedom in love. George is troubled, bewildered, but open, so open to what is in our grasp.

"Pass the wine," I say, as he sits at my table, dressed for dinner.

George and Eugen both reach for it, but my husband laughs and allows George to fulfill my request. His hand trembles as he pours my drink, and the red liquid spills over, staining the tablecloth.

"I'm sorry," George says, jumping to stand and blot the red, but I grab his arm and instruct him to sit. We have dismissed the help during his stay, and we can attend to the mess later. The heat of George's skin is too much for me. I can't breathe.

"George, take me to bed."

Eugen's face is dark, but he tries. He

remains seated when his impulse is to rise. He nods at George as George gets up and stumbles over to me. He pulls out my chair, and I stand. He follows me up the stairs.

I can feel George though we do not touch. His energy is like nothing I've ever experienced. I want to prolong this delicious sensation of waiting. I close the door behind him and lock it, and instruct him to go to the bed and remove his clothes.

I drop my dress to the floor and stand naked before him. He whimpers.

"Please," he says.

"Are you begging me to pardon you or come to you?"

George swallows. "Yes."

I smile, feeling wicked.

I rush to him and he attacks me, and hours pass in a frenzy of lovemaking.

Then days pass and he continues to drink from my well, and from the well of us all.

Then George is gone, and I am wounded like never before.

Weeks pass and there is not a word from him. I demand his return, but he stays silent. I know George hates himself, and I want to convince him that it is all right, but then I turn cruel. I berate him. I apologize. I abuse George again.

And then George returns, and the cycle

repeats itself.

Ecstasy followed by anguish.

Summer followed by winter.

He leaves and I am ferocious.

Months pass and Eugen and I leave for Europe to escape him and what he has done to us, but George drags along behind us, shadows our every conversation and coupling with his damned presence.

The summer comes again and I know that trying to resist him is impossible and perhaps even ungrateful to Sappho, so I beckon George back.

I invite him and as many as I can find to a party, a celebration. I invite people from the town, from Greenwich Village, from Vassar. I invite theater groups, poets, friends, and enemies, and when all arrive, I am determined to dominate.

George is contrite, but not enough as far as I'm concerned. When I see the politician and his wife, the eager conventional people who think they want to dip a toe into this pool, I decide I'll pull them in until they are drowning. I will give them something to take back to their town and I will do it at the cost of George.

I hand Eugen the bottle of absinthe we brought back from Paris, and stand between the trees while he coaxes Marie to try the

Green Fairy. She is charmed by the name, the color, the process. She takes one glass, then another. It is while she drinks the second that I see its effects. Marie stops and looks around her as if seeing the world for the first time. She laughs and says she sees the laugh, and reaches up into the air to claim it with her fingers.

Eugen leads her to the rose garden, where a group has disrobed.

"You are in Eden," he says, when he sees her wide eyes.

All she can manage is, "Oh."

She sits on a tree stump, staring at this strange garden, and while she does, I make sure George sees me stalk her husband. I slide between the trees and coerce Everette to follow me. I feed him from my own cup and brush George with him as I pass, leading Everette by the hand into the house. George follows us to the bottom of the stairs, but I turn and burn him with my eyes to let him know he may not come to my bed. Instead, I will take this average mortal, this wordless, artless, animal creature over George to inflict the cruelest kind of punishment I can.

■ ■ ■ ■

PART TWO:
1930

■ ■ ■ ■

SECOND FIG

Safe upon the solid rock the ugly houses
stand: Come and see my shining palace
built upon the sand!

— Edna St. Vincent Millay

ELEVEN

LAURA

Damn the poet Edna St. Vincent Millay.

I left my bicycle against a tree and climbed the hill to Millay's house, mentally replaying my speech. I'd hoped to spit back at her some of the bitter poison she'd injected into my sister's marriage by seducing Everette at that cursed summer party. I wished to humiliate, intimidate, and shove her costly words back in her face.

It seemed just yesterday that Millay's husband, Eugen, the strapping Dutchman, strode into my shop with a young, pretty man on his arm, surprising me with his presence. Revelers at Steepletop usually had no need of wool and thread.

"My sweet seamstress," Eugen had said, addressing me as the mayor would, "I need a purple cloth for Dionysus here, stained by the ink of grapes like wine to wrap him in. And please make a costume for yourself so

147

you may join us."

I'd narrowed my eyes, wary of Eugen and his unsmiling friend. It had been months since anyone had come into my shop. My daughter's existence had done exactly what I knew it would to my reputation.

The young man had looked as if he would rather be anywhere but in the grip of Eugen. What had led him to Steepletop when he was so clearly ill at ease?

Eugen had spotted plum rayon on the wall display. "Ah! George, look. Just the cloth for gods or men, freshly stained from the vine."

George smiled a little at Eugen's colorful language, and I watched with surprise as Eugen lifted the entire bolt and placed it on the counter. I tried not to snatch the cash waiting in his fingers as I tallied the total. When I looked up, they were both staring at me.

"Seamstress, please consider coming," said Eugen. "The poet-goddess wishes it, and she does not handle denial well."

I looked from him to George. My daughter, Grace, began crying from upstairs.

"I'm sorry," I said. "It's impossible."

"Bring the child."

A spark of pleasure stirred in me that he had been so ready to accept her — to accept us — but I suppressed the feeling, and sent them on their way.

It had come as a shock to me when Marie had told me she and Everette were going to the party. It hardly seemed like the kind of place for two well-respected members of the community. Marie said she wanted to keep her visit a secret since Agnes had gotten word of the celebration. Apparently at the last ladies' tea, Agnes' condemnation of the bacchanalia had done little to hide her bitterness at not having been invited.

"Then why would you go?" I had asked Marie. Public approval meant a lot to my sister. Going against a woman like Agnes seemed suspect, especially when Marie already had the stain of an unwed sister with a baby.

"Everette says it would be rude not to, since we all but told her we'd go at that ball in 'twenty-eight when we first met her. We've been waiting a long time for an invitation. There will be people from New York City there. Not to mention that it never hurts to break bread with the wealthy, especially in times like these."

Marie hadn't met my eyes during our conversation, and had seemed shifty about her involvement. Her neck had even turned red when she spoke of it. Marie's remarks felt like posturing, and though she tried to pin their attendance on Everette's ambition, I had sensed that Marie wanted to go.

When the weeklong party had ended, and Marie had shown up at my back door in tears, telling me that the revelries were everything bad I could have imagined and more, and that Everette had slept with the poet, my shock had given way to anger. I felt anger at Marie for going, at Everette for his terrible deed, and mostly at that poet for being able to live in any way she pleased in the mountain above town, while allowing her corruption to trickle down and poison others without having to face the consequences. Marie's pain spoke to my own — that of a woman having to bear a burden alone, and with the perpetrator left to carry on as if nothing had happened.

Marie had taken to sleeping at my shop away from Everette, having screaming fights with him in my kitchen, spending hours crying, lamenting the fact that she had ever allowed him to encourage her to go. Just when I thought Marie might actually leave Everette, she learned she was pregnant. She had returned to her home, but still hadn't forgiven him. My anger had been building in me for months, but Marie's latest crying fit had sent me over the edge.

The long uphill bike ride to Steepletop had left me panting, so I had to stop and rest against a poplar to catch my breath. I wiped the sweat from my forehead with my arm and stared up at the top of the autumn tree that towered over me. Its posture reminded me to stand up straight, so I drew in my breath and continued up the driveway.

I halted when the tall yellow grasses at the roadside parted and Millay emerged, a waifish imp with a tumble of fiery hair. She wore a white muslin robe, and cradled several apples in her arms like a newborn baby. Her golden green eyes caught sight of me, looked me over, and seemed to approve of what she saw. At once, I understood how a man like my brother-in-law had been ensnared. I took a step backward, but Millay's voice stopped me from moving an inch more. Mesmerizing me with her deep, melodic intonation, she said this:

"I came down a hill, back from raping the earth of her treasures, to see a nymph waiting for me, breathless, angry, uncertain, and I felt the sorrow of seeing the wounded pierce my heart more than she could know."

In spite of all I'd rehearsed, I couldn't find any words. I remembered the day I had first come in contact with the poet, on my sister's wedding day, and sensed that we shared a secret understanding. Now I felt only confusion.

Millay walked to me, into my shadow — for I stood many inches taller than she — and pressed the apples into my hands. She then stood on tiptoe and kissed my cheek. I recoiled as though I'd been slapped. She smiled a wicked smile at me, then pivoted and walked into her house, leaving the door open behind her.

A woodpecker knocked a nearby tree, and the fragrance of a patch of late-blooming anise surrounded me with its intoxicating odor. I could not reconcile the beauty of my surroundings with the anger in my heart. I looked back at the open door, but I did not follow her. Instead, I shook off the spell, walked back down the hill to my bicycle, carrying the apples, dropped them in the basket, and pedaled home like one drunk or deprived of sleep.

What had I really come for? To avenge my sister's pain? Or was my motive selfish, morbidly curious? Did I just want to see the home of one who lived outside convention? No, I told myself that I had come to defend Marie, to insist Millay never again have anything to do with my family. But instead I hadn't said a word, and had allowed Millay to kiss me like some damned Judas.

I wouldn't speak of this visit to my sister. Marie said Millay had mesmerized her and Everette, gotten them drunk, and corrupted them, along with many others. Marie said her reason had slipped, then her control, then her own husband, and she understood why Agnes feared and hated the poet. She'd mumbled something about wishing she could burn her at the stake.

One thing was clear to Marie, and maybe to me.

Edna St. Vincent Millay was a witch.

I passed my old lover on the road back into town, my hair plastered to my forehead and neck with sweat, my cheeks flushed, dust on the hem of my plain dress. Every time I saw him, it seemed I was unkempt, ill at ease, fumbling through an errand, soothing a tantrum. Did he ever wish to help me? Did he ache to be with our daughter? Or did he see me and think, *Thank God, I didn't leave my life to join hers.*

Marie looked up when I walked into the shop, her face drawn and haggard, and her frame gaunt except for her swollen belly, which held her child. Her blond hair was drawn into a careless knot at the base of her neck, and her skin was pale as the moon.

I pointed upstairs and crept to the second

floor to check on Grace. I watched her tiny chest rise and fall. Her golden hair stuck to her face in sweaty curls along her forehead and cheeks, and her arms were raised over her head on the pillow as if she'd fallen backward into sleep. Her little glasses nearly teetered off the edge of her bedside table. How like her to leave them in a careless place.

I crept in and moved the glasses to the center of the table, and looked back at her. Her sleeping form blurred as tears stung my eyes. The day's frustrations had been heaped onto my other troubles, and I felt the familiar sting of pain that my almost-two-year-old girl would be an outcast like me because of our situation. She was so like me in every way — from the tangle of blond curls, to the blue eyes, to the quick temper. There was not a shred of her father in her, at least in looks. That was our one blessing.

Grace turned on her side, now facing me, and exhaled. I crept out of the room so she could continue napping in peace, and walked down the staircase and over to my sewing pile, averting my eyes from Marie's.

"Did you finish your errand?" she asked. Curiosity and suspicion infused her voice, and I pricked my thumb with the sewing needle. I brought my thumb to my mouth, tasting the metallic sharpness.

"Yes," I said. "I did. Thank you for sitting with Grace."

"Of course."

The ticking clock punctuated the silence. Marie held no mending on her lap, worked on nothing, made no attempt to occupy herself. I knew she wanted to talk, but I didn't know if I had the energy.

I rubbed my aching eyes and tried to refocus on my project: a Christmas dress for Mrs. Perth, the only woman left in town who patronized me, aside from my sister. The abandonment had been swift and painful. Agnes and Darcy, Lily Miller, the rest of the choir, Mrs. Winslow. One by one, the accounts went cold, the bell on the door fell silent, and my bank account dried up like a puddle in the sun. Even Mrs. Perth, a progressive woman by our town's standards, slipped into my store after dusk fell and hurried away as if she did not want to be seen in my company. Her husband continued to work as a hand at Steepletop, and I said a silent prayer of thanks that I hadn't run into him on my rash and poorly executed visit.

I looked up at Marie to complain about the lack of business, and saw her crying. Her pain cooled my anger and distracted me from self-pity.

"What is it?" I asked.

"Will I ever be able to stop thinking about him and that woman in bed?" Marie shook her head as if to clear it of the terrible image.

I seemed to catch the thought like a virus, and it made me tremble all over again with fury. I slammed my sewing on the counter.

"Do you want me to kill her?" I asked.

Marie looked horrified, and then smiled when she saw the evil glint in my eye.

"I could make a nylon doll in her image and poke it with pins," I continued. "I'd use the cheapest material, and start on her fingertips so she couldn't write anymore."

Marie shook her head. "It's my fault. I shouldn't have gone to that party in the first place."

I'd never heard Marie acknowledge that she shouldn't have gone, and her words both satisfied the dark place in my heart that wanted to say *I told you so* and softened my judgment of her.

"It was such a time, though," Marie said. "If Everette hadn't strayed, I would fondly recall the wonderful, terrible freedom of it all." Her wistful words poured out before she could call them back. I felt the strangest tug inside myself. Though I knew it was ludicrous, it felt like jealousy.

It was the word *freedom* that had triggered my envy. When Grace came, born from the first thing I'd done only for myself, and as much as I'd fantasized about finding a new town where the shadow of the sin wasn't forever on me, I couldn't tear myself away from the torture of always being near her father without being able to have him. I wanted him to see her even if he couldn't raise her. But I hated what I'd become: a bitter, angry, frigid, trapped woman. Trapped by others and by myself as if in stone, and only twenty-one years old. Most people's lives were just beginning at this age, and mine felt as if it was over.

A noise at the top of the stairs called me from my thoughts, and I saw my little imp scooting down on her bottom, her hair in knots and her glasses askew. She gave me a sleepy smile and crawled into Marie's lap. The light from the window framed the girls, and I felt my love for them like a fire in my heart.

That night, Marie invited me to dinner at her home. I noticed that she had grown bolder in her invitations since Everette's infidelity. Before he'd strayed, she'd respected his wish to disassociate from me as much as possible, and had us over only when he was out of town or at meetings. Now she did as she pleased, and while it heartened me to see more of my sister, a part of me wondered if these dinners were more to punish him than to improve our relationship.

I helped Marie prepare dinner, and kept catching Everette's eye. Did he feel a new bond with me because we'd both fallen? I could sense his guilt reaching out to me, silently begging for my forgiveness so I could help turn my sister's heart, but I couldn't yet give him that assurance.

The window behind where he sat lay open to the night, bringing whispers of the wind to us. The curtains I'd made flapped in and out, brushing along the sill and reaching to touch the empty canvas on the easel Everette had bought for Marie's last birthday. The brushes from the accompanying art set had hardened into fans like miniature brooms, and the paints had long since dried into parched deserts of blue and ocher along the surface of the jars.

Grace sat on the floor near the kitchen, combing her doll's hair and refastening the buttons on the tiny pink overcoat I'd sewn for it. She chattered at the doll, and her high voice seemed to aggravate Everette's unease. After he finished his cigarette, he rose to turn on the radio, and its sharp, loud crackle filled the room.

"Last night, the musical *Girl Crazy* by George Gershwin and Walter Donaldson opened at the Alvin Theater in New York City. Among the rocking-good performances, twenty-one-year-old Ethel Merman is sure to be a big star after knocking out the audience with her number, 'I Got Rhythm.' Other standouts were the graceful and talented Ginger Rogers, and the lyrics of the incomparable Allen Kearns, whose 'Embraceable You' had the lovers in the audience mooning starry-eyed over each other. . . ."

I stopped setting the table and imagined the scene. The station began playing "Embraceable You" and it made me greedy to go to the theater, watch a show, find an escape, even for just a night. I closed my eyes and allowed my remembrance of that night at the Follies to tease me, but Everette snapped off the radio, and the fantasy dissolved. Marie looked at him, her face a film of bitter emotions. When she saw I was watching her, she returned her attention to the chicken frying in the pan.

I'd known Everette would be trouble as soon as I saw those devilish blue eyes at the Valentine's Ball of 1928. The church ladies had been whispering about his new position as city manager and his eligibility. When he caught our eyes over the punch, Marie had stepped toward him. I remembered that I'd felt the need to pull her closer to me, but she'd slipped away and into his orbit.

Everette now sat by the window. When Marie looked back at him, his face wore remorse. I glanced at Marie's belly and then at Grace. I felt the cold emptiness inside me, and the reminder of having a child alone, with no one else to love and help raise her. My own pain made me think that Marie's marriage must be worth fighting for.

VINCENT

They call me a man's name because it is what I want, because I am no woman and no man but a force, alpha of my own motion, limited by no one, guided by the haphazard fancies of my heart. I think if my loved ones and lovers knew my thoughts, they would be frightened and think me soulless.

I may choose to bypass empathy and sympathy because sharing in others' misery is no good for any of us, but I am not soulless or heartless. On the contrary, I am soulfull and heart-swollen. I long for the space

160

to let them all in at once, but one so fully fills my space — the one before me — that I have no room at any one moment for more. But more will squeeze in later and have his share, her share, and then he and she will be addicted.

There is no cure for me.

As it turns out, I only got to take Everette to my bed at that party. It started as my punishment for George, and also because I wanted Everette's wife and then his sister-in-law. I thought he would lead them there, but I was wrong.

He amused me though, the politician. Who knew a man of the government would be so susceptible to a woman of the arts? He told me he needed a fairy-tale romance. It was awful how he thought he sounded poetic. But sneaky blue eyes like his make up for many deficits.

It was not at all unpleasant. I rather enjoyed the rough mannishness that he tried to smooth for small me. I enjoyed the feeling of controlling a man who could have physically snapped my bones. I recited a poem or two, and the oaf thought I'd written them about him. His eyes widened; his forehead creased. I even saw his eyes mist over, and I had to control my impulse to laugh. When I smiled, he thought I was smiling with him. Would he have been so smitten if he'd known I'd composed the lines for his soft, eager wife sitting drunk on the lawn just beyond the window? Would he have pined as I know he does, or would he be outraged and bitter? I get a strange thrill to think of a man of his stature outraged. What could he do in his anger?

But enough about him. I have no desire to allow that vulgar man in my mental space for one minute more. I only want to think of the seamstress, the sister, the sad woman at the church door with flower petals falling around her, about whom I've written. Her tense energy is so much more arousing than the open wanting of her sister. I would much rather a chance at taming that horse.

I need distraction from the control I've lost with George. His resistance is killing me, literally shaving the sinew of my heart, damming the very blood in my veins, turning me cold and gray from the inside out. The seamstress will be a distraction, and one I desperately need. I know she hates me, and I also know that hatred is just a breath away from love, and that in spite of her loyalty to her sister, I still have a chance. Even if it's a small, diaphanous chance.

TWELVE

LAURA

I drew a line on the wall with heaviness in my heart. Grace seemed to grow at double speed. How I longed to protect her from the adult world.

"Revember?" she said, pointing lower on the wall.

"Yes, I *revember,*" I said, imitating her child speak.

"I got Dolly."

"You have a good revembery," I said.

She ran her small, dimpled finger over the line.

The tinkle of the shop bell took my attention to the door, where an elderly woman with thick glasses and a plain, clean face walked into the store. She did not smile, but she looked at me directly and nodded in a friendly way. I rose from where I was crouched on the floor.

"May I help you?"

"I need a dress or two. Nothing fancy. Something that won't show stains in the knee when I garden, or splatters when I cook."

Strangers in search of clothing had been nearly the only customers sustaining the shop, so I was eager to make her order.

"I just got in two new bolts of dark wool, green and charcoal gray," I said. "Those might suit you, especially with the coming winter weather."

"That will be fine," she said. Her eyes flicked to Grace, who stared at her.

"You glasses," said Grace.

"Yes, I do. How do you like them?"

"Owl. Hoot."

"Grace," I said, placing my hand on her shoulder.

The old woman smiled for the first time. "Yours too. We look wise, yes?"

Grace smiled, showing her dimple, and then turned her eyes down, suddenly shy from the interaction and observation she might not have meant to utter out loud.

"How did you come by glasses for such a wee child?" asked the old woman.

"I noticed her having trouble reaching for things. She has always been clumsy, but she started running into chairs and such. I took her to the oculist down the way, and had her eyes checked. Lo and behold . . ."

I motioned for the old woman to stand on the pedestal before the mirror and she obliged, all the time gazing around as if trying to memorize the shop. It made me uneasy. There was no scrap of manliness here, and sometimes that caused old ladies to ask questions, which caused them to judge me. This gave my heart pain because I liked how she'd spoken to Grace and I didn't want her strong, handsome face to frown at me once she knew my situation. I could not explain it, but I felt as if I wanted this woman to like me.

She stood still as a statue while I measured her arms and bust, and took down her numbers on my notepad. As I ran my hand across her back, I admired her strong, straight build. Though small, she held the impression of sturdiness. I'd like to be as sturdy at her age. I caught her wink at Grace in the mirror, and then continue to scrutinize the shop. When I stood from measuring from her waist to the floor, she spoke.

"You live here alone with her." It was not a question.

I nodded.

"Her father?"

I felt my breath catch in my throat and shot my glance at Grace, horrified at the woman's directness. That was not a trait I wanted to embody at her age, though it seemed inevitable, given how many so-called ladies were comfortable asking me the same question without a shred of intimacy between us.

"He's no longer with us," I said. It was the line I'd given Grace since she was old enough to notice. It implied that he'd died, and in a way, he had. To me, anyway. I almost hated to say it to this woman, who seemed too sharp for half-truths. She raised an eyebrow at me.

"I raised my three girls alone," she said. "Sent their father packing. Not an easy thing to do back then. Not easy now."

This was not what I had expected her to say.

"But it was something I had to do. You can too," she said. "Hold your head up."

The stiffening of my posture was involuntary. I did not wish to discuss my personal problems with a stranger, no matter how much I wanted her approval. I passed her the notepad.

"If you'll write your name and address below my measurements, I'll go and pull some patterns for you."

She stared at me for a moment, then took the pad from my hands.

Grace stood in silence, watching the two of us, and when I stepped into the back room, she was at my heels, always my little shadow. As I crouched down to find the patterns I thought would suit the woman, Grace came over and knelt beside me.

"Witchy one," she whispered.

The witchy pattern was for a costume I'd made my sister for last year's fall festival. Grace had seen the costume hanging in a closet, and wanted one for Dolly and herself. I had given in on Dolly, but I'd told her she'd have to wait until she was older to wear the witch costume. I didn't need any more negative attention for my girl than she already drew. Nonetheless, when the pattern wasn't made in black, it had a practical look, and would suit the old woman. I pulled the witchy pattern and two others, and walked them back out to the shop. I almost dropped everything on the floor when I saw the man who stood before me.

Father Michael Ash was not smiling when we emerged from the storeroom, but he broke into a wide, forced grin at the sight of us. His prematurely graying black hair was cropped tightly to his head, and his angular features and shadowed eyes gave him the look of one who was hungry.

"Miss Kelley," he said, almost in a whisper, "I'm sorry to interrupt." He let his voice trail off and would not look at Grace or at my customer. I thought he must have worked himself up for a visit to the shop and was determined to survive it untainted. His pale eyes caught mine and would not let go. "I came to check the progress of the altar cloths."

My heart started hammering in my chest, and the room felt tight and warm.

"I'm sorry, Father," I stammered. "Do you need them today? For some reason, I thought they were due at the end of the week."

"No," he said. "I was only out walking and I thought I'd check."

I worried that the gossips in town would see him in my shop and start talking. Panicked, I wanted him to leave. I glanced at the woman, and her eyes moved from him to Grace, who sat on the floor dressing Dolly.

"I've just got a bit more of the trim to finish," I said. My voice sounded unnaturally high. "I'll deliver them the moment they're ready."

Suddenly, Grace jumped up and thrust her doll at Father Ash. He started as if she were a snake, and dropped his journal. I reached to pick it up, but he said, "No!" He snatched it up himself. "No, thank you, I mean."

"Witchy doll," said Grace.

I pulled her into my side with more force than I intended, and Grace cried out and scowled. Father Ash's eyes stayed on Grace for a moment but then he looked back up at me. His face seemed to have lost some of its color. He gave an awkward nod, and disappeared through the doorway as quickly as he'd come. I turned to the woman. Grace was again the object of her gaze.

"You look as if you made that child alone," she said.

I looked down at my daughter. "She is the image of me."

When I looked back up at the woman, she had turned to the door and gazed out across the street, in the direction of the church.

"A blessing, indeed," she said.

VINCENT

Surgery. Surgery will cure this ailing body of mine. My stomach, my heart, my female organs. I will have them all removed. They have brought me nothing but trouble.

I've been to the Doctor's Hospital. They tell me it's a disease of the bowel, but I know what it is. I am filled with the poisons of my lovers. Their philters have turned sour

169

in the linings of my soft tissue, eroding me to the bone with their dark wishes for my pain.

Why can't they be like me? Why can't they respect the pillars of Beauty, of Love that we have, erecting without corrupting them? Why can't they leave them unmolested, a line of sculptures that would dress a garden more splendidly than the work of Rodin? Instead, they insist on tearing them down, clawing and scratching away at the figures we've made.

I have told Arthur, whose lungs seem more functional for now, that I intend to have surgery, and he shames me for it. He says it will be suicide if I do anything to my body, and I lash at him and declare him simple. How can he not see the physical pain that emotions are capable of inflicting? How can one with such depth refuse to see what is plainly before him?

Eugen understands that he must not try to stop me. He wants to nurse me through whatever ailment I bear. But I do not want his steady arm and his soothing words and kindness. I want my mother, and she is here. Since my youth, ever the nursemaid, always care giving. I can see her in her younger days in a smart white uniform stamping off to this town and that, leaving us girls to care for ourselves while she cared for others. Only our illness would bring her back. She would nurse us with such tender care, and there was no illness she could not conquer. I grew to love my illnesses because they brought Mother back to me, and because then I wouldn't have to keep house or braid my sisters' hair or shop for groceries and make meals. I could recline and be waited upon and simmer in the hot fever of poetic creation. Oh, if I could just burn with perpetual word-giving fever, and never have to deal with the menial tasks of living.

I feel her hand upon my hair and my mind is soothed.

"Stop thinking, Edna."

I turn to look at her, her kind old face gazing down at me with perfect mother love.

"How do you always know me?" I ask.

"You came from my rib, child," she says, her eyes twinkling with mischief through her thick glasses. I smile at her.

"You are the greatest blasphemer I know."

"High praise in comparison to so many."

I laugh, which hurts my abdomen. I clutch my stomach and curl into a ball on the bed.

"Why must I bear this pain?" I ask. "I should be working on my poetry, not thinking of which pills they'll give me after surgery."

"You do not need surgery," she says. "You need newness. Freshness. You should come to the sea. You are too isolated up here."

"I'm not alone. I have Eugen."

"Bah. He is merely a manifestation of yourself when you are happy, which has always been the smallest part of you. I don't even know if he is real."

"Then who arranges our domestic life so carefully?"

"I told you, it's you. On your more functional days. Your worldly days."

"I wish I could be a woman of the world. Instead I am a cloud woman. A tempest."

"Do not begrudge your calling," says Mother. "It is worthy and wild, but it does not come without a price. All great things must be bought at a high cost. Otherwise you'd just live in the town and bake bread or sew things."

"Don't you call sewing common," I say. "Don't belittle that woman. She is far from common."

"Ah, here you are. Waking up," says Mother. "She is common. Nothing but a common girl with a bastard child. A fallen beauty. Oldest story in the oldest book."

Anger rushes through me and pulls me to sitting up in bed. "How dare you? Why do you help connect her to me if you think her common? She makes a form of music with her fingers. Have you seen what she sews? When I saw that dress at the ball, I knew she had magic. When I found out she'd made it, I knew poetry wasn't the only vocation."

"Please," says Mother, dismissing me with a wave of her hand. "She's no conjurer. Any woman with a set of hands and a sewing machine could make those. Why couldn't she make the child's father stay with her if she had such magic?"

"Maybe she wouldn't have him," I yell, throwing off my blankets and sitting on the side of the bed. "Maybe she is like you, and turned the damned useless man out because he did nothing but drag her down."

"No," says Mother. "She doesn't have it in her. She's a begging, fearful seeker of approval. I could see it in her eyes when I went to the shop."

I stand and storm over to my vanity. "You are a heartless crone!" My chest heaves and I stare at Mother's profile in the mirror. A smile lights her face, and she begins to cackle. My anger turns to rage and I slam my hand on the vanity.

"Why do you laugh?"

She stands from the bed, walks over to me, and presses her hands on either side of

173

my face. "Look at you, Vincie."

I realize that I am standing, that my stomach doesn't hurt; the fever, the fever is still there. My heart swells with elation, and I begin to laugh.

"Cured by passion," she says. "Freshness. Vigor. Fight. This is you, Edna. Not the girl curled in a ball on the bedsheets. Take up your lance."

I clutch Mother in a ferocious embrace. My restorer. My healer! I pull away and grin at her.

"You didn't mean all of that," I say. "Clever woman."

I don't bother to get dressed. I run in my nightclothes out to the writing cabin. The cold stones against my bare feet, the dry grasses whipping at my arms, no fire in the grate. Just me and my pencil and my notebook, and my words.

THIRTEEN

LAURA

Early love makes fools of even the most pragmatic of us, but to this day, I could not say that I'd take it back. The sweetness of that short time and the precious consequence of our love — now turning circles with her doll on the path before me — were things I would never undo.

I held Grace's hand as we walked along the banks of the Stony Kill riverbed. I had a special sensitivity to the rush of the waterways running through and around town. Even when I knew it wasn't possible, I heard their fickle noise, even more than I noticed the train whistles. When I needed peace, I felt the murmurs and plash of the water like a sweet balm. When I was troubled by my neighbors' harsh words or gazes, the waters seemed to mock me, adding their whispers to the steady din of gossip.

Today the Stony Kill looked friendly, if a

bit fierce. Recent strong rains had added inches to its banks and it moved with force toward whatever it was seeking. I much preferred its purposeful motion to its meanderings. Industry leaves less time for idle chatter.

Grace and I took the long path in the autumn woods that curved around the mill, the post office, and Crandell Movie Theater. We came out at a grassy meadow behind the small hospital, where acres of wildflowers collected birds and ladybugs, and where Grace liked to run, scaring off rabbits and chipmunks, until she reached the summer stage that had hosted *Romeo and Juliet* more than two years ago, when my lover first knew she grew within me. When we got to the meadow, she released my hand and skipped off into the grasses. I watched her passage part the dried brown stalks, little critters and insects rising from their tips. It felt good in the late October sun, and I turned my head up, forgetting for a moment everything but the golden beauty of the earth before its hibernation.

I heard Grace's little feet pounding on the stage and watched her from afar. Vines climbed the wooden structure, and weeds had overrun the stands. Since the crash of 'twenty-nine, the stage had been vacant.

Only the ghosts of past performances and meandering children on walks with their mothers used it. Our town hadn't been affected right away — most of our residents, even the most wealthy, weren't directly involved in stock market dealings. But little by little, the encroaching shadow of a dying economy had fallen over the country, closing stores, driving up rents and food prices. It was hard to tell if my failing business was a result of my sin or the economy, though I thought I knew the answer.

I had reached down to pull weeds in the first row when Grace bounded up to see what I was doing. She helped me for a bit but soon grew bored, and dragged me to the path, where she again darted away into the meadow. As I walked along, a cloud passed the sun, and the hair on my neck stood. I looked back on the path but saw no one. When I turned toward the hospital, however, I came upon Daniel and Darcy. They appeared to be arguing, but when they saw me, they fell silent.

Grace burst out of the meadow, breathless and smiling, and rolled down the hill at the edge of the path. Bits of grass were stuck in her hair and dirt stains soiled her dress. She ran over and hugged me. I loosened her arms from around my legs and crouched down to brush off her dress and hair while she adjusted her glasses.

Darcy's catlike eyes were fixed on me. Her black hair was set in an elegant wave and she wore a dark green suit and matching hat. Daniel stared hard at Grace. Seeing his scrutiny of my child made anger rise in me. He could at least have the decency to disguise his gawking. He was as bad as the choir ladies.

I grabbed Grace's hand and pulled her past them, down the path from which they had come. She protested but must have sensed my urgency, and soon quieted. When I felt safe enough away, I couldn't stop from turning back and looking over my shoulder. Darcy was also looking over her shoulder at me. I turned away first.

VINCENT

Here we are, at the end of our time together, and Mother is unusually distant. I thought that these weeks of staying with us would not only restore me, but also restore her good cheer and help me to reconnect to the idol of my youth. Yet she became stony. It reminds me of her behavior when she divorced my father, and my sisters and I began to raise ourselves in perfect freedom while she worked to support us.

After the day in my room when she helped me to arise like Lazarus by insulting the seamstress, and the fever of writing that resulted, I again became spent. Nothing she said could stir me to action. I simply didn't have the concentration. Even now I sit with my horse books, the notebooks I keep for my recently acquired hobby in breeding, training, and racing inspired by a nearby neighbor. My new endeavor gives me pleasure, and allows me to live without isolating those around me.

Why does she so disapprove? Yes, it is true I spend an inordinate amount of time on my new hobby, time I could be writing. Never mind that she divorced my father for his compulsive gambling. I am nothing like him.

"I cannot access you," I say over dinner, just nights before she plans to leave us.

I run my hands along the fox-fur collar on my dress and press the silken curls of my newly set hair.

"Vincie," says Eugen as he adjusts his onyx cuff links, "no trouble at the dinner table."

I stare at Mother a moment longer, and then direct my eyes at his. The dressed windows on either side of his chair frame him like an actor on a stage. The light falls earlier in the evenings, shadowing his form, though the flickering candles light his soft, seductive eyes. They crinkle in the corners, and I can't help but return his smile.

"Your hair blends with that foxy stole," he says. "You are a foxy one, Scuttlebutt. Don't bring unpleasantries into the room. Obey the tapestry."

He points over his left shoulder at the Oriental wall hanging of the gods that we picked up on our Asian travels. Four gods at the four corners of the world who would not allow evil to enter the room.

"Forgive my bad manners," I say.

Mother belches without excusing herself and lights a cigarette. I try to hide my disgust at her table behavior, and feel my anger rise. At that moment the cook enters, carrying the tea tray. She places it on the sideboard and lifts the kettle and one teacup to bring to the table, where I smolder.

"Damn it!" I slam the table, causing the service to rattle. "How many times do I have to tell you to set out all of the teacups before bringing over the boiling-hot kettle?"

That loathsome woman has the nerve to glare at me without answering. Her face holds no trace of apology.

"Do you need me to type a list to hang on the wall? Number one: Place the teacups before the master and mistress. Number two: Distribute the tea bags. Number three: Carry the boiling goddamned water last with two hands so you may safely pour it into the waiting cups. Are you deliberately disobeying me, or are you genuinely stupid?"

Eugen sighs long and heavily. Mother continues to smoke. The cook will not take her eyes from mine. Her aggression and hatred are palpable, but I will *not* look away first. When training animals, everyone knows that the first party to break eye contact is the weaker of the two. I can't let her dominate me in my own home. But the woman will not back down. If I had my riding crop, I'd strike her. Eugen intervenes before the situation escalates.

"You are to leave at once," he says to the cook. "Put down the kettle and go. I'll send your last week's wages."

That vulgar woman finally has the decency to look away, and begins begging Eugen. I can see him softening to her pleas, but I will not stand for such a person to soil the purity of my mountain air with her horrid thoughts, no matter what her miserable home situation.

I am tired of employing these stupid townspeople, only to have them fail at their simple tasks, get fired, and return to town spreading vicious lies and violating our privacy with their petty gossip.

"It is unbecoming to share your personal hardships with us," I say. "Do you know that my mother had to work three jobs and stay away from me and my two sisters morning, noon, and night to keep a simple, leaking roof over our heads? We didn't have two pieces of bread to rub together, but no one ever would have known. Sniveling is the lowest form of communication and will get you nowhere. Heeding my directives would have kept you here, but clearly you are unable to follow simple instructions, so you are no longer welcome."

Mother stands from the table and walks out of the room. My eyes begin to blur from the outside edges, and black spots seep into my vision like spilled ink. It is another headache. It comes on so fast, it takes my breath away. I bury my face in my hands.

"Vincie," says Eugen. I hear him instruct the cook to leave at once, and she finally obeys. He slides my chair backward and lifts me into his strong arms, as he's done so many times before, to carry me up to my rooms. "My dear Eddie. You've said too much. Your headaches are fed on high emotion. You must quiet yourself."

I am afraid to speak because of rising nausea. Instead, I cling to him like a child and bury my face in his chest, inhaling the spicy fragrance of his aftershave and the sweet smell of his cigarettes. He carries me up the stairs and places me on my bed. He then draws the curtains, blacking out the remaining light of evening, and undresses me.

"Oh, you sumptuous woman, I want to devour you," he whispers as he tucks the covers up around my naked body. "How could you go and upset yourself like this? Now I won't get my dessert."

I try to apologize, but the pulsing in my head becomes so intense that I nearly cry out.

He runs his hands over my breasts and down the covers until they rest on my thighs. "What can I do?"

"Nothing," I whisper. "You are so good to me. I don't deserve your goodness."

He slides his hands back up my sides, and runs them through my hair.

"You do," he says. "And I will always do your bidding. Call me if you need me tonight."

I nod, though he probably doesn't see, and he leaves me in the dark. As I hear him cross the hall to his room and shut the door,

I imagine him removing his dinner jacket, lighting a cigarette, and pouring himself a digestif. I try to think only of him, but the pain in my head throbs in time with the pain in my broken heart. My splintered mind turns to George and how he refuses to come to me, and to Mother, who allows me to run wild and unchecked, but whose disapproval feels like rubbing alcohol poured in my wounded heart.

How can I be expected to control these tempers when nothing is in my control any longer? Only Eugen obeys me completely, but even that is unsatisfying. Damn the irony of wanting the thing that eludes and not that which obeys.

At least Mother has obeyed. Her quiet marks her disdain, but she has done her part in luring the seamstress to Steepletop. Laura is like a wild filly waiting to be broken. I know of her daughter, who stands as a physical manifestation of her passions, but the experience must have hardened her. I know she turns the pain of the town's judgment on me, because we all need something lower than ourselves to hate. Otherwise we would be left to absorb all of the bad energy and it would destroy us. No, best to pass it on.

I know that if I can tame that woman, I

can use that power to tame George — my true desire. If I can tame her, I can acquire some of her youth and vitality to reinvigorate my body, which has begun to betray me.

Oh, Sappho, let me rise again.

FOURTEEN

LAURA

Sweet mother of God, the old woman lived with the poet.

I stopped my bike as I approached the street leading to Steepletop. The old woman had written only her name, CORA, in all capital letters below my measurements, with an arrow pointing to the next page, where she gave me directions to the house: *Turn left out of your shop, go to the Methodist church, take the country road over the bridge,* and so on. She had left no street names, only crude drawings and landmarks, and I hadn't paid close enough attention to see that she was leading me back to the poet.

My mind catalogued through Marie's descriptions of the party, and I now recalled that she had spoken of the poet's mother, who had sat like an impassive shadow in the corner, watching her half-naked daughter throwing herself at her guests. Marie had been shocked that the old woman seemed to have no judgment of her daughter's behavior.

I considered turning back. My base need for money, however, urged me forward to get the deed over with as soon as possible. On the remainder of the ride, I wondered if Cora knew of my connection to her daughter. Had she seen me ride to Steepletop that day? Did Millay actually share her infidelities with her parent? I found it unlikely, though I knew of the eccentricities of the family. Perhaps her mother was the cause.

The day was unseasonably warm, and I'd worked up a sweat by the time I pedaled the final stretch of the drive and arrived at the house. There was no denying that it was a pretty place. A large white barn faced a handsome white farmhouse. The structures stood on either side of the drive like two wives talking over a fence. Sheep bleated on the hill, and birds flew from the barn to the color-rich trees and bushes.

I took a deep breath and propped the bicycle against the fence. I'd folded and bagged the dresses and placed them in the large basket at the front of my bike, so I took a moment to shake them out. When I looked up, Millay was creeping toward a massive rhododendron bush, holding out her hand to an eastern bluebird. When I coughed, she turned and met my gaze. After a moment, she broke into a smile of the most genuine pleasure.

"You're back," she said.

I cleared my throat. "I have Cora's dresses."

"Put them on the dining table inside the house," she said. "Mother is on a walk, but she'll be back shortly. Make yourself comfortable."

So this is how it's going to be, I thought.

Millay was playing with the wrong woman. She could not push me around like my sister, so she would have to respect my terms. I would get my payment — of that, I had no doubt — so I carried the dresses into the house and placed them on the dining table. I stepped into the parlor and looked around for a piece of paper, which I knew I'd have no trouble finding in the house of a poet. Sure enough, a notebook lay on a table next to a plush chair in the corner. A pencil lay across the tablet, and a half-empty tumbler of some spirit rested next to it.

The entire room seemed staged for visitors. It was strangely formal for a farmhouse, with ornate drapes, heavy antique paintings in decorative frames, and two large pianos taking up most of the space. It smelled of cigarettes, dying violet-blue harebells in mismatched vases, and the books lining shelves and stacked in piles. A large stand holding a black marble bust of some goddess read SAFFO. Her potent, empty gaze watching over the room chilled me.

I couldn't help but wonder if this was the room where Everette had taken her. Or was it upstairs in her bedroom? Was it in one of the gardens? Were there others nearby? And where was Marie at the time? Was she so drunk that she didn't know what was happening, or were her inhibitions down and she'd allowed it to go on? I felt sick at the thought of it all, especially of Everette with Millay. The image of them together seared into my musings and left me feeling dirty and, more darkly, jealous. I had had only one experience of such intimacy and it had left its long and lasting memory. I could see how someone with less control or care might become addicted to it.

A noise on the stair called my attention to the foyer, where Millay's husband descended, buttoning his shirt, humming through lips pursed around a cigarette. Catching the flash of his bare skin and his full mouth turned up with pleasure at the sight of me sent me across the room. I reached Millay's notebook, turned to the next clean page, and tore a piece of paper from it, leaving a jagged half sheet behind. I picked up the pencil and wrote: *Send Cora to the shop for payment and alterations. L. Kelley.*

I left the paper on the table and pushed past Millay's husband. When I stepped out the door, I nearly ran over her. Her fingers seemed to sear my skin as she brushed my arm.

VINCENT

I knew Laura would come, and seeing my prophecy confirmed brings me the greatest delight.

Laura, as flushed as she was at her first appearance but less impassioned, approached me the way one would a wild animal: one step at a time, carefully, full of apprehension. I could see it in the quiver of material she held in her hands like an offering. It was her offering to me to tame me, keep me occupied, turn my intention from devouring her to something else.

Silly girl.

I looked back at the wild birds in the rhododendron and held up my arm to them with my own offering. Within moments, a bluebird landed on my hand and began eating from it.

See, Laura, I thought. *Like this.*

When I told her to go into my house, I could tell that Laura had debated if she should because of how long she remained still. She finally turned on the drive and began making her way to the front door. Once she was inside, I committed to memory the warm rush of emotion I felt watching her walk inside my house for the first time, but I was quickly hit in the face with a cold wind as she walked back out without acknowledging me. She stormed to her bike, and left me quivering in the wake of her tempest.

Rejection. Again. Like a dagger in my breast.

I find myself thinking strange, unreasonable thoughts, but I cannot quiet them. It's as if she and George are cut from the same cloth, a stiff, unwieldy material that refuses to take my shape. My vision shifts a little, and I clutch the porch railing for support until the world again rights itself. I turn my eyes to my hand. It is with shock that I register the gnarled appearance of my fingers, the dry, wrinkled backs, the jagged nails. Are these the hands that used to rest so gorgeously on the piano keyboard, the hands that brought forth such powerful music, the hands that shaped the words like potter's clay? When has time played its cruel jokes on them, and why didn't I notice until now? No wonder George won't have me anymore. Surely he is repulsed.

I stagger into the house, push past Eugen, up the stairs to my boudoir and into my bathroom, where I run to the sink and splash cold water on my face to tighten my skin. I drown my face and hands over and over again in icy sheets until I shake and my skin has turned white and pure, the coldness contracting it, tightening my features, bringing back the young face.

Daylight gleams cruelly through the window, showing the lines around my eyes, crow's-feet, dark black rook trails that would gouge my eyes if they could. I run to the vanity at the window and plunge my hands into the creams and potions, rubbing layers of lotion over my face and fingers. Pushing the oils into my skin, turning it red and waxy, but not erasing the lines, the years.

Then I see it: a line of silver through my foxy hair. Oh, my crown, my red crown. I can't lose it. Not yet. Dyes, I must get dyes to color it. But how can I ever find a dye the color of my hair?

I weep in my arms, but then I smack my

cheeks. No! I mustn't cry. It will puff up my eyes and make me look more like the hag I am becoming. I stand tall and erect and walk into my sitting room, pull the curtains closed, and pour myself a glass of gin from the bottle on the fireplace mantel. I drain it in one long gulp. I pour another and drain that. Inhaling and exhaling in a rhythmic pattern, I feel my heart calming, my breath steadying. I look at my hand that grasps the glass, and it looks softer, blurred, younger.

There. That will do for now.

But as soon as I recover, I see the edge of an envelope from George, another letter in which he refuses to come to me, and I am back in a state.

I begin to scribble a letter full of venom.

"I am at my crest and you will drag me to the trough with your small-minded jealousy, cruelty, and youth that make you think you know more than a man decades older and a woman older by ten years, when you know nothing."

Nothing, I spit at you.

I want to take it back and undo the night we ever met. I want to throw the flask at the mirror and uninvite you from my bed and my heart so I can start living again. Start to reclaim my youth instead of being forced forward in time.

You and time: You are relentless.

FIFTEEN

LAURA

A stranger arrived at the rectory late last night.

He came on the late-night train from New York City, carrying a military duffel bag, a large leather satchel, and some kind of case. I watched him walk from under the lights of the station to the rectory, where he knocked on the door. Strangers did not often stay in town, and if they visited, they were usually picked up by Eugen Boissevain and hauled up the mountain to Steepletop. I turned out the electric light I used to see my needle-work, and peered outside. The clock in the square showed eleven o'clock, but a light burned upstairs, where Father Ash resided.

Much to my interest, Father Ash soon opened the door and greeted the man. I saw that Father wore only his undershirt and pants, but no shoes. It was disconcerting to see him so casual, so human. He embraced the man with a warm hug of old friendship, of men who share a past and feel great affection for each other. Father Ash bent down to retrieve the duffel bag and closed the door.

I'd never known Father Ash to have a friend. He was always so alone in spite of being so often surrounded by people. I couldn't imagine how he bore his existence. He'd never spoken much of his past, so I didn't know a great deal about it, only that he had spent part of the Great War in Italy with the Red Cross. He must have many stories of loss of which I couldn't conceive.

The light in the room next to Father Ash's went on and the silhouette of his visitor moved to the window. He placed his hands on the sill, slumped his shoulders, and turned his head toward the center of town, where a rotten, half-dead maple's turning leaves shivered in the night breeze. The tree stood alone in a large circular area of grass at the roundabout in the middle of Main Street. The side streets reached out from the center like a mandala, or toward it like many streams draining into a pool.

When I looked back at the stranger's room, the light went out, but the window stayed open to the chilly night. I crossed myself and was compelled to think a little prayer for him. I sensed that he was lonely, though I didn't know why. That must be the way God sees us. We think we are alone, but He watches from the shadows, hoping the best for us.

Grace was at my bedside early the next morning, waking me to tell me about the commotion on the street. Coffin's Coal & Wood truck idled out near the circle, where a group of workers began to chop down the maple tree with an audience of townspeople. I looked at the clock on the bureau and was horrified to see that I had slept until eight o'clock.

I arose from bed, pulled on my robe, and allowed Grace to crawl into my lap on the chair by the window to watch the action. Her wild curls tickled my face and her body warmed me. I snuggled into her.

"Why they hurt it?" she said.

"The tree?" I asked.

She nodded.

"It was dying already. Do you see how easily the branches break?"

Another nod.

"Maybe they'll plant a new tree," I said.

"I hope flowers. Pink and blue."

"Blue flowers?"

"Hydras."

I smiled at her and kissed her cheek. "Hydrangeas would be very pretty. How did you remember those?"

She shrugged without looking away from the circle.

"It's fall though," I continued. "The best flowers to plant now are bulbs that will bloom later."

A movement at the rectory door caught my eye. Father Ash stepped out, looking like a proper clergyman, followed by the man who had arrived last night. In the morning light, I could see how tall he was. He wore his hair short, a few-days-old beard, and a scowl. As he stepped into the street behind Father Ash, he looked up at me. His eyes appeared light, but were underlined in shadows. He did not smile, and looked away after a moment. I rubbed my arms. I placed Grace on the wood floor. My bare feet felt like ice.

"All right, no more lazy," I said. "It's time to dress and eat. We need to get ready to open the store. Go wash your face."

Grace scampered to the bathroom and I heard the scrape of the stool across the floor, and the splash of the water. She enjoyed doing things all by herself, and I loved her independence at such a young age. I wondered if a boy would be as capable.

A shout came from outside, and I returned to the window to see the tree crash to the street. The workers swarmed over it and began sawing it apart to clear the road for traffic. Father Ash stood with his back to me, but his visitor had a notepad in his hand and turned a slow circle until he faced my building. The rising sun warmed his face. He closed his eyes for a moment, and then opened them, his eyes so light they appeared white. He looked down and wrote something on his notepad, then turned back to the circle and pulled a measuring tape from his pocket. He nudged Father Ash's arm, and the two of them spread to either side of the circle, measuring its diameter. Father Ash called something to the man, and he made more notes.

I turned from the window when I heard the water in the bathroom shut off and went in myself to prepare for the day. I couldn't imagine what the man was doing. He didn't seem the landscaping sort, though I could hardly discern what sort he was.

No matter. In a town this size, I'd know soon enough. And regardless of what he was up to, it would have no bearing on my small life.

■ ■ ■ ■

I clenched my jaw when Boissevain's Cadillac pulled up in front of the shop that afternoon. Millay's mother sat in the backseat, the poet in the front.

Eugen let the old woman out first. Then he opened the door for Millay, helped her up, and escorted the ladies, one on either arm, into the shop. I glanced over their shoulders out to the clock tower in the distance. It was ten minutes to two, and Marie was due in soon to pick out material for the baby's clothing. *Please, God, let her be late!* If she found out I worked for the witch woman, she'd never forgive me. I cleared my throat and grasped the counter, where I stood, when I noticed they had brought none of the dresses I'd sewn for Cora with them.

"Did everything fit well?" I asked, addressing Millay's mother, and trying to ignore the poet.

"Very well, thank you," said Cora, extracting herself from her son-in-law's arm. "Finely made. The finest I've ever owned. I'm leaving for home today, and I look forward to wearing them once Indian summer has had its say."

200

"I'm glad," I said.

Cora walked over to the display of winter coats I'd assembled yesterday in the front window. I felt Millay's eyes burning me, but I did not look at her.

"Then you've brought the final payment?" I said, directing my attention to Eugen. I hated to be so blunt, but I wanted these people out of my shop as soon as possible. Millay stepped forward.

"I have," she said, trapping me with her arresting green eyes and a tight smile on her red lips. She pulled a blue check out of her coat pocket, her name in block letters on the side. She passed it to me with some flourish, as if to show it was she who paid the bills. I was unimpressed, since I'd been in charge of my own household for years. Perhaps I'd get my name printed in block letters on the sides of my checks too.

"You've overpaid me," I said, holding the check back out to her.

"It's a down payment," Millay replied. She made no move to retrieve the check. I groaned inwardly and raised my gaze to the ceiling. I did not want any more of their business, no matter how badly I needed it. "I want a velvet gown with white fur trim to keep me warm at home in the winter months."

I nearly laughed in her face. Would she like a crown and a scepter with it? Ladies-in-waiting?

"I'm sure Lurie's Department Store in Albany would have what you need. In the costume section."

I heard a snort and saw that Cora covered her mouth and turned away so Millay would not see her laugh.

"Are you in the regular business of sending customers away to giant stores that will devour you?" said Millay.

"Only those whom I do not wish to serve."

Eugen let out a nervous laugh. Cora turned back and watched me through the bottle-thick lenses of her glasses. I looked back at the clock tower. Five minutes to two! I placed the check on the counter.

"Please, I am very busy this afternoon," I lied. "I'm glad the dresses worked for you, Cora, and I apologize for my rudeness, but it is how it must be. I will issue you a new check for the difference."

Eugen stepped forward. "My dear, I know why you do not wish to serve my wife, but it would be good for your shop, for your daughter, to do so, wouldn't it?" He spoke with charm and ease, his voice like warm honey. Millay followed his lead.

"I know you want to hate me," she said,

202

"but the simple fact is that I never make anyone do what they do not wish to do. Please think about that before you judge me. Besides, whatever *was* is finished, so there's no need to hang on to the past."

I felt shocked by Millay's lack of discretion around her mother and her husband. What a strange family. I wished to flee, but I had nowhere to go, so I had to stand firm.

"It is not for you to tell me what I should do or think," I said. "What passed might be over for you, but I have a sister still very much wounded from whatever it was that went on, and my loyalty to her prevents me from doing any more business with you. She will be here any minute, and I do not wish to disturb her delicate condition by your presence."

"Come, Vincie," said Eugen. "We do not wish to bother Miss Kelley any longer."

"Just one more thing," said Millay, her voice firm. "Not everyone is what they seem to be, and you, of all people, should understand the danger of judging others."

Grace cried out from upstairs, where she was napping. All eyes looked toward the ceiling, and I reddened at Millay's meaning. Damn her for throwing my bastard child in my face.

"Get out," I said, as Grace began to wail. "Out!"

Millay turned with some reluctance, and Eugen escorted her and Cora back to the car. The two o'clock train announced the hour, but mercifully, Marie was nowhere in sight. Once the car pulled away, I turned to see to Grace, and ran right into Marie.

"Oh," she said, grabbing the chair for support. My heart pounded.

"Where did you come from?" I asked, nearly breathless.

"I came in the back," she said. "What's got you so rattled?"

My glance returned to the street, but the car was out of sight. "Nothing," I said. "Grace, I mean. She's woken up crying from her nap. I need to see if she's all right."

"Has the baby fabric arrived?"

"Yes, it's in the storage room." I started up the stairs. When I entered Grace's room, she cried from her bed. I reached down to pick her up and saw that she was covered in sweat. Her sheets were drenched. I lifted her and felt her body burning.

A fever.

"Oh, no," I said, cradling her in my arms while I sat at the edge of her bed, gripped with raw maternal fear. Grace whimpered and sucked her thumb. I placed her in the rocking chair and stripped her bed, quickly putting on new sheets. I removed her sweat-soaked dress, put her in soft cotton pajamas, and tucked her back in with her dolly.

"Mommy is going to get the doctor," I said.

I hurried downstairs to see Marie holding up yellow and green fabric. "Which do you think?"

"Grace has a fever," I said.

Marie opened her eyes wide. "Oh, no! Poor thing." She picked up the bolts of cloth. "I'd better go so I don't get sick."

My impulse was to feel angry at Marie for thinking only of herself, but then I chastised myself. She was thinking of the baby, and she was right. It wouldn't do for her to become ill.

"I need to fetch Dr. Waters," I said. "Can you stay downstairs while I run for him?"

Marie looked up at the ceiling with uncertainty.

"Or can you go and tell him, if you don't want to stay?" I said.

"I'll get him," she said, setting the fabric down and rubbing her back. "You really need a phone installed."

"Yes, and I'll just do that with all the extra money I have lying around," I said. As soon as I spoke the words, I remembered

Millay's check, still on the counter.

"You don't need to snap at me," Marie said, pulling on her coat. "You know, you're really changing, Laura. I know it's hard with Grace, but you're becoming so cold."

How dared she? How dared a respected woman with an employed husband criticize me? And I wasn't the only one who'd changed. Since Everette's infidelity, Marie's outbursts and fits of temper had been just as sudden. I opened my mouth to retort, but Marie cut me off.

"Maybe if you exposed her father, you'd get some peace, or at least force him to take responsibility."

"No," I said. Concealing his identity seemed to be the only way I could preserve my dignity and protect Grace. I was also aware that my silence was a form of self-punishment, but it was what I thought I deserved. "No, he's dead."

"He's not. It's you who's dying a little more every day. I'm sorry to say this, but it's for your own good. I know I'm one to talk about bitterness, but I can see that it's a poison. I try to remember that every time I walk in the door of my house. And it's working."

"I'm so glad my misfortune is able to help you," I said. As soon as I'd uttered the words, I was sorry.

She picked up her pocketbook and started toward the door, but didn't look at me. "I'll send Dr. Waters as soon as possible."

Once she left, I crossed the shop and shoved Millay's check into the cash register. I walked to the window and watched Marie hurry off down Main Street, wishing I could take back my nastiness, and acutely aware that I was driving away my only ally.

I went to the kitchen to wet a rag and then to the cellar to chip some ice off the block I'd had delivered that morning. I ran the little cup up to Grace and slipped the ice in her mouth, where it could melt and help ease her temperature. Hideous remembrances of my mother's death from the flu years ago threatened to push me into a panic, but I willed the memories away. Grace didn't need me in hysterics to add to her misery.

Once Grace was sleeping easily, I sat in my front window, from where I could see the clock tower, and watched the hands move slowly around its face for two hours before Dr. Waters walked up the street as fast as his girth would allow. He passed the center of town, where my eyes found Father Ash's friend using a shovel to fill and smooth the hole left by the maple's roots.

His shirt was soaked with sweat in spite of the chilly autumn air, and he lifted his hat often to wipe his brow. He barely looked at those passing by, but remained focused on his work.

Dr. Waters left me with a package of five aspirin, and a bill we both knew I could not pay.

I promised him half once I cashed the check from Millay, but I still needed to come up with the rest of the money, and to find a way to pay Millay back her so-called "down payment." At moments like these, I thought how foolish I was never to ask Grace's father for anything. He should be helping us — if not with his hands or his heart, then with his wallet. I allowed myself to imagine sending him blackmail notes, demanding financial support or I'd make our secret known, but my pride and principles recoiled at the thought.

I barely slept that night. I lay in Grace's bed with her, waking up from her cries, feeling the draft coming in through the thin window in her room, agonizing over whether Marie would find out about Millay, worrying over Grace's illness, remembering what Millay had said about my judgment of others. Somewhere deep inside, I knew she was right, at least a little bit. I was the definition of passion and sin in this town. If I had run away that night, early in my pregnancy, where would I be now? Had I made the wrong decision by staying?

But, no, it was impossible. I had no money for such a move. I had no child care. My only family was here, and Marie would need me once her own baby was born. And, like it or not, this town was a part of me. I could feel its dust on my feet, its rivers like blood in my veins, its street patterns etched on my skin; to leave would mean amputating a part of myself.

Marie's words came back to me. I had changed, and not for the better. My determination had become stubbornness ruled by pride. I had withdrawn from the townspeople in as many ways as possible, thinking my isolation would be less painful if it came on my own terms. Maybe that had something to do with the silent bell on my door.

But, no, the bell went silent first. They had turned away from me first.

VINCENT

The seamstress vexes me.

She wears plain clothing in spite of her talent, and her shoes are so old, she must feel the ground on her toes. There are no ornaments in her shop or on her person, and she looks very much like one who would appreciate decoration. I can see her vanity in her soft, well-tended curls, her clean face and fingernails, the way she dresses her daughter, who is more fashionably outfitted than her mother. The girl would be happy in stained cotton, but she's starched, pleated, and plaited. Is the seamstress punishing herself?

But then, my mother was just the same.

We send her on the train, this time in first class. When I watch her small, slouched form climb the steps with effort and disappear into the car, only to reappear in the window, smiling, eyes obscured beneath her thick glasses, I feel as if I'll cry. Why does this one seem like the last good-bye?

I hear the whistle and how I wish to climb aboard with her. Instead, my large husband has his arm around me. Sometimes I feel he will crush me with his great weight. Everything he does is so big, every movement, every word. It is intolerable that someone as small and delicate as I must be pushed and steered by this bear of a man. How I long to extricate myself from Eugen and rush to George. If he could have me without my husband, he could fully surrender.

Without Eugen's shadow, we'd be free to partake of each other with chests full of air, speaking poet language, exploring our soft contours.

"Don't be sad, Vincie," says Eugen. "We'll see her soon."

I wrench myself away from him. Damn him for intruding on my longings. He will suffocate me. I storm to the Cadillac and sit in the backseat, wanting as much distance as I can have from him. He will serve me separately now. I can't stand his closeness.

He lights a cigarette and walks around to close my door. When he turns from me, I see the tightness in his eyes and his pursed lips. He is controlling his temper. This infuriates me more. I want him to blow his top. Scream, argue, insist. Anything but this stubborn acquiescence.

He has the audacity to hum on the way home.

He motors us past the dress shop, and I see Laura standing at the doorway, wringing her hands and watching down the street. I don't know why she is so troubled, but I wish I could stop and ask her. I wish I could go into her shop away from this man, from the men working at Steepletop, from all the damned men in the world. Even living in poverty with her would be better than the

211

dullness on the mountain.

She doesn't see me, but I have a sudden memory of my mother standing at the door casting out my father after he gambled away our money. It was the last time. She boldly dismissed and divorced him.

Can I cast out Eugen for no sin? Can I send him away from me for having done nothing but serve me? It seems a cruel act, but cruelty has its merits.

SIXTEEN

LAURA

It took Grace four days to get over her fever. During that time I received a notice from the New York State Gas and Electric Company that I would lose power if I didn't pay my delinquent bill, a request from the grocer to pay down my account, and not a single new customer. I also received a letter from the New York School of Fine and Applied Arts notifying me that my acceptance would expire at the end of the school year unless I made plans to attend classes. I held on to it for a day, and then crumpled it into a ball and threw it across the room into the fireplace. The new day's mail slipped in through the door slot. I picked up the pile and noticed a letter addressed to me in fine script. When I turned over the envelope, I saw that it was from Austerlitz, and when I opened it, I noted the Steepletop letterhead.

Millay had written in hurried, nearly illegible script to request that I reconsider my offer for her velvet gown. She noted that the nights were getting very cold on the mountain, and that she and Eugen dressed for dinner, and would appreciate a new frock to admire.

Dressed for dinner? In their secluded mountain estate? Was there no end to their pretense?

I dropped the letter in the cold fireplace to burn later with the art school notification, and decided that I needed to walk.

I bundled Grace into her wicker pram with a quilt I'd made for her out of fabric with nursery rhyme characters. She pointed to the picture of Humpty Dumpty, and I had to say the rhyme. Then she pointed to the cow jumping over the moon. We went on like this through the backstreets of town and along the river until I tired of reciting poems or she began commenting on our surroundings. We rarely stuck to the main roads to avoid running into her father, and because I hated when her waves or greetings were not returned.

Today I wanted to cross the Stony Kill Bridge, where the autumn views were particularly beautiful, so we had to walk up Main Street for quite a ways. I was in a reckless mood and thought I might not hold my tongue if provoked or cast down my eyes if they met disapproval. The firemen outside nodded to me, but most pedestrians avoided me. The choir ladies stood gathered on the church steps, and I had the audacity to wave at them. One or two of them reacted with a wave on instinct, but most simply gaped at me. I held Agnes' gaze until she turned away.

Grace pointed to the stars on her quilt and I recited "Twinkle, Twinkle, Little Star" to her until we approached the center of town, where my footsteps slowed. A massive, gleaming slab of marble rose from where the great tree had been removed, as if it had erupted from the earth. The stranger leaned his forehead and palms against it, as if in pain.

"Whassat?" asked Grace, as we passed. The man turned and glared at us. He seemed to soften when he saw Grace, but he did not smile. The darkness in his eyes reflected some mental agony, and I felt both sorry for him and worried that he might be a danger. He looked as angry as I felt. Maybe he harbored old war wounds or recollections of lost loves. Or maybe he was just out of jail, and I'd do well to stay far away from him. Recalling that he was Father Ash's friend, however, put me at ease.

"Rock," said Grace.

Before I could answer, Father Ash was at my side, and said in a low voice, "It will be a statue. Of Our Lady of Grace."

"Grace?" said my Grace, pointing to herself.

He smiled. "No, dear child. Jesus' mother."

"Closer," said Grace, and I pushed her to the circle.

I looked at the large lump of marble, fascinated that it could be transformed into a statue.

"My old friend Gabriel will carve her," said Father Ash to Grace. "Mary's hiding in the rock."

Grace's eyes widened and she moved to get out of the pram. I began to protest, but Father Ash said, "It's all right."

I stared hard at him for a moment, and then at Gabriel. He seemed to notice me for the first time. Grace had climbed out of her seat, and was already at the marble, running her hands over it, when I caught sight of Agnes and her fellow choir mate, Sissy, approaching where we stood. Agnes would, no doubt, be the first to spread the gossip. *That seamstress Jezebel was making eyes at the sculptor.* I stepped toward Grace and lifted her back into the buggy, covering her legs with the quilt in haste. Grace let out a wail in protest, and pushed back out of her seat. My face flamed with embarrassment.

"We have to go," I said, trying to keep her seated.

"See Grace," said Grace. "In rock."

She broke out of my grip, and I felt all eyes on me as I lunged after her and shoved her back into the pram while she struggled to get away. I said a silent prayer for patience and placed her firmly in the seat, tucking the quilt around her legs, feeling sweat collect under my clothing.

"We'll see her later," I said, brushing my hair out of my eyes.

Grace stood again, but I pushed the pram with enough power to force her into the seat, and hurried away, mortified that they'd all seen that I was unable to control my child.

I could hear Agnes' cool, proper voice as we left them. "My goodness, how anyone could think to take a walk in this late-fall weather is beyond me. No wonder the child is so unruly." Her provoking appraisal of my walk and parenting felt like a dare, but I would not take it. My shame had overridden my courage.

I put space between us as quickly as possible, forcing all of them out of my head.

Gradually the colored leaves drifting off their sleeping branches cooled my embarrassment.

"I'm upset with you, Grace," I said as we neared the bridge. "When Mama says we have to go, you must listen."

She turned her head to look at me. "But I like rock."

"I do too. But I don't like that lady, Mrs. Dwyer."

Grace raised her eyebrows, and turned away. I regretted saying such a thing to her, but I couldn't help myself. I hoped my words would never come back to haunt me on the tongue of my impish girl.

When we reached Stony Kill Bridge, there were no cars, so we stopped for Grace to drop a couple of leaves over the side and into the current. She waved at them until they disappeared from sight. When she tired of this, we continued on, mingling the recitation of nursery rhymes with natural observations. I enjoyed the calm, and became more relaxed the farther we traveled from town.

About a mile beyond the bridge, I realized I'd gone too far. Grace was hungry, and the air had grown uncomfortably chilly. Grace coughed, and her hot breath came out in a puff in the cold air. I was angry with myself for keeping her out so long immediately after her illness, and cursed my own recklessness, especially as the first icy drops of rain landed on my shoulders.

I turned and saw at our heels a great cloud bank moving swiftly on the increasing winds. It seemed to have chased us from town. We would have to walk back toward it to get home. The pram did not have a visor, so I wrapped Grace's blanket over her head and around her face to keep out the rain, which began to fall harder. Grace started to cry.

"Oh, Gracie, I'm sorry," I said, as I quickened my pace. I hated to run because it seemed to make us colder and wetter, but I had to get my little one out of the elements. The rush of the river down the embankment signaled to me that the rain was increasing, but this lonely stretch of road had no house where we could stop. Half of the forest trees above us had already lost their foliage, leaving us little covering over our heads.

Water wilted the brim of my hat and dripped over my coat. Grace cried harder. I too wanted to cry, thinking of the danger in which I'd put my poor child's health in the name of calming my heated nerves. Agnes would really think I was a terrible mother if she saw me, and I feared she was right.

An old farm truck came puffing up the road, but the driver either did not see us or did not care, because he came uncomfortably close and splashed us as he passed. I vowed revenge, though I'd never seen him before, and had a thought that I might enlist the witch, Millay, to put a curse on him.

The rain had become a relentless downpour, and I knew I had to find shelter, or Grace would surely catch pneumonia. The bridge was in sight, and I thought I could lift her out of the pram and carry her underneath to hide from the storm. I quickened my pace, and as I neared it, I heard a car approaching me from behind. I stopped and pulled as far off the road as possible to avoid being struck or soaked further, but the car slowed until it was at my side. I was shocked to see Eugen and Millay staring out at me.

"Miss Kelley, please allow us to help you," said Eugen.

I looked at the sky and then at the bridge, thinking I would rather wait out the storm than accept charity from these people. I began to walk again when Grace sneezed.

Damn it!

Millay surprised me by opening her door and walking around the front of the car, where she promptly lifted my daughter and hurried to the passenger side. Eugen also got out, picked up my pram, and slid it into the backseat, dragging muddy wheels over the Cadillac's spotless interior. I came to my senses, horrified that they had rescued me and messed up their car, but I wedged myself into the backseat next to the stroller, and allowed Eugen to close the door.

The warm, comfortable car smelled of cigarettes and chamomile. Grace seemed mesmerized by the beguiling woman with red hair and green eyes, who was holding her and gently rocking her in the front seat, as was I. I'd made a very clear judgment of this woman in my head. Kindness to children did not fit in with what I thought I knew.

"Miss Kelley," said the amiable Dutchman, "why ever did you decide to take a stroll in the cold rain?"

"She was certainly caught unawares, Eugen," said Millay as though I was not there.

"You are lucky we were just returning from Pittsfield," he continued.

My stomach clenched, and flashes of memory from the night at the Follies tormented me. I thought of the poor woman for whom I'd bought the ticket. I looked down at my worn dress and coat, feeling the weight of the damp hat on my head, thinking of my loneliness and poverty. I must appear to Millay as that woman had to me years ago, and I hated being the recipient of her pity.

We crossed the bridge and the car moved slowly down Main Street, back toward my shop. When we passed the marble slab, I saw that it had been covered with a tarp, and a small canvas tent had been erected over it. Gabriel stood inside, tying the canvas to the poles. He did not look up as we motored around the circle.

"A beautiful stranger," said Millay. "I wonder if he likes parties." She seemed to say this out of the side of her mouth, directing the comment at me as if to provoke me, which it did.

"I'm quite sure he does not," I said, surprised at my own vehemence and presumption. I felt my temperature rise further when I saw Millay smile.

"There she is," she said.

"Lady in rock," said Grace.

"Is she, now?" said Millay. "That is something I'd like to see. My work is a little like that, but I work with paper and pencils."

Grace sat up, unafraid and at ease in the car. "Mama sews clothes."

"I know," said Millay. "Do you think your

mommy would make me a pretty gown?"

"Yes," said Grace.

"And what color should it be?"

"Purple."

Eugen laughed. "Yes, my little one, purple for the Royal Duchess."

Millay laughed, and Grace joined them.

I couldn't abide their familiarity with my daughter or the way she had taken to them, but thankfully, we had arrived at the shop. When Eugen stopped, I opened the door and pulled the pram out, no longer caring about the mess it had left, only wishing to get away from them. Millay carried Grace under the awning at the front of the shop. She stood maddeningly close to me as I fumbled with the key, and then walked in ahead of me once I opened the door. I flipped on the light switch next to the door, but nothing happened. The electric company must have turned off my utilities. I wiggled the switch back and forth to confirm my suspicions.

Millay placed Grace on her feet and patted her head.

"She is a beautiful child," she said. "The very image of you: soft blond curls, an aura of vulnerability. Although she seems as light as a firefly, while you carry the burden of your past."

I suddenly felt very tired, cold, and unable to defend myself. I just wanted her to leave.

"Laura." My name seemed to echo in the room. Millay's voice held such weight, such layers. In her address of me, she'd conjured kindness, sympathy, sweetness. I raised my eyes to hers. "Please. Make me a gown. This is not charity. It is the wish of one businesswoman with the means to afford a high-quality service to the businesswoman who may provide that service. Nothing more."

"Miss Millay," I began.

"Please, call me Vincent. Or Edna — most of my new friends call me Edna."

"Edna," I said. "You must understand that it is my loyalty to my sister that prevents my service to you."

"Your loyalty is admirable," she said, "but I'm quite sure your sister wishes you to have working lights. A business. Rooms of your own. I don't want to coerce you. I want you to want to make me beautiful things because that is what you love to do. I know you love to do it because I've seen your work and your attention to detail. I saw that costume you made for your sister at the hospital ball, the frocks you made for my mother. They are the nicest she's ever worn. I just want you to think about it. Will you do that? And you don't have to tell your sister. Does she require an accounting of every one of your customers?"

"No."

"Good. Please think about it."

She smiled at Grace, met my gaze once more, and left us standing in the dark.

VINCENT

Keeping Eugen in his own rooms at night has given me new life. I can tolerate him more if his hand isn't on my breast or my arm all night long. I know he used to sleep that way with his own mother until he was a grotesquely advanced age, and I do not wish to be his mother. If anything, I am his child, but I won't stand for such incessant closeness. Conjugal activities, which I still enjoy with him, are separate from sleep and may take place anywhere and anytime, but I must enforce my insistence on separate sleeping places.

I will not have breakfast with him in the dining room any longer if I do not wish it, either. Sensible people of means should take breakfast in bed alone. And while I am taking control of my household, I will inform Eugen of exactly what is expected of these horrid, pedestrian people: people without vocation whose lives are spent in toiling misery shining the banisters of others' homes. I can't imagine such an existence, but they must be of a different mind from someone like me, so I must instruct them how to exist around me. No more slopping water on the floor and chattering to me like finches when I am trying to compose a sonnet in my head. I can't think of the thousands of words and phrases I've lost to the questions "When do ya want the linens taken to wash?" or "Which brand of dog meat do ya want us to buy?"

Really? Asking me such questions when I have goddesses and muses delivering timeless poems to my brain? Scattering their gifts with solicitations my husband can handle.

Control. I must take control. I have allowed it to slip from my fingers for far too long, and this lack of order poisons everything. It poisons my feelings of power so I cannot properly manage my work or my George.

I gaze out the window and see Eugen walking up the drive. The clouds are moving swiftly, throwing him in and out of shadow. From this distance, I love him wholly. He sees me smile at him through the window, and raises his eyebrows as if to say, "May I come see you?" I nod, giving him permission. In moments, the door opens and he is before me in the front room.

"You are radiant today," he says. "Your eyes are sparkling. What spells are you at?"

"Sit, sweet man. We need to talk management."

"This sounds very serious, love," he says, taking the chair and gazing at me with adoration.

"It is," I say. "You may have noticed that I have been mercurial lately."

He laughs in his warm, open way.

"I mean, more than usual," I say, with a grin.

"I just thought it was the curse," he says. "No need to explain."

"But it isn't the curse. It is this household. It needs tighter management. It's too noisy and loose. You must explain to the servants that if they wish to stay employed, I have to work, and I can't work with all of their distractions. You understand?"

"I do. I'll lay down Edna's law."

"Good. Also, my mother is ever in my thoughts. She keeps writing, asking for small amounts of money. This is distracting because of the pain it brings me. I know she needs more but is ashamed to ask for it, and I can't abide her shame. She gave her life to care for my sisters and me, and I want her comfortable."

"What do you suggest, Vincie? We've tried to have her live in the cottage before but that didn't work out."

"No, we all need our own space. I mean that I want to give her a large sum."

"How much do you mean?"

"A fortune. One thousand dollars."

He widens his eyes and then smiles. "You are so generous. You know we are not exactly in our best financial place, though, yes? The stock market has gone to hell."

"I know the numbers, Uge. But since I have claimed more control here, my words are in abundance. When I finish these sonnets, we will have quite a windfall."

"Then let's do it. Write her the check."

We are grinning at each other. The room is lit from warm sunshine. A true radiance. Order. When I do this good, good will come. But I don't do it for any reward when it comes to Mother. I would give her my very breath if she required it.

SEVENTEEN

LAURA

A terrible wind battered the house, slipping in through windows and flimsy doors in need of sealing. I had boiled hot water over the fireplace to warm the cold tub water, and given Grace and myself a bath. We dressed in our flannel nightgowns, tights, and socks, and sat by the fire eating cold ham sandwiches and apples. She was frightened of the windstorm, so I let her sit with me past her bedtime, braiding her hair, which was growing in and making her look more like a child than a baby, and following the aimless sweetness of her chatter.

"I make purple dress," she said.

"What dress?" I asked.

"For witchy lady."

Goose bumps rose on my skin. I wondered if Grace had ever overhead me say Millay seemed witchy or if she'd intuited that on her own. I stopped pondering that question, however, when the front door burst open, causing Grace and me to jump. Marie entered on a gust of wind, and slammed the door behind her.

"Damn him," said Marie, wiping her eyes with her sleeve. She flinched and held her back, which had been giving her pain. Marie's angry visits and overnight stays had lessened in frequency with each passing month, but still came, erratic and unpredictable as the currents in the Stony Kill. I wondered what had set her off. When Marie saw Grace sitting with me by the fire, she looked mortified.

"I'm sorry," said Marie. "I didn't know she'd still be awake."

Marie reached for the light switch. "Why are you sitting in the dark?"

"I haven't paid my electric bill. I'll run to the office tomorrow."

"Do you need something from us to hold you over?"

"No," I said. "Everette doesn't need to support me. It's just you that you need to worry about."

"I'm going mad. I spend half my day wishing for Everette to hold me and half wishing to strangle him. I need a hobby or employment. When I suggested I try to come back to work with you to bring in business, he said it would reflect poorly on him, but the truth is that he has taken a considerable pay cut as town manager since the crash, and we are barely making ends meet. If I could still work with you, I might be able to contribute."

"As you can see," I said, "we'd need customers for that to be so."

"Why haven't you told me it was this bad?"

"For you to do what, worry right along with me? We'll be fine. Someone always seems to walk through the door just before I think I'll need to shut down for good."

I thought of Millay with guilt, but I pushed her from my mind. Marie began pacing the room.

"It's time for bed, Gracie," I said.

"Stay," she said.

"No, you need to rest so you keep getting better."

She protested all the way up the stairs, but as soon as I laid her in bed with her blanket, she turned on her side and snuggled under the covers. I kissed Grace's head and went back downstairs to see to Marie. In the front room, I found her rubbing her back.

"Sit down," I said. "You'll have the baby right here if you continue like this."

"I wish I could. I don't even care any-more," she said. "Then he'd really pay."

I recoiled from her as if slapped. Did she mean that she hoped the child would die? Marie's eyes met mine and appeared remorseful.

"I didn't mean that," she mumbled. "Not at all. I just want him to hurt."

Her words didn't soften me. Her willingness to give voice to such a thought chilled me.

The wind rattled the panes like hands shaking the glass, trying to get in. I gazed back at Marie and saw real fear. I realized how horrible it must be for her, circumstances so different from my own and yet somehow the same. While I was alone, she certainly felt alone, and having a child under such anguish was its own kind of hell. I reached for her hand and saw her relief. Our silent remorse knit us back together.

"Would you like to stay the night?" I asked.

"No, I should go back," she said. "Forgive my tantrum. It's just that if I don't let it go here, I'll fling it at him, and we're too unstable for more pressure."

"It's all right."

"I hate to leave you here in the dark and cold. Are you sure you and Grace wouldn't want to sleep at our house, at least until the electricity is turned on?"

"No," I said. "Thank you. We'll be fine." What I didn't say was that I would rather Grace not see and feel the turmoil in their house. She got enough of that at home with me.

Marie left me with a hug, and I locked the door behind her. Seeing Marie so frantic felt like looking in a mirror. I could understand why she said my bitterness helped cure hers. It was ugly and unsettling to witness, but hard to control.

I knew I should go to bed, but my mind felt too active. I sat by the fireplace and stared into the flames. Then, almost as if hypnotized, I reached for my sketch pad and pencil on the end table. Inside the pad were my ideas for costumes. I'd kept it since that night at the Colonial Theatre. There were hundreds of pages of designs: a parade of costumes for the Follies, Shakespearean plays, interpretation of songs from Beethoven's *Appassionata,* to Handel's *Messiah,* to George Gershwin's "Rhapsody in Blue." The sketchbook had become a diary of my dreams. I fantasized that if I ever became a seamstress for a theater company, I'd have my design blueprints ready.

I flipped to the next clean page and put

the pencil on the paper. As if overcome by a force outside of myself, I drew a curve, a shadow, a bell-shaped sleeve, a fur cuff. I noted *velvet* and *ermine* in the margin, and then retrieved my colored pencils and began to shade in the folds of the gown with a deep, warm shade of purple. A shade that would complement locks of copper hair. A hue that would provide a perfect contrast to the golden green eyes looking out over it.

A gown fit for a Royal Duchess.

VINCENT

I need this storm. The weather is a mirror for the tempest building inside me.

The household has fallen into line. Silence is my gift. But the words are erratic, in my poetry and from my poet.

Eugen comes from the post every day with nothing from George — not a letter, a note, or even a telegram. My headaches have become so severe that I can only write in the darkness, where the light cannot torture me. It seeks the place in my skull behind my eyes and makes it throb until I can only curl up in my bed covered with the blankets that still hold his smell, which I refuse to have laundered.

George is breaking me. I don't know if he means to do it, but with every day that passes without a word from him, I feel more sure I will run to the train station and travel to him to force him to look at me, confront me, love me.

The rumble of thunder has called me from my bed. I open the curtains and am able to watch the wind in the stubborn, clinging leaves without the damned sunlight to torture me. I'm suddenly overcome with the need to be in the storm, conjuring, one with nature in this form. We are the same today.

I slide my silk robe around my body and throw open my bedroom door. Eugen emerges from his rooms next to mine but sees the wild look in my eyes and my hair loose around my shoulders, and senses that he is not to impede my progress.

I move down the stairs with the elegance of an apparition, and the maid scrubbing the stone floor looks at me as if I were indeed a ghost. She gasps and clutches her brushes and buckets to move them from my path before I kick them at her. She is no idiot like the cook, and keeps out of my way.

I open the door before she can get to it, and the wind throws it back to slam into the wall and blasts my hair, lifting it up behind me. I inhale deeply and push out into it, feeling the electricity from the clouds and the landscape. A lightning bolt hits the ground so close to me that I feel the earth tremble, but I know it will not harm me. I even court it, wishing it would slice me through so I could exist in the peace of the grave.

The dried husks of my summer flowers have not yet been flattened, so they still conceal me on the path to my writing cabin. My heart is beating fiercely, and I both relish the feeling and wish to clamp my hands around this organ of torment.

My cabin is made of crude wooden boards and heated with the fire of an old stove. Here it is just me and my pencil and my desk. Here I don't have to feel the pulse of my husband's energy, disturbances from the help, or predictable knocks on the door from the Fickes, who seem to need us to exist with each other.

Ficke's wife won't allow Arthur and me to consummate any longer, and as much as I wish we could reclaim that freedom, we cannot. The past cannot be resurrected. This hurts me because it reminds me of my own fading youth and the death of all of those throbbing bohemian nights in Greenwich Village or the Left Bank or on the coast of Maine, where one never felt the isolation of being surrounded by mountains and forests.

It is there that I will escape soon — the

shore. The only place where I can truly breathe.

I will visit Mother. That will make her happy.

I imagine a seaside at night, a woman born of its tides in the stark moonlight, crawling out of the surf spitting shells and seaweed upon the sand, while dry sand clings to her wet hair, her hands, her eyes. I imagine a house with windows lit with the warm glow of fire while the woman shivers on the shore. There is a longing in the woman that the man inside the house will come and minister to her, but he does not come.

In the salty silence, the woman becomes aware of the weight of darkness all around her and sees the truth. Only the night, her sister, will watch with this woman, and she must pick up herself, and dry the briny drippings, and expel the death from her own lungs.

EIGHTEEN

LAURA

My heart banged in my chest and I had difficulty breathing as I approached Eugen. He was waiting for me in his car, behind the cemetery, as I'd asked. He smoked and stared off in the distance. I could have turned away; he still hadn't seen me. I stopped once, twice, but felt the weight of the sketch pad in my satchel and continued toward him, all the time telling myself I had to survive; I needed money. I thought of the lie I'd told Marie, who was keeping Grace, that I was meeting with a client for some housedresses, an elderly woman who preferred not to come to the shop. Half-truths, full betrayals, a sister preoccupied enough with herself not to ask too many questions.

When Eugen caught sight of me, he smiled and tossed his cigarette out the window. He opened his door and came around to open mine — a true gentleman. I thanked him and faced forward, reminding myself that I was a professional, and this errand was necessary to support my daughter.

"I'm so glad you've decided to help Vincie," he said. "You have brought a light to her that she hasn't felt in weeks. I was beginning to worry about her state of mind approaching the cold dark of winter, but now, with your kindness, I think you will restore something in her."

I was coming just to make a dress. Why did he place so much importance on my visit?

"Where is your darling daughter?" he asked, driving fast on the curving slope of road that snaked through the forest.

"My sister has her," I said.

He raised his eyebrows at me. "And did you tell her where you were going?"

"No."

"Ah. A secret among sisters. It is for the best," he said, almost to himself.

He took the next turn sharply, and I fell into him. I scooted back to my side of the seat, and he laughed.

"Feel free to stay there, *chéri.* You are a pleasant weight on my shoulder."

I inched closer to the window and looked out at the passing forest, the evergreens shrouded in mist, the gray sky looming low over the mountainous landscape. Eugen laughed next to me.

"Forgive me, Miss Kelley. I don't want you to feel uncomfortable. I want you to be happy. Maybe someday I will make you smile."

"I doubt that very much," I mumbled, and was again met with his laugh. He was maddeningly cheerful. His joviality put me off because it disregarded my feelings. But perhaps that was his strategy for calming others. I'd seen him effectively use it with Millay. Perhaps he felt that acting like a child meant he never had to deal in the muddled complications of adulthood.

"How much older than her are you?" I heard myself blurt.

"Twelve years."

That surprised me. It was quite a gap.

"Vincie needs taking care of — not with money, but with her fragile health. Isn't she like a tiny girl? A precious, tiny girl."

The way he spoke of her made me uneasy. These people were not like me. Their natures seemed predatory or spoiled, like large children who wanted to collect things.

I felt nauseous on the fast, twisting ride to Steepletop, and it struck me that if anything happened to me, no one would ever know. If these strange, covetous people wanted to

keep me locked up in a basement or prisoner in an attic, I'd have no way of being
rescued. But this thinking was ridiculous. I
needed to stop reading the whodunits at the
library. My imagination was being contami-
nated with nonsense.

Still, as I gazed over the acres of mountains and trees, and felt my ears pop as we
climbed the road, the extreme isolation of
the farm weighed on me. I had admired
Millay's freedom away from town, but I realized it might not be as ideal as I'd imagined. As much as I longed to escape the gossips in town, perhaps I did not wish to
escape people or civilization. Maybe I
needed new people with whom I had no
past, people who would smile kindly at me
and my daughter, invite us to dinner, not be
afraid to take a walk in the park with us,
not hesitate to patronize me for my services.

When we finally reached the gates of
Steepletop, I couldn't believe I had managed bike rides up these hills without collapse. My anger must have fueled some well
of dark energy inside me. The darkness sat
heavy in my chest. I hated myself for being
here. I hated Millay and her husband for
participating in my sister's undoing. I hated
that I'd ever let myself get into such a situation.

Eugen drove a bit slower as we motored up the driveway, calling my attention to the barn assembled from a Sears and Roebuck kit, pointing out the horses running in a high field, greeting the handsome English setter that ran alongside the car. The bare branches of the dragon willow that hung over the drive parted like a frayed stage curtain as we pulled up to the front of the white farmhouse. As soon as I stepped from the car, the hair rose on my neck.

Steepletop sounded like a hive. Bees infested the air over the flowers and grasses. Gnats swarmed my face, unfazed by my swats. Eugen came around the front of the car and held out a cigarette to me.

"Here," he said. "Light this. It will keep the bugs from assaulting you."

"I don't smoke," I said.

"Of course you don't," he said, not unkindly. "Just let it smolder in your mouth. No one will be here to see you."

I hesitated, then took the cigarette, allowed him to light it, and held it in front of my face, thinking how odd it felt here. How unholy.

I slung my satchel over my shoulder and followed Eugen to the door. He opened it for me and allowed me passage into a stone foyer, where a set of tiny women's riding boots sat in a border of drying mud next to a .22-caliber rifle.

"She's a good hunter," said Eugen. "Bloodthirsty, but with ample remorse."

I suspected his assessment had as much to do with people as with animals.

"Wait in the dining room," he said, gesturing through the door ahead of me. "She will be with you shortly."

While Eugen climbed the stairs to the left, I walked forward into the dining room. The hardwood floor gleamed in the light shining from the windows on either side of the far wall, framed in red-and-cream toile curtains. The wall was painted bloodred beneath the chair rail, and there were many heavy pieces of furniture. On either side of the room at my left and right, corner shelves held rows of seashells, brilliantly formed, creamy as pearls, and somehow at odds with the opulence. A tapestry hung on the wall next to a fireplace, where the hearth blazed, heating the room beyond what was comfortable.

I dropped the cigarette into the embers, removed my hat and coat, and laid them on one of the high-backed dining table chairs. As I slid the scarf from my neck, Eugen returned.

"She wants you to come up to her rooms," he said, looking subdued and somewhat uncomfortable. "She's . . . not well. It has been a difficult day for her."

"Should I come back another time?"

"No," he said. "She suffers heartsickness. Her lover is not cooperating with her. He is breaking her."

Her lover is breaking her. Words flowing from the mouth of her husband as if he were speaking of a coming storm or a farming matter. A woman with men orbiting her like moons while I sat cold and alone with my former lover a gaze away. A woman sulking in her rooms while a doting, indulgent husband made offerings for her amusement.

I rewrapped my scarf around my neck and put on my coat.

"What are you doing, Miss Kelley?"

"This was a mistake," I said. "I don't know why I'm here. I wish to go."

"Please stay. If you leave, she'll collapse."

"I hardly think that's true," I said, pressing my hat on my head and starting out of the room.

"No, truly. I don't know what she'll do if she gets one more rejection," he said in a quavering but insistent whisper. "Her poetry has been uncooperative, her lover, the weather, her health, her horses, her mother, now you. How much is one woman expected to endure? I'm afraid she will take that gun and blow her own pretty head off; you must help me."

He had me by the arms, and I saw that there were tears in his eyes.

"Please, Laura. Please. Don't do it for her. Do it for a husband in agony. Do it for your daughter."

I pulled out of his grip and moved to the hallway, where I opened the door and started down the stairs.

"I would never have taken you for a hypocrite," he said.

I ignored him.

"You say you don't help us because of loyalty to your sister," he continued, "but you know it is more than that."

I stopped and stared straight ahead of me, down a hill and into a rose garden. Something in the air had changed. Thorny branches reached toward the sky, and crows moved from the tree limbs hanging over the path. A breeze stirred the willow. Shafts of sunlight dropped from between moving cloud banks. A line of men walked on the crest of the hill and waved down to me. The setter came back, and greeted me by placing his head under my hand. I stroked his silky fur and tried to think what was different when I realized that I could no longer hear the bees. Their terrible droning had stopped. No bugs flew at me. A crisp wind traveled up the driveway and into my face, opening my lungs.

I turned back to Eugen. "What strange magic is this?"

He closed his eyes and inhaled. "I think it is winter, just arriving."

"But it has only recently turned fall."

"The seasons are advanced and fickle up here. You are in another world, don't you know?" He grinned at me, and the tension left my body. I returned his smile.

He clapped and said, "I made you smile!"

I laughed and felt almost drunk from the sensation. When had I last felt a release like this? I walked past him back into the house and removed my hat. He helped me with my coat and scarf and hung them on pegs in the foyer.

"I could kiss you, kind woman," he said.

"If I'm going to ever return to this place, you'll have to stop saying things like that."

"And if you return, you'll have to understand that I am harmless, jovial, and full of love. It is my nature — I cannot help it, nor do I want to. But I will try to respect your prudery."

"I wouldn't call myself a prude," I said. "I just . . ."

"No, I only tease you. I know you are full

246

of passions. I can see it in your eyes," he said. "Now, come. We've kept the Duchess waiting long enough."

She stood in the darkened room with the curtains drawn, wearing a translucent coral negligee. She stared at dying embers in the fireplace while fondling an empty bottle of wine on the mantel. Shiny tracks of tears lined her cheeks. Then, theatrically, almost as if posing for a movie still, she turned her head. Her copper hair fell in waves to her shoulders, and reached the middle of her back as she tilted her head and finished the clear contents of the tumbler in her hand, which she then held out.

Eugen ran his hand over my back as he passed me. He took the glass and set it on her vanity behind us, where he gave her another pour from the half-empty Fleischman's Gin bottle. He placed it back in her hand, and she sipped from it before clearing her throat.

"This wine," she said, indicating the empty bottle on the mantel, "this curved, supple bit of blown glass, was emptied the night we heard that the poet Elinor Wylie had died, and I keep it here always as a reminder of why I must do the things I plan to do the moment I intend to do them. I had planned to save this wine for Elinor upon her visit to my rooms, where she spent so much time in tender communion with me, and she was never able to drink it."

Millay drank again and looked at me. "Would you like a drink?"

"No," I said. "I'm here to measure you for your gown, but then I must get home. No one knows I'm here."

She stared at me for a moment, drained her glass, and placed it next to the wine bottle.

"Oh, the impatience," she said. "Gene, shut my door on the way out."

Eugen winked at me as he closed the door to her bedroom, leaving me alone with her. I followed her tiny figure through a door to a bathroom with a black-and-white-tiled floor, two toilets, and another vanity facing a window. I turned my attention back to the dual toilets.

"A bidet," she said. "Have you ever seen one?"

I shook my head.

She crossed very near to me, filling my nose with the scent of alcohol and an herb of some kind. She turned a nozzle and water shot up and trickled back into the bowl.

"I first saw these in Paris in the twenties, and now I can't live without them. I love the freshness, the cleanness." She took my hand. "Come."

We passed through another door to a workroom, where a large table covered in notebooks, scribbled papers, and ashtrays took up most of the space. She pushed aside the papers and crossed the floor to open the curtain, allowing in the late-morning light. I placed my satchel on the table and removed the measuring tape, relieved to see the light of day, and to be at my business. I pulled my sketch pad out of the bag and opened it on the table to the page with the purple gown, allowing myself to enjoy this moment. It was as close to costuming as I'd ever get.

I turned back to Millay. She stood in front of me, lit a cigarette, and untied her negligee, allowing it to drop to the floor, exposing her nakedness. I averted my eyes.

"There is no need to remove your covering," I said. "I can get a good enough measurement through your robe."

She let out a rich, throaty laugh, and put her hands on her hips, clearly at ease with my discomfort. It occurred to me that this need to provoke seemed like adolescent behavior, which made me feel superior to her. In spite of our age difference, I was the mature woman dealing with a naughty girl, and that gave me courage.

I circled her, noting how very small she was, almost freakishly so, like a pixie. She relaxed her arms at her sides while the cigarette burned between her lips. From behind she could have been a young girl, if it wasn't for the slight spread of her hips. I wrapped my arms around her from either side and pulled the measuring tape across her chest, joining it in the back and noting her bust size.

Thirty-four inches.

Millay had ample breasts for one so small in stature. She turned her head to the side as if watching me, and raised her hand to her lips to remove the cigarette and flick it over the ashtray on the table. As I let the tape slip off her breasts and down to her waist, she sucked in her breath.

I tightened the measuring tape on her small waist, and as I did, my hands grazed her lower back. She again pulled in her breath and raised the cigarette back to her lips. Her skin began to flush, and I knew that this woman was working herself into quite a state at my touch. I felt curiously removed from the situation. Perhaps my separation from what I was doing allowed me to continue.

Twenty-two inches.

I moved the tape a bit farther down and allowed it to open around the swell of her hips. As I noted her perfect curvature, thirty-four inches, she reached over and stubbed out the cigarette, and then turned to me. Her eyes were half-open, and she was nearly breathless. A fine sheen of sweat glistened on her freckled neck.

"Put out your arms," I said. She obeyed me and I measured their length. I knew I had to measure her legs, but I didn't want to be at her feet with her naked over me. I went around the back of her again, and measured from behind, careful to keep my fingers away from any place that might further arouse her. The graceful curve of her back ignited an image in my mind of purple velvet outlining its slope. I could almost feel the material in my hands as I worked, and became dizzy.

"You have such a gentle touch," she said. "Like wind moving over my body."

I shook my head to scatter my fantasy, and walked over to my notebook, where I recorded her measurements.

"Once you've put on your robe, I'll discuss my ideas with you," I said, meeting her gaze. "But only once you've dressed."

Her face fell, and she replaced her expression of drowsy anticipation with a sulking scowl. She looked like a lascivious child. I turned my back on her to hide my smile, pleased that I had won some control. Soon, she was at my side, close enough that I could feel the heat radiating from her body.

"Can you at least tie my robe?" she said. "My hands are trembling."

I gave her a look of annoyance, but decided to give in a little if it would mean that her breasts would no longer be poking out at me. I closed the negligee over her chest and tied it in a double knot. She could barely take her eyes off me, but managed to glance down at the sketchbook. She ran her hand over the purple gown, tracing the fur collar as if she could feel it. It made the hair on my arms rise.

"Yes," she said. "This is exactly what I envisioned. Velvet. Ermine. You have a special sight."

"No, Miss Millay —"

"Vincent."

"Vincent, I simply listened to what was asked of me."

"How much will it cost?"

"That depends on the quality of fabric —"

"The highest."

"Then I imagine it will cost close to twenty dollars, payable up front, as soon as

I have the exact figures."

Millay walked over to the bureau in front of the window and opened the middle drawer, where she removed a white banking sleeve from under a pile of sweaters. She found a twenty-dollar bill and held it out to me. I longed to snatch it from her fingers and get as far away from her as quickly as possible, but I willed my composure and took the money gently, pressing it into my notebook, which I slid into my satchel.

"You are an innocent," she said, almost to herself.

"I don't think most people in town would agree with you."

"You are wounded too. Deeply."

I couldn't argue with her there.

She reached out to touch my face, and I flinched.

"Forgive me," she said, drawing back her hand. "I am very sensitive — to touch, to the environment, to the interior lives of others. You have a tempest in you at odds with your softness of feature and manner that I find irresistible."

I did not answer her comment. I did not want to acknowledge her advances, though her boldness fascinated me. I was determined to keep my composure, although I'd begun to feel the same wrongness in the atmosphere that I had earlier, with the buzzing bees. I longed to get out of these rooms, which felt too close and intimate, and no doubt held the impressions of countless strange and promiscuous rendezvous.

"I should have the gown finished within several weeks," I said. "Mr. Boissevain can pick it up at that time. On appointment, of course. We must be discreet."

"Why don't you bring it up to me?"

"I don't have a car, and the trip is difficult by bike. Also, there's my daughter."

Millay sighed and started back through the bathroom to her bedroom. I followed her in, but instead of leading me out to the hallway, she walked to her bedside, lit a candle, and untied the knot on her robe, again letting the negligee fall to the floor. She leaned back on the bed and narrowed her eyes.

"I'm glad you came," she said, stroking her hair and letting it fall across the tops of her breasts. She slid her hand down her stomach as I turned to leave. "Tell my husband to hurry back. I'll be waiting for him."

VINCENT

I once told George we were doomed because our love began its bloom when there

254

were no leaves on the trees for sighing under. No flowers for him to place in my waiting hands. No birds to christen us, no spring rains to baptize us, no sun's blessing.

Bitter wind, heavy snow, gray skies cracked by black rooks were all we had.

He'd disagreed with me. He said that our winter love would grow like the fire's ember, a cozy place against a battering storm. He said it would drink the melted snowdrifts until it burst open and coiled its roots and shoots out to meet the spring, where it would flourish.

He always was a silly poet.

But thoughts of George always mingle with those of Elinor.

While I recline in my bed, my eyes fall on the empty bottle of wine that I was to share with Elinor Wylie before she passed. I think of that night I was to read, when just a breath before I went onstage I was told that she had died. As I walked out before the audience, I could not hear their welcoming applause. A thousand smiling faces behind two thousand clapping hands were like actors in a silent film. They made no sound. I could only hear the rushing of blood in my ears, pumped from my vital heart, reminding me that my life had no power to infuse her life any longer. I had recited her poetry

255

that night, instead of my own, until I could barely stand. Then I wrote to George.

It seems our love was born in the death of that time, a phoenix rising from Elinor's ashes. I can't think of Elinor's death, her stroke at such a young age, without it being followed by the way George pierced my heart.

I am overcome with a little poem, a neat stack of words that will be my dedication. I will dedicate my sonnets to Elinor; the essence of what I felt for her will be a prelude to my love with George. It will be a perfect marriage, more perfect than this marriage in which I now exist.

The last word in the dedication is *grief.* My pencil clings to it like a magnet. I am suddenly trembling.

I look down and see that I am still naked. My breasts are heavy and sore with my coming courses. My belly is swollen. How I wish one of them could be here to see me, ripe like this. Full as the moon. As soft and open as I'll ever be.

Nineteen

Laura

Eugen dropped me off behind the cemetery, just as I'd asked. Once he had pulled away, I walked to the stone in the wall and dislodged it. There was no lover's note, of course. He hadn't left one in years, and I hated that it still hurt me. I began to press the stone back into place, but decided to put an end to that hope. I searched until I found a large rock, which wasn't difficult being so near the mountains, and brought it down on the stone, cracking it into pieces. Smashing it felt exhilarating, and I was smiling to myself as I turned to the homeward path, only to halt in surprise when I came face-to-face with the sculptor Gabriel walking toward me. His hat hung low over his eyes.

"Feel better now?" he asked.

"I do," I said, trying to hide my embarrassment. "You should try it sometime. It would do you good."

He laughed. "I'll start tomorrow, as a matter of fact. With the marble, that is. The first strikes can be free and careless. Not as much after that."

"I'll have to bring my daughter to see you work. She's dying to see the lady in the rock. If you don't mind an audience."

"I don't have much choice, being out in the middle of town, do I? But it's what Michael wants. And I'll take your daughter over those other women any day."

He must have meant Agnes and her friends.

"Father Ash is an old friend?" I asked, my curiosity getting the better of me.

"We were in Italy together during the war. Michael's a great man. A brave man."

I tried to think of Father Ash outside the context of our town, framed in a different window from the one in which I often found him watching over the street, but I could not. I couldn't picture him with a group of men, sharing insults or injury. He seemed solitary to me. An island. I wondered if Gabriel was the same.

A novel suddenly came to mind — *A Farewell to Arms* by Ernest Hemingway. Mrs. Perth had snuck it to me after it was banned from the library. I'd loved it, but had been devastated by it. What if Gabriel's heartbreaks were like those of Frederick Henry's? Whom had he loved and lost in the war?

"Michael wants the town to see the transformation of a crude rock into a pure, holy being. To show what we are all capable of becoming in spite of our sin. To show what God does with us. Those are his words, not mine." He sounded cynical.

I was further embarrassed to feel tears spring to my eyes. "I must be going," I said, and continued on the path away from him.

A breeze sent a shower of leaves falling over me and the sun warmed me as I hurried back to my home, to my daughter, to my sister, who waited for me. As I walked, I prepared in my head the lies I'd tell to hide my betrayal, and it hurt me deeply in light of the symbol on display in the center of town that was meant to change me — to change all of our dark hearts.

Marie didn't ask me a single question about my outing. I supposed her preoccupation with herself had its benefits.

She complained about her aching back, her distaste of Everette's new approach of simpering remorse, the way winter seemed to be coming down early from the mountain. I stifled a smile at that comment, remembering how I'd said just those words to Eugen, but she did not notice. She kissed Grace on the head, kissed me on the cheek, and was market-bound before I could get a word in edgewise.

The next day, I was glad I'd thought to prepare the fireplace with kindling and logs the night before. Winter had arrived, and the sharp cold had made its way under the door, around the windows, and through the floorboards. I set the rice pouch I'd made for Grace by the fire. My mother had shown me years ago how to sew a flannel pouch, fill it with dry rice, and warm it on the hearth. This little sleeve provided comfort on cold winter mornings and in bed at night. Grace loved it. She called it her rice baby.

When she awoke, I gave her the heated rice baby, boiled a pot of water for the percolator, and used what coffee I didn't drink to make gravy for the biscuits I'd saved from yesterday morning. Once we'd eaten our fill, the fire had warmed the downstairs, so we hurried upstairs to wash our faces, brush our hair, and put on dresses, then return to the toasty room.

I kept an eye on the door, knowing Marie would come through at any moment. She wanted to work on the layette for the baby, but I was eager to place fabric orders for Millay's gown. I kept the samples in the back room and told Grace to call when Aunt Marie arrived. As I flipped through the velvet samples, I reveled in their softness. I couldn't imagine spending so much money on fabric, but I was glad someone else could.

I filled out the order form, and placed the money for the electric company in an envelope to run to the post office. While I waited for Marie, I tidied the storeroom, and prayed that someone would come in with more business for us. After a short time, I heard the bell on the front door. Someone did enter the shop, but he was not looking for business. Gabriel staggered into the room holding his hand, which was covered in blood. His pasty skin glistened with sweat.

"I had an accident," he said.

It was jarring to have a man in this shop, especially one who required my assistance. My impulse was to feel guilty, and I looked over his shoulder to see if anyone on the street had seen him enter. Gabriel squeezed his eyes shut for a moment, then opened them halfway. He looked like he was going to pass out. I dispelled all thought of the townspeople, and hurried to help him to the sink, where I instructed him to put his hand under the faucet. He looked at me from inches away, before returning his gaze to his hand. Once the blood had gone down the drain, I could see his thumbnail smashed and bloody where he must have struck it with the mallet. He leaned his elbows on the sink's edge and put his head down.

Once the blood had been cleared, the injury didn't look very serious, but he seemed quite affected.

"Are you all right?" I asked.

"I guess," he said. "I hate when I do that."

"Do you do it often?"

"Yes. Common sculpting injury," he said. "Don't you often poke yourself with the needle?"

"Daily," I said. "But I don't turn green over it."

He gave me a half smile as Grace came into the room.

"Ouchie," she said.

"Yes," said Gabriel.

"Here." She held up a strip of pink cloth with tiny purple violets in the pattern.

Gabriel turned off the water, wiped his hands on the towel at the edge of the sink, and reached for the cloth. He looked at it a moment with a furrowed brow, then held out his bloody thumb, and wrapped it with the material.

"Thanks," he said.

"Thank you, Gracie," I said. "But let's get him something a little thicker."

As we walked back into the shop to my cloth basket, Marie entered with Everette at her heels, holding her baby fabric. They were arguing, but when Gabriel stepped into view, they both stopped and looked from him to me. Marie's face was unreadable, but Everette, ever the politician, broke into a smile that didn't touch his eyes. He put the layette cloth on the counter, and came toward Gabriel with an extended arm. Gabriel gave him his good hand.

"You're the sculptor," said Everette, his voice tight and too loud for the small space we all occupied. "I've heard all about you from the ladies at church."

"I am. I've never eaten so many baked goods in my life."

"They feed those they want to devour," said Everette. Marie smacked him.

"Ouchie," said Grace, pointing to Gabriel's hand.

Gabriel smiled at her, and then turned his attention to us. "I'd better get back. I left all my tools sitting in the square when I ran in here."

"I wouldn't worry about them getting stolen," said Everette. "You've come to a pretty sleepy town."

"Oh, I don't know," said Marie. "People steal all kinds of things around here." She glared at Everette and I kept my head down. I wished she didn't have to stir up trouble while strangers were in the room. Marie pushed around Gabriel and headed to the kitchen, leaving Everette clenching his jaw.

"Pregnant women," he said. "So volatile."

I wanted to strike him for his comment. Instead I handed Gabriel a thick cutting of cotton cloth and bade him farewell as he walked to the door. "Good-bye. I hope your thumb heals quickly."

"Thanks." He nodded and closed the door behind him. Everette watched Gabriel until he was out of sight.

"He seems nice," he said in an icy voice. "I haven't found out much about him though, so you might not want him in your shop with Grace."

"Do you have any reason to suspect a problem? He's friends with Father Ash."

"No, but there's something about him that sets me on edge."

You enjoy being the center of attention, I thought. *Gabriel's a threat.*

"I doubt he'll have any reason to come

back," I said.

"I wouldn't be so sure about that."

Marie walked into the room with red eyes, and Everette rearranged his face to look contrite. He went over to her and put his arms around her.

"Focus on the baby," he said. "Look forward. Make his clothes —"

"Or *her* clothes," said Marie.

"Or *hers.* That will make you happy."

She looked up at him with doubtful eyes, but allowed him to kiss her on the cheek.

"Don't stay too long and tire yourself out." Everette nodded at me and patted Grace on the head. "Bye, girls. Don't get into any trouble while I'm gone."

The door opened and closed, bringing in a sharp gust of wind. I crossed the room to tend the fire.

"You can count on it," said Marie.

An hour later, Marie and I looked up from our sewing, surprised to see Agnes and Sissy, a fellow choir woman, walk through the door. Agnes glanced with distaste at Grace, who sat at a small table pretending to feed her dolly bits of jellied toast. I cringed when I saw that Grace had jelly all over her cheeks and fingers, and must have touched her hair, because the left side had pulled out of its barrette. I jumped up and hurried to the kitchen, where I wet a dishrag, and returned to wipe Grace's face and hands so she wouldn't appear so unkempt. Marie welcomed the women and I heard the three of them discuss Marie's impending arrival, as Grace squirmed under my grooming.

"I'm so delighted for you and your *husband,*" said Agnes, emphasizing the last word. "It is so nice to see such a fine family rising to political prominence."

I laughed inwardly at Agnes' assessment of Marie and Everette's family situation. If she only knew that the junior politician had so recently spent time in the bed of the Jezebel poet on the hill, how her mouth would have dropped. My mind raced with spiky barbs I wished to throw at Agnes, but all that ever came out were polite responses to questions and resolute acceptance of her cruelties.

"What can we do for you today?" I asked, trying not to appear too eager.

"I'm afraid I've come with a rather impossible errand, but Father Ash insists, strangely, so I'm afraid I must ask it of you. It seems that he wants the choir to have new robes for Advent, less than a month from now. Ten of them. Why he is so insistent on this and the creation of the statue in town at this time is beyond me, but he is absolutely firm."

My spirits sank over the impossible task. The time it would take to complete this job and the other I'd promised to do stacked up in front of me. On the other hand, Father Ash had given me the job as a kindness, and we needed the business. Perhaps I could persuade Marie to sew a robe or two while I worked around the clock.

"I'll do it," I said. "I mean, I would be glad to try."

I found it coincidental that I had been commissioned to create robes for a witch and for saints in the same color, and thought that Millay would appreciate the irony, though this thought startled me. Millay was the enemy, just as Agnes was. How strange to think of Millay as an old friend with whom I might share a laugh.

"Of course you will," Agnes said. "I don't really think you have a choice. It's been awfully dark here in the evenings. You aren't without electricity, are you?"

"No, ma'am," I said. "I mean, we had a mix-up, but that's all taken care of."

Grace stared between us, and I wished my daughter were not here to witness my cowardice. I hoped she was too young to understand. I caught Sissy peering at Grace, and it unnerved me.

"I'm so glad to hear that," said Agnes. "In any case, the choir budget will allow for a small down payment for materials, and we'll pay the balance upon completion of the work."

"I usually require half up front to cover some of the labor in addition to materials," I said.

"But that is not what has been approved in our budget," she said. "And time is running short. I had assumed this would be a suitable arrangement. If you don't think you can do it, however, one of the ladies has come across a catalogue where we might order exactly what we want, with a due-date guarantee. I'm sure I can persuade Father Ash."

"No," I said. "Please, no. I'll be able to get your robes to you. I agree."

I knew the church could be relied upon to pay me in full, especially if Father Ash had suggested me, so I agreed to her terms, wrote up a work order, and led Agnes and Sissy to the large table to select materials for the robes. Agnes picked out warm purple shantung with complementing gold trim that looked festive enough for the coming liturgical season. Sissy nodded in agreement with everything Agnes said. Sissy was in awe of Agnes — the woman fond of big, public gifts followed by the recognition of bigger ceremonies and plaques. Half the public buildings in town had her name bolted to their facades — the library children's wing, the firemen's living quarters, the church for the stained-glass windows she'd financed. It was a shame that a better person wasn't behind such philanthropy.

Marie thought that I was too hard on Agnes and that in spite of her haughtiness she was very generous. Marie would also remind me of the rumors of Agnes' early heartbreak. But every time I had tried to give Agnes the benefit of the doubt, she had insulted me. I knew that she saw my unusual family situation as a threat to the moral order she wanted in her town. I also knew that Darcy was the center of her life, and ever since our school days, I had sensed Agnes' general disdain for me and any other girls with good looks or talent. She had a terrible need to be best.

When they left, though they'd been in my shop for only fifteen minutes, I felt so exhausted, it was as if the encounter had lasted an afternoon.

"I suppose you'll need my assistance to finish these robes," said Marie. "Perhaps

Everette won't mind if I help, though I do have these baby clothes to work on."

"I will appreciate any help you can give," I said. "Leave me to it for now. When it comes down to the final week, I might call on you for trimming."

"I trim it," said Grace, wielding a large pair of cutting shears. I jumped up to remove them from her hands and placed them high in the cupboard.

"Lord, that child," said Marie. "Fearless! I think babies must be easier."

I thought of the sleepless nights, the painful breasts, the worry over her weight gain and colic, the endless laundry.

"Yes," I said. "I think so."

VINCENT

Eugen returns and takes me savagely. I know Laura did not have to tell him I'd be waiting — he would understand. He can read the vibrations in the atmosphere.

When we finish, he lights one of my Egyptian cigarettes for me and passes it over, then lights a cheap Lucky Strike for himself.

"She is so bound by her self-judgment," he says.

"Laura?"

"Yes. She is held prisoner by what the oth-

270

ers think of her. It must be hell."

"Aren't we all in that hell, though?"

"Not you and me. We live freely, open, as we wish."

"That's not true. Tell me, does one of our friends know about my affair with George?"

"No, they do not."

"They don't because even we fear what they will say. We are as bad as she."

Our smoke is mingling over us. I don't like how the cheap smell from the Luckys overpowers the spice of my cigarettes, but I don't tell Eugen to stop smoking them. There would be fewer for me.

"We must live completely without fear," he says. "We must live like we did in the summer. When George came to the party, maybe some of them saw. Someone must have realized."

"There was so much free love going on, even if they saw, they would have simply thought our connection to be one of many, like electric sparks. And remember, I took Laura's brother-in-law. I used him as a weapon to cut George."

"That was beneath you," he says. "You are not made for that kind of smut."

I stiffen at his judgment. How dare he say such a thing when he has lanced many a woman to satisfy the very smut of which he

271

judges me?

"You are one to talk," I say. "How many fair maidens have ridden your horse for the pleasure of it?"

"That's different. I'm a mere mortal."

"Then go," I say. "If you're not worthy of the attention of a goddess, you best get away from me."

"Blasphemer," he says, throwing back the covers and walking naked toward the door.

"Hypocrite."

He slams the door.

I stub out my cigarette in anger. He has left his clothes and shoes in an untidy mess around my room to anger me. I stand and collect his things, open the door, and throw his clothing in a pile in the hall before again slamming the door.

I walk to the window and look out at the night, uneasy about our quarrel. I sense so many unspoken words, a real fissure in our foundation, which I once believed was impenetrable. It seems George has left a wound that might never heal.

TWENTY

LAURA

I cannot escape the clink of Gabriel's hammer. It rings in the square, from sunup to sundown, every day of the week except Sunday. When I think of the hammer, I think of the arm working it, the fine dust, the debris of the marble, which coats his skin as he removes it from the rock.

He is relentless in his noise, and it calls to Grace. She begs to go see the "rock man," again and again, and though he rarely talks to me, he obliges her toddler speak. He crouches down to her level, and lets her hit odd pieces of marble that litter the ground around the slab until they crumble into shards sharp enough to draw blood from her dimpled fingers, if she were to touch them.

Clearly he has no children, and isn't married, but why? Where is he from? What happened to him in the war or after it to bond

him to Father Ash? Why does he feel indebted to a priest to do this act in public
when I've never seen him set foot in the
church except to pass to his rooms in the
rectory?

On the second of November, I awoke to
his steady noise and heard it all morning as
I prepared a chocolate cake for Grace's
second birthday. She kept peering out the
front window at Gabriel, and begged me to
allow her to show him the tiny toy xylophone with fairies on it that I had given her
as a present. While the cake cooled, I
consented, and she pulled me by the hand
to the center of town.

"My birthday," she said, thrusting the
xylophone at Gabriel.

"Happy birthday," he said. "I must have
known because I brought something for
you. And it will go with your xylophone."

How kind of him to think of Grace.

He reached into his satchel and produced
a small sculptor's mallet. He held it out to
her, and her eyes widened with pleasure.
She snatched it from his dusty hands,
placed the xylophone on the ground, and
began banging it as hard as she could. I
crouched down and tried to soften her force.

"Gracie! Say thank you."

"Fanks!"

She continued to bang until I wrestled the mallet from her hands and lifted her and the xylophone into my arms.

"Thank you," I said, breathless with embarrassment.

He grinned at us. He seemed to enjoy her antics.

I started back home with Grace, negotiating all the way about when she could have the mallet. I gave it to her once we entered the shop, and watched her do violence to the musical instrument before shaking my head and returning to the kitchen to check the cake. As I entered, Marie came in the back door with a big box wrapped in flowered paper. She stopped when she heard the noise coming from the shop.

"What is that?"

I shook my head. "I thought it was a good idea to buy her a xylophone. Then the sculptor gave her a mallet. This is the result."

Marie gave me a strange look. "Hmm."

Grace must have heard us talking because she ceased her concert and ran into the kitchen.

"Look what Auntie has for you," sung Marie.

"Birthday!" shouted Grace, grabbing for the box.

I knelt down and took her hands in mine. "Grace, you must be polite. Say please."

"Please birthday!"

Marie knelt and passed Grace the box. She tore through the paper and squealed with delight when she saw the little sleigh for Dolly. While Marie took the sleigh out of the box, Grace ran to get Dolly, and then began to pull her all around the house. My heart hurt a little because I couldn't afford a gift like that, but I knew at Grace's age, she didn't notice the difference between a simple present and an expensive one.

"Thank you," I said to Marie. "That was very generous. Would you and Everette like to join us for cake after dinner?"

"I'm sorry, but I can't. There's an event to benefit the firehouse tonight. I would much rather stay and eat cake with you girls, but you know . . ."

Marie left shortly after her delivery to visit the hair salon, and Grace spent the rest of the afternoon hammering every available surface in the store. The *tick-tick-tick* of Gabriel's chisel and the *thump-thump-thump* of her mallet were beginning to drive me bats.

"Gracie," I said as I worked on Millay's velvet gown, my gaze darting between my work and the door in case Marie returned. "Can you sort colors for me?"

"No. I hammer."

I raised my eyebrow at her and shoved the basket of extra fabric toward her. She sighed as if I'd asked something very hard of her, and dropped the hammer on the floor. She took the basket and mumbled under her breath while she carried it over to the rug by the fireplace. I waited to smile until she turned away from me. When she looked back, I made my face serious, and she began to sort the cut lengths of extra cloth by color and material for me, throwing out the scraps that were too small or jagged for future use. It wasn't long before she'd abandoned the basket, and begun to instruct her dolly how to sort the cloth. I felt I'd burst with love for such a cheeky little person.

I turned my attention back to Millay's dressing gown. After using the machine to sew the body of it, I would hand-stitch the fur collar and cuffs. If Millay wanted to rule her domain, she would surely look the part in this sumptuous frock. I admired my own exquisite work that I had enjoyed creating. I'd sent Eugen a telegram to fetch the dress behind the cemetery tomorrow, so I'd stay up all night working at the fireside if necessary. The material for the church robes had already arrived and I needed every moment possible for that project.

The doorbell rang and the Western Union boy slipped a telegram through the slot. Grace ran to pick it up before bringing it to me. It was from Eugen. Vincent was in bed, suffering from a nervous attack, and he couldn't leave her side. Could I possibly deliver the gown?

I crumpled the telegram and threw it across the room into the fire. Grace watched me with large eyes. I wanted that gown out of my shop. Every day it sat folded in the back was a day when Marie might discover it.

"Bad news?" Grace said. I laughed at so small a child sounding so grown-up.

"No, just extra work," I said. "I have to deliver the purple gown."

"For queen?"

"Yes, because the queen is stuck in bed."

"I see her?"

"No," I said.

"I stay with Auntie?"

Yes. Yes. And what would we do once Auntie Marie had her own little one to look after? She was already tired all the time. I couldn't imagine how she'd take the demands of new motherhood. At least she'd know what to expect. She'd been at my side for Grace's birth and afterward, valiantly so. Just thinking of the nights she'd rocked

Grace while I tried to steal consecutive hours of sleep washed me with guilt for thinking of her with such negativity now. Where was my compassion? The woman was pregnant, and had a husband she'd rather leave. It was almost as bad as not having one at all.

I didn't want to waste money sending another telegram. I decided that I'd just bike the gown up the hill and hope it was for the last time. With the income from the choir robes, I'd be able to pay my delinquent bills, and hopefully not have to crawl to Millay ever again.

When the next morning dawned, a damp mist cloaked the river valley and penetrated my skin to the bone. It took me longer than usual to persuade myself to get out of bed, and when I did, my head ached. I hoped that a little coffee would fix it, and also the raw feeling in the back of my throat. Had I slept with my mouth open all night? Was I coming down with a cold? I had no time for sickness, so I forced myself out of bed and dressed in layers.

Marie had asked that I bring Grace to her for sitting while I delivered the gown. I told her it would likely take at least two hours because the old woman lived in Spencer-town, about a forty-minute bike ride from

Chatham, and enjoyed conversation. I reflected that the lies were beginning to roll off my tongue with unsettling ease, and I thought I was caught when Grace told Marie the cloak was for a queen.

"What does she mean by that?" asked Marie.

"Oh, silly Grace. There are no queens in the Hudson River Valley," I said, trying to distract her with Marie's cat.

"But you said."

"I was being silly while we read fairy tales," I said. "Now be good for Auntie Marie."

I hurried back to the store, made sure the gown was wrapped securely in the bag in case I dropped it in the mud, and started the long ride to Steepletop.

In truth, a piece of me had been looking forward to this visit. In general, I enjoyed physical exertion, I looked forward to being alone for a change, and I was eager to see a client's reaction to my first truly creative endeavor. In my mind I pretended that Millay was any rich old woman in search of a disguise, a frock, a dress-up piece to adorn her life. If her acquaintances saw the gown, perhaps they too would want similar pieces, though I couldn't imagine anyone as eccentric as Millay.

My view did not extend beyond several yards into the woods and up the road because of the thick fog. I could feel the presence of the mountains, however, looming in the mist. My chest felt tight, and I coughed as I pushed myself onward. My headache had intensified, and I began to care less about Millay's reaction to the gown and more about getting home as quickly as possible.

The sense of unease I experienced whenever I approached Steepletop grew in me, and when I reached the last lonely pass before arriving at the long driveway, I was exhausted from pedaling with a cumbersome load, soaked to the bone from the water vapor and my cold sweat, and anxious because again no one knew where I was, and if I never came back, no one would ever search for me there. I had to stop and get off the bike until a coughing fit passed. I realized I would need to walk the final climb up the hill to the house, and resolved that it would be my last.

My mouth was dry, and I felt dizzy. I stopped to prop my bicycle against a tree, picked up the gown, and made the final ascent, certain that the mountain had grown since my last visit. I rested against the fence post to catch my labored breath, and Ghost

Writer, the English setter, ran up to me and nuzzled my leg. I pet him on the back, and his hair felt damp from his forest adventures.

"Shoo," I said. "Don't muddy the Duchess' gown."

I gave the dog a pat on the rump and waved him off, and he ran ahead of me to the house. When I reached the front door and knocked, Eugen opened it before I could finish.

"Ghost came around the back and told us you were here," he said. "Are you well?"

I felt the opposite of well, but I just wanted to hand over the gown and pedal down the mountain. I wiped my muddy boots and stepped into the foyer. As soon as I entered the house, I saw flashes of light, and then I collapsed.

Someone toyed with the hair on my aching forehead.

"I knew I'd get her into my bed," said a female voice, followed by a laugh.

"Though not quite under the circumstances you imagined," said a man.

I opened my eyes and blinked until the room came into focus, but it was dark. A candle burned on the table next to me and the moon hung like a half-grin framed by the window. For a moment, I thought I was

282

dreaming, and then I remembered: the delivery, the dog, my dizziness.

Oh, no!

"Grace!"

I bolted up in bed too fast, and had to drop back to the pillow. My head felt as if someone had slammed it with an ax, and my mouth was dry as cotton. My heart pounded.

"You have to help me," I said in near hysterics. "They won't know where I am. They'll think something awful has happened. You must have him take me home."

"*Shhh*," said Millay. "You are in no shape to go home."

"You can't make me stay. I —"

"I don't wish to make you do anything, but you fainted in my foyer, and I want to see you to good health."

"Oh, my Lord," I said. "Marie will think I'm dead. My daughter must be frantic."

"They'll know soon enough that you are all right."

I rolled over with my back to Millay, certain that my sister would never speak to me once she found out where I'd gone.

"My goodness," said Millay, running her hand over my back. I shrank from her touch, and scooted as close to the edge of her bed as I could. "I would have never taken you for such an alarmist."

"But I never told Marie where I was going. I thought she'd be angry with me. I told her I'd be home in two hours. What day is it?"

"Settle down. It's the same day you arrived, and the sun has only just gone down. Eugen can take you back. Just tell her he found you passed out on the side of the road. That's mostly true."

I turned over and looked at Millay, and noted that she wore the purple gown, which set off her green eyes as I knew it would. Her hair fell in gentle waves around the white fur collar, and candlelight cast a flattering color over her features and muted the lines around her eyes, which had seemed so prominent in the light of day.

I sat up slowly in bed and hung my legs over the side. Eugen came to help me stand.

"Can I at least persuade you to eat some soup before you go?" he said. "It's here and hot, waiting for you."

I noted the steaming bowl on the table next to the chair by the fire, and my stomach growled, but, no, I had to go. Right away.

"I'm sorry," I said. "I have to leave. Please."

He looked at Millay and she gave a slight nod, granting her acquiescence. He escorted me past her, and to the door of the bedroom. I looked back once more, where she lay arranged on her bed like a small queen.

"I hope you like the gown," I said.

"I love it more than I can say."

I attempted a small smile, but I felt so pulled away that I could not remain to admire my work any longer. Eugen helped me down the stairs and into the car, where my bike was already shoved in the backseat. As we raced home, I clutched my stomach when he took the turns too fast in the misty dark, but I could at least appreciate that I would be home soon to see my little one. I closed my eyes and tried to rest. Eugen respected my wish for silence.

When he pulled up in front of my shop, it was dark, so we continued down the lane to Marie's house. From the outside, her Victorian home looked so cheerful — a comfortable front porch with a swing, electric lights blazing in every room, tidy landscaping. Yet inside, cold and bitter winds blew between my sister and her husband, winds stirred at the place from which I'd just come. I stiffened and thought about the people who had helped me tonight — that ultimately, their desires guided their lives, and they didn't have to deal with the consequences because they lived in voluntary exile.

I opened my own door while Eugen removed my bicycle and leaned it against the oak tree in Marie's front yard.

"Your payment is in your bag," he said.

He opened his arms to me, looking for an embrace, but I'd had enough of him, no matter how kind his manners, and I hurried by with only a nod and a muttered thankyou. I did not stop to see if he'd been hurt by my coldness. I cared only about seeing my daughter. He got in the car and drove away, and the minute he was out of sight, I raced up the steps. Marie threw open the door, pulled me in, and slammed it behind me.

"Where have you been?" she yelled, her eyes wild and rimmed in red. Everette darkened the space behind her, his brow furrowed.

"Where is Grace?" I asked.

"She's upstairs, asleep. Poor thing kept asking all day where you were, and I had to make up lie after lie. I thought you were dead at the bottom of a ditch. I made Everette drive all over Chatham and Spencertown looking for you."

"I knew she wasn't dead," said Everette, lighting a cigarette and walking into the parlor.

"Oh, hush," said Marie. "He wouldn't call

the police. I begged."

"And thank God, I didn't," he called from the other room. "Do you want to invite more scandal into your sister's life? Into our lives? I can't afford more of that."

"I'm sorry," I said. "So sorry. I wasn't feeling well all morning. My head ached — it still does — but I wanted to make the delivery so I could get paid. I did, and she did talk awhile. When I left to go home, I felt dizzy and miserable. I pulled off the side of the road to sit for a moment, and I must have passed out. When I came to, I raced home as quickly as I could."

Marie squinted her eyes at me and looked me up and down. "Then whose car brought you? I thought I heard one stop."

"I don't know. Someone must have driven by when I arrived."

Everette flipped on the radio to listen to *The Eveready Hour* and opened *The Chatham Courier.* Marie watched him through the doorway for a moment, and then pulled me into the kitchen. I was desperate to see Grace, but I knew I had to finish with Marie.

"May I have a glass of water?" I asked as I slumped at the dining table and placed my head in my hands. "I've never had such a bad headache."

"It's the weather," she said, filling a glass and placing it before me. "And your worries."

She pulled out the chair across from me and sat down, resting her elbows on the oilcloth, and not taking her eyes off me. I couldn't stand the scrutiny much longer.

"You have a lover," she finally said.

I choked on my drink and coughed and sputtered while she crossed her arms.

"I knew it."

"No," I said. "Heavens, no. That's absurd."

"More absurd than that ridiculous story about fainting on the side of the road for hours? Your dress isn't even dirty. Why aren't there twigs in your hair? Someone dropped you off here."

I gazed at her, and part of me wanted to relieve myself of the burden of the lies, but I held back. If Marie found out where I'd been, if she knew who had employed me, she might never speak to me again, and I couldn't bear to lose her. So I continued with the lie.

"No one dropped me off. I don't have a lover," I said. "This has been a terrible day, and I still feel awful. Can I please just see my girl? I don't want to talk anymore."

"Fine. Sleep here. You can have one of my nightgowns."

I felt so relieved I almost cried. Instead I hugged Marie and apologized for worrying her to death. Then I climbed the curved, narrow staircase from the kitchen to the back of the second floor, where servants must have slept years ago. Everette and Marie had converted the room to a guest bedroom, and the small room between it and theirs would be the nursery.

I peeked in and saw Grace on the large bed curled in a ball around her dolly and sucking her thumb. I crept across the squeaky wood floor and climbed into bed with her. She stirred when I wrapped myself behind her, and she smiled before closing her eyes. I inhaled her sweet scent and fell asleep.

VINCENT

Eugen has decided that we should go to New York City. He thinks a change of atmosphere will blow away the disturbances between us. I hope he is right.

We're lately in love with the Vanderbilt Hotel, on Thirty-fourth and Park Avenue, an impressive three-towered monument in gray brick. As we drive up to the valet, I inhale. Sometimes one needs the fumes and mists of motorcars, subways, and speakeasy gin to dull the senses. Smartly dressed men

289

and women walk in and out of the terra-cotta-framed doors with energy and authority. Here, for a hundred a night, I can enjoy the city in perfect comfort and intoxication, and that is exactly what I plan to do.

"Let's ring Deems and Mary," I say. "We need partners in crime."

"Perfect," says Eugen.

He walks to the desk to check in, and I stand in the middle of the foyer, gazing at this spectacle of stone and earthen material. The architects of the Vanderbilt understood that gaudy ornament wasn't necessary for opulence, and that crude material often yields the most impressive transformations.

Eugen escorts me to our rooms, and produces a bottle of 1921 Lanson Champagne. The cork pops. We drink the whole of it in less than an hour. There is another bottle. We take a taxi to Deems Taylor's place.

"Edna! Gene!" he says, opening the door. He wears his black framed glasses and a huge smile, and we embrace. Mary comes from the kitchen. She is smiling out of politeness instead of joy, which really doesn't concern me at all. I wave her off, and the three of us recline in the sitting room around the piano, recalling that glorious night in 'twenty-seven when we were at our collective summit.

It was February. Deems and I had nearly worked ourselves to death on a commission from the Metropolitan Opera Company to produce a great American opera. My head-aches and poor vision had reached a terrible low, but in my writing shack, I had managed to create a most impressive libretto. The story of *The King's Henchman* was one I knew well. It was a tale of love and betrayal among friends. It was the story of my heart.

That night, drowning in a gown of red velvet, I was escorted by Eugen, my sisters, and my mother. A young and open Gladys Ficke was there. Elinor Wylie was too, though I barely knew her at the time. I could hardly breathe in the sold-out auditorium, where even standing room had been filled to capacity.

At eight o'clock sharp, the harp began playing, announcing this tragedy of tenth-century England. I watched the very cells of my imagination take full form through the performers onstage, and felt as if I were living a dream. My elation did not cease until the last of the seventeen curtain calls, and the ending of twenty consecutive minutes of applause. No, it lasted even beyond that.

"You sold ten thousand copies of that

libretto in twenty days," says Deems.

"I beat the sales of that shit Hemingway," I say.

"His *Sun* couldn't rise above your *Henchman*," says Eugen.

"His member probably can't rise anymore, for that matter," I say.

Deems howls with laughter.

Eugen is shocked. "Vulgar Vincent!"

Mary serves us a sober dinner. How I sometimes wish these simple spouses could disappear. I know it is cruel of me to think it, but they only intrude with their petty insecurities. Do something or don't, and be confident in it, but don't sulk.

When we finish our dinner and another bottle of champagne, we go to the piano and sing loud, raucous songs. Mary has loosened up a bit, and joins us. I loop my arm through hers to smooth any hard feelings. Eugen is proud of me for doing so.

But as the hours pass, the drunkenness turns sour. The city becomes too noisy; it is a beast clawing at the window. I begin to feel the intrusion of Elinor's loss. I can't ignore her.

"If only Elinor were here," I say. I see Eugen doesn't want me to spoil our fun, but I don't care. I must give voice to this pain. "She wrote the most glowing review in the

Herald Tribune for *Henchman.* Uge, do you remember when she stayed with us at Steepletop, and you served us breakfast in bed?"

"And we walked and read and picnicked in the hills," he says, quietly.

I am weeping. There are arms and hands of consolation trying to reach me, but they can never help me. They can never bring me back. Grief has not been tended properly in me. I did not care for it and it has run through my organs like a weed, choking every good and healthy thing.

Eugen has to carry me to the taxi that night, and up to our rooms at the Vanderbilt. I cling to him like a life preserver in this terrible sea that wants to drown me.

TWENTY-ONE

LAURA

The sight of the marble's changing form caused me to stop.

I pushed Grace in her pram to the library to return our fantasy books — Grace's fairy tales and my collection of pictorial costuming books. Grace noticed the sculpture too. The rock had a shape, a definite outline that was more something than nothing, more a figure than an inanimate object. The tools Gabriel used were finer, more precise, as were his motions. He wielded a tiny hammer and a chisel, and made long vertical lines around the base of the slab. The piece he carved stood taller than his ample height by more than a foot. A stepladder rested on the grass to his right, but he didn't need it at the moment since he was concentrating his energy on the bottom portion of the rock.

Down he chiseled, his vertical lines at irregular intervals along the bottom half of the slab, until he switched hands and slashed a horizontal line across the lower portion. His action and the result were jarring and seemed out of sync with the rest of his creation, but I knew better than to judge. If I'd been designing a dress, I would have crumpled and crossed out a half dozen pieces of paper by now. Rock wasn't as forgiving.

Several townspeople stood and watched him from different vantage points. He rarely noticed any of us. His concentration was singular. Grace, now used to him, had lost interest and turned her attention back to the book in her lap. She didn't call out to him, so he did not address us as we passed. I felt a curious sinking in my chest, and realized I was disappointed not to talk to Gabriel.

As we neared the library, I was in a state of distress. For two years, Grace and I had existed in our small sphere. We had learned to get on by ourselves, mostly, and I had learned to live with the dull ache in my heart over my lover's abandonment. Now our quiet was disturbed, and I didn't know what to make of it. I was further annoyed when we ran into Darcy Dempsey leaving the library as we entered. When her mother wasn't around, she smiled too brightly, stood too close, spoke too loudly. She always mentioned my father's sad end and how terrible it must be for me and my sister. Her words never seemed intended to bring consolation.

"Girls," she said. "It's always so nice to run into the beautiful Kelleys."

Grace adjusted her glasses and stared up at Darcy with curiosity, but she did not speak. I wondered if she felt the same way I did about Darcy, who crouched down and looked at Grace's book — *Hans Christian Andersen Tales.*

"I had a book like this when I was a girl," she said. "I only wish I had a little girl of my own to share it with. Your mother is so lucky to have you."

I felt uncomfortable with Darcy's words, knowing she had miscarried. Since she still did not have any children, it was possible she'd had more troubles. And her statement that I was lucky seemed sinister. Lucky to be an unwed mother? Lucky to have the scorn of half the town, led by her mother, Agnes? Yes, I knew I was blessed to have a child, but I was not lucky. Did Darcy mean to inflict wounds or was she unaware of how her words sounded? No, I couldn't believe she was innocent.

When Grace did not respond to her, Darcy stood to face me.

"Mother told me about her generous order for robes," she said. "It's wonderful how the church takes care of you."

"Yes, I'm very *lucky,*" I said.

"I just hope you can maintain such a quality standard in so short a time. I hate to say it, but it would be so much easier if they just ordered premade robes. Times are changing."

"They are, so every moment I spend standing out here is a moment when I'm not working on your mother's robes. Excuse me."

I pushed past her and returned the books to the desk. Mrs. Perth gave us a small wave from the fiction shelves and recommended a new mystery. I allowed Grace to pick up several picture books, and then we started for home. When we arrived, a telegram from Millay waited for me.

Millay requested I return to her as soon as possible to design costumes for her spring and summer reading tour. Her new book of poetry would be released then, and she was planning an extensive tour of readings throughout the country. I needed to read the sonnets, she said, so I would know what colors and styles she'd want. Would I do it? Would I come?

The telegram seemed to weigh more than the slender paper on which it was printed — almost as much as a bag of coins. I looked at the fireplace with the heavy thing in my hand as a parade of gowns, cloaks, and dresses moved through my mind in black, royal blue, and scarlet. I could almost hear the swish of the material. Then the bell on the door rang, and I rushed to hide the telegram in the top desk drawer.

Everette entered, and his eyes followed my hands to the desk.

"Have a moment?" he asked.

"Of course," I said, feeling odd that he was here without Marie.

He glanced around the room. "Where's Grace?"

"Napping."

He took one more look around the store, and then he spoke. "You've made a nice life with Grace here."

I did not answer him. I suppose I would have called it nice when business was strong and the electricity wasn't turned off. But even on those nights, I had no company except her chatter, no one to talk to about raising her, no one to consult about whether I should allow myself to work for Millay.

Everette walked over to the mantel and looked at the wedding portrait of my parents — a serious and formal representation of two people who were neither serious nor formal. I wondered when the picture had been taken. My father would have been better in a photograph in the outdoors wearing snowshoes and framed by the sagging branches of snow-covered trees. My mother — Well, I'd hardly known her, but I could still conjure the music of her quick laugh, and her even quicker temper. But that thought slipped away as quickly as it had occurred to me.

"If I asked, would you tell me where you really were the other day?" said Everette.

"I'd tell you what I told Marie — I made a gown for an old woman."

"Who?"

"Why do you care?"

"Because I care about you, and I don't want you to invite any more trouble into your life."

"Do you mean my life or yours?"

"Ours." He turned and looked at me. "I saw Eugen drop you off in that rainstorm weeks ago."

Damn.

"I got stranded in the rain after Grace was sick," I said. "I let them drive us home to

299

get her to shelter."

"And then you took that woman on as a client."

"No —"

"It's no use lying to me. I won't tell Marie, but sooner or later, she'll find out. And when she does, you will lose her."

He'd spoken aloud the very words I'd known deep in my heart.

"What am I to do?" I said. "I need money to support my daughter. Half the town won't patronize me because they don't want my stain. The other half is already migrating toward the bigger stores and mail-order catalogues, if they can afford new clothes at all."

"I don't know the answer right now," said Everette. "I only want to warn you to be more careful. And also, to tell you that Millay is a witch. She takes power over you. If I could, I'd try to find a way to run her out of Columbia County."

I could see that he didn't blame himself for their dalliance. He blamed Millay as Adam had Eve in the garden, as my lover left me alone to deal with the consequences. Why did it seem that no man would take responsibility for his actions?

I was disgusted with Everette when I knew he wanted my gratitude, my esteem, my praise of his assessment of Millay. I felt oddly protective of her when he'd condemned her with the same words I myself had thought again and again. Hearing them spoken aloud, however, confirmed more about the one judging than its subject. My thoughts returned to the telegram.

"Thank you, Everette," I said. "I'll keep that in mind."

He stared at me without a smile. His eyes darkened, and a passing cloud shadowed the room. On his way out, he let the door slam. In a moment, Grace cried for me, awakened too soon from her nap.

VINCENT

His murder of me is torpid, almost languid.

He doesn't hire the sharpest swordsman for my execution. There is no gun to my head, no knife to my breast, no quick poison.

No, George is a vine that has slowly crept up me, winding its way about my legs, my breasts, my heart. Its tendrils reach into my nostrils, my mouth, my ears, rendering me insensate so I am unable to enjoy a simple walk through my garden, a drink, a poem. His vine mingles with the weeds of my grief for Elinor, chaining me like a prisoner in this dungeon. I can barely move my hands to write; but write is what I must do. I must put this pain on paper to honor the process, to show future lovers the way, to reinforce that anguish is better than sterility, experience better than bareness.

When I think of 1929, and how George loved me so well, and our art flourished for it, I know it was all worthwhile. Our mutual adoration allowed us to serve our vocations to poetry, so even if we kill each other in this death of our love, the precious words will remain.

I come from the country and I live in the country, so I know the future, the cycle, the seasons. Any fool can tell you that autumn follows summer, that the short, dark days follow the light, that the trees will lose their coverings. How could it be another way with love or beauty, profession, health? It all spins on the wheel, so that even in the golden, glorious days of vigor, the shadow of death covers all, and we cannot know the high without the low, the sun without the moon, the good without sin.

Eve has long been crucified for her great folly, for showing us what sin was, but without it, could we know beauty? Can we fully appreciate the summer without the winter? No, I am glad to suffer so I can feel the fullness of our time in the light. Don't

ever take the dark away if, without it, I cannot feel the light.

TWENTY-TWO

LAURA

The holy women's choir produced an eerie sound. It undulated on the harsh November wind in the prematurely dark sky, bringing its sadness to the empty street. It seemed strange that just months ago Grace and I had taken walks under the trees on the cobbled stones after dinner. We'd skipped rocks along the stream banks while the woodcocks courted and flew across the rippling waters, making magical-wing noises.

I hesitated on the steps before continuing into the church to present the robes I'd nearly lost my sight over, sewing at all hours this long month. I hoped the Advent robes of rich indigo-violet would be a royal offering to show them I was worthy, to respect their place in the church and to inspire a little of my own. I'd had foolish fantasies that they would gasp, rub the fabric, and smile at me — real smiles that reached their eyes.

But, no, that was not to be. And I was shamed and humbled by the vanity in me that thought it might be so.

They did stop singing when I entered, but not to stand in awe of my creation. They looked on me as a contagion. No one made a move to take the heavy robes from my arms, ten of them, pressed, folded, and wrapped. I placed the box on the front pew while the women stared at me.

"I've finished," I said. "Just in time."

Agnes stood still in front of the choir, wearing her customary look of distaste. I could sense a sinking in her. She had wanted me to fail. I scanned their faces, some wrinkled, some pinched, some as young as mine. My peers would not meet my eyes. Lily Miller gave me a small smile laced with pity.

Agnes reached up to caress her hair while placing her baton on the music stand, and finally stepped toward the box, peering over the end of her nose as if she'd stumbled upon a pit of snakes. The rings on her wrinkled fingers clicked over one another as she rubbed her hands together. Finally, she lifted the lid.

The way she widened her eyes and leaned closer, I could tell she coveted the robes, but as soon as she allowed the emotion to run through her like a current, she shut off the switch and her face became stone.

"I'm sorry, Miss Kelley," she said in a voice that held no apology. "I distinctly remember requesting silver piping and you've gone and used gold."

I clenched my fists into balls and took deep breaths to steady the flare of temper that rose in me, willing myself not to strangle Agnes.

"Mrs. Dwyer," I said through clenched teeth, "I am quite certain you requested gold to reflect one of the gifts of the wise men to the infant Jesus, and to complement this particular warm shade of purple."

"Well, now, that's part of the problem too," she said. "This is not the hue I ordered."

I could hear my heart beating in my ears. She wouldn't. She couldn't dare make me lose money on a month's work. The choir had already paid a portion up front from their budget funds, but that wouldn't be enough to feed us for the next month. She knew how we struggled to pay the rent, but I'd never dreamed she would deliberately act to set us back. Her anger felt personal.

I summoned the strength I possessed and willed it to help me change my tone. I unclenched my fists and tried to rearrange my features to appear less aggressive.

"I'm sure this is the shade you selected because it is the only shade of purple shantung from this manufacturer. Sissy, can you help me? You were there."

Sissy looked from me to Agnes. I could sense her dread, and I regretted putting her in such a position. My heart lifted when I saw her take a step toward us, until Agnes lifted her hand.

"That won't be necessary," said Agnes. "I am quite capable of seeing what is before me without assistance."

Sissy looked down at the floor.

"Let me make this clear to you," said Agnes. "I did not choose that fabric and I did not select that color trim. It was probably left over from something else you made, and the fabric I ordered is probably wrapped in bolts in the back of your shop."

"That is most certainly not so," I said, my anger rising. "I have the purchase order at the shop, and it has all the information I need. I'll just go get that and show you —"

"There is no need to do that because I won't believe this is the fabric you will say I chose. It seems to me that the question arises as to whether or not the choir here at Our Lady of Grace would like to continue patronizing a seamstress who does lazy work, and I know what I think in response to this question, but being a democratic woman, I will put it to the group. What say you?" she asked, turning toward the women who looked like they would like to die. Mostly.

Lily spoke first in a quiet voice. "I would give her a chance to correct herself."

"In the future we might consider the mail-order robes Sissy found in a catalogue last week," said another.

My mind raced. How to keep this account? I could change out the trim. It wouldn't look as striking as it did now, but those old hens wouldn't be able to tell the difference, and if it meant appeasing Agnes, I knew I had to do it.

"I'll change the trim," I said. "It would be a terrible sin to waste all this material, whether it is correct or not, but I think I can find the right shade of silver to comple-ment the purple of these robes."

Sissy spoke. "Honestly, it would save the church money to just go through the cata-logue for our linens. We can get almost two robes for the price of one of these. We should be good stewards of our funds."

No, no, no. I was in charge of sewing the linens, the robes, the vestments. I needed this account.

"Please," I said, aware that I was begging but unable to see the alternative. "I can offer a discount because of the confusion, and I can have them resewn by Sunday."

What was I saying? I had two days and a child to care for, and I was supposed to unstitch and resew ten robes?

Agnes softened her glare and turned to the choir. "Ladies, as much as I know we are right, we must indeed be good stewards and not waste these robes. I vote that we allow Laura to restitch the robes, but we must have them by Sunday."

I knew the task was impossible, but I found my voice. "All right."

The women of the church looked from Agnes to me and back again. It was particularly painful to see that most of them wore looks of shame. They sided with me but wouldn't speak up. The injustice made me dizzy. I needed to get away before I was sick on Agnes' patent leather pumps.

I pressed the lid onto the box, lifted the package, and walked down the church aisle, holding my head as high as possible. In spite of the cold night, I felt liberated to be free of those women. I stood on the stairs, taking deep gulps of breath, when I soon had the feeling of being watched. I gazed down the shadowed street, but saw no one there, so I turned back to the rectory and could have sworn the curtains of an upstairs window snapped shut and the light went out in the room. I imagined that Father Ash watched the square at all hours of the day and night, and wondered if it was him I saw in the window. As I turned back to go home, I ran into Darcy's husband, Dr. Dempsey.

"Excuse me," I said, as I tried to push around him.

"Are you all right?"

I gave him my most withering glare. "Yes, I'm just fine. As fine as I can be in my present circumstances, and having to re-make ten robes in two days because your mother-in-law wants to torture me."

He looked at the doors of the church and back at me. "I'm sorry. Is there anything I can do?"

What did he expect me to say? Was he going to take off from his shift at the hospital to help me sew robes? Or perhaps I could ask him and Darcy to watch Grace for me. I wanted to say those things, but it felt too cruel, even for my savage mood.

"No," I said, my tone full of ice.

I walked away from him on the sidewalk and toward my store, feeling the weight of his gaze on me. I glanced up and again saw a curtain in the rectory twitch. Another set of eyes on me. Always, eyes watching me.

I could not bring myself to mutilate the robes. That's what it would be: mutilation for the sake of humiliation. I decided at midnight that night that I would not remake the robes, no matter what the consequences. But I also knew that I would win this battle because I'd take it to Father Ash himself, and in front of Agnes if possible. He would love the robes because they were not only beautiful but also liturgically correct, and because it had been an act of charity on his part to commission them from me.

On Sunday, I brought the robes boxed and ready to church, ten minutes before Mass. I instructed Grace to sit in the back row, where we always sat, and strode up the aisle toward the choir where they were rehearsing, and where Father Ash was lighting the candles. I could see that Agnes thought I had remade them, and she looked triumphant. I could barely contain my satisfaction.

Father Ash smiled at me when he saw the large box I carried, and hurried over to relieve me of my burden. He placed it on the pew in front of the choir, and I lifted the lid. With a great flourish, though my hands trembled, I raised one of the robes and shook it out.

"This is marvelous," he said, running his hands along the gold trim.

Agnes gasped, as did several of the choir women. Father Ash turned to them.

"Do you see, Miss Kelley?" he said. "Even they are speechless. You have outdone yourself."

"Thank you, Father," I said in my most humble voice. "It was my pleasure to sew for these holy people in honor of God."

I felt a little ashamed for my theatrics, but I couldn't help myself. Perhaps I'd confess later if it became a burden. I didn't look at Agnes, but I felt her hatred.

Father Ash placed the robe back in the box and I helped him carry it to the sacristy. I placed my hand on his arm. He seemed to shrink from my touch, so I withdrew it.

"Thank you, Father Ash," I said quietly, now truly humble. "You have done me a great kindness."

His face turned red, and I felt bad for being so familiar in a sacred place. "It is you who have done the church a kindness. You have great talent."

"Thank you."

Being alone with him became uncomfortable. We made quick work of hanging the robes. When I turned to leave him to prepare for Mass, I saw that Agnes was waiting in the doorway, watching us. Her eyes had a wild look in them, and her neck was blotchy and red. Her anger prevented me from fully enjoying the moment, and my courage failed. I put my head down and walked past her to where my daughter sat alone in the back of the church.

VINCENT

I am disgusted by the suited men who run our country.

Pale, bloated things without hearts.

They called me an anarchist. What a laugh. Anarchists are optimistic beings, those who believe the goodness of humans should allow them freedom to rule themselves as they will.

I am no anarchist. Men are not good. They might do good things, but they are fundamentally cruel, selfish, and murderous. I know more than anyone because I fight these impulses with my every waking breath.

I stare at this box of papers I've saved over the years. I'm stuck on the periodicals published after the executions of the Italian immigrants, two innocent men framed for murder because they were different.

313

The silence in the Berkshires sometimes feels the same as the quiet that night in August of 'twenty-seven when we all waited to hear if the governor would pardon them in light of so much spotty evidence, the mountains of reasonable doubt.

I think that night was the night it all started changing. It was the night my youth, my freshness, my joie de vivre was choked. I have been dying a little with every breath since. It permeates my work, and try as I might, I cannot change that. I can only testify to it.

If my life was a quilt, there would be squares I'd want torn out. I'd unstitch the block where I learned of the doomed immigrants. I'd use my teeth to tear out the square where I allowed Laura's brother-in-law in my bed. I'd cover George Dillon's square with another color to hide him away so no one, not even my Eugen, could know about him.

But the past cannot be unmade, and I suffer for it.

TWENTY-THREE

LAURA

As November turned into December and the darkness and the cold grew more oppressive, I began to receive letters two and three times a week from Millay. Some begged, some commanded, and some didn't have anything to do with her request at all. I found those letters the most unsettling — about the weather, her mother's poor health, her nerves, the houseguests visiting her and Eugen — because I thought she must be lonely to write to me, a near stranger. Receiving the letters gave me a strange thrill because they seemed forbidden, and I was only human, and just as tantalized by secrets as the next person.

The silence of the shop's bell gave me ample time to consider her requests, constantly deciding for and against working for her. I'd also begun designing in secret. Millay had been enclosing samples of her sonnets as they were published in *Poetry Magazine, Harper's,* and *The Saturday Evening Post.* As much as I wanted to resist her, I found the sonnets entrancing.

They were about an ill-fated love, captured in mythological language but clearly written from her heart. They were intensely personal, even disguised in their elevated vocabulary and ancient imagery. At places cruel and aloof, at others the poems exuded a vulnerability that spoke to me. I hated to admit it, but I felt I was reading about my own failed love, and I was inspired.

My hand seemed to have a mind of its own as it flew over page after page, drawing frocks representing emotion through color, texture, and form — costumes that I realized came from my own pain amplified by a woman who knew how to chisel emotion out of black marks on a white page. Thinking over my lost love and also about what Millay must be feeling — no matter how sordid — connected me to her. I stopped trying to resist it, and indulged in the thoughts because of the beautiful designs they yielded.

When Marie came into the shop, I stashed the book away and helped her with her crib sheets and baby blankets. I made new clothes for Grace and her dolls, and I took long walks down by the pond with her, where I could avoid Gabriel and the ever-changing lady in the rock, who had now begun to emerge in startling clarity. Sometimes at night, while Grace slept, I'd venture out to see the statue up close in the moonlight. The tent kept her face in shadow, but the rays struck the hem of her dress, giving it a cold, clear blue befitting the robes of the Blessed Mother.

The horizontal line Gabriel had made that day had become a snake under the foot of the Virgin. I loved the imagery of this calm, lovely woman with full power over evil, this new Eve crushing that old devil. And it was in the dark of night where I felt most at home, unjudged and free to do as I pleased.

One evening in mid-December, after being cooped up in the house all day, I had a wish to walk in the anonymity of the crisp, dark night to restore my calm. Even down by the streams meandering out of Borden's Pond, I could peek at my house for quite a while to be sure Grace was safe, so I felt no misgivings about leaving her. She slept like Rip Van Winkle at night, and mostly had since she had been six months old. After checking her one last time, I went out the back door, locked it, and headed for the pond.

The water made barely any noise at this time of year, frozen from the edges inward. In a few weeks, we'd be able to skate on it, but now the soft whisper of the current continued. Last night's slick rain had turned to snow, encasing the empty branches in glittering shells of ice and dressing up the woods in white. As much as I hated the chill in my bones, I loved the beauty of the winter landscape in the moonlight, and it loosened the knot inside me.

I heard something, however, that caused me to stop walking — a noise that had not come from an animal. I looked back at my home and wondered if I should return, but I picked up a wisp of a melody, and crept along the path until the music grew louder, and I could make out voices, male and female, in song. The noise was joyful, and as I rounded a bend, I saw a group, upstream, sitting on logs around a blazing fire.

The men and women laughed, and sang, and drank steaming liquid from tin cups. Warmth emanated from them, and I was intrigued to see several children playing at the group's periphery. A striking woman with shiny brown hair and big brown eyes led the song, while a young man with long, curly hair and a bowler hat played the guitar, wearing fingerless gloves. A heavyset man used a ladle to refill cups, and a tall, fastidiously dressed man played the fiddle. There were others — a woman with a blond bun under a woolen cap, who kept an eye on the children; a middle-aged woman with a great mass of curling gray hair, who played a flute; and a young colored man with a harmonica. They looked like a band of Gypsies, and I wondered what Agnes would say about a group like this in the woods so near town.

As fascinated as I was, I knew I'd been away from Grace for too long, so I forced myself to head home, and hoped that these people would return so I could listen again to their music.

The Gypsies did return. Each night I waited until Grace fell asleep, and then crept out into the woods to watch the singers. Members of the group came and went, but there remained the same palpable joy, the camaraderie, and the hot drink. I began having fantasies of joining them. I started to recognize some of their songs, and hummed along to myself while I sat in the foliage of a fallen tree. What would they say if a single woman emerged from the trees to join them? Something told me I'd be welcome.

I watched on and off throughout the

weeks on the nights I wasn't too tired and the weather wasn't too cold. I had recently missed three nights in a row, due to Grace having a cough, but she was soon well again, and I planned to go back. I put a pot on the burner to make tea to take with me. While the kettle heated on the burner, I went to the front of the store to close the curtains and saw a figure coming toward my house on the street. Who was out walking so late at night? As the man drew closer, I noticed that he held a bucket in his hands. He passed directly in front of the store, and I moved back so he wouldn't see me.

It was Gabriel.

He looked at my store, and then continued around the side, heading toward the woods.

I rushed to the kitchen window in the back, and saw him cross the field. My heart sank because I wanted to watch the musicians, but I couldn't risk running into him alone at night. And what was he doing carrying a bucket into the woods?

The teakettle whistled, and I poured the water over my tea bag and returned to the window, but Gabriel was out of sight.

I had been looking forward to the "show" all day, and I didn't want to let Gabriel's presence in the woods deter me. After all, I knew the paths well enough to hide if I saw him, and I wasn't afraid of him anyway — not at all.

I thought for a few more moments while I checked to make sure Grace still slept, and then put on my coat, hat, and gloves. I picked up my thermos, locked the back door, and headed across the field to the woods.

A light snow fell and stuck to my eyelashes. I realized that Gabriel would see my steps in the fresh powder if he returned this way, but I didn't care. I was tired of worrying about others all the time. His footprints led straight to the path I took to the musicians, and before long, I heard their music reaching out to me, bringing a smile to my lips.

As I crept to the bend where I could watch unnoticed, the smile froze on my face. I was shocked to see Gabriel withdraw a set of drumsticks from his pocket, and join the group in their music making. The beautiful singing woman kept looking at him, and he returned her gaze once or twice, but he mostly talked to the man who I presumed was the leader of the group.

When had he met them? How did he know to come here? Did he know them from before, or had he stumbled upon them?

A lot of kids were playing that night, and I wondered where they went to school and why they were allowed to stay up so late. I tried to check my judgment and just enjoy the show, but I couldn't. The idea that Gabriel could walk up and join these people, even if he stayed quiet most of the time, mesmerized me. It seemed so unlike him.

When the music making ended, the beautiful woman walked over and sat next to Gabriel. He kept his eyes on the fire, but spoke to her. She seemed at ease and graceful, and not at all intimidated by the brooding stranger. She placed her hand on his arm, and I could have sworn he flinched, but he did not pull away.

She rose to get two cups of cider, and brought one back for him, and while she went, he watched her walk away. My loneliness was more acute here on the periphery than it ever had been, especially when she made him laugh. I stayed longer than usual, and as they began to pack up, and Gabriel stood with his bucket, I realized I needed to hurry home so he wouldn't discover me. I walked as quickly as I could along the path, and broke into a run when I reached the field. Once home, I locked myself inside and watched out the window for a while, but I never saw Gabriel return the way he had come.

VINCENT

The cottage where my dear old lover Lulu and his wife, Alyse, stayed with us last fall is empty. I wish I could fill it back up with them. With Mother. With my sweet, terrible George. Perhaps I will have them back, and take Lulu like I did in the past.

But I don't want Llewelyn, not really. I want what he symbolizes.

I want to reclaim the twenties in Greenwich Village.

I walk into the empty guesthouse and it is as if their ghosts rise around me. The year slips away and I remember.

We were endlessly drunk. There were sleigh rides and fancy meals, but also regret, a feeling of playacting what we all thought this time together was supposed to be, creating stories to tell our other friends and ourselves about what fun we were having.

From a full revolution of the earth, a complete passage of seasons, I can see now that the fun was hollow, shadowed, underscored by spirits like me and Lulu thinking of lovers we had elsewhere — me of George, and Lulu of a poetess he left in Dorset. Alyse plagued us for her own reasons. Eugen was high and low like I'd never seen him. We all must have sensed an explosive end to all the recklessness, but we couldn't stand to look straight at it.

I now sit on the bed of our guesthouse, where our visitors read and slept, and made love, and I stare out the window at the gnarled tree limbs. I am reminded of the trees that grew from the sidewalks in Greenwich Village near our place in December of 1920.

I ruled the Village then. They called me the Great Queen.

My lovers, Edmund and John, escorted me up Christopher Street. We were a merry threesome — or, rather, I was merry. The young men tolerated each other because they knew I only wanted them together. Edmund saw a display of my poetry books in a window, and a woman with scarlet lips lifted a copy of *Figs from Thistles* from its stand. There were none left.

"They can't keep you on the shelves," said Edmund, with the enthusiasm of a child.

"Like we can't keep her between us in bed," said John.

Dark and light, yin and yang, my boys appealed to different aspects of my character, and together, we were a force. But I began to tire of them. They were becoming too attached. It's why I preferred to take married men as lovers. They never pestered me when we were apart.

A writing assignment for *Vanity Fair* became the answer to my wish for freedom. I was sailing for Paris in a few days to start my new life, the next chapter. But all great stories should end with fresh moments, and I found mine in an English writer we called Lulu.

"What sweet goddess is this?" he'd said.

I'd been reclining on a settee in a mid-afternoon salon, indulging in a rogue ray of sunlight that had pushed between buildings and winter clouds to find me. I turned to look at this new man, a gentleman by the tailoring, and allowed him to kneel beside me and grasp my hand. My peers were already drunk, but I hadn't yet begun. In truth, I'd been ill in my nerves and my belly, and the touch of his graceful fingers seemed to permeate my chill, and send warmth through my body. I knew the sunlight must have turned my hair a hundred shades of copper, and brought out the gold in my green eyes, and I gave him my softest, most welcoming gaze.

"Finally, a man who knows how to treat me," I said.

"Don't fault them," he said, gesturing to

the room behind him. "Mortals don't know how to behave in the presence of angels."

"Ha!" I laughed. "A fallen angel, perhaps, but I think goddess would be more appropriate."

"Or Jezebel."

"I consider that a high compliment."

"You won't be good for my soul," he said.

"Then put it on a shelf while I attend to your body."

I thought he would die of pleasure, and for the next few days, I let him learn all about me. This man almost ten years my senior was a child in my willing hands, moldable like clay, a puppet without strings. I allowed him to stoke his obsession of me because I knew I'd be leaving him soon, but I had to teach him to be like me. Otherwise, he'd be in for a lifetime of devastation. He still would, no doubt, but a healthy dose of distance from love might save him some heartache.

We lay in a steamy tumble of limbs on the last night I would bring him in my bed, and I unthreaded myself from him, and sat up to light a cigarette. He gazed at me as if trying to memorize my every feature.

"Lulu, I command you to take control of your senses," I said.

"I can't. I don't want to. I only want to

adore you."

"And you have, but this swell of feeling must be stifled. Step away from this room in your head. Look in on it. What do you see?"

"The very definition of beauty, animated by cruelty."

"Good," I said. "At least you see the dark with the light. Move farther out. What is there?"

"The poor man who can see nothing else beyond the beauty, whose heart is about to be torn from his ribs."

"Excellent. Now go farther away. What's the view now?"

"A building of young people, exploding with ideas and creativity. Revolutionaries, artists, and poets at the start of a movement, getting high on each other."

"Farther."

"A city, teeming with magic and energy. A fresh continent. A big world. A tiny planet. Just another universe."

"And there you have it," I said. "Our bodies are insignificant to the whole, but what we do with them, the energy we exchange, feeds some large thing. Don't personalize it too much. Accept it. Revel in it. Find a new way to create these fresh connections. The worst thing you can ever do is to grow stale."

"I can't accept that," he said. "Not with your flesh so near. When you go away, I will try."

"Good boy."

He buried his head in the pillow. His lean back and strong shoulders were all I saw. I ran my hand down his spine, and he pulled his head out. His hair was tousled and his eyes were sleepy.

"Once more," I said.

He groaned with a grin, and dove into me.

I am back in the parlor of the guest cottage when Laura steals into my thoughts. I look around the room and think a wild thought: Could she and her daughter live here? I could offer her this place of respite from the town that shames her. She could create in freedom, her daughter could learn about the birds and the seasons, and, in the nights, gradually, Laura would grow comfortable with me, eat out of my hand, take me on her lap, and then to bed. This vision is so clear, I think I've nearly conjured it. I can almost smell her in the room with me, and my heart pounds in response.

A sharp wind rushes down the fireplace, sending ash over the room and blowing away my sweet fantasy. I cough and wave the air until I notice my reflection in the mirror. My hands are spotted and there is a fine dust on my hair. It is as if the past has disintegrated all over me. There is no youthful glow left, only my older self, ashamed that I cannot be what I was.

TWENTY-FOUR

LAURA

Eugen came into the shop early the next morning, carrying a sled. He must have noticed my panic, as I watched to see if anyone had seen him enter.

"Don't worry," he said. "I parked at the end of the street and walked on the opposite side. No one saw me."

"Is my fear so easy to read?"

"Yes."

Grace came down the stairs, holding Dolly.

"There she is," he said. "The Duchess wanted me to send this to you."

I had an impulse to refuse the gift, but Grace had already run over to where Eugen placed it on the floor and bounced up and down on it, begging me to take her sledding.

"It's a brand-new Flexible Flyer. You can sit up and steer, or go headfirst."

330

"Sitting up will be just fine," I said.

"And there is a rope if your lovely mother would like to guide you."

Grace jumped off the sled, left Dolly on it, and began pulling the sled over the floor.

"What is this for?" I asked.

"Pure bribery. I won't pretend otherwise."

"Another down payment?"

"Yes. But this time, she's trying to get to your heart through your daughter."

I appreciated his honesty and the gift, but I wanted him to leave.

"Well? Is it working?" he asked.

The clock tower chimed nine o'clock, calling my attention out the window. Few cars drove by, but some townspeople strolled on the streets, and shopkeepers began opening their doors. Gabriel passed the store and looked in the window, pausing when he noticed the man inside, but continued without stopping.

I thought of the Gypsies by the pond and people living so free. I couldn't imagine any of those people caring about the silly judgment of a town. And I glanced at my work ticket book and saw that it lay open to the same clean sheet it had been on for weeks. This thing that Agnes had wanted, what I had feared — it was done. Clearly. I couldn't turn Eugen down.

"It is working," I said.

Smelling of spicy aftershave and tobacco, he smiled and wrapped me in an embrace. I kept my arms at my sides, and he pulled away. He held my shoulders with his big hands. Grace had stopped pulling Dolly and stared up at us, blinking behind her glasses like a baby owl.

"You are an angel," he said.

"But you must leave," I said.

"All right, all right. Just one more thing. When can I pick you up to discuss Vincie's needs and make some designs?"

I glanced at Grace, trying to think what excuse I could make to convince Marie to watch her.

"Bring her," said Eugen, as if he read my thoughts. "I promise, it's safe. Vincie will behave."

"Who Vincie?" asked Grace.

"The Duchess."

"She have crown?"

"I'll see if we have any polished."

"How about this evening?" I said. "We'll meet you behind the cemetery."

"Yes! We'll serve you dinner."

"That won't be necessary."

"Please," said Eugen. "Please, let us."

"But I thought you dressed for dinner. We don't have the clothes for that."

"Tonight we will be casual. For you. Please. I have venison I'd love to have the cook prepare. You will dine with us, and design dresses, and it will be perfect. Five o'clock, behind the cemetery."

"Auntie!" said Grace.

My heart began to race as I pivoted to see if she'd come in the back.

"No. There."

"Go!" I yelled to Eugen, hustling him to the kitchen and out the back door. When I returned to the front room, Marie was about to enter.

"Grace, go upstairs and get ready for sledding."

"But . . ."

"Now!"

She looked hurt that I had spoken so harshly to her, but she lifted Dolly and obeyed. Marie entered a moment later, and her eyes went immediately to the sled.

"Are you taking Gracie sledding today?"

"Yes," I said. "Just got this new sled for a song."

"Where?"

"Oh, I ordered it."

Marie narrowed her eyes and looked as if she wanted to ask more, but changed the subject.

"Those choir robes are gorgeous," she

said. "Everyone is saying so. Has it brought in any more business?"

"Some," I said, thinking of Millay with guilt.

"That's a relief. Well, I'm on my way to the market. Can I persuade you and Gracie to come to dinner? Since it's Advent, I'm trying to be a more forgiving wife. Everette and I haven't fought in two whole days."

"I'm glad to hear it," I said. "But, no, thank you. I have some leftovers I need to eat before they go bad. You and Everette should take this time to get to know each other again."

"I suppose," she said. "It seems better than the alternative. Sometimes. Well, enjoy your sledding and dinner."

"Thank you."

Marie left, and started for the market, and I finally felt as if my heart had stopped beating so fast. It seemed ironic that Marie was working on remaking herself during Advent while I was working at sewing gowns for an adulterous witch. I knew I shouldn't go to Millay's house and I scolded myself for agreeing with Eugen so easily. I thought that perhaps I wouldn't show up at five behind the cemetery, but my eyes again found the empty appointment book, and I knew I would meet him.

■ ■ ■ ■

On the climb to Steepletop, Eugen took the roads a bit more slowly with Grace in the car, but not much. I had her pressed to my left side, while I held my satchel with my drawing materials on the other. The flutter of excitement that I felt at showing Millay the designs gave me the courage not to ask Eugen to turn back, but I wanted to many times.

Grace expressed her excitement at riding in their car, and chattered about the snowy woods in the dark. I hadn't figured out how I'd keep her from telling Aunt Marie about the visit. If I told her it was a secret, she'd be even more likely to slip. I would worry over that tomorrow. First, I had to make it through tonight.

When we arrived, the house was dark upstairs and looked almost vacant. Candles glowed through the downstairs windows, and the scent of wood burning in a fireplace hung in the air.

"It's dark," said Grace.

"We don't have electricity up here. Just a few appliances powered by the generator. Maybe someday we will. Vincie likes it primitive for now."

Grace nuzzled closer to me, as if she was scared. I didn't blame her.

The dogs greeted the car as it slowed to a stop, and Grace dislodged herself from my side and stared at them through the window. When Eugen opened the door, they licked her face until she giggled, and reached for me to carry her.

Eugen showed us into the foyer and took our coats to hang by the door. I noticed that the gun was not there, but Millay's riding boots were in their designated place, alongside a well-worn saddle. It had been so long since I'd ridden a horse, and I remembered how I had loved the sensation of sitting high, racing over the grass with the wind in my hair. My father's friends at the dairy had let us ride anytime we wished. I wondered how often Millay rode and how many horses she owned. Did she need a smaller breed to accommodate her diminutive size?

We entered the dining room, and Grace's eyes grew wide at the elaborate display before us. Polished crystal and silver glinted from the table and sideboards and a cheerful fire burned in the grate. The table settings of orange plates painted with witches leaning over steaming cauldrons amused me. How fitting. Grace and I were directed to sit on either side of the set table, but

Grace would not let me put her down, so I kept her on my lap.

"I'll go and inform Vincent that you are here," said Eugen.

He disappeared up the stairs, and while we waited, I pointed out the shell collection, the witchy plates, and the tapestry in the corner. Grace ventured off my lap to get a closer look.

"Bad guys," said Grace, pointing to the demonlike figures on the wall hanging.

"They are meant to scare away the bad spirits," said Millay. She entered with the pageantry of royalty, again having donned the gorgeous purple robe, and spinning in a circle for Grace's amusement. Grace walked over to her without fear and ran her hands over the velvet.

"Didn't your mother make me the most beautiful robe?" she asked.

"Yes. I say purple."

"I remember," said Millay. She motioned for Grace to take the chair at her left, which she obeyed, to my surprise.

"I can't tell you how pleased I am that you agreed to come here," she said, walking to her seat at the head of the table.

"Thank you," I replied. "And thank you for the sled. We had fun today."

Eugen pulled out Millay's seat, and moved

her to the table. Then he went and sat on the other side. Once the lord and lady of the house were settled, a man and a woman entered with small steaming tureens of tomato soup, garnished with fresh, warm fennel bread, followed by a course of greens, and then tender venison rubbed with garlic and rosemary. The meat nearly melted in my mouth, and it interested me to learn that Millay had killed the deer for our feast.

"Have you ever hunted, Laura?" she asked.

"Never," I said. "I don't think I could."

"You should try sometime. As humans, we do, after all, have dominion over the beasts. When necessary we must take their power to nourish us."

I glanced at her, and back at the food, conscious that every word out of the poet's mouth had many meanings.

"I'm glad there are those who can stomach the act," I said, "for I am happy to enjoy the fruits of your labors, but I would not want to fire the mortal shot."

"Someday I will take you hunting with us, and you will see that you not only can do it, but also enjoy it. Power is its own drug."

Throughout the evening, the goblets seemed to refill themselves. I allowed myself to indulge in the wine. So deep in the woods, the Boissevains had no need to hide from law enforcement, and had the means and privacy to enjoy alcohol whenever they desired it, which seemed often by my observation. Grace ate more than I would have guessed, but grew restless and began inspecting the paintings and furnishings in the dining room before venturing into the living room. I called her back, but Eugen insisted that she was fine to explore, even when she began experimenting with the keys on one of Millay's two parlor pianos.

Millay lit a cigarette and listened to Grace's noise for a moment before speaking.

"I could have been a great pianist," she said, "if only it weren't for my hands."

I glanced at the tiny freckled fingers tapping the ash from the cigarette, and noted their graceful lines.

"What's wrong with them?" I asked.

"Only that they are too small to reach far along the keys. It became impossible, really. I tried to stretch them, but it didn't seem to work."

"But they have found their home resting in paper notebooks, scribbling marks that make magic meaning of these words we speak," said Eugen. "So I must be glad that you were designed exactly as you are."

Millay smiled and blew her cigarette in the opposite direction of where I sat.

"This is all distraction," she said in a sudden harsh manner. "Damned small talk. Did you read the sonnets? What do you have to show me?"

I stared at her for a moment, sensing that I must not jump the moment she asked it of me. I was determined not to act her serf.

"I have read what you sent me," I said, taking a large gulp from my goblet and finishing what was left of my red wine. Soon the cook had refilled my glass and vanished into the background.

"And?" said Eugen. "What did you think?"

I thought of the words she chose as symbols, used over and over. Words like *dust, feather, heart,* and *moon.* Words with weight that moved through one's lips with clarity of meaning. I could not translate into words my feelings of love and loss that had arisen when I had read the sonnets, so I finally left the room, pulled the sketchbook out of the satchel, and presented my notebook to her. When she gasped, I knew I had pleased her. Her tiny hands flipped through the pages, and her eyes misted over as she took in each design.

"Fit for a goddess . . . Oh, that color, I would have never thought it, but it is perfect. . . . This will be heavy, but the slits will give me air. . . . Silver, over and over. Cool blues. Trimming in feathers and pearls." She placed her small hand on the book. "Laura, this is exquisite."

"I wanted to conjure the recurring images of the moon and the night in this one," I said, running my fingertips over the silver cape trimmed in pearls and lined in pale blue.

She flipped to another sketch.

"And here," I continued, "I know it's dramatic with the white feathers on the trim, but there are so many bird and flight images — the swans, thrushes, the winged heel, nests and cages. . . ."

"It is perfect," she said.

"Or here," I said, flipping farther back, unable to contain my enthusiasm. "Black on forest green, black vines crawling up from the hem, so dark they nearly blend in."

"How will I choose?" she asked. "Uge, do you see these?"

Eugen winked at me and drained his glass. Millay closed the book, rested her hands on the cover, and reached for me. Because I felt warm and loose from the wine and the pleasure of having designed costumes pleasing to a discerning and demanding client, I took her hand, unafraid.

"You have no idea how these will elevate my readings," she said. "So many people think a reading is just words, volume, timbre. You and I know that it is more, that I can't become the persona on the page, I can't complete a transformation without these clothes to assist in my metamorphosis."

I knew she spoke the truth. It was something I'd sensed for a long time, and knew it applied to more than just the stage. It had taken a sequestered, lascivious, half-drunk poet to help me fully understand this. What did that make me?

Later that night, after Millay had played the piano for me and Grace, after they'd fed us chocolate cake and digestifs, chosen their designs, and lined my satchel with money to cover fabric and half of the labor, Eugen delivered me and Grace home safe and unmolested. He left us at the end of the block and watched us until we entered the shop. Grace had fallen asleep on the ride home, so I carried her up to bed. I could not rest, however, and my fingers itched to begin creating the gowns. Without fabric, I was unable to do anything, so I forced myself to put on my nightgown and prepare for bed.

There was another clear sky, full of stars and crisp air. I pressed my hand to the warm skin on my chest, trying to cool the heat that had risen there. I walked to the window and touched a pane to feel the chill, lifted the sash and leaned out. Glancing around town, I saw that many lights in upstairs rooms were out, and most of the town slept. Dr. Hagerty's downstairs light was on, however. Caroline's silhouette darkened the window. She held a book, and John sat at his table behind her, bent over his work. I wondered if she read to him while he repaired frames and polished lenses, and this glimpse of their intimacy touched me. After a moment, he stood, walked to her, and turned her chair to face him. He reached down and lifted her, and then disappeared from sight. My skin tingled from where the night air found the tears that slid down my face. The Hagertys' companionship moved me, and I realized that I shouldn't pity Caroline. I should envy her and everyone in town and up the mountain who had a partner, even with all of their imperfections. At least they had another person with whom to share ideas, a book, or a simple meal.

For the first time, I thought of Agnes, alone in her large house, her husband dead, her only child married, her grandchildren too weak to come into the world. Perhaps her losses had hardened her, and being alone, she had no one to challenge her or soften her rough edges. Maybe loneliness had chilled her and closed her heart, and caused her to envy others who had anything she did not, even if those others appeared to have less than she.

I shuddered at the thought of how much we had in common.

VINCENT

I cannot be satisfied.

I long for visitors, but wish them gone as soon as they've arrived. I desire city energy, but can't bear it once I'm there. I wish my husband would go away and leave me alone, and I am helpless without him.

This capricious, dizzying response to my world is only quelled by Laura. When I desire that she come and she does, I am calm. She seems to feed the good things in me. I knew I could tame her eventually, but the result is not what I expected. The softening of her heart toward me hasn't further ignited my desire for her. Strangely, it has cooled it. But it is not a frigid cooling; it is like the river in the spring. After the thaw, before the heat, when it is refreshing.

Cleansing.

The feelings I have for her resemble mother love, with our roles reversing. I want to be her mother. I want her to mother me. I want to hold her hand and sit in silence working next to her — Laura with her needle and thread, and me with pencils and paper. I want a Sapphic relationship, abundant with mutual admiration through creation.

But I know that sexual love is what fuels me, so it is George I desire. George must come to me. I won't wait any longer. I will command that he come.

I write to him on Steepletop letterhead, reminding him of what poetry is born from our passion, chastising him for letting our love turn dry and cold, telling him that this is the anniversary of when our two galaxies collided and why the hell can't he revisit that place? Suddenly I am savage, writing that he isn't big enough for our love, that he is nothing but a child, that his palate is not refined enough for my sophistication. But I know exactly what his lips are capable of, and I am again reduced to begging, pleading, caring not that I sound like a madwoman, only hoping that he gets the letter soon, sees the urgency, and makes the trip.

If he does not, I will. I will go to Chicago.
But I know he will come to me. I know it.

TWENTY-FIVE

LAURA

I awoke in the morning to a fresh blanket of snow. The following day provided even more. I'd already tromped through the frigid mounds to post the order for materials for Millay's reading tour wardrobe, but day after day of terrible weather prevented trains from delivering the fabric. While I waited for their whistles, I pored over pattern books and designed my own, selected linings that might complement the colors, refined details on bodices and necklines.

I pulled Grace around town on her sled, stopping at Marie's house to help her finish sewing diapers and bibs for the baby, and then started for the hills near the school to sled. Gabriel didn't look up while working on the back of Our Lady's robes, but I noted that his eyes didn't appear as dark as usual. He'd also trimmed his beard and lost his scowl. Did meeting the musicians have anything to do with that?

Before I passed, he spoke. "Will you come tonight?"

He was crouched down at the base of the slab at Our Lady's feet. There was no one else nearby, so he had to be talking to me.

"Pardon me?" I asked.

He did not speak for a moment, and it dawned on me that he must be referring to the musicians. He'd seen me. I felt like a fool for spying on them.

"You'd be welcome, you know. Both of you," he said. He stood and brushed off his dungarees, and finally met my eyes. "You don't have to hide."

"Hide and seek?" asked Grace.

"Do you like that game?" he asked her. "I know some kids who do too."

Grace nodded. "We sled now."

I was troubled by his words, torn in two by a strong impulse to go and another that scolded me for even considering it.

"They are good people," he said.

I couldn't help my curiosity. "How do you know them?"

"I met Sam, the guitarist, at the lumber-yard where I've been doing some side work. He invited me. How did *you* find them?"

"I heard the music while I was walking by the pond."

"I never hear," said Grace.

I had almost forgotten that she sat there listening to us. She shook the rope and I looked down at her. "I never hear," she said.

"Maybe sometime you will," I replied.

Gabriel redirected his attention to the statue. I said good-bye, and he nodded as I walked past him. Just before he was out of my sight, he turned and caught my eye. I paused and he held my gaze longer than I could his. I resumed our trek to the hills. At the last moment I turned back. He was still watching me.

After Grace and I baked and ate raisin bread and shared an apple for dinner, I tucked her in early. Our snow play had exhausted her, so she went without a fight. I looked out the window toward the woods, trying to decide what I should do. Young Laura — Laura before the change, as Marie had pointed out — would have gone willingly and with enthusiasm. But I wasn't that girl anymore.

As I walked downstairs, I noticed my boots next to the back door, pointed toward the forest. How could going hurt my reputation any more than it already was? It couldn't. No one would know, first of all, and second, there were families there —

nothing sordid except maybe a little taste of gin, which I could refuse. Grace would want to make the adventure, and if she weren't so sleepy, I would have taken her. If I was ever going to take Grace to the forest people, I should learn more about them first. Without thinking beyond that, I checked Grace once more, bundled up, took the bread I'd wrapped in a towel, and locked the door behind me.

Moonlight bathed the landscape, making the covered hills and snow-burdened trees appear frozen in time. I placed my feet in the tracks that preceded me in the snow. Before long I arrived at the bend, and the revelers came into view. All the usual visitors encircled the fire, including the children, too cold to venture far from its warmth. The beautiful woman sat next to Gabriel and passed him a cup. They hadn't yet struck up a song. A branch near where I stood shook in the breeze, causing a rush of snow to fall beside me, and Gabriel saw me standing there. He stood, and they all turned their attention to me.

Suddenly the group surrounded me. Many of them embraced me, a few mentioned that they'd hoped I would come, and the heavyset man thanked me for the bread, which he proceeded to pass around the circle. The young man with the guitar, Sam, invited me to sit next to him and his husky, Blue, and introduced me to the group.

"For those of you who don't know, this is Laura, the woodland fairy we thought was watching over us. She has actually turned out to be a beautiful woman bearing baked goods."

A cheer went up in the crowd, and I colored from the heat of the fire and the embarrassment of being known in spite of my hiding.

"I'm glad you finally joined us," said Sam, patting his dog on the head. The husky looked at me out of wise blue eyes. "Gabe told us you might, one of these days."

"I'm Sam's wife, Callie," said a young woman wearing a cap over her blond hair. "And while I'm glad you're here, I'm a little sad you aren't actually a wood nymph."

"If it makes you feel any better," I said, "while I watched you, I often thought you were just such creatures."

"I'm glad," she said.

The colored man dipped a ladle into a steaming pot over the fire, and filled a tin cup for me. The scent of the cider tickled my nose as he placed it in my hands and gave me a shy smile.

"I'm Darren," he said. "I work a farm,

just north."

I nodded at him, a little wide-eyed at seeing him with a group of whites in the woods.

"Tim," said the large man. "When I'm not making music with these people, I'm at the post office in Austerlitz."

The kids began to grow restless and started slinging snowballs at one another on the periphery of the clearing. I thought of how much Grace would love to be here with these warm people and a dog in this secret place, and was pleased with myself for coming. The woman with the long brown hair spoke last.

"Liza," she said, extending her hand to me. "I work in set design for the Colonial Theatre and some other local theater companies."

I felt a rush of envy, but I took her hand and attempted a smile.

"And it's your turn," Liza continued. "Tell us who you are and what you do, besides being a voyeur."

"I'm just a seamstress," I said. "I work in town."

"Ah," said Callie. "If we ever get that Chatham theater group going, I know who we'll call for costumes."

"Look at us," said Sam. "Gabe's a fallen-away papist. Tim's a moonshiner. Darren is a colored farmer. Randall there is a Jewish lawyer." A tall man with glasses and a bow tie raised his violin at me before directing his attention back to tuning its strings. "Is there any more base creature than a lawyer?"

"You're nuts," said Randall, with a half smile.

"But we've all got one thing in common. The music. So we meet and let the rest fall where it may."

"You play?" Liza asked me.

"No."

"You have ears that can listen?" asked Tim.

"I do."

"Good," said Sam. "Then let's stop chattering and start playing."

For the next couple of hours, I sat among them and allowed the music and the laughter to mend me in places I didn't know could be healed so close to town. I sang along to some of the tunes I'd heard before; I drank the cider and absorbed the fascinating conversation and debate that rose between sets. Blue had come to sit next to me and nuzzled me until I began to pet her thick, warm coat. I could see her swollen belly, and thought she must be pregnant.

Gabriel sat next to Liza, across the fire from me. Our gazes barely met, but I was acutely aware of his presence. When I did gather the courage to look at him, I noticed that he seemed calm here. His intense eyes were softer, and he laughed more than once.

After almost no time at all, Darren announced that it was approaching midnight, and a great grumbling arose about early work times and long walks home in the cold. I felt suddenly nervous about how long I'd been away from Grace, and said my good-byes. While I stuffed my bread towel into my jacket, I saw Liza whisper something to Gabriel, and he laughed and gave her a hug before she waved to all of us and started up the snowy path with Callie, Sam, and their girls.

"I'll put this out," said Tim, shoveling dirt and snow over the fire.

As I entered the darkest part of the woods, Gabriel joined me. "I'll walk you home. I'm going this way too."

"All right," I said. As we climbed, the chill began to overtake the luscious warmth of the past few hours. It made me long for the fireside and the kind people. "I'm glad I came tonight."

"I can tell," he said. "You looked different down there than you do in town."

"I felt different," I said, shoving my hands deep into my pockets. "You seemed changed too, I'd add."

He made a sound of assent. "Next time, you should bring Grace. I don't like you leaving her alone while you're down there."

I bristled at his comment. "Really? And just who are you to criticize?"

"It's not criticism; it's concern. What if there was an emergency?"

"Like what? After my mother died, my father left my sister and me alone as children all the time. I'm less than five minutes away. I can see the house from here."

"What if a candle catches the rug on fire, or robbers break in, or she has a nightmare?"

I fell silent, suddenly embarrassed and ashamed that I'd left Grace alone so often. What kind of mother was I?

"Hey," he said, "I'm sure she's fine. I didn't mean to upset you. I just want you to bring her next time so she can have some fun. I don't see her playing with little ones in town."

I was glad of the dark so he couldn't see my shame. The back of my shop came into view, and as we crossed the meadow, I felt exposed, and then worried that I'd be seen walking at night with a man while my daughter slept alone in the house. I widened the space between us. Gabriel looked over at me and then back at the town, and didn't say anything more.

When we reached my back door, he wished me good night and waited for me to go inside. I locked the door behind me and rushed upstairs to check on Grace, who slept soundly. I thanked God for it, and rubbed my temples, alarmed at my bad judgment.

That night I crawled into her bed, holding her close to me. There would be no more leaving her. I would take her with me to the forest at night and let her play with other children. I'd show her what community looked like.

VINCENT

George has refused me.

I wrote him; I telegrammed him from New York City when we went for the weekend. I begged him to call me or I'd be on the next train to Chicago. He finally called us at the Vanderbilt to calm me, to say he could not get away at the moment, but that he would come as soon as he could.

I know he lied to me to keep me from coming to him, and it makes me want to hang myself.

In the newspapers, I recently read that a scientist used penicillin, a fungus of some kind, to cure an eye infection. The implications are profound, but I cannot help but wish there could be a cure for my emotional suffering. Alcohol and morphine dull me, but they do not fix me. The hurt comes back stronger when the blurring wears off, and it seems I need more and more of the drugs to deaden my heartsickness.

I wait in bed for Arthur Ficke. He is coming to me today, and without Gladys, thankfully. If I have to endure her stuffy, soul-sucking fussiness for another minute, I'll put a gun to my head. She is the worst kind of female, one who pretends to be open, but inside her a Puritan minister waits in judgment. She is high on women's rights, and yet she's crueler to women than to any man, and is an appalling bore, to boot.

Gladys is prone to lecture me when I disappoint her. When Uge and I had decided to stay in the city and celebrate last New Year's Eve with Deems and Mary instead of going to Hardhack, Gladys had a tantrum that lasted for weeks. I told Uge that she could kiss my derriere, and I've tried to avoid her the whole of this long, strange year.

But it is Sunday, and the Fickes are so damnably married to their routines, we can count on them to arrive like clockwork.

Sometimes we leave to go somewhere before we know they'll show up, and make excuses afterward, but today, with the snow in the roads and my strain over George's refusal to come to me, I cannot leave my bed.

Sunday is the only day when we are free of employees. The servants aren't here; the farm staff is off. When the weather is nice, we don't put on a stitch of clothing all day. We work in the garden and sunbathe by the roses, where we'll put in a pool one day soon. Our skin becomes deliciously dark and freckled, and we make love surrounded by bees and birds in our private Eden.

Oh, we didn't always mind the Fickes joining us. They would strip with us and flirt. We'd take nude photos and dally with one another. I hope all of that is not over, but it will be if Gladys doesn't learn to hold her tongue, or at least use it for good.

I giggle at this luscious thought just as Arthur walks in. My robe is open, baring my breasts, and I smoke my cigarette like a butterfly takes nectar from a flower. His face opens in a smile.

"I thought you weren't well, sweet Vincent," he says, coming to my side and burying his face in my neck.

"Gladys won't like this. We can only partake of each other when she's there. You know the rules."

"You have enchanted me, you goddess. I am helpless in your gaze. Surely she'd forgive me."

"Never. And how is your dearest *wife*?"

"She's fine. Visiting friends. Jealous that I'm spending the day with you."

"I'm still bitter that you married her, even though it was aeons ago."

He is taken aback that I have voiced this. I don't know why he is ever shocked by a thing I say.

"You may be more sensitive than I," I say.

"You are too inconstant for me," he says, gruffly. There is dark emotion in his voice and he pulls away. "I require loyalty."

"All great hypocrites do, love," I say, and stub out my cigarette. I close my robe over my breasts and cross my legs at the ankle.

He rises from my bedside, understanding that he is no longer welcome.

When he gets to my door, he turns. "Will you come to the table for dinner tonight?"

"I haven't decided if I'll forgive you by then."

He leaves the room, wounded, and I take comfort in the knowledge that I can still control some men.

TWENTY-SIX

LAURA

I wiped the sweat from my forehead with the back of my sleeve and leaned on my shovel. Another winter storm had dropped a fresh six inches on the six we already had. The snow mounds on either side of the walk were almost as tall as Grace, and she loved using the mallet Gabriel had given her and a stick of kindling to chisel away at the snow, while he worked at his sculpture just up the street.

"You're dropping little piles all over the walk I just shoveled," I said to her in mock exasperation. She looked up at me with an impish smile, the lenses of her glasses foggy, wet, and covered in smudges.

"Honestly," I said, removing her glasses and sliding them under my coat to polish them with the bottom of my sweater. "How can you see anything?" Once they were shiny, I noticed a crack in one of the lenses.

"Gracie," I said. "When did this happen?"
She shrugged.

"Now we'll have to go back to Dr. Hagerty," I said, dreading the thought of disturbing him, being around his mournful wife, putting out money I didn't have. I tried to put the damaged glasses back on her face, but she dodged me and refused to wear them, so I folded them and slid them into my pocket. As I did, Everette came up the walk with his shovel in hand. He looked me up and down, pausing to consider my jodhpurs.

"You look like Amelia Earhart," he said with a forced laugh.

"If you're referring to my snow pants," I said, "I couldn't very well wear a dress to shovel snow."

"Mrs. Miller down the street is wearing a dress and boots, and I'm sure she's both warm and comfortable."

"Did you come here to give me fashion advice or help me shovel?"

"The latter," he said, "and to invite you to dinner tonight."

"Where's Marie?"

"She saw you shoveling while she shook out our rugs, and insisted that I help you."

"I don't need help," I said. "And besides, it might hurt your chances at reelection to associate with someone like me, out in the open."

He laughed. "Actually, it might help. Politicians should be democratic, helping all kinds of people."

There was something invigorating about standing in the snow sparring with my brother-in-law. As much as he frustrated me, I found honesty — no matter how cruel — to be a comfort. I still didn't want to accept his dinner invitation, however. The thought of an uncomfortable meal with them instead of sneaking off into the woods for talk and music with the wood nymphs, as I had affectionately begun to think of them, did not appeal to me. I had been putting off Marie and Everette quite a bit, however, and did miss my sister.

"Will you join us?" he again asked.

I took a deep breath. "All right. I'll bring a side dish."

"Fine. I'm glad to hear it." His voice softened and he looked down at his snow boots, kicking at a frozen pile. "We could use a little friendly chatter at the table."

Everette's humble posture took me aback. It wasn't something I'd often seen in him, if ever. He looked up at me.

"Five thirty all right?"

"Yes, that will give Grace time to finish

listening to *Uncle Don* on the radio."

"Good. I'm glad that's settled."

Everette began shoveling the fresh snow on the sidewalk by the street while I worked on the path to the shop. I noticed that Everette kept stopping to watch Gabriel at work on the statue. He'd stare at him for a little while, then turn back to shoveling, then stop again — on and off, like a light switch. I didn't know what he expected to see. At one point, Sam and his dog walked up to Gabriel and Sam shook the other man's hand. They gestured back and forth a bit, and Sam talked with great animation about the sculpture. After a few minutes, Sam shook Gabriel's hand once more, and set off toward the bridge with Blue. He did not carry his guitar with him, so I imagined that he must not live far away.

"Where do you think he's from?" Everette asked. "He looks like a hobo with that long hair and wolf dog."

"The man talking to Gabe? I'm not sure."

"Gabe? Are you on such friendly terms with him?" Everette rested his arm on the shovel's handle, peering at me. I cursed myself for my slip.

"No, that just came out," I said. "Gabriel seems like such a formal name."

Everette narrowed his eyes before returning to his chore. We made quick work of it, in spite of Grace's fresh snow tracks. I wanted him to leave me alone, but he seemed intent on staying. Perhaps he wanted to escape Marie. I couldn't be rude, so I offered him some of the soup I had on the stove.

His face was unreadable. "No, I'd better not."

I nodded in agreement.

On the front porch, Grace and I stamped the snow off our boots. Everette watched me sit her on my lap and pull off her tiny boots, and when I finished, Grace raised her arms to him. He hesitated, then reached for her and carried her inside so her feet would not get wet. When he put her down, she insisted he take off her snowsuit. He looked at me, helpless. I shrugged.

"You'll have to get used to it," I said, "with your own little one on the way."

He removed her snowsuit and placed it by the fire, while I stirred chicken noodle soup on the stove, and slid two slices of bread into the oven. I put on a kettle of hot water for tea, and sliced a small block of Swiss cheese. Everette was just leaving when the bell on the front door rang, and the fabric vendor stepped in, carrying two large boxes. I was surprised to see him despite all the snow, and silently lamented that he had picked now, of all times, to arrive. He placed the boxes on the floor with a thump and stamped his boots, leaving hunks of snow drying in pools on the wood floor.

"Cash on delivery today," he said.

"That's quite an order," said Everette. "More work for the church, or is the *old lady* in need of more gowns?"

I ignored him and wrote out a check. The man thanked me, and helped me carry the boxes to the supply room. Once he left, I closed the door and went to set the table, trying to avoid Everette's eyes.

"I guess I'll be off now," he said. "We'll see you tonight."

I nodded, and as soon as he was out the door, I rushed to the closet and tore open the boxes to see what treasures lay inside. Glints of silver, white, and ice blue fabric were stacked like layers of snow. I knew I'd need to work at night to make sure no one caught me sewing the witch's wardrobe. Even if I stayed late at Everette and Marie's house, I knew I'd work tonight. I'd begin creating for the woman I said I'd never serve.

I imagined I could hear the fabric calling to me on the winter gusts that rattled the windows of Marie and Everette's house while we dined. If the fabric were animated, it would be a long, pale woman with platinum hair and ice blue eyes, like Gabriel's Madonna. She'd be sad and lost — a drifter with no place to settle her love-weary bones.

"Laura," said Marie, a look of annoyance on her face.

"I'm sorry. What?"

"Where is your head tonight?"

"I guess I'm just tired. Distracted. The winter feels heavier this year."

I glanced at Everette, and he looked down at his lamb chops.

"I was saying that the doctor says the baby is measuring large. I'm not due until March but maybe I'll deliver early. I do seem to have a lot of false contractions."

"You hear that, Gracie?" I said. "Are you getting excited for a baby cousin?"

She smiled. "I like babies."

"You'll look so grown-up next to him or her."

"I want boy," said Grace.

"Really," said Marie. "Why is that?"

"Like baby Jesus."

"How nice," I said.

Our Lady of Grace Church had recently put out the large Nativity set with the empty, waiting manger. Grace had been asking about it every time we passed, and she was excited for the day they'd finally add the infant to the display.

I enjoyed church more these days, though my primary reason was shameful. Watching the choir in their gorgeous new robes while Agnes wore a look of stony distaste was deeply satisfying. I wouldn't indulge too much reflection on the other reason the building had felt warmer: Gabriel had started attending.

While Marie and I cleaned up dinner, Grace pulled Everette into the parlor to play pickup sticks with her. If he wasn't comfortable with her, she wouldn't let up until he was. I looked out at them with a small clench in my heart. How nice it would be to have a husband to play with Grace while I tended to chores or work. It would make life so much easier to have another set of hands to tuck her in, bathe her, take her sledding, if such a husband existed. I cherished Grace, of course, but it was exhausting being the only parent.

A finished painting on the easel above where they played caught my eye. It was an oil on canvas of Stony Kill Bridge from the banks of the stream. Icicles that had frozen at the edges reached down toward the water. The trees were done in blacks and browns in sharp contrast to the cool whites of the snow. Their limbs hung like hunched skeletons and cast deep shadows. Glimpses of gray sky between the branches and the sharp icicles gave one an ominous feeling.

"That's a striking picture," I said. "I'm chilled just looking at it."

"It's reflective of my soul."

Marie's flat voice troubled me. I would have rather seen high emotion — fiery tantrums, bold statements, anything but this terrible blankness. I worried about her mental state. She seemed so melancholy. And suddenly the danger of what I was doing with Millay hit me in the gut.

"I wish you wouldn't say things like that," I said quietly. "What can I do? How can I help?"

She stared out at Everette and Grace until her face crumpled with tears. I pulled her into an embrace and rubbed her hair. She clung to me, and I felt another stab in my stomach. She pulled away, and I wiped her face with my fingers.

"Have you spoken to Father Ash?" I asked.

Her face contorted in horror. "No! What, am I to tell him that we got intoxicated at some wanton female's house, and instead of leaving when we saw what kind of place it was, I got drunker while my husband dallied with her?"

I flinched at her description and tried to imagine such a thing before shaking the image from my head. "It's what confession is for," I said.

"I'm sure he's never heard anything like that."

"And I'm sure he has. It's why there's a sacrament for it. The burden is too heavy for you to bear."

"I don't think I can," she said.

"I've confessed everything about what brought Grace into this world, and while it hasn't fixed it, it has allowed me to live and to breathe. You have to try. You have to make Everette try. Give it away or it will continue to haunt you."

She looked out at Everette once more, and he turned to us in the kitchen. When he saw Marie's tears, he went to her, and she began to cry again, but allowed him to embrace her. He held her head to his chest and stared at me over her shoulder, his expression troubled. It touched me the way he held her, and I left them alone in the kitchen.

Grace and I cleaned up the pickup sticks.

"Why Auntie cry?" she asked, staring into the kitchen through her cracked glasses.

"She doesn't feel good," I said.

"She sick?"

"Yes," I said. "But she will get better."

I bundled Grace for our walk home. We left soon afterward, and once I'd put Grace to bed, I sat at the window and stared at the half-finished statue, thinking, praying, making peace with what I knew I had to do.

The next day I sent Millay a telegram with only two words.

I can't.

VINCENT

I throw the full vase of roses at the wall, sending glass and broken flowers showering the hard wood in a sopping mess.

"I can't!" I yell.

I cross the room and snatch the paper from Eugen's hands. Two miserable words. Where am I in these words? How can she dismiss me after all our progress? Laura is so selfish. I throw the paper in the fire and clutch the mantel.

"This is madness," I say. "I've never seen one as inconstant and capricious as this damned seamstress. She has no respect for me, for who I am, for what these robes are. Doesn't she understand that she will drape a piece of herself in history by her creation? Thousands of people will see her work. Her art will be asked about, noted in columns, sought out. But, no, she *can't.*"

"You must stop this fit, Edna," says Eugen. "You will strain yourself. You are taking on too much."

"Don't you tell me what I know," I say, feeling the tears hot on my face. "It's as if I've become irrelevant. My wishes are ignored, swept aside, rebelled against. I have no say! Not with George, my mother, my sisters, not even some damned lowly, outcast dressmaker in a nothing town."

I collapse in a heap on the hearth rug, and feel Eugen lift me and carry me to the bed. He is mumbling and frightened. I've disturbed the only constant presence in my life. I know I will never drive him away — only death will separate him from me. But what if I drive him there through my hysterics?

Maybe that would be best. Then I will have lost everything and I can fully embrace the grave, which waits for me like an open mouth, wanting to swallow me, tuck me in the earth, cut me off from everything of beauty.

Twenty-Seven

LAURA

December passed like a sleepless night.
Christmas came and went. My telegram had
gone unanswered, and the boxes of unused
fabric tormented me from their hiding
place, deep in the closet. I refused to touch
any more of the down payment they'd given
me, so I again ran out of money, and I
wondered how I would pay them back.

Grace continued to wear her broken
glasses because I could not go to Dr.
Hagerty without a way to pay, obligating
him to help us for free. I would not take
advantage of him. He had already been kind
enough to fashion these tiny glasses for a
child. He'd written papers on optometry for
children using Grace as a case study and
had assured me it helped him more than it
did me, but I did not believe that could be
true.

After shivering in the cold for three nights

after the New Year, I awoke the next morning with new resolve. I couldn't sit passive any longer; I had to seek work. It couldn't be at the church. I didn't want to put Father Ash in a bad position. Agnes' friends would no longer use my services for dresses. I decided to offer to provide linens for the hospital. My parents had done so years ago, but with the expansion of the facility, the need had become greater than what we could offer. I was determined to find a way to reinvolve myself with the hospital, even if in a small way.

The new maternity ward might be the best place to start. While sewing blankets and diapers for Marie's baby, I'd remembered how easily such tiny items could be made. Perhaps they could use my services. Marie thought it was a good idea, and volunteered to keep Grace for me while I went to inquire.

Approaching the building brought back a tumult of painful memories. Marie was resigned to having her baby there, in spite of her proclamation after my father's passing that she would never enter its doors. I hoped Marie's birthing experience would give us new, positive associations to drive out the bad ones. When I stepped through the front doors, however, Darcy Dempsey was leaning on the front desk chatting with the admissions secretary, a woman with whom we'd attended school. It humiliated me that Darcy would see me begging for employment, and I tried to turn around, but she spotted me.

"Good morning," she said.

I was trapped. "Hello."

"How can I help you?" asked the secretary.

I tried to think up a lie as to why I'd come when I was further mortified to see Daniel round the corner. He stopped when he saw us at the desk, then continued toward us.

"Hello, Laura. What brings you here?"

I looked from him to Darcy to the secretary, and blurted out, "Maternity."

Their faces were horror-struck, and I realized that they thought I was pregnant.

"Not for me," I said. "I'm looking to see if I can provide linens for the babies in the ward."

"Oh, well, you'll have to talk to the secretary there. Just down the hall and to the right," he said.

"Thank you." I hurried away from them, imagining their whispers and speculation. I wished I could have turned around to leave, but now that they were watching me, I felt obligated to continue.

I rounded the corner and proceeded to

the shiny new wing of the hospital, born of Agnes' fund-raising and planning. Employment in its construction had kept many men in town, and their families, from destitution. The wing looked out over the meadow, and I could just see the overgrown amphitheater at the bottom of the hill. I turned my attention to the woman seated at the admissions desk.

"I'd like to speak with whoever is in charge of linens for the maternity ward," I said.

"May I ask what this is in reference to?" asked a woman of about fifty, whom I didn't recognize.

"Sewing opportunities."

"For volunteer?"

My face flamed. "No, for pay. I own the town dress shop, and when my parents were alive, they sewed linens for the hospital. I wanted to see if I could renew the partnership for the new maternity wing."

"I'm sorry," she said. "We have a virtual army of volunteers who knit and crochet everything from diapers, to booties, to blankets for the ward. The ladies' choir of Our Lady of Grace is in charge of coordinating volunteers. In fact, Dr. Dempsey's wife just left after delivering a whole box of booties."

My stomach roiled and I trembled with frustration. "I understand," I said. "Is there anyone with whom I can discuss whether my services would be useful in some other capacity?"

"I apologize, but you'll need to speak with Dr. Dempsey about that. You will have to visit his secretary and schedule a meeting. She's on the second floor, at the other end of the hallway."

My head hurt. I turned and began to head down to the other corridor, hoping to run into Daniel again, and this time without Darcy nearby. They had both disappeared, however, so I had to go upstairs to find his secretary. She politely informed me that his schedule was booked solid. I agreed to see him in two weeks, and after she penciled me into his appointment book, she handed me a card with the date and time of my appointment.

On the way home, I stopped at the library to see if they had any need for linens, window treatments, or table coverings, and Mrs. Perth was kind but could not help me. Their funds had been sharply reduced since the crash. I asked at the Crandell Movie Theater, noting the tears in the curtain, but the manager said they didn't have money for repairs. As a last resort, I even went to the church to see if anything needed to be replaced, if any albs or coverings were needed, but since I had made them not long ago, they were still holding steady from my craftsmanship.

Gabriel wasn't working on the statue, and because of the frigid temperatures, there were barely any people on the streets and sidewalks. The clock tower chimed the hour, reminding me that I'd told Marie I wouldn't be longer than an hour. Today's search having proved fruitless, I decided that I needed to look in nearby towns for work. I'd have to brave the icy roads on my bike, but if I took it slow and if Marie could watch Grace, I'd make it. Perhaps I could place an ad in the paper, and being removed from my own town, people wouldn't judge me.

A thought suddenly occurred to me. The necklace my lover had given me: I could sell it. It was only costume jewelry, but it looked expensive. Besides, I didn't know why I'd held on to it all this time. When I visited another town, I'd take it to a pawnshop and rid myself of it.

Late that night, I again stared out into the blackness, trying to think of a way to support Grace and myself. I felt too tired and discouraged to attempt a visit to the wood nymphs, so instead I searched through my library pile for a book to take my mind off of my troubles.

At the bottom of the stack I found *The Harp Weaver and Other Poems* by Edna St. Vincent Millay. I had picked it up in a moment of weakness and curiosity, and wished I had not. I stared at the book for a long time, and finally opened to the first poem. The candle wasn't throwing off much light, since it had burned down to a nub, but I was soon so immersed in the words, I did not notice. It was as if Millay was reading in my ear. I could hear her voice speak the words of the ballad of the poor mother who would do anything to provide for her son. Her devotion to him led her to a magical harp, on which she spun clothes for him. She wove all night, the finest garments she could, until she died, and all that was left of her love for him was the clothes she had made.

When I shut the book, tears were running down my face. How did a woman like Millay create such poetry, such words that spoke to the human heart? How could she know my soul, years before she'd even known me?

I crawled into bed, miserable and confused. My thoughts snuck to the fabric in the closet, but as they strayed, I pulled them back. Instead, I imagined happy times, good things, adventures like sledding and ice-skating with little Grace. My fantasies soon gave way to sleep, but it did not last. At eleven o'clock, a banging on the back door awoke me. I bolted up in bed, my heart racing, terrified for Grace and myself. I tried to ignore the sound, but it continued insistently.

I stepped carefully down each stair until I reached the final riser, and was able to peek around the corner. The large, shadowy figure of a man showed through the curtain. My heart was pounding. With no weapon of any kind, I had no way to defend us. Should I pick up Grace and try to run out the front door? I crossed the kitchen and grabbed a knife, praying I wouldn't have to use it, and rushed back to the bottom of the stairs.

"Miss Kelley." A muffled voice came through the door. "Please, let me in. It's Eugen."

He seemed too large for my house. My small rooms and furniture didn't suit his big frame, his high emotion, his raw and uncensored speech.

"Why must you torture her?" he asked. "You don't have to make love to her. You just have to fulfill a contract. You broke a

379

contract. You have our check but you have provided no service when you said you would."

"I . . . I know what I said, but things changed. I'll get your money back to you."

"What changed? Nothing has changed. All that is different is your mood, your whims. They are like the wind in the trees." He put his face in his hands.

"I'm sorry, Mr. Boissevain," I said. "Truly."

"What, then? What was said to make you go from a woman smiling at my table to a rash and fickle lover, giving and taking away as her young lover gives and takes away?"

"It's this! All this talk of lovers! How can you stand to live that way?"

"Why is that your business?"

"Because my brother-in-law was one of those lovers and it has nearly driven my sister mad. She can't move forward, and if I take up with you people, she will never understand."

"You are not making a deal with the devil. You are making a couple of capes and robes."

"It feels like a betrayal."

He stood, scraping the floor with his chair. I looked up at the ceiling, wondering when my little one would come scooting down

380

the stairs, awakened by the arguing in the kitchen. Mercifully, she slept on.

Eugen walked to the window and placed his hands on the sink, gazing out into the moonlight. I followed his gaze and saw a horse-drawn sleigh down by the road at the back of the field.

"They are reliable, the horses. More so than any automobile," he said. "They could take you to and from Steepletop if you'd like a place to work where you will not be found. We could harbor you, your daughter, for any number of hours or days. We would do anything to accommodate you."

"How can I explain?" I asked.

"You can tell the truth," he said. "You can't starve for the indiscretions of your family. Your own have nearly done you in."

It was my turn to sit at the table. I felt weak, defeated. From town, to family, to these people. It was getting too hard to keep up with all the battles.

"Why tonight?" I asked. "What brought you here in such a panic?"

"Vincie had a breakdown. Her mother wrote her a poem that stank of death, and now she thinks her mother will be gone. If her mother dies, Vincie will lose her soul. I thought I might have to take her to the Doctor's Hospital in New York, and I might still, but I thought that one last try with you, a diversion and realization of what she imagines for her book tour in the form of a goal, might help to align her again. When she has focus and goals, she can cope. When things are in her control, she gains the strength she needs to persist. If you don't come, it will seem to her that she can control nothing — from her mother's health, to George Dillon, to the passage of years — which will lead her further into despair and drinking and, ultimately, destroy her."

I looked at this man, plain and honest before me. His love for his wife over-whelmed me. I felt a terrible surge of jealousy that a woman like her had a man like this who would quite literally do any-thing for her, even if it made him unhappy, or inconvenienced, or half-mad himself. Why wasn't he enough for her? Why all these extraneous people? But larger than my feeling of jealousy was my pity for him, and my wish to survive.

"I won't come to Steepletop to work," I said, "but I will do the work. I give you my word."

He began to cry. This large man began to cry in my kitchen, quiet, moving tears of gratitude. I stood and picked up from the counter a clean cloth, which I handed to him. After he wiped his face, he reached for my hand and pressed his warm lips to it.

"Thank you, sweet girl."

The pleasure of working with exquisite fabric filled my nights as a lover would.

I'd fantasize about the work all day, the feel of the silks, velvets, furs, the glint of shiny silver lines in crumpled silver fabric, the sheen of moon blue spread over my lap like light on a snowy field, the precise stitches and birth of plans from sketches on paper. Eugen had advanced me more money, so I again had electricity. We ate well. The release of pressure gave way to lightness. In a strange way, it was one of the happiest times of my life. Why was it always in the times of selfish secrecy that I gained the most calm and pleasure?

A small bit of hurt and longing remained inside when I'd watch Gabriel walk to the forest at night and glance back over his shoulder at my house. Sometimes he'd see me in the window and nod. Sometimes he wouldn't look up at me, though I thought he might want to.

The first of the wardrobe was complete in a week, and Eugen arrived mere hours after I'd sent the summons. He parked far away, snuck to the back door, embraced me, and poured out his exuberant gratitude, a wash of words so heartfelt, it brought a smile to my face. I promised I'd start on the cape as soon as I received word from Millay that it met her standards, and that word came in a touching note on Steepletop letterhead and written in her hand, praising my creation as an act of perfect art, a conjuring of emotion through fabric that would amplify her meaning to her audience and even to herself. Like an eager pupil, I began the next garment in earnest, thrilled by the new project, the regular pay, the praise of my talent, which fed my daydreams until I could barely concentrate on anything else.

I'd been making such fast progress that one night I decided to take off and visit the wood nymphs with Grace. She was excited to go to the pond at night, and even more excited when I told her about the musicians, the dog, and the other children. I had her bundled and ready, and when Gabriel passed behind our house that night, I stepped out with my little one to join him.

"Rock man," said Grace.

His face lit with a smile.

We started off over the field together, pulling Grace behind us on her sled. Gabriel took the rope from me, which I appreciated in the deep snow. I looked up at the quarter moon and inhaled, enjoying the open feeling in my chest, and then at the path before me, where Gabriel and Grace had pulled ahead, silhouetted against the forest.

When we arrived at the fire, a hearty cheer welcomed us. Two girls about seven or eight years old ran to Grace and reached for her hands. Grace looked at me with a question in her eyes, and I could barely see her through the tears in my own. I gave her a smile and a nod, and she brightened and allowed them to lead her to the edge of the circle, where Blue lay with three puppies nursing from her.

"She had babies," I said, as we walked up to the dogs.

Sam beamed. "Man at the lumberyard had a husky, and we let them have a night of it a while back. It proved fruitful."

As silly as it was, I felt embarrassed for him to say such a thing while I stood so close to Gabriel.

Grace and the girls kneeled by the dogs, whispering and remarking on their sweetness. When the puppies finished eating, two of them tumbled about while one stayed snuggled against her mother, half-drunk on milk and warmth. The girls giggled and shrieked when the puppies nibbled their fingertips, and Sam showed them how to clamp the puppies' mouths to teach them not to bite.

"This one has a red eye and a blue eye!" said one of the girls.

"It's actually brown, but it sure looks that way in the firelight."

Gabriel moved away from me, and when I stole a look at him, I could see him talking to Liza. She wore a smart dress in forest green with a white collar, and a matching jacket and hat. I wondered if the flush of her skin came from the fire, the alcohol, or Gabriel's company.

Randall, the Wall Street violinist, brought a steaming cup of cider to me.

"Thank you," I said.

"Would you like a shot?" He held up a flask with a large RGL engraved on it.

"No, thank you."

Randall looked from me to Gabriel and Liza, and back.

"You'd better tell your friend to watch out," he said. "Gabe, that is."

"Why?"

"Liza has a theater house full of broken-hearted suitors."

"Do you speak from experience?"

"Indeed I do."

The firelight reflected off his glasses. He

stood a full head taller than me, but he was so thin and tidy, he looked as if a strong wind would knock him over. He gave me a weak smile.

"I barely know Gabe," I said. "He'll have to figure that out on his own. As for you, I'm sorry for your hurt heart."

"It's all right. I knew what I was getting into," he said. "It's just that your friend seems sensitive. I don't think he'd take it with a grain of salt."

"I see what you mean," I said, though I had a feeling Gabriel was a sharp judge of character. His comments about the towns-women had shown me that.

I turned my attention back to Randall. "If you'll excuse me for saying it, you don't seem like a shrewd Wall Street type. I mean that as a compliment."

"I'll take it that way," he said. "I can relax here. I'm a bulldog at work."

Sam whistled through his fingers and motioned for the musicians to pick up their instruments. Randall tipped his hat and moved to join the others. Liza winked at Gabe. I felt a small thrill of satisfaction to see that his face remained dark. He turned his gaze back to me, and I looked away.

By now, the puppies were sufficiently exhausted, but the children still ran in circles. Grace seemed to have opened like a butterfly. The realization that it was the first time she had ever really played with other children unleashed a storm of emotion in me: gratitude that they'd been so kind to her, sadness that this had never before happened, pain like a snapped thread between the two of us as she took her first steps away from me.

"You are impossible to read," said Gabriel. He had come to stand beside me without my noticing, and I was startled to hear his voice so close to my ear.

"I'm sorry. I shouldn't brood while I'm here."

"Don't apologize," he said. "It's fascinating. But it makes me see how limited I am in my artistic medium."

"How so?"

"Well, if I were to sculpt you, for example, I'd have no way to fairly represent you. Would your brow be furrowed or relaxed? Your eyes squinted in concentration or wide with wonder? And your mouth — pursed or open, with a small smile around the edges? There is no stillness in your features. Like the stream."

"With language like that, you could be a poet," I said.

Gabriel smiled.

Liza turned her eyes on us across the fire. Her gaze was not kind. Gabriel stared into the dark forest, but directed his words to me. "She's angry."

"Who, Liza?" I asked.

"Yes," he said. "She can't understand why I'm not romantically interested in her."

"I can't either," I said. "She's beautiful, talented —"

"She's not you."

In spite of the noise around us, we might have been alone in the woods. I dared to look at him, and he at me. My heart pounded as if I'd been running over hills, and the short moment of warmth I'd felt at hearing his words cooled and shriveled like a blackened vine when I reminded myself that he was just another man.

"There you are again," he said. "Unreadable."

"How could others be expected to read what I can't understand?"

I looked away from him and toward Grace making snow angels on the ground. For her protection, I could not allow myself to start a relationship, at least not at this time in our lives when she was beginning to understand people. It would be bad for her to get to know Gabriel as someone connected to me, only to have him wrenched away when the inevitable split occurred. But my young self would have hated me for such negativity. My young self would have taken her cup and clinked it against his, and leaned into his arm, and enjoyed herself.

Damn the man who had done this to me. Damn myself for allowing it to be done.

I placed my empty cup on a nearby stump, and then went to Grace to take her home.

"No," she said, staring up at me from the snow.

"Don't tell me no," I said. "Up. Now."

She curled herself into a ball on her side and refused to look at me, even whispering no under her breath. I crouched down to pick her up and she thrashed back and forth, wiggling out of my grasp and running to hide behind a tree. I lunged to grab her, and she darted behind another tree. My anger and embarrassment grew, and I hated that I would have to drag her away.

After several more slips and dodges, Gabriel finally came over, scooped up Grace, and swung her under his arm. "Don't give your mother trouble, little imp," he said. She giggled in his grasp and allowed him to hang her upside down while he carried her to the sled. He passed her a caramel from his pocket, and tucked the blanket around her legs. I gave the group a halfhearted wave as we started back to my house, mortified that Gabriel had had to help me control my own daughter.

"Thank you," I said, as we emerged from the forest. "I'm embarrassed that she behaved so poorly."

"What, like other toddlers when they have to leave a place of fun?"

I shoved my hands deep in my pockets, and tried to concentrate on the shafts of moonlight slipping through the trees. I hated that I couldn't find a single word to say to him. I was sabotaging something real, and possibly good. Every time I thought of something to say, it sounded silly in my head. I didn't want to lead him on, nor did I want to apologize for my response. Gabriel couldn't understand what these years had been like, alone, ostracized, tainted by scandal.

To him, I was a regular woman, without stain. He knew that I had a child alone, but I could have been a widow, for all he knew. I hated to let another person in on my secret. If I allowed him to get close to me, I'd have to do that. The thought made me weary.

We reached the field, and the unspoken words seemed to sizzle in the air between us. A train issued its mournful whistle in the distance, and as I looked at the lay of the town before us, I noticed how charming it appeared in the glowing, snowy moonlight. Candles and lights dotted upstairs rooms. The pleasant scent of wood-burning fireplaces drifted on wind gusts.

"I love this town," I finally said. "I think of my parents here. I have my sister and my shop. My daughter. It's familiar, like an old robe. But it's hard to live here, Gabriel. It's hard. I don't know how else to put it."

"Whatever your situation," he said, "it doesn't matter to me. I mean, it matters, but it doesn't bother me."

"How can you say that when you don't know anything about me?"

"I know all I need to know. You're a hard worker, a deep thinker, a good mother. What else could matter, really?"

"I'm touched by what you say, but it is all very complicated."

"Of course it is. What isn't?"

The walk that I hadn't wanted to begin now ended. How I wished we had miles more to go. But perhaps this was for the best. I shooed Grace indoors and propped her sled against the cellar doors. Then I turned to Gabriel.

"I'm sorry I can't give more right now," I said.

I turned and started up the stairs to the kitchen door when he reached for me, his hand on my arm.

"Just so you know," he said, "there's no charity in what I said. It's purely selfish."

He pulled his hand away, put it in his pocket, and left. I went into the house and bolted the door behind me. Grace had fallen asleep halfway up the stairs. I carried her to her room, pulled off her snow clothes, and put on her pajamas while she continued to sleep. I placed her in the bed and her smudged glasses on the night table.

I went to my room, thinking of Gabriel's words. He'd understood that I hated charity, and he had appealed to my sense of self by talking in terms of his own gratification. His honesty and directness stirred me, and I knew I was attracted to him. I also knew that he was just a passerby, a rover. He'd be gone once the statue was finished. I didn't know a thing about his past, and I knew I wasn't as open-minded as he seemed to be.

I didn't bother with sleep. Instead, I worked all night by the window in my room, where I could glance between the dark rectory and the unfinished statue. By early morning, I began to pity my own loneliness. I felt sorry for Grace. I hated that I was a prisoner of my past. As I worked, I felt almost feverish. My fingers manipulated the fabric in ways that extended beyond what I could have ever imagined in my sketches. My tears fell on the cape of midnight blue, and once, without showing any discoloration, the fabric absorbed a bead of blood from where I'd pricked my finger with the needle. This robe would reflect the goddess who walked at night, with the moon and the darkness her only friends. It would recall the nights she spent with her lover and wished for winter because those nights were the longest.

VINCENT

I open the curtain when I see the horses draw up to the house, delivering Laura to me. She has surprised us with a telegram asking Eugen to bring her to Steepletop for the fitting. Eugen climbs down and walks through clouds of horse breath to Laura's side. He lifts the dress box from her hands while she carries Grace bundled in a plaid blanket to the front door, where I hurry to let them in. The moonlight reflects off Grace's glasses, winking at us. I feel a satisfaction I haven't felt in many nights — of firm footing that makes me stand erect, relaxes my features, allows me to take deep, full breaths.

It is a perfect night. We drink wine; I play the piano well while we sing; we eat chocolates and cinnamon toast. I remove the cape from the box with great flare, and stand in front of Laura while she wraps it around my narrow shoulders and comes kissing close to me to fasten it at my neck. I feel myself bloom. I approach the mirror, and I am in awe of myself and the cloak. I run my hands over the material, lift it to my face, and close my eyes.

"You are all over this cape, Laura. Your scent — like apples and a glowing hearth. A scent of home."

There's more of me on you than just the scent of my home. I can almost hear her voice, but when I look at her lips, I realize she hasn't said anything aloud, and yet I understand her thoughts. *My blood. My tears. My past, folded and put to rest on the yards of fabric wrapped around you.*

I wonder if I have hallucinated her response.

Later that night, I drive the sleigh to take her home. She holds Grace on her lap, and Eugen sits on the rear-facing bench, dangling his legs behind us and whistling. The clear sky of stars enchants us. We marvel at the icicles reflecting the moonlight, the owl sounds, and a shooting star. I think I hear fairy music on the breeze, but when I say so, Laura smiles in a secret way, and the sound vanishes.

On the approach to the road behind her street, just as we round the bend, the unfinished statue of the Blessed Virgin glows in the moonlight. I reach back and touch Eugen's shoulder.

"Look, Uge," I say.

He turns around in his seat and looks between us where my finger points at the Virgin. He whistles long and low.

"That is something," he says.

"Your favorite saint," I say.

Laura laughs. "*You* have a favorite saint?"

He gives her a playful nudge. "Yes, Miss High and Mighty, I do. Us heathens are capable of the occasional chaste prayer, you know."

"She reminds me of *The Miracle*," I say. "You know, the play we saw when I was on my last reading tour in Texas?"

"Ah, yes! That wonderful, awful play," he says. "In it, a statue of the Virgin comes alive to take the place of a troublesome nun in a convent, while the nun experiments with life. But when the statue is gone, there are terrible droughts and such."

"How interesting," says Laura. "How does it turn out?"

"After the nun has slept her way through numerous men —" continues Eugen.

"We don't know she sleeps with them," I say. "It is implied."

"Yes, but clearly, she sleeps with them. Anyway, when all is said and done, the nun returns to the place from which she came, satisfied that it is actually where she belongs, and the statue resumes her place over the town."

"Restoring nature's order," I say.

We ride the rest of the way in silence. When we stop, Eugen jumps down from the back of the sleigh and lifts Grace to help Laura down. She thanks him, and bids me good night.

We turn for home, and again look at the statue of the Virgin. From this angle and the progress of the moon, she is cloaked in shadows, and I can no longer make out her form.

TWENTY-EIGHT

LAURA

Grace and I set out for the market the next morning to pay off our account with the money I received from Millay, and to visit Dr. Hagerty to fix Grace's glasses. I was surprised and somewhat relieved to see that Caroline was not in the window. Her incessant watching unnerved me. Dr. Hagerty welcomed us, but I could see that he was agitated in the way he kept looking over his shoulder. I thought I heard crying from the back room, but when I turned my head, it stopped.

"Broken," said Grace, shoving her glasses at Dr. Hagerty.

"And how did you do this?"

"Hammer."

I looked at her and she returned my gaze without a shred of guilt.

"Did you hit these with the mallet?" I asked.

"By accident."

I knew it couldn't have been an accident, and I intended to scold her once we were out of Dr. Hagerty's shop. As it turned out, we'd have to come back in a few days. He would need time to fix the lens and adjust the frames.

"Will you be careful not to bump into anything while these are fixed?" he asked Grace.

She nodded and was already pulling me out the door. I was grateful, because I was now certain I heard weeping from the back room, and Dr. Hagerty looked pained.

On the way home, we passed Gabriel. He seemed to concentrate harder than ever before, but in spite of my shushing, Grace claimed his attention. He stopped chiseling and smiled when he saw her. I looked up at the statue of Our Lady of Grace. Most of it had come together, but the face was still indistinct.

"When will she get her features?" I asked.

"She hasn't shown me how she'll wear them yet. I'm patient though."

He stared at me until I had to look away, and I continued past him.

These feelings were agonizing. His attention lifted me like a wave. Then I'd remind myself that I had to ignore it, and the crash would come. I decided that I'd take the backstreets like I used to. I could avoid him and, thus, save myself from disappointment.

I thought of the statue and his process, and of the work I had left to do for Millay, yards of fabric to cut, shape, and sew. I'd left her scarlet cloak for last. I knew this cape would symbolize the pain of love lost, love scorned, regret, sin — like a scarlet letter on her breast, born from my own heart — to close this chapter in my life that had been left open for so long. I was finally ready to sew it. It was the right time to fully own the pain of the past and let it go.

Something about watching Gabriel in the act of producing art in public stirred me, and I wondered if the cloak would be more authentically beautiful if I made it at Steepletop, with my subject an arm's length away. It seemed to me that it would bring about a perfect communion in our working relationship by uniting subject to artist, sitter to sewer. I'd send for Eugen as soon as he was available, and Grace and I would spend a day at Steepletop completing Millay's reading wardrobe.

When we returned to our shop, Sam was there with his wife, Callie, and his dog, Blue. He invited me to dine with them and a few others that evening at their house over the bridge. Father Ash was standing in the door of the rectory, clutching his journal. He watched us for a moment, and then disappeared. I turned my attention back to Sam and Callie. I dared not ask if Gabriel was invited, but I assumed he would be there.

"Come on," said Sam with a smile. "You'll see the girls, and the puppies."

"We go?" said Grace.

I looked down at her eager face. It would be good for her to play with her new friends. It would be good for me on some level too, and I agreed. They gave me their address.

"How long have you lived there?" I asked.

"Just a few months," said Sam. "You know I work at the lumberyard, and Callie takes care of the girls, and wants to start giving music lessons. We hope to meet more people once the weather improves."

I didn't reply that they would have a hard time making friends here, being from far away and looking the way they did in their eccentric clothing and with their long hair.

"What can I bring?" I asked.

"Whatever you have around the house," said Callie. "Don't go to any trouble. I have a roast I picked up for a steal."

"Then I'll make something of these potatoes," I said, holding up the bag I'd just purchased.

"Swell. Come around four, before it gets dark. Sam'll walk you home after dinner."

After I tucked in Grace for her nap, I spent the rest of the afternoon worrying over Gabriel and cooking potato pancakes. I couldn't get out of my head the old Irish rhyme *"Boxty on the griddle, boxty on the pan; if you can't make boxty, you'll never get a man,"* and I thought I'd go mad.

I hunted down a pile of table napkins in jeweled colors I'd sewn. They would make a nice housewarming gift. I tied the napkins with a ribbon, and then woke Grace at four o'clock. I placed her in the pram with a towel in her lap, and set the dish in her hands. It would be a miracle if we made it to dinner without her letting the potatoes tumble to the ground, but I'd wrapped it tight with another towel and hoped for the best.

I took the side streets in case Gabriel was still working, and on our way, we passed Lily Miller's house. Her backyard lay in shadows, but I looked twice when I saw the orange glow of a cigarette on the back porch. I was surprised to see her smoking in public, but as a widow, Lily had a degree of freedom that younger women didn't. Also, she was out of plain sight.

"Good evening," she said.

"Hello, Lily."

"We see puppies," said Grace.

"Oh, where?" said Lily.

"We met the new family that moved in over the bridge," I said. "Their dog had puppies, so Grace can play with them while we dine."

"How nice," she said. "It's good for you girls to have friends."

I waved and continued on, warmed by our interaction, and happy at the thought of dining with neighbors. I was determined to make a pleasant night of it, even if Gabriel came. I resolved to treat him with polite distance. I would not allow him to upset me.

Disappointment and relief claimed me when I did not see Gabriel.

Tim had joined Sam's family, as had Callie's sister, Lydia, who was staying with them for the week. Sam and Callie's daughters fussed over Grace, and took her to the shed outside to see the puppies. Tim poured me a glass of his homemade wine, which I gladly accepted, and I joined Lydia in setting the table. Callie loved the napkins.

"There are eight of us, but nine plates. Is anyone else joining us?" I asked, trying not to sound too curious.

"Gabriel said he might if he meets his sculpting goals today," said Callie. "I told him not to worry about it one way or another. I made the same amount of food whether he's here or not."

My stomach began to twist in knots, and I drained my glass of wine. Tim noticed and poured me another, with a wink. Sam carried the carved roast to the table and I placed the potatoes at the other end with boiled carrots. Lydia filled the water glasses, while Callie carried out a bowl of steaming gravy. A cheerful fire burned in the dining room grate, and the napkins brought out the colored landscapes hanging on the walls. I walked close to one and touched the frame, entranced by a painting of mountains at sunset. The sun's fiery glow transformed the trees and river, and the brushstrokes brought motion to the canvas.

"Callie painted it," said Sam, his admiration evident.

"A musician and an artist," I said.

"It's just a hobby," said Callie.

"Not quite," said Sam. "She's brilliant."

My old companion jealousy stung my belly. I admired their love for each other and wished I could experience it. I tried to imagine what it would have been like if my lover had forsaken his old life and come to live with Grace and me, but I simply couldn't hold on to the thought. It dissolved as quickly as it had formed. I took a generous swallow of the wine and set my glass on the table. I noticed that the candles were not lit.

"Where might I find matches?" I asked, suddenly feeling very cold and empty, and in need of setting my eyes on my daughter.

"I left them on the porch with my pipe," said Sam.

"I'll get them," I said.

I passed through the front room, and opened the screen door. It felt good to be out in the cool evening air. Grace and the girls were by the shed, and I smiled when I saw how happy she looked. I glanced around the porch, and spotted the matches on a crude wooden table. As I went to retrieve them, a small statue of a goddess with a lyre caught my eye. I picked it up and ran my hands over it, recognizing the cool white-blue of the marble.

"She's Terpsikhore," said Gabriel.

I turned and found him on the steps, his eyes shadowed by the brim of his hat. He walked over and cornered me on the porch. I no longer felt the night's cool.

"The muse of music, dancing," he said. "I

carved it for Sam and Callie from a shard that fell from the Virgin."

He stepped forward and closed his hands around mine on the statue. I could barely breathe. I looked up at him and could smell the faint scent of alcohol on his breath, mingled with a hint of incense. I imagined that he carried it on his clothes from living at the rectory. I pulled my hands from his just as Grace hopped up the stairs.

"See puppies," she said.

Gabriel stared hard at me before letting Grace take his hand and lead him to the shed. He crouched down and petted the huskies, which had grown at an astounding rate. I put down the statue and lifted the matches. When I turned to look back at them, Gabriel came toward me. I hurried into the house and to the table to light the candles. Sam and Callie greeted Gabriel and announced that dinner was ready. The shuffling and seating of guests left me on a corner between Gabriel and Grace. I instructed Tim to top off my glass of wine, and he was happy to oblige.

"You're enjoying the wine tonight, Laura," he said.

"It's going down smoothly."

"You're flushed," said Callie. "It's very becoming."

Gabriel watched me, but didn't comment. I thought I saw a smile lift the corner of his mouth, but I couldn't be sure.

"Your statue is a real looker," said Sam. "She's almost finished."

"I'm just waiting for her to show me her face. She's elusive."

"A frustrating part of the process, no doubt," said Callie.

"You have no idea," said Gabriel.

I took a long drink.

"What will you do once it's finished?" asked Tim. "Do you plan to stay around here?"

I put down my glass and reached to cut Grace's dinner, straining my ears to hear his reply.

Gabriel cleared his throat. "I thought about applying for the maintenance supervisor position at the hospital, but now I don't think I'll stay on after all. I don't think there's anything for me here. My brother in New York City knows of a hotel that wants someone to carve sculptures for the facade. I can also work with him at his tavern for extra money."

"Is it a speakeasy?" asked Tim.

"No, it's an honest place. It used to be a bar, and hopefully it will be again in the future. I guess I'll have to come back around here from time to time for the goods."

"You won't have any trouble finding places in the city," said Lydia. "I live in the Village. There's no shortage of watering holes. You'd be welcome."

I noticed Callie nudge her with her elbow and give her a frown. I wondered if that was for my benefit. I didn't know how to tell her that Lydia should feel free to flirt.

I couldn't get out of my own way for the rest of dinner. As much as it pained me, I felt myself shutting down. I accepted praise for my potato pancakes and smiled at the girls as they babied Grace, but the large, brooding man at my right arm disturbed me more than I could bear. Every time we brushed against each other in the close quarters, I felt as if my skin had been seared. Clearly, the turbulent energy we emitted made others uncomfortable, and relief came when people began to stand and clear the table.

I insisted on washing the dishes so Callie could rest in the sitting room and talk with her guests. The girls braided Grace's hair and showed her how to braid Dolly's hair. Lydia sat at the old upright piano, and began playing jazzy songs I'd never heard. I had only a few moments of peace before Gabriel was at my side with a dish towel and a scowl. We worked in silence, each of us in a kind of competition to convey our aloofness. The steady flow of adults and children in and out of the room thwarted the few chances we had at conversation. When we finished, I gave a perfunctory, "Thank you."

He didn't reply, but walked out into the room where the merry crew continued to sing and laugh. I saw Grace curled up in the corner of the couch, yawning, and I knew I should go, but I hated to ask Sam to leave his own party to walk me home. I could also see that he was a little drunk. Tim lived in the opposite direction. Yet again, Gabriel was the obvious choice, but I didn't want him to think I needed him. We'd go on our own.

I lifted Grace from the couch, and she wrapped her arms around me without protest. Her body was so relaxed, I knew she'd sleep as soon as we started walking.

"Thank you for playing so nicely with Grace," I said to Sam and Callie's daughters.

They smiled, and the older one spoke. "We love her."

Her simple words touched me. Today had been a gift in so many ways.

I thanked Callie for her hospitality.

"Do you have to go already?" she said.

"We do. Grace is exhausted. I am too. But thank you for the invitation. You have no idea how good this was for us. I'm afraid we aren't popular dinner guests around here."

"Nonsense," she said. "I hope you'll join us often. I'll have Sam walk you."

"No, please," I said. "It's not much more than a mile. We're used to walking."

"But not alone at night?" she said.

"I walk alone at night a great deal," I said. "Do you remember how I found all of you?"

Callie smiled and embraced me. "All right. Just watch for cars."

I waved to the group, avoiding Gabriel's eyes, and bundled up Grace and myself. I placed her in the pram and started on the long, dark road back to town.

I'd overstated my bravery. I'd never traveled this road alone at night. It led to the main highway to Pittsfield, and I worried about motorists failing to see us and running us down. Punctuating my unease was the long, high cry of a wild animal. I picked up my pace, and was glad to see Grace asleep so she wouldn't be frightened.

When I reached the end of the long driveway, I heard the door slam to the house and looked over my shoulder to see Gabriel's large silhouette. His hat was pulled

410

low and his shoulders hunched high, brac-
ing against the cold. Puffs of breath came
from his mouth and encircled his head. He
reminded me of a bull.

As nervous as I'd been, I was angry now.
He was relentless. And why? If he planned
on leaving, why bother to start a relationship? His cruelty appalled me, but I reflected
that he'd once told me he was selfish. Now
I could see it was so.

In spite of my quickened pace, Gabriel
caught up to me. He looked down and saw
that Grace was asleep.

"Lord, woman, what is wrong with you?"
he hissed.

"Me?" I whispered back. "You won't get
the message."

"What message, that you're a fool who'd
deny herself happiness because she's so
damned stubborn?"

"How dare you — thinking you know me?
You don't know a thing about me. And you
don't care about me. All you care about is
scratching some itch before you're off to
New York City and your bohemian lifestyle."

He had the audacity to laugh.

I slapped his arm. "You're going to wake
her."

He covered his mouth and quieted down
for a moment, but then continued his rant.

"I can't believe your hypocrisy. You blame the town for judging you. What about your judgment of others? You think you have me figured out from watching me carve a statue."

"You're wrong. I can't figure you at all. I can't understand why you'd try to get involved with someone like me when you know you'll leave. What kind of man does that to a woman, especially one with a young child?"

"Is that what you think?" he said, raising his voice. "Did you ever stop and think your coldness has something to do with my leaving? Why would I try to stay?"

Grace stirred, but resettled when we fell quiet.

"You've spoken of betrayal like you're the only one who has ever known it," he continued. "I know betrayal."

We had reached a bend in the road and I shivered. I didn't know what to say to Gabriel, but I wanted to know what he meant. Whatever it was, I couldn't believe it compared to what I had experienced. Soon he continued.

"I was supposed to marry a girl after the war — a wealthy American girl studying art in Italy. I let myself believe that someone like her could love someone like me, and I was a fool. I found her in bed with my best friend. She'd told him she loved him too, and then left us both for a rich Italian doctor. So don't talk to me about betrayal."

All I could hear after his speech was his heavy breathing and the crunch of our steps on the road. I felt sick to my stomach for jumping to conclusions. There was so much about him I didn't know — so much about everyone. I'd allowed my own self-pity to blind me to the pain of others, and worse, I'd made assumptions and judged them. It was the very hypocrisy for which I blamed the town.

A sudden vision of Gabriel being intimate with a beautiful woman intensified my unease. I was sick at the thought of him with another and angry with myself for having allowed my desire of him to grow into something more. A sharp wind blew and I leaned down to cover Grace more snugly. When I stood up, I dared to look at him. He stared ahead, and I had an urge to touch his face. Instead, I squeezed the handles of the pram.

We crossed the bridge under ice-encased branches. So much of the stream in that place had frozen, and the world seemed suspended in time. I could scarcely remember what it looked like in the spring with the cherry blossoms drifting on its currents, the long tips of the willows grazing the surface of the water. But I knew that season would come. It lay dormant under nature's sleep, waiting for its resurgence.

The darkness gave me courage.

"I'm sorry, Gabriel."

He glanced at me, and then back at the road. I knew I'd have to explain, so I let the words spill out, as if I were in a confessional. I felt reckless, with nothing to lose since I'd already lost it all.

"Grace's father lives here, in town. Our relationship is a scandal that no one knows about. I can't involve you in it. And I can't risk the fragile place I've reclaimed in this community."

"Do you love him?"

I thought about Grace's father, how much I'd once loved him. I couldn't understand this longing that remained. It could be for him or for what was. The two seemed the same in my mind. No, it was a longing for companionship, not for him.

"No," I said.

We walked on and passed the Virgin's form shrouded in darkness. I had an urge to stop and touch her, but I hesitated only a moment before continuing. When we arrived at the shop, I unlocked the door. Gabriel lifted Grace and carried her inside for me while I pushed the pram around the side of the house and came in the back way. He met me in the kitchen, and I took her from his arms, and started up the stairs. I placed her in bed, took off her boots and coat, and pulled up her covers, then returned downstairs.

Gabriel stood in the front room, looking out the window with his hands in his pockets. I walked up beside him and stared out at the night, toward the statue. It was difficult to see in this light.

"I'm going away soon," he said. "I'll be back for visits to look in on Michael from time to time. He's lonely, and I hate to leave him. He helped me during the bad time in Italy. He taught me how to trust again."

"You're lucky."

"Not in all matters." He stepped toward the door and put his hand on the knob. "I hope I see you again."

A lump formed in my throat and I clenched my fists. I had let this tension come between us. It was my fault, and now we'd both suffer for it.

He closed the door on his way out, and walked back to the rectory. I wondered how many more nights he'd lay his head on the pillow across the street from me.

VINCENT

When we went to Europe in 'twenty-nine, the separation from George was excruciating.

My sweet boy with his soft Kentucky accent had transferred his mother love to me, so when the wrenching away began, it held more force than usual. The death of Elinor clung to that time like a parasite, with its relentless reminder that we'd all meet the same fate. We would all end.

I'd put such prophecy in the sonnets. Perhaps if I'd written them more happily, things would have turned out differently. But, no. Mortals cannot stop the passing of the seasons or the turning of the earth.

While Eugen directed porters and bags, I walked to the railing of the *Rotterdam,* thinking of my first trip to France when I was twenty-nine years old. A decade had passed, and I felt no more wise or worldly than I had in 1921. I felt used. Empty. I thought of the people whom I'd allowed into my body. Each one of them had left a scar or a bruise, but no laceration stung more than that of yours, George Dillon. I hoped that leaving you and sailing for Europe would help the wound heal to a benign scar I could still see, even admire, but one that would no longer plague me.

I was wrong.

In my room, I found a piece of stationery. At the last moment, I scribbled a little message to you, a simple farewell I had wired, but it was a mistake. The note tethered us. It kept me bound to you across an ocean and would not break.

April in Paris was a prolonged, inebriated fantasy, an endless parade of artists and ideas, lightness and darkness, a crush of heaven and hell. The phone rang endlessly. "Why aren't you here? Everyone's asking. Come to the *Oubliettes Rouges*!"

Eugen would button and brush me while I ran the tube of lipstick over my lips, staining them more like blood, trying to ignore the throbbing in my head from yesterday's champagne. That place was hell — a medieval dungeon turned bar on the Left Bank, decorated with devices of torture, human bones, a guillotine. How could these people make merry in such a place, surrounded by all this death? It was like stepping into the hollow, abused cavern of my heart. The chains and cuffs hung from its fleshy walls, stained in blood. I wrote this to you so you could know that though I wasn't with you, I carried you, always. How I wished for the cruelty of my youth. How I wished for the divine cynicism I once held.

In a haze of absinthe, I clutched Eugen's arm. "We must go. Get me out."

"Vincie, you're not having fun? Drink up!"

"No, I am haunted. I need the light."

In spite of his annoyance, Eugen threw back his glass and took me outside, where I could breathe.

"I'll never go there again," I said. "I could feel their suffering."

"It is your own," he said. "Reflected."

He escorted me to *la Closerie des Lilas*. We sat in the open air, staring at the shadowed linden trees, when suddenly I saw you. A young man walked by, his face like a cherub, and I knew you haunted me. But then you were gone. I began to shake uncontrollably, and felt like I was drowning. I knew then I'd never be free of you.

TWENTY-NINE

LAURA

Two nights passed, and while I waited for Eugen to take us to Steepletop to finish the scarlet robe, I grew restless to begin. I pushed Gabriel from my mind, and avoided looking at the rectory or the square. To fill the hours, I prepared, packed a few items, and spent time with my sister, making sure Grace and I saw enough of her so she wouldn't notice one day's absence.

Dr. Hagerty delivered Grace's repaired glasses, and she delighted in the new red frames. I paid him and invited him into the shop, but he declined and set out for home as quickly as he'd come.

The morning Eugen was scheduled to pick us up behind the cemetery at ten o'clock, I took Grace to Marie and Everette's house for breakfast, and to give Marie the new baptismal gown I'd sewn for her baby. I was proud of the small ivory creation embroidered with ivy in the same shade as the rest of the gown. Boy or girl, the frock would become an heirloom, and I'd add his or her initials, and all of their subsequent children's initials, to the band along the hem.

"Oh," said Marie in a whisper, laying the gown over her growing belly, "it's precious."

Everette ran his hand over the material. "Very nice."

I could see he didn't care about baby baptismal gowns, but that didn't bother me. In truth, I wanted him gone. His presence gave me the jitters since he'd told me to watch out for Millay. Knowing that I'd be in her home in mere hours made me even more nervous, and I spilled a small pitcher of cream on the table when we began to eat.

The pumpkin loaf and poached eggs smelled delicious but stuck in my throat. My anxiety rose with each passing movement of the clock on the mantel, and when I saw that it was nine forty-five, I began to panic that we'd never be able to leave without it seeming unusually hurried. I was also frustrated to see a new snow falling in tiny flakes that accumulated at a frightening rate. It was the snow, finally, that gave me a good excuse to go.

"I'd better get Grace home, where it's warm and cozy, before this snow really starts to pile up," I said, nearly knocking over my chair as I stood. Everette grabbed the headrest and righted it for me, while giving me a strange look. I slipped out from behind the table, and cleared the empty dishes in haste.

"Don't worry," said Marie. "I'll get that. Just take Grace home. I'll send Everette to check on you later this afternoon."

"Oh, that won't be necessary," I said, with perhaps too much emphasis because they both stared at me in surprise. "I only mean that I enjoy shoveling and our electric is working, so we'll be just fine. Really."

Sweat formed on my neck and I glanced at the clock in the town square. It was three minutes to ten.

I hurried about bundling Grace in her coat and gave Marie a kiss before I left. By the time I locked the front door, it was five minutes after ten. I ran to the kitchen and strained my eyes through the falling snow to see if Eugen was already there. He was, of course, so I opened the door and waved my red hat to show him that I had seen him and would be there soon.

"Grace, put Dolly and your blocks in this bag to take with us. We'll be gone all day."

While she worked at filling her small bag of amusements, I made sure I'd packed everything I needed to complete the cloak. I'd done all of the machine work, and wanted to hand-stitch the rest. I grabbed my sketchbook and Grace's sled, and pulled her over the field to where Eugen waited.

"Winter is best enjoyed in an open sleigh," said Eugen.

I had to agree with him. It thrilled me to dash up white forest paths, catching glimpses of the jagged trail of the frozen river through naked trees. I pointed out a streak of orange to Grace, a fox that dashed from the underbrush. A wink of red on the wings of a male cardinal. Two spotted brown deer.

The way winter revealed the rise and fall of the hills in the woods caught my interest. It was a pleasure to see the graceful texture of the forest floor, which was camouflaged during the leafy parts of the year, now revealed in the carpet of snow. A gust of wind sent a large branch nearby crashing to the ground, relieved of its snow burden and in preparation to become a shelter to some small woodland animal. The sharpness of the air invigorated me.

"How is she today?" I asked, now well

acquainted with the ever-changing tempest of emotions present in the small poet.

"Today is a day of light and cheer. Visitors usually bring that satisfaction to her. Every time you come, it is a gift. She was toasting your arrival with an early glass of wine just as I was leaving."

"It's my last gown for her tour. I felt compelled to work on it at Steepletop."

"I'm glad you listened to your compulsion," he said.

When we arrived, Eugen carried my bags and I carried Grace into the house, where friendly fires blazed in the hearths. Millay sat at the larger of the two sitting room pianos, playing an impressive rendition of Beethoven's *Appassionata* with the intensity of a concert performer. She did not look up when we entered. I noted a nearly empty wineglass and bottle on the table next to her. Millay's cheeks were flushed and her hair blazed as orange as the coat of the fox we'd seen in the forest.

Grace, seemingly at ease in this house, walked to the sofa and found a book of paper dolls. After a short while, she removed her coat and let it rest behind her on the seat. Eugen crouched at her feet and asked about the paper dolls while I strolled the perimeter of the room, running my hands along tables, the mantel, musical instruments, and lamps. I came face-to-face with the massive ebony bust of Sappho in the corner and stared into her black eyes. She was an intimidating representation of the ancient lyricist, and I thought that if I had stood before her months or even weeks ago, I would have turned away. Now I tried to know her, to look unflinchingly at her to decide why she was worthy of my attention. I imagined that she did the same with me.

When the piece ended, silence seeped into the room. I turned to Millay, expecting an open smile and a thrill that I had come. Instead, she trembled and appeared ill. The flush no longer looked like passion but fever. Other than her cheeks, her skin was as cold and pale as marble. I crossed the room and knelt before her.

"Are you well?"

She looked down at her hands, and then her eyes darted to Sappho and to Eugen.

"Vincie, are you all right?" said Eugen, coming to her and wrapping his arm around her shoulders. "Look, it's Laura. Your friend. Your seamstress." She looked at me and seemed to see me for the first time. Her eyes opened wider and a lazy smile touched her lips.

She was drunk.

I was frustrated that we'd made the trip for what I'd hoped would be a time of creativity, and I had this dull, blurred woman before me. So much for my lofty ideas of working with the subject of my art. I began to feel foolish for the way I'd built these two up, imagining this artistic salon. Spending time with the river people had put fantasies in my head of meeting others on such terms even outside their circle.

The cook entered the room with a tray of cookies and tea, and smiled at Grace. She placed the tray next to her, offering her sweet treats and asking about her toys, telling her about the sumptuous dinner of roasted pheasant they'd make just for her. Grace glowed under the attention.

Eugen left and returned with a glass of water and an apology in his eyes. Millay suddenly stood and walked past him up the stairs. After she disappeared from view, Eugen made a move to follow her. I put up my hand, took the glass, and went after her.

When I reached her boudoir, she was already reclined on the bed against a mound of pillows, waiting for me with eyes half closed and the strange smile still on her lips. I hesitated for a moment, and then went to her bedside. I held the glass to her mouth as if she were a child, and encouraged her to drink. Then I put it on the bureau and sat on the edge of the bed.

"I have drunk till I'm drunk," she said with slurred words. "My heart hurt, so I drank him away, but now you're here and I'm like this."

She giggled to herself, but a tear slid down her face. I felt pity for this creature before me. I reached up and wiped away the tear with the back of my hand.

"There," she said. "When my tears dry, I will be on your skin. You will carry me with you."

"I've lately carried you with me, anyway," I said. "Your generous commission has invigorated me. I am grateful."

"Good," she said. "But you have it backward. You are helping me."

I lifted the glass to her lips once more, and she drank. Then I removed the pillows behind her back, except for one, so she could lie down on the bed.

"I'll sleep for a while. Then I'll be better," she said. She closed her eyes and soon breathed deep breaths. Her hands were clasped together as if in prayer. Her copper hair fanned out around her head in silky waves. I reached out to touch it, leaning closer to study its exact shade. I thought of the red of the cloak, and was glad that it looked more like fire than blood. It would complement her coloring.

When I went downstairs, Eugen had arranged a sewing station in the corner of the room by the window with the most light. Grace still sat showing the cook her dolls. The fire glowed in the hearth, reflected in the marble poet's eyes.

I felt at home.

Two hours passed, and I'd made much progress. I knew the cloak would be used on Millay's spring tour, so I'd selected a light fabric for the lining. The velvet was thin but soft, and the trim and the collar were made of cool silk. It was a pleasure to touch, and I knew it would be so to wear.

Grace had played outside the window with the dogs for a while, and now sat drying by the fire with Dolly, telling her how she wished she had a dog, speaking loud enough for me to hear. Eugen was outside digging the Cadillac out of the ice and clearing the driveway, and he kept coming in to see if I was comfortable. If I needed anything. If I was hungry or thirsty. If I wanted to put Grace down for a nap in the office on the oversized chair. I assured him that we were comfortable, and each time, he beamed as bright as the sun. I'd never seen such a man.

Eugen clearly ran the household and farm. I witnessed him discuss the menu with the cook, instruct the groundskeeper on which bushes to bag, and oversee the laundry and the mending. I watched the farmhands converse with him multiple times through the window. He shoveled the front walk and the garden path. He called the pharmacy in Pittsfield, placed an order with the grocer, and made lists of hardware supplies to fetch on his next visit to Chatham, and all while Millay slept upstairs.

I tried to imagine what it would be like for a husband to devote so much of his energy to me while I created costumes. I pictured a man at the stove cooking dinner while I pored over fabric books and completed orders, a man taking Grace on a walk while I finished a dress and matching gloves, a man to read to me by the fire at night while I sewed cotillion dresses. For the first time, I could not see a face on this imaginary man.

But the temporary lift in my spirits from such fantasies came crashing down. No such man existed, or if he did, he was here at Steepletop, not only supporting his wife but also encouraging behavior that would no doubt lead to their ruin. He indulged her drinking, antisocial behavior, erratic moods, and whims for stimulation outside of her marriage.

Eugen was an optimist, and life was his grand experiment. I could see from his tortured wife, however, that such indulgences would not support their relationship, but erode it. How could I show that to them without sounding like a haughty church lady? These observations were not moral; they were true. A heart divided could never fully unite to another's. Split affections couldn't fully ripen before being ripped from their trees.

At least, I didn't think they could.

My thoughts were interrupted when Grace stood from the hearth and brought her coat to me. I fastened the buttons up to her dimpled chin, and helped her with her hat and mittens.

"Dry already?" I asked, squeezing the coat. I removed her glasses and wiped them on my dress before setting them back on her nose.

"Yes," she said.

"Play where I can see you."

She ran outside with the dog at her heels and, in a few moments, waved to me from the side yard. The snow that had begun that morning had already left three inches of fresh powder, and continued to fall. I glanced at the clock and thought that I should ask Eugen for an early supper so we could get back before the roads became impassable, even by horse-drawn sleigh.

"You are lost in thought," said Eugen.

I turned my attention to him at his desk, where he was writing in a ledger.

"My mind wanders when I sew," I said.

"You have a poet's heart," he said. "You looked like Vincent for a moment. Racing through a world in your mind. Tell me, what did you find there in the dark forest of your thoughts?"

"I'm afraid you don't want to know."

"Ah, but that entices me more. Did you fantasize about a lover, the man who helped make your girl, but who is not here with you?"

"You are direct," I said. "Plain speech must be so freeing. I have too much of my own constraint to allow it, I'm afraid, so I will keep my thoughts to myself."

"There is none of that here," he said. "We are open, as you know. Speak your mind."

A gust of wind sent a swirl of snowflakes against the window, obscuring Grace's form for a moment, and then drawing back like a veil, showing my girl running in circles with the dog.

"Yes, speak your mind," said Millay. She

leaned on the doorframe in a severe black dress with a high collar. She'd put on pearl earrings and a necklace, and would have looked entirely formal if it wasn't for her hair, which she wore loose on her shoulders. Her eyes looked tired, but sober.

"My sweet," said Eugen, rising to escort her into the room. He led her to the sofa near my chair and kissed her on the neck before returning to his seat.

"Every sentence you utter is like the tip of an iceberg," said Millay.

"I think not uttering them fully has allowed me to carry on as well as I have."

"I cannot bury my self," she said. "Or rather, I won't. I must give it voice. Otherwise it will eat me alive. This worm inside is a parasite."

Grace shrieked with delight, and we all stared out the window.

"All of you Kelley girls have that same fair beauty," said Millay. "I would love you less if your eyes weren't so blue, but blue's my favorite color."

"My mother was fair," I said. "Both she and my father had light eyes, but we get our hair and skin from her side of the family."

"Are your parents living?" asked Millay.

"No," I said. "My father fell from the falls before Grace was born, and died from his injuries. My mother died in the influenza epidemic of 1918."

"I'm sorry," she said. "Those years claimed so many. How old were you when your mother died?"

"Ten."

"What happened to the shop when she died? It was a family place, yes? You and your sister must have been too young to sew."

"I was actually quite adept at that age, but you're right. We couldn't have taken over a shop. My father did. He was trained at the Chatham Shirt Factory, which closed in 'twenty-two, and was able to keep the business going until Marie and I had completed home economics in high school."

"Do you remember your mother?"

"Not really," I said. "I remember emotions connected to her or small moments with her. She instructed me to stand up straighter. Try harder. I remember her temper — quick, harsh words. But I also recall careful instruction in sewing. Teaching me how to pair colors and fabrics. Her hands around mine, showing them how to work the material."

"That is a beautiful series of memories," said Millay. "Like a poem."

"I feel her quick temper inside myself," I

said. "Grace has it too."

Grace walked in at that moment with rosy cheeks and wet clothes. I sent her back to the foyer, where I removed her boots and snowsuit, and carried her into the room to sit on my lap by the fire.

"I couldn't have gotten along in the world without my mother," said Millay. "I still couldn't. She is divine perfection, a loving angel watching over me. Of course she's trouble, but of the best kind. My father, however, was lost to us when my mother divorced him."

"That must have been quite a scandal."

"Indeed," said Millay. "But he and my mother were like weather fronts, and he had a capacity for cruelty. And for gambling. It was for the best."

"Your mother raised you and your sisters alone?" I asked, privately weighing how Millay had turned out against my own child. Would Grace always live on the fringe, without regard for societal rules? I did not want that for her. I didn't want her to be forever fighting the tide of public opinion. If she did, she might end up on a mountain, half-mad, overindulged, and out of touch. Was there a way to live freely without being wild, to live a balanced and satisfied life? To have good fortune in love, parenthood, and work?

I didn't think so.

"Yes," Millay said. "We lived on our own, in harmony with one another. Mother supported us, and we made do."

"Now you support all of them," said Eugen. "Good, good Vincie. Mother to her mother; mother to her sisters; but no one's mother."

"Mother to my poetry," she said. "It's a selfish thing, the need, the longing of the words to find homes on paper. The writing is like a hungry child, demanding more and more, never satisfied, keeping no regular hours, depleting me while making me love it, guard it, swat the outside world away. I am forever pregnant with words."

I thought her comparing poetry to children was dramatic, but I could see that she believed every word she spoke.

"You remind me of my mother," she said. "You are the harp weaver."

I was moved, and rested my chin on Grace's shoulder, pulling her closer into me.

"Vincie won the Pulitzer for that collection," said Eugen. "You must read it."

"I know," I said. "I have."

I thought of Millay with a growing awe, and some jealousy. Whether she was a witch or not, her words meant a lot to many people, including me. I felt pride at the thought of creating for this woman child. A woman who needed a well of experience from which to draw her words.

And a husband willing to allow it.

When dinner ended, I walked to the front door and opened it with a feeling of dread. The great drifts and banks still growing from the persistent snowfall confirmed my fears. We should have left hours ago.

Millay walked up behind me. "You aren't going home tonight."

It was not a question, and I had to agree with her. Knowing we'd have to stay brought a strange and sudden peace to me. The inevitable confrontation with Marie was coming. I'd known it for a long time. I would have to face it. *This* would be the catalyst for *next*.

I wrapped Grace snugly in blankets and lay with her until she slept on the reading chair in Millay's library. The **SILENCE** sign hung above her. Dolly looked out from Grace's embrace. When I got downstairs, Eugen had just kissed Millay.

"This old man is tired," he said. "I'll leave you two to each other."

"Good night," I said.

435

Millay sat by the fire, the pattern of orange light and black shadow on her, reminding me of a tiger. I wasn't scared of her, though, as I had been. I was no longer her prey.

Eugen proceeded up the stairs. I waited until I heard him close the door to his rooms, and joined Millay by the hearth. She'd poured a glass of wine for each of us, and left the bottle uncorked. I sat in the chair next to her and stared into the flames.

"I'm glad you decided to stay," she said.

"It would have been madness to try to leave in this storm. And secretly, something inside me must have wished for exile, even if it's only temporary."

"It's a hard place to live," she said.

"I'm tired of being watched in town," I said. "It's better here, on the mountain, away from their eyes."

The wood popped in a violent manner, sending sparks up the flue.

"Their eyes never leave," said the poet. "Their eyes are your eyes, your conscience reflected back at you. They never leave, but down there you can blame them. You can live with it. Up here you can blame only yourself. You cannot escape yourself."

I turned my eyes to our shadow forms on the wall, and noted that they overlapped. I could not make out one of us from the other. When I looked at her, her face became alive and active in the changing light. The set of her forehead gave her the appearance of vulnerability. It was a new look on her, and one that unsettled me.

"Tell me a secret," she said suddenly. "Tell me about the time that the little Grace seed was planted. Tell me of when your passions ran unchecked, when you may have even embraced them."

"Isn't it best to let sleeping beasts lie?"

"No," she said in a whisper. "Never."

With the snowdrifts piled against the house, amplifying the quiet, it felt as silent as an empty church. It felt safe.

"It's a long story," I said.

"We have all night."

I drank from the wineglass until my shoulders tingled and warmth rose from within. "It began on the night of my nineteenth birthday," I said, staring at our blended shadows. "It began with a car accident."

THIRTY

May 1927
Our heads crowded together to read the headline in *The New York Times.*

Lindbergh Does It!
To Paris in 33 1/2 Hours!

Father Ash stood in the doorway of the drugstore and soda fountain and whistled through his teeth, which sent Marie and me into a fit of laughter. We were high on ice-cream floats and the knowledge that in just three hours we'd be heading to Pittsfield for a dance on my nineteenth birthday. Our father had given his reluctant approval for the Winslow brothers, two town boys near our ages, to motor us to the dance and then straight home when it was over. We knew that we were old enough to make our own plans, but we indulged our father to make him feel that he still had control. And though neither of us was interested in the Winslow brothers, they had a car, so we played along to get to the dance.

"Do you think we'll ever be able to fly to another state for a dance?" I asked. "Like Lindbergh?"

"I don't care much about flying," said Marie. "But I'd go along for the ride if Lindbergh was the pilot."

All afternoon, as we did each other's hair and makeup, and ironed the gorgeous dresses we'd sewn — pastel blue for me, lilac for Marie — we talked of our own dreams. We imagined bridal boutiques or fancy dress stores on Fifth Avenue, upscale establishments where we wouldn't have to sew a button on a farmer's winter wool coat, or a frumpy mourning frock for a widow.

When Billy and Tom had arrived, we promised our father we'd be careful and come straight home from the dance, but we never made it there.

Billy drove, his slender knuckles white from his tight grip on the steering wheel. When Tom's joking got too loud, he shushed him and lectured him on the importance of paying attention to the road. Marie and I rolled our eyes, certain that there could be no danger at the slow speed Billy was going. But when a deer jumped out of the brush and darted in front of the car, Billy flinched and turned the wheel too sharply. The car crossed the yellow line, clipped a massive oak, and shot down a ravine, where a thicket of holly trees caught us.

Marie and I whimpered in the backseat. Tom held his head in his hands where he'd struck the windshield, and a thin trickle of blood slid down his face. Billy cried like a child. I didn't know if he was injured or devastated about the crash, but the way he sobbed scared me. I leaned against the door to get to Billy and see what ailed him, but searing pain ripped through my shoulder so hard, I couldn't breathe. I noticed my arm hung at a strange angle, and a bone on the top of my chest appeared to be trying to poke through my skin.

Nausea welled up in me. I leaned back on the seat and closed my eyes, trying to find a position that didn't feel as if someone was jabbing a knife into my shoulder, but there was no relief.

"Is it broken?" asked Marie, in a panic. She slid open the collar of my dress and covered her mouth, slowly arranging the material back in place.

Billy had stopped crying, and our sorry quartet began trying to figure out who could seek help, while we lost more and more evening light by the minute. I didn't want to be stuck at the bottom of a ravine without anyone able to see us. My poor father would think we'd run away or died.

"Marie, you have to go. I can't move," I said.

"I'm afraid," she said.

"Please," said Tom. "My head's going to split open."

"Billy," said Marie, "come with me."

"I'm stuck," he said in a hoarse voice. "My door won't open and the steering wheel is so close, I'm lucky to be breathing right now."

Marie shut her eyes and laid her head back, then leaned up and looked out the window. "It's almost dark. And we're miles from town."

Suddenly we saw a flash of lights.

"Go!" I said.

Marie threw open the door before she could change her mind, and began to climb up the ravine. For a moment, I heard nothing, but then a male voice. Another woman. Shouts.

Dr. Daniel Dempsey was at my window, peering through at me. I gave him a half-hearted smile, in spite of the pain, and he began pulling on the door. It was dented in toward me and jammed tight, but with a hard tug, he was able to open it.

"I don't want to move you," he said. "Tell me where it hurts."

"Here," I said. My skin grew clammy, and to my embarrassment I leaned over and vomited all over the back of Billy's car. He groaned in the front seat. I was sure it was more because of the mess than his pain.

"I'm sorry," I said.

"It's all right," said Dr. Dempsey. He pressed his handkerchief to my lips and slid his hand along my neck. "It's your collarbone. Broken. You may have other injuries as well. The way you're flinching has me concerned about your internal organs."

"There are others here, Daniel," said a sharp voice from behind him. I glanced over Daniel's shoulder and saw Darcy, his girlfriend. She'd snatched the young doctor up as soon as he'd started working at the hospital. Marie and I had often thought of sending him anonymous letters of warning, having grown up with Darcy and knowing her nature, but we decided to let him find out for himself, confident that it wouldn't take long.

"Of course," he said.

Marie worked to open Billy's door while Daniel moved around to the passenger side and checked on Tom, who had begun to shiver. After using a penlight to check his eyes, Daniel said that we needed to get him to the hospital immediately.

"There goes our night," Darcy mumbled under her breath.

She wore a pink silk dress with layers of fringe from the waist to the hem, and matching pink high-heeled shoes. They must have also been heading for the dance.

"I don't want to move them," said Daniel, "but it will take too long to fetch an ambulance. Darcy, help me get them to my car."

Darcy looked down at her dress and shoes and then at me, half covered in vomit and blood, and didn't move. Billy crawled out of the driver's side, and helped Daniel. They looped Tom's arms around their necks and started up the ravine. Marie came to my side of the car.

"Forget it, Darcy," she said. "I'll help her. We wouldn't want you to get dirty."

I winked at Marie as she leaned into me.

"This is going to hurt," she said.

I nodded and took a deep breath.

"I want you to slide to my side of the car so I can get you out on your good side," she said. "I'll meet you there."

Each movement brought a new blast of pain, and by the time I'd scooted the short distance, I felt dizzy.

"I can't climb up that hill," I said, finally allowing the tears to come.

"Just close your eyes for a moment," she said. "Open them when you think you're ready."

I tried to focus on my sister's calming words. She held my hand and I felt comforted by her simple presence. She leaned in and whispered in my ear, "Darcy gathered our purses. Isn't she helpful? I hope she slips and gets mud all over that dress."

I smiled, but even that hurt my shoulder.

I heard a rustling, and in a few moments, Daniel was back and breathless. I opened my eyes and watched him loop his scarf around the back of me and tie it as gently as possible over my arm to keep it immobile. I winced as he pulled the knot.

"I know," he said. His mouth was at my ear and he smelled faintly of aftershave. I tried to concentrate on that as he slipped his arms under me and lifted me from the car.

"I'll walk behind you," Marie said, "and support your back."

Up he carried me. It was no easy task. His breath was so labored by the time he reached the top of the hill, he had to place my feet on the ground. He leaned over with his hands on his knees while Marie walked me the twenty or so more feet to his car, piled with wounded people. Marie settled me in the front next to Darcy, and then went around back with Billy and Tom. Soon Daniel was in the car and we were off, racing to the hospital.

"I got their purses," said Darcy.

No one replied.

When we arrived, we were lifted and scattered to various rooms. Tom had a concussion but would heal. Marie had escaped with only scrapes and cuts. Billy was fine, but mourned the ruin of his beloved car. Because they worried my bruised spleen might rupture, I stayed in the hospital for two weeks. I took comfort in the steady presence of Dr. Dempsey, whose visits to me lasted longer and longer. We'd talk late into the night, and laugh, and he tended to me with a gentleness I hadn't known since my mother's touch.

The night before I was scheduled to go home, after my father and Marie had left and the lights in the room were darkened, I dozed until I saw at the door the familiar shape that I had grown to love in that short time. Daniel looked up and down the hallway, quickly entered and shut the door, and leaving the lights out, went to my side. I smiled at him in the shadows.

"I thought you weren't supposed to work tonight," I said. "We said our good-byes in the bright and honest daylight."

His face was serious. I began to worry that something was wrong. He pulled a chair up to my bedside and grasped my hand. His palms were moist and his breath was quick.

"Are you all right?" I asked.

"I am," he said, finally smiling. "Look at you. Asking after me while you're wrapped in bandages in a hospital bed."

He brought my hand to his lips, something he'd never done, an acknowledgment of our growing affection for each other. I felt the air shift between us.

"I know this is sudden," he whispered, "but I love you, Laura. I hope it's all right that I'm saying this to you."

At that moment I imagined a secret space opening between the two of us, where our feelings met. In spite of my battered body, my heart felt warm and alive.

"I love you too, Daniel."

His face collapsed with relief and he smiled. He leaned in and kissed me on the lips. The space I'd felt between us seemed to grow around us. We existed there alone for a few blissful moments, but then he pulled away. He kept his face close to me, and again grew serious.

"There is the problem of Darcy," he said. "I hate to hurt her, but she just isn't right for me. We've been together for less than a year, and all she talks about is marriage. I can't marry her. Does that make me a scoundrel?"

"No," I said, relieved that he saw her for what she was. "I knew you'd figure that out sooner or later. I just didn't know why I cared so much. Now I realize that crash must have been fate. That sounds so silly."

"Not at all," he said. "It took the accident to really show me what she was made of. Or what she wasn't made of. She's a good actress under most circumstances."

"I know."

"All right," he said. "I have to slip out so I'm not found, but the next time you see me, I will be yours. I promise."

My emotions prevented me from speaking, but I knew he understood. He leaned in and kissed me once more; then he disappeared into the night.

I would later learn that he went to Darcy's house, was admitted by her mother, and met Darcy on the back porch, where she told him that their wedding would have to take place very soon because she was pregnant.

THIRTY-ONE

January 1931

VINCENT

Though it is midday, Laura instructs me to drive the sleigh to the front of the store. She does not speak of it now, but I know she no longer wishes to hide from Marie. She is tired of untruths. She sits up straight next to me with Grace on her lap. Eugen is bundled on the backseat. I point out birds' nests to Grace as we travel, but when we approach Main Street, we become silent. We are all watching for Marie.

The first sight that comes into view is the completed statue of the Virgin. The tent over her has been removed, and she stands in awe-inspiring glory. The light shines on the statue's face, and Laura draws in her breath as I do the same. We are distracted by the beauty and pure humanity the sculptor has infused into the Virgin's countenance. So many likenesses of her are impersonal, gazing at nothing, passive, anonymous. This woman is distinct. Her gaze faces downward, but not with a demure turn of the head. She lords over the snake. Her brow is pulled high and back, and a smile of satisfaction touches her full lips. Her eyes, though still unsettlingly white and round in marble, are heavily lidded, and her hair escapes her veil in pieces, rather than parting in neat chunks.

The second sight in town makes me pull the reins to stop the sleigh.

There is a mob. The townspeople fill the street between the church and Laura's shop. They stand in clusters in boots and coats, staring at the front of the church.

Laura mutters, "What is this?"

I recognize Father Ash, Mrs. Perth and her husband, and Dr. Hagerty as he joins the crowd. There is also a heavyset man with a black doctor's bag at his feet, a group of finely dressed women, and Agnes Dwyer, who stands next to a man in impressive clerical vestments. Agnes wears a strange smile, and when she sees us, she gets a wild look in her eyes.

"Is the statue being dedicated?" I ask.

Laura looks from the Virgin to the crowd and relaxes a bit, though she pulls Grace closer to her side. "I guess so. I must have forgotten."

But this does not feel like a dedication. There is tension in the air. While the clergyman I don't recognize speaks the blessing, Agnes drops her hand to the purse on her arm, and slides it in front of her as if protecting its precious contents. Her gaze keeps slipping from the purse and back to us. Father Ash looks lost, and fidgets with his hands. Something is wrong.

I catch sight of Marie and Everette, though they have not yet noticed us. "Do you want me to come closer, or turn back?"

Laura nods that I should proceed. She told me last night that she is prepared to confront her sister with the truth and face whatever the consequences.

As we approach, townspeople emerge from the houses and storefronts. The brothers who work at the market arrive, as do Agnes' raven-haired daughter and her doctor husband, whom I now know was Laura's lover. They begin to notice us. We stop behind them and listen to the words of the prayer the clergyman says as he raises his arm toward the statue. Father Ash lights incense in the censer and they begin to process toward the statue when Agnes suddenly shouts.

"Wait!"

The group halts. Some of the women wear

expressions of unease.

"I wasn't going to do this, but seeing Laura Kelley with *that woman* is a sign that I must. From God. For the sake of this town."

As the townspeople turn to look at us, I realize I am the woman to whom Agnes has referred. She assumes a position on the top step of the church entranceway, and I feel strongly that she thinks she is on a stage and we are her audience.

"Women like them," says Agnes in a shrill voice, "are poison to this town."

There are gasps, and I dare to look at Laura. She is clearly confused.

"It's all here in *Father* Ash's diary," she says. Agnes reaches into her purse and lifts out a brown leather book. I hear an intake of breath followed by furious whispers. Father Ash loses his color. He might faint.

"His journal," whispers Laura. "Why does Agnes have that?"

"Allow me to enlighten all of you," says Agnes. She clears her throat and begins to read:

"Laura stands with her hands out, one clutching her hat, and her head thrown back. Tears glisten on her face, the sun warms her soft blond hair, and her ripe,

451

round body is like fruit on a tree — sweet enough to pluck. She looks like the Madonna herself."

Laura looks at me with shock, and then at Father Ash, who makes himself a shadow, an impotent thing with no fight in him.

"If Laura knew how often I watched her, she might be frightened of me.

"The window of my writing desk in the rectory faces her shop across the square. From my room I can see Laura — her soft blond curls mingling with those of the child as they bend over a book, the light catching the child's glasses. I ache at their vulnerability. Watching them is like watching the same girl at two phases of her life — before and after innocence — and as much as they break my heart, as much as the mother does something else to it, I can't tear my eyes away."

It occurs to me that someone needs to stop this horrid witch from exposing the priest's private thoughts, but not one of us has the strength of character to stop listening in morbid fascination.

"The great irony is that I can watch and love anonymously, while her sin must be forever tethered to her. I've tried to tell her of my sorrow so often with my eyes, but she rarely meets them. No matter how I've assured her in the confessional, she never truly believes that her sin was long ago forgiven, while mine simmers like a slow burn from the inside out. I imagine my insides scorched as my longing flares up in those blessed, cursed moments when she is inches from me, on the other side of a screen. Veiled.

"I try to embrace the purer aspects of my feelings toward her: my great sorrow for her loneliness, my admiration for her strength and the way she loves the child, her love of her sister.

"The crackle of the candle distracts me. I turn my eyes toward my homily book and see that I've written two words: Loneliness. Loyalty. I stare at them until Laura's relationship with the words blurs into mine, and the lesson I needed to find makes itself clear to me. My loneliness is a virtue. I must stay loyal to my vows.

"Ready now to write my homily, I pray that no one will find me hidden in the words. Preaching to others the lessons I need to hear is a delicate dance. From my youth, I never suspected the priests as being anything less than perfect. I thought their words came from their wish for our purity to match theirs, and ultimately God's. Now, being on this side of the altar, I feel a new kinship with my brothers. To stand before people who respect me so much, and to know that their idle worship is so misplaced is humbling.

"No. It is agonizing."

Some saint emerges, climbs the stairs, and grabs the diary from Agnes' hands. She is shocked that a man would make so violent a move toward her. It is the sculptor, who has been approaching slowly, but who hurried as he caught her indictments on the wind.

"For God's sake, what are you at, woman?" he shouts.

"I am showing this town that the depth and breadth of scandal with Laura Kelley at its epicenter are more awful than any of us could have imagined," she says.

Laura shakes her head as if she can't accept what she's hearing, this confession of deep love that no one was ever meant to hear. This malicious woman has somehow gotten her gnarled claws in the priest's chest and pulled out his heart for all to see. And then I realize why. She thinks he is Grace's father. I can see by the panic in Laura's eyes that she realizes that fact too.

The choir women reveal a curious mixture of emotions. None will look at Laura. Some stare with open horror at Father Ash. Some hold arms crossed over bosoms, calculating how they can say they knew all along. One is heartbroken. Simply devastated. She cries into her handkerchief.

"How did you come by this diary?" asks the impressively dressed cleric, whose incense has made a cloud over them.

"Sissy cleans the rectory." The witch points at the sobbing woman. "She saw it open and read Laura's name. She thought she'd give it to Miss Kelley, but she couldn't help read it. When she discovered the scandal on its pages, she knew what she had to do. And thank goodness for that. We can't allow this vile corruption to poison our community any longer."

Now interrupting this horror comes Marie, the sister. Swollen with pregnancy and in a rage even greater than Agnes'.

"How could you?" Marie emerges out of the crowd, approaching the sleigh where we sit and speaking in a dark voice that comes from deep inside her belly, behind where she grows her child. Her anger is bigger than her sorrow, so no tears touch her eyes. Her hatred is stoked every time she sets her eyes on me.

Laura's breathing is shallow and quick. She thought she would come home to a private confrontation with her sister. Now she is being flogged in public by a madwoman. I want to take her back up the mountain, out of harm's way.

"You've betrayed me," says Marie, walking closer. "You are worse than Everette, worse than anyone."

"She is with us because she needed money," says Eugen. "That is all. Don't add to this trouble."

"Shut your mouth," says Marie. "We don't need the help of another philanderer."

"Marie, please," says Laura. Her voice is somehow steady and resigned. This was the argument she'd been expecting, after all, though not in the middle of the street.

"I'm not finished," pronounces Agnes. She cannot stand that the attention is slipping away from her performance. "I've also heard rumors of Miss Kelley leaving her child alone in the house on multiple occasions to go down to the pond where those Gypsies have been drinking. No doubt the bacchanalias would draw a harlot like her, but I don't think we are safe with such people nearby."

"Silence," says the sculptor. "You are in

the presence of an innocent child."

I've almost forgotten Grace, but now feel her shivering beside me.

"That is where all of this is leading," says Agnes, turning to address the clergyman. "I would like to call the police and report Laura Kelley for adultery, fornication, imbibing, and child endangerment. That girl will have no kind of life with that woman. A report needs to be filed immediately with the New York Society of the Prevention of Cruelty to Children."

Laura wears a look of sheer terror. "No," she whispers, drawing Grace closer to her.

The cleric places the censer on the ground. "Enough," he says. "We cannot address this here."

He takes the priest by the arm and begins to lead him into the church. Father Ash says nothing. He makes no move to defend himself. He is defeated. He must feel he deserves this condemnation for harboring such feelings. I ache for him, and for Laura, and panic rises in my own chest. Laura must speak out. She must tell the truth.

"With these charges," continues Agnes, "shouldn't the child be taken into custody until there may be a hearing?"

I move to shake the reins, to remove Laura and Grace from this madness, when Laura shouts, "No!"

She has found her anger. Grace finally understands the trouble and begins to cry. Laura tightens her arms around her. Father Ash's face turns red and he looks as if he would like to run. The sculptor strides over to us, still clutching the diary, and stands next to where Laura sits in the sleigh.

"There is no substance to this woman's lies," he says. "You cannot take the words of this madwoman as evidence. We are a group of workers from the neighboring towns. We meet at the pond to sing and we're forming a theater company. The child has been with us. There is no mischief."

"You expect them to take your word over mine?" says Agnes. "Some shell-shocked hobo to whom Father Ash has given a charity job. We all see what he's about."

I am aghast at the depths of this woman's animosity, and I don't shock easily.

As Father Ash is led back into the church, Laura stands and screams for them to stop. "He is not her father," she says. "I swear it."

"How do you expect any of us to believe that?" says Agnes. "His diary, the way he is forever giving you charity through business. I saw the two of you alone before Mass, buried in the robes."

"You see what you want to see," says Laura.

Daniel Dempsey has moved to the back of the crowd, and is attempting to pull his wife with him. Laura has seen. No one notices them but the two of us. I look at Laura and feel a shift in the air around her. She no longer trembles. She is tall, erect, and devastatingly beautiful. I would fear her if I did not know her. She says a name.

"Daniel."

The doctor stops, and all at once, the crowd quiets. Heads turn slowly to him. It seems that each person makes meaning of his name, one after another. His wife wrenches her arm out of his grip.

"The man you seek to expose is your son-in-law, Daniel Dempsey," says Laura. She is holding Grace so close to her that they merge into one. I realize that Laura has not used the word *father.* She will not give that weak man who attempted to slither away just moments ago the honor of that title.

Gasps and exhalations rise all around. Marie lets out a sob and hurries away, down the street. Everette remains, his face still as stone. Father Ash looks at Laura with pity and gratitude. Daniel's wife stands next to her mother. And Agnes is shocked. Really and truly shocked. She falters and her

459

daughter grabs her arm, but it's too late. Agnes has fainted on the church steps.

While the crowd closes in on the woman, I see Laura's dry eyes, her calm face, the child clinging to her. Daniel hesitates for a moment before he goes to his mother-in-law. He repels the crowd around him. Laura squeezes Eugen's shoulder and bends to embrace me. Her strength has moved me. I hold her and her daughter tightly to communicate my feelings because I am at a loss for words.

The sculptor holds up a hand to Laura, and helps her and Grace down from the sleigh. They walk to the shop and enter together, closing the door behind them.

THIRTY-TWO

LAURA

Grace wouldn't let me put her down. She sensed my turbulence and the aftershocks from the scene outside the church. Gabriel hadn't left. He kept peering out the front window and pacing like a wolf, though I assured him we were all right. The danger was over.

"I am humbled by your care for us," I said.

"I couldn't stand by and let that woman get away with such scandal."

"She has just stepped into her own private hell."

"And now you can be free of yours."

Perhaps, but I did not yet feel free. My separation from my sister was my new yoke, the one I'd been anticipating.

Grace's arms encircled my neck, and her weight began to burden my back. I sat in the chair by the fireplace with her still clinging to me, and kissed her hair, which

461

smelled like winter.

"You okay, Gracie?" I asked.

"Mm-hmm," she muttered into my neck.

I held her away from me and looked into her owl eyes.

"You're safe," I said. "Hoot."

She giggled and pulled Dolly into her neck.

I looked up to where Gabriel stood watching us, wearing the strangest expression.

"Would you like to stay for lunch?" I asked.

He blinked as if under a spell, and then shook his head. "No. No, thank you. I should be going now. If you feel safe, that is."

I nodded and smiled, hoping to give reassurance. He smiled back at us and paused before closing the door behind him.

After an hour, Grace was finally calm enough to climb out of my lap and pull Dolly around the shop in her sled. As I prepared a fire, the store bell rang. I was surprised to see Sissy. She held a large basket full of apples and oranges. Still reeling over the words in Father Ash's diary and Sissy's theft of it, I didn't know how to welcome her into my shop. I was shocked that she would come in so soon after the scene in the street.

Her red-rimmed eyes confirmed that she had been crying. She carried the basket and placed it on the counter. Then she turned to me and wept. Grace saw her and became troubled. When she rushed to me to pick her up, Sissy flinched.

"To think I could have harmed you girls," she said. She wiped her tears on the sleeves of her coat, irritating the skin on her red cheeks.

I walked over to a pile of handkerchiefs under the counter, picked one up, and handed it to her.

"Thank you. I do not deserve your kindness," she said.

No, she didn't, and I wished she'd leave, but I was aware that my daughter had witnessed many troubling exchanges, and must learn how to treat people. I stood straight.

"I brought you this fruit basket," Sissy said. "I . . . I mean it as an apology. The beginning of an apology. I know it will take time."

"Thank you, Sissy," I said. "But perhaps you should take it to Father Ash. I believe he has been hurt worse than we have been."

This caused her to cry harder. I waited for her outburst to subside.

"I can't," she said. "I just can't. I'm so

ashamed."

"Confess it to him."

She stopped crying and nodded her head, and silence grew around us.

Though I appreciated her gesture so soon after the trouble, I wished she would go. I was exhausted and did not wish to upset Grace any more. Mercifully, Sissy too seemed fatigued, and turned to leave. She muttered one more apology, and then shut the door.

I watched her walk home through the snow, slipping a bit on the road. Many people still lingered in town, talking in groups. They looked at the church, my shop, and down the street toward the hospital. I knew many of them would still judge me for my relationship with Daniel, but Sissy's visit might represent a shift. A moving on. A welcoming.

This heartened me for a moment until I remembered the look of pain and anger on Marie's face, the way she had clutched her belly and tried to flee from us. I thought I'd prepared myself for confronting her, but Agnes' performance added so much confusion to my return that I found the rift with Marie infinitely more insurmountable. I didn't know where to begin to build a bridge.

Marie's anger weighed so heavily on me all day that by eight o'clock I knew I had to turn in once Grace was in bed.

"Stay," Grace said, and I didn't refuse. I curled myself around her and rubbed her arms until she slept soundly in my grasp. I waited for sleep, but it did not come. Only a hazy half-consciousness that confused me, and reminded me of how Marie and I had slept this way as children when one of us was scared. Before I knew it, I was crying, trying hard not to wake Grace with my shaking. Exhaustion stole over me, and I finally succumbed to sleep, but it felt as if not a minute had passed when I heard a knock on the back door.

My eyes refused to open, and I prayed that the knocking was a bad dream, but seconds later, it came again with more insistence. I didn't want Grace to awaken and become further troubled, so I slid away from her as carefully as possible and crept down the stairs. I peered around the wall at the bottom of the staircase and looked at the back door's window.

It was Daniel.

I didn't think I should let him in — not because I felt a stirring in my heart, but because he did not deserve a chance to explain himself. He would not stop knocking, however, so I was forced to admit him.

"I'm sorry to come . . . so late." The words hung between us.

He had dark circles under his eyes, disheveled hair, and trembling hands. I stepped aside and motioned to the table, where he sat so heavily, it was as if he did not possess the strength to remain upright.

After I closed the door, I heard a sound and saw Grace scooting down the stairs into the kitchen. Daniel looked at her with an expression of such pain that I was moved to pity. I lifted her into my arms and thought that he would never get to hold her like this.

"Hello, Grace," he said, attempting to put lightness in his voice. She did not speak.

"Say hello," I said. "Be polite to Dr. Dempsey."

She shook her head and shoved her thumb in her mouth, burying her face in my neck.

"It's all right," he said. "She doesn't know me."

She doesn't know me.

The words seemed to echo in the air. He was wretched, indeed. Then he sat up as if remembering that he had something to say.

"My secretary said you wanted to sew for the ward. For money. We get our linens now in bulk from a supplier, but our waiting room could use some new curtains and cloths for the end tables. How about it?"

My softened heart suddenly flared in anger.

Curtains? Cloths? To think that we stood here in this room, with this child between us, after all that had happened, talking of such things. My fury rose and my face burned. Without a word, I climbed the stairs, tucked in Grace, and instructed her to go to sleep. She whined a response, but the wild, dark look in my eyes quieted her complaints. Back in the kitchen I stepped toward Daniel, standing over him.

"How dare you come here and ask me to make curtains for your waiting room," I said.

"Laura, I'm sorry. I wanted to see you."

"Really? Now? Haven't you seen me often enough? *Alone,* pushing my daughter in her pram. *Alone,* sledding with her on the hill. *Alone,* running into your wife at the library. *Alone,* in the back pew of the church while your mother-in-law throws spears at me with her eyes. *Alone,* in my window at night sewing so I can feed this child and keep her safe and warm."

He had the nerve to allow his lips to quiver.

I pushed him with all my force. "Get out," I said. "You're too late."

He grabbed my arms and knelt in front of me. "Please, Laura, I'm so sorry. I didn't know what to do. I don't know what to do. I want to help you. I love —"

I wrenched myself out of his grip. "Don't you dare."

He crumpled and buried his face in his hands. I was disgusted to see him like this.

"What would your wife say to see you? Your mother-in-law?"

"Darcy left. She went to stay with Agnes. My marriage is over."

My fury began to scare me because I wished to do this man violence — this man who finally came to me because his wife had left him.

"There's more," he said. "Darcy wasn't pregnant when we married."

His words didn't make sense to me. "Of course she was, until she lost the baby. But by then you'd married her."

"She lied. She told me earlier tonight. She wanted to keep you and me apart."

My mind raced. I thought of how Darcy had stolen our happiness, stolen a father from Grace's life; forced me to live alone, scraping together funds and working for Millay in betrayal of my sister to make ends meet. I thought of how the love between Daniel and me had persisted even after his marriage, and how it had led me to disobey my father, which resulted in his death. I thought of what could have been, and put my face in my hands. Emotion came howling up and I pushed it down. Far down. It was the only way I could cope.

"I'm sorry to burden you now, but don't you see?" he said. "It means we can finally be together. I can have my marriage annulled because of the lie that started it. We can move away. Grace will no longer be a bastard."

I lifted my head upon hearing the horrible word he uttered about my daughter. The spell of regret was broken. Only anger remained.

"My daughter is no bastard, and damn you for saying that."

"I mean, she'll be legitimate."

"She was *legitimate* the first day I knew she grew inside me. She was born of love — something that grew between us, separately, and continued even after you were too cowardly to face it. You are not worthy to *legitimize* her."

I knew the man across from me was broken and sick. An emotional cancer plagued him, a true hatred of Darcy, which was actually of himself. As much as I wanted to hate Darcy, I felt a stab of pity for her. She had to pretend to be pregnant to hold on to a man who didn't love her and who never would, and an unworthy man, at that. At least I had my daughter, and a chance at real love.

Daniel grabbed my hands.

"Please, Laura, don't you see? We can be together. We can be a family!"

I was suddenly sick for the lost years — for the time I'd spent pining for him.

"Leave," I said.

He stared at me in shock. He hadn't expected this conversation to go as it had, and he had no retort. After a moment, he walked toward the door and paused there. "You are tired and need time to think. Think about it for me. And for Grace."

It was astounding but I was still surprised by his selfishness. I thought of the angry fire burning in me. I imagined fighting it from the outside in until it was but a candle I could snuff. I knew that I must speak so he understood me, so that there was no spark of hope in him.

"Daniel, you have failed me in every way a man can. You are selfish beyond imagining. You left me alone with our daughter, and only come to me now when your marriage is over. I will not allow you to disrupt my life any longer. You are nothing to me."

Daniel's eyes looked as if they would bulge from his head. He made a move to the back door, but I stopped him.

"Wait."

I ran upstairs and to my room to dig through my closet. Before long, I found the box holding the triple-stranded pearl necklace from our night at the Follies. I was glad I had never sold it because I wanted him to know that at no time had he ever had any part in supporting us. I carried it down to him and passed it over. He lifted the lid, and when he saw what was inside, he looked as if he would shatter.

I crossed the room and threw on the front lights, opened the door, and thrust him out. He stumbled down the stairs, but turned once more to me.

"I know there is nothing I can ever do to make up for these lost years," he said. "Nothing. But please know that I put myself through torture every day. Every single day. Seeing you and your — *our* — beautiful daughter, and not being able to have either of you, it is hell."

"A hell you created," I said, suddenly calm. "It didn't have to be this way."

"I'm so sorry," he said.

I noticed the moon and the stars in the sky, breathed the crisp winter air, and felt purified. I realized that I was not sorry.

Not at all.

Marie would not see me. Everette told me as much at the door each day. He apologized, but there was nothing he could do.

I turned away, holding Grace's mittened hand. She took great strides, crushing snowballs like a giant stepping on boulders, and we walked together up the stairs of the church. It was quiet and dark, with only the glow of votive candles and colored light filtered through stained glass. The aroma of incense lingered in the drapery folds. Lily Miller arranged flowers on the altar.

"Good morning," she said. "You girls are up and about early today."

"We know the choir has rehearsal this morning. We wanted to hear the pretty singing, and see how Agnes is doing."

Lily stood up straight and widened her eyes.

"You are very kind to check on her," she said. "She is resting under doctor's orders for an indefinite period of time. She's under a bit of nervous strain, I'm afraid, after her attack of apoplexy. There is danger she will suffer another."

There was an awkward moment of silence until I spoke again. "Have you seen Father

Ash? I wanted to speak to him too, after all that."

Lily's eyes welled with emotion, and she reached for my free hand. Her voice trembled. "You are good, Laura."

I was embarrassed to feel my own tears, but I quickly blinked them away.

"The last I saw him, he was shoveling snow on the path to the cemetery," she said. "I think he would be very glad to see you."

I squeezed her hand and smiled. "Thank you."

I led Grace to the back of the church and we exited onto the path. Father Ash stopped shoveling, and wiped his brow with a handkerchief. When he saw us, his expression changed from one of pleasure to panic. I willed myself to be courageous. We must talk openly if we were both to go on with our lives.

"Miss Kelley," he stammered. "Grace. What a gift."

"Good morning, Father," I said, suddenly unsure of what I wanted to communicate.

Grace pulled away to chase a group of cardinals flitting between the bushes and the snow. He watched her, but could not bring his gaze to meet mine.

"I'm so sorry, Laura," he said.

"Please —" I started to say, but he cut me off.

"No, I must apologize. I was wrong, so very wrong, for allowing myself to feel those things. I've been thinking and praying, and for your comfort, I will request a transfer. The bishop thinks it is a good idea."

"No," I said. "I don't want that. You are a good priest. We are blessed to have you."

"It will be for the best. I need to start again."

"Perhaps *I* should go," I said, with a sick feeling. I'd so often entertained thoughts of leaving town, but now the real possibility filled me with dread. Still, it might be for the best. "I don't want to burden you, and this seems like such a good place for you. You shouldn't have to go."

"No," he said, looking into my eyes. "You and Grace belong here. You have family, friends, a shop. This is your home."

My home. That it was, and I felt both guilty and relieved to embrace it. It was finally clear that the judgment I felt from the town wasn't only theirs, but a reflection of how I allowed others to treat me, just as Millay had said.

This was a lot to take in at once, but I didn't have long to think on it, for Grace was back, pulling my hand to take her sledding. Father Ash gazed at me, and I stopped Grace's motion for a moment. Looking at him alone on the path, with nothing but the birds to keep him company, I was filled with compassion for him.

Unable to speak, I tried to smile. Then I left with Grace.

Later that evening, Everette showed up at my back door. When I allowed him in, he walked to the kitchen table and sat without being invited. He put his face in his hands, and rubbed his eyes.

"I have to go to the city for a couple days," he said. "I hate to leave Marie so close to her due date, but I want to take care of something before the baby comes."

"Is everything all right?"

"Yes," he said. "I have some business, and then I'm meeting with the priest at St. Patrick's. I want to see if he'll bless our marriage. I'll also reserve a room for Marie and me at the Plaza like we did on our honeymoon. You know, to start over before the baby's born."

"I think she'll love that," I said, touched by his efforts. "I'd offer to keep an eye on her, but she won't let me."

"I know," he said. "But if you can watch her from afar, please do so. You might even try to talk to her when I'm not here. Maybe she'll feel freer to yell and scream. I don't know."

"I'll try," I said. "I'll never stop."

"Good."

"What has she said to you about me?" I asked.

"What you can imagine. That you've betrayed her worse than I did because of your connection. That the witch has gotten her claws into you. That you could have come to us for help with money before crawling to Millay. She's also hurt that you never confided in her about Daniel."

Stung, I looked at the floor. Marie's anger had not waned; it seemed to be building.

"And what do you say to her?" I muttered.

"I don't say anything. I don't know how to answer her."

We were quiet for a moment before he cleared his throat. "Well, I just wanted to tell you that I'll be gone. Thank you for watching out for her."

He stood and pushed the chair under the table. I locked the door after him, and watched him walk home, his shoulders slumped.

I was unable to work that night, and when I slept, I had terrible dreams about my father. I hadn't dreamed of him in so long, it felt like the reopening of an old wound. I knew he would be saddened by my division with Marie. What I couldn't decide, however, was whose side he'd take.

VINCENT

I've been in bed for days. Laura's strain has affected my nerves as never before.

Just when I think I cannot take another blow, word arrives that Eugen's mother has died.

My poor husband. He weeps freely, lamenting her passing and that he hadn't seen her in so long. She lives — lived — in the Netherlands. We haven't been back since we were newly married, when I was swallowed into the vast Boissevain tribe. I could feel their judgment of me, the way they compared me to Eugen's first wife, Inez.

Inez was a suffragist and fellow Vassar alumni whom I'd admired since my Village days, a tall, charming, well-spoken light of a woman. Eugen was devoted to her as he is to me, supporting her on trips across the country so she could speak for women's rights. The duo made a strapping pair, but pernicious anemia sent her to an early grave.

How is it that Eugen had a whole life before he married me? How is it that we almost never speak of Inez anymore?

Once a bright star has faded, it is nothing. It scarcely leaves a memory.

I allow Eugen to sleep in my bed this night. I take him into me and comfort him however I can, allowing him to fall asleep with his head on my breasts, crushing me with his weight, suffocating the dread in my heart all the night long. A bobcat's moan comes to me on the winds that batter the house. I am achingly alone.

A letter arrives in the post the next day from my mother. It contains a poem she's written about the mountain laurel bushes we gave her. I crumple on the settee, and begin to sob. Eugen races into the room.

"She will die," I say. "All our mothers will leave us."

"No, no, Vincie. Your mother is alive. She is all right."

"She is dying. Read it. She writes of laurels and of sleep. She means the eternal sleep."

He holds me the way I held him, whispering to me assurances that I do not believe.

We don black after that. We leave the lights low and read poetry and write letters. I sit in the shadow of Sappho's bust, gazing up at her for guidance. She rests strong and erect, a dark virgin, a muse I can cling to, a well from which to draw strength.

Days later, as we eat a quiet dinner, I hear the crunch of gravel. I look to my left, turning my ear to the door with dread. I put my utensils on the table and clutch the arms of the chair. Eugen waves the cook away and answers the door himself. I turn in my chair a little more and see a taxi, a driver, the handing over of a telegram.

When Eugen turns to me, his eyes are wide with horror. He cannot speak.

"Bring it to me," I say.

It is a telegram from my uncle. Mother is sick. She may be dying.

We send a message with the driver that we are coming.

We leave the hot meal on the table, full glasses of wine. We pack in haste, and rush to the garage in the darkening night. I tremble so badly, Eugen must open my door for me and help me into the car. We still cannot speak.

Eugen reaches for the throttle and tries to pull it out a bit to keep the engine from stalling in this cold, but the throttle is stuck. We won't move an inch.

"Damn!" he says.

He tries and tries, but we are going nowhere.

I refuse to return to the house. Eugen promises he will get the Cadillac started.

He promises we will get to Mother, but the damned hunk of metal junk won't move.

He disappears, and returns minutes later dragging the horses. He attaches their reins to the bumper and smacks them forward. They pull the Cadillac out of the dark garage. He returns them to the stables and again tries the throttle. I am still in the car. I will not move until we are at Mother's side.

I watch the night outside my window, mumbling prayers I haven't thought of in years, begging the deity in charge to get us to Mother's side before she dies. My husband labors and swears next to me, and suddenly, miraculously, the car starts and we shoot forward. We race down the long driveway and out to the road. Eugen is half-mad with determination.

"I will get you there. I promise. You will see your mother."

He has stopped saying she will be all right. The night is treacherously dark and frozen. The snow causes us to slip and spin out as much as we move forward, and the farther we get from Steepletop, the more I begin to panic.

"What if it stalls?" I say. "No one will find us. We will freeze to death."

"I promise we will not stall. I will not stop the car. We will drive straight through."

It is at least ten hours to the coast of Maine, probably longer because of the snow and ice. Eugen is exhausted. He will need to sleep along the way. I must say this out loud because he answers, "I will not sleep. You will get there."

The night passes like a terrible dream. The car makes horrid noises, and patches of black ice send us slipping more times than I can count. It seems that as soon as I doze off, I am shaken awake by the lurching of the car. Over and over again, it is as if I am falling from a dreadful height and snapped back into consciousness. I am convinced we will die on this trip, and I'm half glad.

But we don't.

Twelve hours later, we motor into Camden as the sun peers over the edge of the horizon. I feel ice-cold and stiff in spite of its warming rays.

"She is gone," I say.

"No," he says. "She is not. Do not say it, Vincie. She's not. We drove all night."

Eugen turns at the lily pond, and takes us down Chestnut Street to the address from which Mother's letters have been coming. I check the numbers on the envelope and stare at each passing house, searching for her place. Suddenly I grab Eugen, and he slams on the brake.

At a cottage — a place as tidy and humble as Mother — the door is covered in black crepe.

THIRTY-THREE

LAURA

I lifted my hand to knock on Marie's door as she spilled out of it. I grasped her arms and saw that her face was red, her hair disheveled. She was breathing heavily.

"Marie!"

She pulled from my grip and I saw the suitcase she held.

"Is it time?" I asked. "You're early. Like when I had Grace . . ."

She looked at me with a horrid glare. I'd only ever received such a look from Agnes. To get it from my sister inflicted new pain.

"Let me help you," I said.

She tried to pass me, but was gripped by a contraction. She squeezed her eyes closed and leaned on the porch railing. I moved her hand from the spot on her back she held and pressed deeply into her. She began to protest, but the pressure must have brought her some relief, because she allowed me to massage her until the contraction passed. Once it was over, she continued on. I followed her as she headed down the sidewalk toward the hospital.

"Please, Marie, let me find you a ride."

"By the time you find a ride for me, I'll be there," she snapped. "It figures Everette goes away now, of all times."

"It's an errand for you," I said. "For both of you."

"How do you know?"

"He told me. He wanted me to look out for you while he was gone."

"He barely watches for me when he's home," she said. "Do you expect me to believe that?"

Marie resumed walking. As we approached the statue of Our Lady of Grace, Marie rested her arm on the folds of the dress and squeezed her eyes shut. I again applied pressure, and this time, she leaned into it, allowing me to help her. Once the contraction ended, Marie pushed away. I stopped and looked back at my shop. Grace had not yet awoken for the day. I had anticipated leaving her alone only long enough to get turned away from Marie's house.

"Marie, I have to see about Grace. I'm sorry."

Marie did not turn. I watched her until

she was out of sight, and then I hurried home.

Grace was asleep and would likely be for another hour, but I felt pulled toward my sister. Marie had delivered Grace, and I wanted to be at my sister's side for the birth, at least until Everette returned. I could have the hospital phone him at the Plaza and leave a message that he needed to come at once.

Could I get anyone to watch Grace? I thought of each person I knew in town, and it occurred to me that perhaps Lily would help me. I could offer her pay or sewing services in exchange. I made up my mind to wake Grace and call on Lily. If she refused, I would have to go home.

Grace fussed when I awoke her, and sucked her thumb until I fetched her a glass of warm milk. I looked out the window at the clock tower, and time seemed to move at double speed. I was frantic to get to Marie.

I pulled on Grace's socks, boots, and hat while she finished her milk. Then I dressed her in her coat and mittens. I grabbed Dolly and a few books, tucked all of them into the sled, and hurried out the door and down the block to Lily's house. Once we arrived, Grace climbed out of the sled and walked up the shoveled path with me to mount the steps. No one answered our knock, but a cat jumped into the window and stared at us. I knocked again.

"I hope Miss Lily can watch you while I help Auntie have her baby."

"I see baby?"

"The baby isn't here yet," I said, trying to hide my impatience. I knocked again, but clearly no one was home.

"Damn," I said. Grace's eyes widened behind her glasses.

"I'm sorry," I said. She suppressed a smile.

I placed her in the sled and started along the street, trying to think of an alternative, but there was none. I decided to take Grace with me to the hospital. At least I could show Marie that I wanted to be with her, even if I couldn't stay through the birth.

By the time we reached the hospital, it was snowing again, and the wind took my breath away. Great piles of snow fell from branches, and drifts blew across the walkways. I looked up to where my father's room had been and said a prayer for him and for Marie. Before I entered the hospital, I was surprised to see Gabriel coming out. His hair was longer and beginning to curl at the ends. It suited him. I wondered why he was there.

"Hello," I said.

He was surprised to see us too, and ushered us in from the cold into the lobby. We left the sled propped against the building.

"Are you well?" I asked.

"Me? Yes. I was just hired. Chief maintenance engineer."

This sat between us while the implications settled in my thoughts. He was staying.

"How wonderful," I said, a bit more breathless than I would have liked.

He looked at me with an expression I couldn't decipher but continued. "Now I need to look for a place to live. As kind as Michael has been to let me stay in the rectory, I'll need to pay my own way. No more charity."

He looked down at Grace and his face wrinkled with worry. "Are you well?"

"Yes," I said. "My sister is having her baby. I'm coming to see if I can help."

"Do you plan to take Grace in with you?"

"I don't have much choice."

"I could take her," he said.

I was so surprised by his offer that I didn't know what to say. I trusted him, but how would it look to allow him to watch my daughter? Then I stopped myself from this kind of thinking and reconsidered his offer.

"Actually, I would appreciate that very much, if it's all right with Grace."

"What?" she said.

Gabriel crouched down to her level. "Would you like to come with me to see the puppies and maybe sled while your mother sees to Aunt Marie?"

She nodded her head with enthusiasm. I was so touched by his offer and her excitement that I had to look away to regain my composure.

"I'll take her to Sam's," he continued. "We'll check in with you in an hour or so, after we see the dogs. Then we'll sled on the hill behind the hospital."

Grace was already pulling Gabriel by the hand. He looked over his shoulder at me.

I mouthed, "Thank you."

He nodded and smiled before hurrying after her.

When I reached the maternity ward, I was grateful I hadn't run into Daniel, and I prayed that I didn't see him at all. Instead, I asked for Marie.

"Last door on the right," said the receptionist.

I hurried down the corridor and soon heard Marie's cries. When I rounded the corner, I found her alone in the room. The high ceiling made her look small. At the sight of me, relief crossed her features before she rearranged herself to look proud and distant. I walked in and placed my coat and hat on the chair before going to her bedside. I grabbed her hand and wouldn't let her pull away.

"Marie, you must let me help you."

"You've done enough."

"What? What have I done?"

"You've betrayed me."

"How? Really, how? Would you have had me lose my shop? Lose everything? Would you have Grace and me living under your roof or in a poorhouse?"

"No," she snapped. "All you needed to do was come to us. We would have helped you. Instead you . . ." She suddenly squeezed her eyes shut and began breathing heavily. I rubbed her hand and allowed her to tighten her grip on my fingers until she nearly cut off my circulation. After a minute or so, she relaxed.

"God, how much longer will this go on?" she asked.

"Has a nurse seen you?"

"Just to admit me. Then they left me here alone."

Marie began to cry and I placed my hands on her cheeks. "Listen to me. You are my sister. You are mine and you always will be. Millay is a customer."

"She is a friend," said Marie. "I saw it. I saw it as you rode into town with her."

"I cannot deny that," I said. "But I can promise you, Everette is nothing to her and she will never go near your family again."

"That is supposed to make me feel better?"

"No. Yes. I hope so."

"But Everette still pines for her. I can see it in his face."

I thought that what she sensed was true, but I also knew that it was just a spell. Millay would never dally with him again. If anything else, she wouldn't do it for me.

"I don't know anything about Everette's heart," I said. "All I know is that he is in New York for you, to recommit himself to your marriage. He is with you because he loves you. I believe he deserves a second chance, if for no other reason than the child you are about to bring into this world."

"For all I know he's meeting a mistress." Marie squeezed my hand again. Sweat glued her hair to her forehead, and she whimpered.

"That is not true," I said once the contraction passed. "I know why he's there, and it's not true. I love you, Marie. I can't live

490

like this. Grace and I need you in our lives."

Marie looked over my shoulder and around the room. "Where is Gracie?"

"She's with Gabriel," I said. "He offered to take her so I could be with you."

"That was very kind," she said. Marie closed her eyes for a moment. I reached up and smoothed her hair, and she opened her eyes. "Can the hospital ring Everette wherever he is?"

"I'll see to it immediately."

"Will you stay with me until Everette gets here?"

Tears spilled over, and I wiped them away with the back of my hand as I nodded.

A group of nurses and a doctor entered the room. I stepped out of the way and watched the nurses surround Marie, taking her blood pressure and temperature and asking her questions about her pain. I heard Marie gasp. The doctor pulled a curtain around her bed, and I heard something about her progressing quickly and Twilight Sleep. I stepped away to have the front desk phone the Plaza for Everette, and then hurried back to the room.

I stayed with Marie as long as possible, holding her hand, brushing hair off her forehead, and massaging her back until the doctor returned, and she was wheeled away

491

for the birth. Just before they administered the ether, Marie smiled and I felt as if we were rejoined.

I pressed my hand to my heart and walked to the window, where I saw Gabriel and Grace outside in the snow. Grace smiled while he watched her coast down the hill. I looked past the sledding hill and saw the amphitheater, overgrown with ivy and encased in frost. I stared at it for a long time, imagining the ivy cut down, a new coat of paint on the stage, a strong red weatherproof curtain. I allowed the fantasy to grow and sit in my heart until the church bells called my attention to the center of town, and to the statue of Mary. She was far away and small, but I felt her presence.

I walked over to Gabriel with my arms crossed, trying to keep out the cold. Grace ran to me with an open, happy face. Her cheeks were red and her glasses were foggy. She jumped toward me, and I opened my arms to her.

"I want a puppy," she said.

"Gabriel, is this your influence?"

He smiled and walked to me, pulling the sled behind him.

"She's drawn to the little one in the lit-ter," he said. "He has one blue eye and one brown. She calls him Brownie, and he comes to her every time. Sam says he's free to a good home."

Grace placed her mittened hands on either side of my face. "Can we?"

"You girls could use some protection," said Gabriel. "Brownie will be a good watchdog one day."

I liked that Gabriel thought of our protection.

"We'll see," I said. "But we'll be busy helping Auntie Marie. Don't you want to know if you have a boy cousin or a girl cousin?"

"What do I have?"

"A boy cousin! His name is James, after our father."

"Wonderful!" said Gabriel. "And Marie is all right?"

"Yes. And speaking to me."

"Very good to hear."

"And Everette arrived on the train not long ago, so the little family is getting to know each other."

Gabriel looked at his watch. "I have to run. I have an appointment about a rental not far from Sam and Callie. Can you come to the pond at four?"

"What's going on there?"

"Haven't you seen the flyers Callie's

hung? Singing, potluck, a bonfire, ice-skating. All out in the open."

"Can we?" asked Grace.

"Now that Auntie has had her baby, yes, we can."

"Good, then," he said. As he turned to leave, I reached for his arm. "Thank you. You have no idea . . ."

I gave his arm a squeeze, and he left us, looking back over his shoulder to wave to Grace. She waved until he was out of sight.

A crowd had gathered at the pond. Apparently the wood nymphs had hung flyers all over town inviting folks to join them. I had been too preoccupied to notice.

It was a pleasure to see the musicians in the open, and to note how many people came. Tables were crowded with steaming casseroles, warm breads, and fresh pies. The great cauldron bubbled with cider. Tim took a quick nip of his flask and replaced it inside his inner coat pocket. John Hagerty pushed his wife on the path to the clearing. Pale but smiling, Caroline caught sight of me and lifted her hand in a wave, and I returned her greeting. Sam's dogs attracted the children's attention, including Grace's. She ran up to her friends. When the children from town saw her in a group, they approached and were folded in. Acceptance covered them like fresh snow.

I felt the absence of those not present like a weight. Darcy, Agnes, Daniel — I didn't know what to do about these people. Something dark and savage inside me wanted to make them pay; it wished for no reconciliation, desired to show them I would be all right without their forgiveness or approval. But I knew that to allow that darkness to root itself in me would replace my old hell with a new one. It would scratch my skin like a hair shirt. It would show my daughter what I did not want her to see.

"You are still unreadable," Gabriel said as he walked up beside me, ice skates flung over his shoulder, his hat at a jaunty angle.

"Perhaps you should consider photography," I said. "Take a series of pictures to show the progression of my emotions."

"Or writing. I could write the phases of your reflective face," he said. "Phase one: relaxed forehead and smile. Soft eyes. Head at an angle. A warm response to seeing all of us together."

"And phase two?"

"Alert but open. Watchful. Seeing her child join a group, a touch of sadness is introduced into the subject."

"She wonders if the children are being

kind to hers," I said. "She thinks that her daughter is getting older before her very eyes."

"Phase three: pain. Regret. Longing. That is the moment when I see her. What is she thinking that has caused the line to appear between her eyebrows? Her mouth turns down. Her eyes grow dark and shadowed."

"Yes, regret. Wonder. Will it be all right with those who aren't here? What have I done to make this separation, and how can I stitch it back together?"

He looked surprised that I'd said as much. I surprised myself, but it felt right. I needed to start making healthy connections with others, and honesty lay at the heart of that desire. Courage was important too.

I turned my concentration back to the moment. I was fascinated that it was no longer the eyes of the town watching, but the eyes of the sculptor. He read me like the weather. I felt the stirring begin again in my belly. I allowed this feeling to touch my face, to show him that I welcomed his attention.

His eyes narrowed and the side of his mouth lifted in a grin.

He knew.

There was a pleasant soreness in my legs

from the skating we'd done all evening under the white lights hanging from the trees. I ran my hands along my thighs, massaging them as I sat in front of my fireplace at home. Then I stretched both legs, pointing and flexing my toes.

I thought of Gabriel's hand in mine while we had tried not to fall on the frozen river, glove to glove, and imagined if it had been skin on skin. His hands would feel rough, callused. The hands of a workingman. My mind tried to take that further, to leap into the future, but I quieted it. I didn't want to think too far ahead. I accepted this day for what it was, and I'd do the same with tomorrow.

I was barely conscious of picking up the book, and of what I sketched, but after a few moments, I was caught up with the creative spirit that hovered at that time of night, waiting to inhabit my fingers to fashion its designs. I drew a pair of soft leather gloves, lined in lamb's wool. Hand-stitched. Men's gloves to match a hat that I also drew. The hat was brown with a black band.

When I picked through my closet, I found an old brochure for the design school, but I slid it into the fire. I'd set my sights on the neglected amphitheater a short walk from home. I thought I could do what I enjoyed here, in my place of origin, where I wanted my daughter to grow in a happiness I thought I'd forever lost. Her good years here would balance my bad.

I would make dresses and cloaks for whomever I desired. I'd allow anyone who wished to use the front door. I would make plans for a theater company with Sam and Callie and the others.

I turned the page and allowed my imagination to roam new landscapes, landscapes of ceremony, of celebration. White tulle, lace overlay, or maybe satin? I jumped ahead in my mind again, but I couldn't help it, so I gave in to the fantasy.

In spite of all the joys of the day, I had a small sadness in my heart. I missed Millay. I wanted to tell her what had happened to me, to the town, since that terrible afternoon. I knew she would welcome me. I decided to send her a letter asking if Grace and I might join her for lunch one day.

I grew tired, so I poked the logs, locked the front door, and began to climb the stairs. The sound of approaching footsteps stopped me. I didn't want to open the door because I was afraid a visitor would destroy the fragile happiness taking root in my life, but somehow I sensed that I must.

■ ■ ■ ■

Dr. Waters' hands trembled on the teacup.

"Thank you," he said. "I hate to bother you. Especially after all your . . . trouble."

"It's all right," I said, eager for him to disclose why he had come. He took another sip of tea, however, and looked around the room as if seeing it for the first time. I heard a car drive past out front, and the distant cry of an animal in the woods. Perhaps a bobcat. How strange it was to live between civilization and the wild. Dr. Waters cleared his throat, scattering my thoughts.

"I'm going to tell you some things," he said. "These are patient secrets. It is wrong for me to tell you, but I've been thinking long and hard, and after what I saw that woman do to you and to this town, I realized you deserve to know. Maybe it will even bring you some peace."

I widened my eyes and leaned forward on the table.

"Remember the night Grace was born and I told you she certainly wasn't the first child in this town conceived and brought into this world out of wedlock?"

I nodded.

"Over the years I've delivered dozens. You

know some of the women. While some hastily married to prevent scandal, most gave away the babies. I'm not here to expose all of them, but to tell you about one who may be of particular interest to you."

I began to imagine the women he meant. In truth, I couldn't, nor could I see what any of them had to do with me.

"I delivered one such child of Agnes Dwyer."

I gasped and sat back in my chair, covering my mouth with my hand. He sipped his tea and continued.

"When she was a teenager, she fell for an actor — an out-of-towner — in a traveling theater group. He got her pregnant and left her heartbroken and alone. Her father wanted to disown her, but her mother begged, and her father conceded to let her stay as long as she remained hidden during the pregnancy, and gave the baby up for adoption once it was born."

He stopped to finish his tea while I tried to make sense of his story. I still couldn't believe he was speaking of Agnes.

"It was a black time for her, and I worried she'd do herself harm, but she made it through in secret. No small feat for a socialite about town. Her parents told the world she was abroad with an aunt and kept her tucked away at a house they owned in Austerlitz. I attended to her health and eventually the birth. It was a boy, and she put up a terrible crying fight after he came, but her father got his way."

I let Dr. Waters' words sink in, and I was shocked at my compassion for Agnes. I couldn't imagine being forced to give up Grace. What if I had lost not only my lover, but also my girl? What kind of person would I have become?

Dr. Waters stood and put on his hat. "Please keep this between us."

"Of course," I said.

I opened the back door for him. He passed me to go outside, and at the bottom of the staircase turned to wish me good night.

"Doctor," I said, "thank you for telling me. Knowing it helps me . . . understand."

He nodded, and opened his mouth as if he wanted to say more, but the moment passed and he started off down the path. I watched him until the night folded in behind him.

VINCENT

Knowing death was coming did nothing to lessen its blow.

For a while I've known deep in my soul's roots that Mother was dying. She kept speaking of the mountain laurel we'd brought with too much enthusiasm, too much gratitude for so small a thing. She wrote with a weak hand, making no effort to align her words or disguise the truth that she might not live long enough to see the spring.

Oh, her body will see spring, because it will be the very food on which the blind worms feed to enrich the soil. The laurels will bloom from her very hands. Her stomach. Her eyes. She will feel the vibration of the rain on the earth above her, and how it will decompose her bed and her body until she is one with the earth. And she will be in my earth, here at Steepletop, with me for as long as I take my breath. How I wish that I could curl up with her, deep inside the belly of the place where we will bury her.

They are coming. The dogs, Alstair and Ghost Writer, have been circling me and my sister Norma. Our other sister is across the ocean in Paris with her husband, begging us to conjure her and give her love to Mother. Norma's husband, Charlie, is here with us and the hired men. I wish Laura could be at my side, but she cannot make it in the terrible snow that has fallen. She has sent a scarf patterned in small harps, honoring the harp weaver. I do not know if it is intended for me or for Mother, so I wrap Mother in it to keep her warm.

I follow the dogs to the front door and open it to the night. She reaches in her cold fingers and steals my breath as the sleigh approaches. I feel as if I am in a tomb, hit with this savage chill, this pure silence. As they come closer, bearing the coffin, I see the breath of the horses, the swinging lanterns, my husband, who has just lost his own mother across the ocean, tall and dignified, honored to escort my mother here for a final time.

He pulls up to the house and our hired men and Charlie carry the coffin inside to lay my mother out in the front room, where dear, dark Sappho will watch over her when my eyes are too heavy to do so. We will bury her on the east side of the property, with the laurels.

While the men begin preparations for the burial, we sit at the coffin's side and sing songs like we used to when we were three young girls with our mother, alone in the warm cocoon of our home at the shore, where the miserable stink of death had not yet reached us.

Norma and I are half-mad with grief.

We have been with her body for four days,

while each hour is announced with explosions. It is as if we are in a winter war zone. It is Argonne and the enemy is attacking in the hard, cold snow. But it is not an enemy. It is Eugen and the men, blasting the rock in the laurel grove where we must put her body. She must go there in the grove, but the damned mountains' roots reach so far through the hills that only dynamite can hollow her cavern.

Boom.

Norma and I flinch. I return to the piano and play another song. We drink another glass of champagne and tell another story. I want Laura. I want George. I want Kathleen to get on a boat and come home.

Eugen tells me to sleep. Charlie tells Norma. They don't understand that we cannot leave her or she will die for real — a soul's death from abandonment.

We've left her alone too much as it is. While she lived and complained of stomach pains, we allowed the acid in her to dissolve her from the inside out instead of helping her. We thought that she, a nurse, would seek her own medical help. Now she is dead. She will be cold in the winter rock, alone, a mile away from the house. I wonder if her grave should be closer.

Eugen looks at me with some new emotion I do not like.

"She will be buried where we blasted," he says.

I pull on my riding boots. My leather coat. My cap.

I take my coat off again, and slip on the purple robe. This is a procession. She is royalty, my mother. I must attend her as such.

I pull the coat back over my robe and grab my gun. Norma carries the gladiolas Eugene O'Neill sent. Charlie has a lantern. Eugen, a bottle of champagne.

I am coming undone.

We hike the mile across a path the men have dug. They have dug for two days through ten feet of snowdrifts. They have blasted the mountain so we could tuck our mother in it.

When we arrive at the grave, I am nearly broken. This place is stark and cold. It is lonely and strewn with burned rubble. We cannot leave her here.

I start to say as much, but I am silenced. I think it is Eugen who silences me, but it is actually the large and dreadful presence of some *thing* that is not of us. I am almost mute.

The men lift her coffin from the sleigh.

Norma covers Mother with a blanket of yellow roses. The men lower her into the ground.

I find my voice in a hymn we used to sing. "Lead, Kindly Light."

Then I lift my gun and fire.

Once.

Twice.

Three times for Mother.

I pass the gun to Eugen.

He fires thrice for his own mother.

How I wish to be a bird circling high overhead so he could put a bullet through my heart.

Thirty-Four

LAURA

Before Father Ash left Chatham, I brought him a new hand-stitched stole, and Grace drew him a picture of the "statue of Grace," as she called it. Gabriel and several others joined us to wave him off as he boarded the southbound train. Father Ash promised to come for a visit in the summer for the blueberry festival. I tried to tell him with my eyes how much he meant to me, and that I wished him well. His leaving filled me with great sadness, and I was still in the grip of the melancholy and my confusion over my feelings toward Agnes after Dr. Waters' confession.

I spent the next nights in a state, in and out of sleep, plagued by nightmares of my father, Agnes, Daniel. I questioned that I had turned Daniel away — denying Grace a father — and wished desperately that I could talk to someone about it. I considered

Gabriel, but at this beautiful, fragile place of beginning in our relationship, I could not introduce doubt. I wished I could lie nose to nose with my sister and talk it out with her, but she was rightfully consumed with little James.

As dawn snuck into my room, I turned to look out the window I had not bothered to cover, and saw the steeple of the church illuminated by the sun. I watched as the light moved over it and knew what I must do. After I dressed and made breakfast for Grace, I took her hand and crossed the street to the church.

Our new pastor, Father O'Leary, was much older than Father Ash, with a stiff countenance, lines around his eyes and mouth, and thinning gray-blond hair. Everyone said he came with the highest praise from his last church, but I didn't yet know him outside of polite greetings after Mass.

I instructed Grace to sit quietly with Dolly, and entered the confessional. I felt that gripping fear, like standing on top of the falls, knowing I'd have to jump. How could I ask a priest if I'd done the right thing by denying my daughter a true father? How could I ever forgive Agnes for trying to have Grace taken from me?

After his greeting, I took a deep breath

and began telling him everything. I had a sensation like hovering outside of myself, separate from what I said, and dreaded the moment when my body and mind would reunite to face judgment. When I finished, he was quiet for a short time. I felt disoriented from my conflicting emotions. He began to speak in a voice gentler than I would have imagined.

"My child, calm your troubled heart."

I looked up through the screen, wondering if I'd heard him correctly.

"The chance you had with that man is over. He is married to another, and if he gets a divorce, Church law would prohibit him from remarrying. You have confessed your earlier sin of lying with him before marriage and when he was with another, yes?"

"I have."

"Then you are absolved from that. Your duty is to your child and her best interests, and it seems that marrying that man would not be in her best interests."

I was moved by grace.

"There is healing of our souls in suffering, though it is hard to understand when we walk those valleys. You have suffered these years, but have faith and allow your future to give you a chance at joy. God wants that for us."

My tears began and I felt a great release.

"As for the woman who hurt you, who wanted your daughter taken away, please pray for her, as the Son prayed for those who persecuted Him. When you pray for your enemies, you see them as God sees them — with all of the pain and heartbreak that have made them what they are. She has a wound from where her child was torn from her, and when she sees you with your daughter, that wound bleeds."

He raised his hand to the screen and asked me to place mine on his. Then he raised his other hand and said a blessing over me.

"For your penance, go to the statue of Our Lady. Pray for your daughter's father's soul, and for that of his estranged wife and her mother. Ask for guidance in raising your daughter, and pray for all those whose suffering is so great that they lose their senses."

We concluded, and I pulled a handkerchief out of my purse to wipe my eyes before leaving the confessional. I thanked him, and stepped out to see my girl waiting in the colored light of the stained glass like a benediction.

Dinner with Gabriel that night was charged

with more undercurrents than the Stony Kill.

I had seen him in the street after leaving the church earlier that day, and blurted an invitation before I knew what came over me. He did not hesitate to say yes. He brought a bag of caramels for Grace from the Candy Kitchen.

All through dinner we played an unspoken game with each other: How many ways could our touch seem accidental yet have purpose? How could we communicate to the other without looking in the other's eyes?

Our knuckles met when we both reached for the butter, and we waited to pull them apart while laughing at Grace's silly chattering about how happy she and Dolly were to be wearing matching pajamas at the dinner table.

"Salt, please," Gabriel said.

I rested my face on my hand and answered one of Grace's queries about why the grown-ups weren't wearing pajamas while passing the shaker to Gabriel. When he touched it, I didn't let go. His laugh was for me but Grace thought it was for her, and in a way, it was. The slow weaving of our lives together would benefit her.

The dance continued through dinner until

Gabriel made the boldest move. We sat across from each other at the table, and he slouched down a bit until our knees met. Then he arranged his legs between mine, and I couldn't help but look at him with heat burning up my neck.

"I need water," I said. "Ice-cold."

"Gracie," he said, "your mama's burning up. She needs cold water."

"On fire?" said Grace, with some alarm.

"No, silly Gabriel," I said. "Just thirsty."

Grace pushed her glass to me and I took a long drink.

Gabriel suddenly stood. "Clean or read?" he asked me.

"Clean."

Gabriel carried Grace to the fireside while I cleared the dinner dishes. She nestled into his large lap with Dolly, and he read to her from her library books. While I washed the dishes, I could hear his deep voice and her high laughter from the other room. Before I knew it, and without fully understanding why, I wept. I stifled my cries so they couldn't hear me, choking down my own emotion. I collected myself, and a few minutes passed before I felt his hands on my shoulders, and heard his voice in my ear.

"You deserve this," he said. "And more."

He reached for the towel and I turned to him. He lifted the cloth to my eyes, and then rubbed my sudsy hands dry. I tried to laugh and apologize, but he shook his head.

"It's all right."

He moved to embrace me, when we heard glass shatter in the front room. We ran to check on Grace. She was crying, and my parents' oval wedding picture was facedown on the floor. I rushed to see if she was all right, and asked her what happened.

"I try to reach it."

I saw that she had pulled a footstool in front of the mantel, and I was in a fresh panic over what could have happened if she'd fallen into the fire.

"Never do that!" I said. "You could have gotten hurt."

"I want to show you," she said.

"Show me what?"

"I want you to be like that."

I stared at her for a moment until I realized that Grace wished I was married. I was speechless because I thought she was too young to understand such things. I caught Gabriel's eye, and saw that he understood.

With such an idea taking up the room, it was hard to call myself to action to clean up the glass, and I decided instead to take

Grace to bed. I started to walk her up the stairs, but she twisted and wiggled out of my grasp, and ran to Gabriel.

"You do it," she said to him.

He looked at me, helpless, and I nodded, and gave her a kiss on her forehead.

I returned to where the picture had fallen, and saw that the frame was destroyed. Careful not to damage the photograph, I removed each piece of glass and wood, and placed them in the wastebasket. When I reached the wedding picture, I saw the date December 3, 1907, written in my mother's hand on the back, and flipped the photograph over to look at my parents. I brushed off some of the smaller fragments of glass and noticed how much I resembled my mother. This thought comforted me, as did my father's likeness. How I wished they were still here to meet their grandchildren.

I placed the picture on my sewing table and had turned to fetch a broom and dustpan from the closet when I was shocked still.

December 3, 1907.

I was born in 1908 on May twenty-first. My parents were married five months before my birth. I was so shaken, I had to sit down. Dr. Waters' words about how he'd dealt with cases like mine didn't apply just to

Agnes, but also to my parents. They must have fled their hometown, gotten married, and started over here.

It was a strange progress of emotions marching through me as Gabriel joined me by the fire.

"She's in bed," he said.

"My mother was carrying me when she and my father married."

"Excuse me?"

"It's true. Look at the date." I passed him the photograph and he read it aloud. "My birthday is five months later."

"You're only just learning this?"

I nodded, still dumbfounded.

"Does it upset you?"

It took a moment for coherence to disperse my confusion, but I shook my head. "No."

I gazed into the darkness outside, thinking of Agnes. I thought of how much she had given up in her life and of how desperately she'd wanted love.

"Gabriel, can you stay here with Grace while I run an errand?"

He nodded, and I pulled on my coat and left the shop, heading toward Kinderhook Street.

I saw what must have been Agnes' silhouette

in the window. She was a dark form in an upstairs room blazing with light.

I forced myself up the path to her front door, though I wanted to run in the other direction, but like that night at the Follies, I was full of energy that compelled me onward.

A young woman answered the door, clearly a maid by her dress.

"May I see Mrs. Dwyer?" I asked.

"Is she expecting you?"

"No. I . . . I just need to speak to her."

The young woman frowned and looked me over before allowing me into the foyer. "May I have your name?"

I hesitated, almost certain Agnes would not see me. I half-hoped she'd turn me away so I could at least know I'd tried. "Laura Kelley."

The woman's eyes widened. My name meant something to her.

"Wait here." She hurried up the staircase, which turned at a landing before rising higher.

I gazed with awe over the foyer and the rooms that lined it. Every surface gleamed: polished wood floors, marble fireplaces, golden lettering on book spines, glass-covered photographs of her family that led to painted portraits of ancestors. I noticed a space next to Agnes' wedding picture, where only a nail jutted from the wall. I thought I knew what used to hang there.

The piano in Agnes' front parlor reminded me of the one in Millay's home. I had a sudden thought of Millay, inebriated and in misery following her mother's death, and resolved to visit her as soon as possible, before she began traveling for her reading tour.

The maid returned, jittery as a loose electrical wire. I imagined that she couldn't wait to tell her fellow servants who had come to visit their employer.

"She'll see you."

I was surprised to hear it, but stood straight and followed her up the stairs.

The second floor was carpeted and the walls were lined in pale, cool rococo rose wallpaper with a coordinating frieze border. The vases, curtains, and bedspreads were heavily floral with competing patterns, and I couldn't help but wonder if my mother had sewn any of the drapes and bedding. As we approached the large, carved maple doors at the end of the hall, my palms began to sweat. We passed a bouquet of dying flowers, and the combination of the foul water in the vase and the antiseptic smell in the air made me nauseous. The maid opened the door at the end of the hall with some drama, and stood aside to admit me.

Agnes sat in a wheelchair at the window, her back to me. Her view encompassed a number of houses and the Methodist church on Kinderhook Street, but didn't quite reach the center of town.

As the maid closed the doors, I stared at the woman who hated me. I was struck by how her hair hung limp, thin and steely gray in a short cut. What had happened to her glorious crown of white?

Then I saw it, just inside the white marble bathroom on the vanity: a wig on a stand.

I was horror-struck.

"Why are you here?" she asked. Her voice was small and trembled, so different from when it had projected over the crowd from the church steps.

My shock made me unable to respond at first, but I forced my gaze from the wig back to Agnes. I offered a silent prayer that I might find the right words.

"I wanted to inquire after your health," I said.

Her bitter laugh was followed by silence.

I continued. "And I want to tell you that I . . . I hope you'll return to Our Lady of Grace soon."

"You are quite the saint, Miss Kelley," she

said, her voice flat. "I have no wish to reenter the society of a town like this. What it has become."

I realized this was a fool's errand, but I ignored her words and continued. "The choir isn't the same without you. And our new priest is very kind."

Her bony fingers gripped the wheelchair, her hands like claws. "You know," she said, "I think I always sensed the truth about you and Daniel. It's one of the reasons I loathed you. One of them . . ."

Knowing the other reason was what kept me calm.

"I understand," I said. "I do hope that, over time, you'll be able to forgive me. And I will pray for you so that I'm able to do the same."

I waited for her reply, but she said nothing, so I turned and opened the doors to leave. I paused once more to look back at Agnes. She placed her face in her hands. I had an urge to go to her, but I knew that it would not be a comfort, at least not now.

As I walked home, I touched the hem of the dress of the statue, and felt lighter. Unburdened. Renewed.

VINCENT

I should telegram Laura to come and comfort me after Mother's death. I should spend these coming weeks and months with a fallen beauty who can show me the righteous way to reclaim my power in the light.

Instead, I place two large canning jars on the table by the fireplace, filling one with pure water and the other with bloodred wine. The firelight gives me glimpses of two scenes from my future. In the water shimmers a reflection of what my chaste night with Laura would offer: a renewal, clean air to fill my lungs, a recognition of my grief. The wine reveals a cosmos of flesh and chemical stimulation waiting for me in the pulsing veins of New York City.

I know what will happen if I choose the wine. Our bender will last the year. It will make the reading tour for *Fatal Interview* a blur. It will lead me to George in distant cities, with or without my husband. New poetry will emerge.

I lift my gaze to meet Sappho's black eyes and feel her urging me toward the wine. I reach for it and drain it in a long drink that leaves tracks of red running down the sides of my mouth and neck. When Eugen enters the room, I don't bother to wipe my face.

"Pack our bags," I say.

■ ■ ■ ■

PART THREE:
1939

■ ■ ■ ■

FROM RENASCENCE

And as I looked a quickening gust
Of wind blew up to me and thrust
    Into my face a miracle
Of orchard-breath, and with the smell, —
I know not how such things can be! —
    I breathed my soul back into me.
              — Edna St. Vincent Millay

THIRTY-FIVE

LAURA

I arrived at the theater early to meet Millay before her reading, as she had asked. We were at Clark University in Worcester, Massachusetts, where she had sold out the house. As we moved through the lobby, an announcement was made that the program would be starting fifteen minutes later than projected. I wondered if she was well.

I left Gabriel at our seats. My outdoorsman was uncomfortable in his fine suit, but so handsome. I kissed him and ran my thumb over his mouth, where I'd left a trace of red lipstick. Then I walked away, sashaying a bit, and glanced over my shoulder to wink at him. He smiled broadly and used his hat to fan his face.

I'd gone a little daring with the evening dress I'd sewn, allowing the neckline to plunge, selecting a sumptuous shade of burgundy, roping a long strand of pearls twice around my neck. The pearls were real — an anniversary present from Gabriel that he said he'd been saving for since our wedding day, years ago. It was our first night out without the children in longer than I could remember.

I caught a glimpse of myself in the tall gilded mirror in the hallway, and noticed the flush in my cheeks and the swell of my chest. I wasn't certain, but I thought I might have a little secret growing inside me, a new member to add to our tribe. Grace would be delighted, and would surely hope for a sister to balance her two little brothers. Gabriel would too. He just said at the dinner table that it felt like someone was missing.

We lived in a house we'd built an acre from Sam and Callie's place, by the river. My old house was now entirely my shop, with the upstairs used for sewing and storage, and the downstairs a showroom. I loved to sit at the windows in the room that used to be my bedroom, and work in the light of day while watching over the town and taking in my view of the statue of Our Lady of Grace and the far-off mountains. I'd started a theater company with our friends, and I costumed the actors in the amphitheater in the creations that had lived in the pages of my sketch pad. Caroline Hagerty had written and directed several plays for us. Gabriel built sets and sculpted on commission from local businesses and wealthy families on the side. His full-time job was as the grounds and building supervisor at the hospital. We still heard from Father Ash — now a bishop in Pennsylvania — several times a year, and he came back for the annual river potluck festival.

Everette was the Speaker of the New York State Assembly, and he and Marie had two boys and a girl, who folded in nicely with our brood. They were a loving bunch of cousins, whose adventures took place on the same paths Marie and I had hiked, in the same school we had attended, at the same soda fountain where we'd flirted. They didn't know how much they missed by not knowing our father, and how much richer their time together would have been with a grandfather like him, but there was no use dwelling on the past. Not for any of us.

I walked through the halls behind the stage, glancing around doors and corners in the gloomy shadows. The dark wood walls and musty spaces smelled ancient. Out of the corner of my eye, I saw a woman who looked like Darcy Dempsey, and my heart pounded. On second glance, it was clearly not her. Darcy had left Chatham after Agnes had died from a second stroke, mere weeks after I'd visited her. Daniel had had his marriage to Darcy annulled, and it was said that she had married again. Daniel had resigned from the hospital and they had both moved away. No one knew what had become of him.

I gathered my senses, and was about to turn around and ask for directions when I heard Eugen's voice. I followed the sound, and as I ran my hand along the wall and around the corner, I noticed that he was speaking in the high and patronizing way one would use to address a small child.

"Little Nancy, we mustn't fuss," he said. "You are always a beautiful girl."

A simpering, babyish voice responded, "No, no. You're just saying that."

"Tsk, tsk. Drink these down, Scuttlebutt. It will be over before you know it."

"Promise?" the voice said. "Little Nancy needs her beddy."

"And she will have her beddy and her big teddy, too." He giggled, and as I approached the door, I stopped short. It was only Eugen and Millay in the room. He placed pills on her waiting tongue, and held a glass of water to her mouth. When she finished drinking, he patted her lips with a handkerchief. I tried to slip back into the shadows but they saw me. Their heads turned at the same moment, and their eyes widened.

"Laura," said Millay, in the voice I knew.

I hesitated a moment, and then stepped into the doorway.

I was shocked at how the two of them had aged since I'd last seen them, which must have been at least a year ago. We'd kept in touch over the years; she allowed only me to create her reading wardrobe, but with her travels and my family and business obligations, we'd let time get away from us.

Eugen's hair was nearly white, and deep lines had formed under his eyes. He was slightly hunched and he lit her cigarette with a trembling hand before having a coughing fit. She patted his back from her chair, and motioned for me to approach. Her skin was puffy and white, her lips pale and cracked. Gray streaked her copper hair.

"Hello," I said, trying to hide my shock. "Has it been a whole year?"

"Too long," she said.

A woman emerged from the corner of the room. She helped Millay stand, handed her burning cigarette to Eugen, and supported Millay as if she were an invalid while they stepped to the rack of cloaks and gowns. I felt a flutter of excitement, seeing my creations hanging so beautifully together.

Millay slid her robe to the floor, exposing her mostly naked, aging body. She wore only a brassiere and panties, and I could see how her breasts sagged and that she had accumulated weight around her stomach. I was astounded at her appearance. Had it been only nine years since the first fitting? How did I not notice this deterioration the last time I measured her? I recalled that she had invited me to Steepletop at night. We'd drunk wine. She had me measure her with a nightgown on. That was why I hadn't noticed.

The woman instructed Millay to lift her arms, and slid a silk slip over her body. I tried to avert my eyes, but Millay had seen my shock. She stared daggers at me.

"Aging is hell," she said.

I rearranged my face to appear more relaxed. "Oh, I don't know," I said, lamely. "We all do it."

I was suddenly aware of myself in her dressing room mirror. My blond hair shone in the soft light. My curves were accentuated. My lipstick was a perfect match for my dress. I wanted to shrink away from here.

Millay walked up to me.

"Would you kiss me now, Laura?" she said with her smoky, alcoholic breath. "Would you press your supple lips to mine to give

528

me some color? I'd do anything to drink from your youth."

Not a day might have passed since the first time I'd felt that she wanted to consume me. I was a mother of three, a respected businesswoman, an aunt, a wife, yet before Millay, I felt like the shivering, stained girl from a decade ago. I looked at myself again, and reminded myself who I was.

I reached into the small clutch in my hand and pulled out my lipstick. "Here," I said, willing strength into my voice. "Take it. The fountain of youth in a scarlet tube."

She smiled, but it was more of a sneer, and she took the lipstick from my hand and held it up for her maid. The small woman took it and placed it on the dressing table.

"You are a cruel beauty," she said to me. "You always have been, but I suppose I wouldn't have you any other way."

She took a step back and faltered a little, seeming on the verge of fainting. The maid and Eugen came to her sides and held her propped between them.

"Almost there," said Eugen. "We need you to be strong tonight. It's the last night of the tour. Put on Laura's gown. All will be well."

As the maid stepped over to the rack, I held up my hand to stop her, and selected the gold dress myself. I walked it over to Millay, holding it like an offering. The maid and Eugen moved aside while I slid it over her head, and fastened the hooks and buttons. I smoothed the brocade and lace with my hands down her arms and back, and knelt behind her to arrange the train. I walked around the front of her and picked up the lipstick, touching it gently to her mouth and holding the blotting paper for her when I finished. She leaned her head on my shoulder as if it was too heavy to hold erect. I applied her mascara, and brushed her hair so that it fell in soft waves on her shoulders.

I saw a hint of her former self, but I wondered how she would summon the strength and sobriety to make this last night of her tour a success. The lights flickered, and I knew I must leave her.

I lifted her hand to kiss it, but at the last moment, I leaned in and pressed my lips against hers. I didn't know what came over me.

Blood rushed to her cheeks.

I excused myself as I moved past the already seated theatergoers. When I reached Gabriel, I was trembling. He took my hand in his and looked at me with concern.

"Are you all right, love?" he whispered. "You're pale."

"Fine," I said, breathless.

The lights went black. The crowd hushed, and it seemed that an eternity passed. Then a single spotlight appeared over the center of the stage, where she stood. She was so small on the grand space she occupied, but then her voice began. It was deep and wide. It filled the auditorium so that it was as if she spoke in each of our ears. The gown gleamed gold in the light, and she was animated as I'd never seen. She seemed to grow like a tempest before our eyes. The gray in her hair had disappeared. The color in her cheeks complemented the dress. Her eyes gleamed, green as jade. They seemed to look right at me.

She was mythic, a goddess. The audience was transfixed.

We did not breathe until the stage went black and she was gone.

AUTHOR'S NOTE

The poetry of Edna St. Vincent Millay is a great inspiration to me. Here is a list of poems that informed this text:

"The Ballad of the Harp-Weaver"
"Winter Night"
"Dawn"
"To a Friend Estranged from Me"
"Buck in the Snow"
"Justice Denied in Massachusetts"
"West Country Song"
"The Anguish"
"To the Wife of a Sick Friend"
"To a Musician"
"Dirge Without Music"
"Lethe"
Fatal Interview: Sonnets

I set my novel in the village of Chatham, near Austerlitz, New York, but it is a reimagining of Chatham to suit my fiction. This

533

particular church does not exist. The Stony Kill Bridge does. The hospital situated as such does not exist, but the train station and clock do. There are other truths and fictions surrounding Chatham in my novel, but what I hope to embody is the spirit of a small town undergoing great changes. This is, after all, a work of fiction.

There is no record of Cora Millay visiting her daughter in October of 1930. I made it so to suit the story. Also, I combined several of Millay's 1928 parties into one. To the best of my knowledge, all other dates and times in Millay's life are accurate. Any mistakes are entirely my own.

ACKNOWLEDGMENTS

I continue to follow the bread crumbs of dead writers from one to the next, so I must thank Zelda and Scott Fitzgerald for leading me to the fascinating poet Edna St. Vincent Millay.

I thank God for granting me life experiences and people to enliven the page and support me on this journey.

I am grateful for the encouragement and guidance of my editor, Ellen Edwards; my agent, Kevan Lyon; and the entire team at New American Library/Penguin Random House for their enthusiasm, vision, and support. It is a true pleasure to work with all of you.

To the Edna St. Vincent Millay Society and Peter Bergman for his detailed tour of Steepletop and fascinating wealth of information, and to the Library of Congress Special Collections Division for their help with research materials, much gratitude to you.

To my family, particularly Robert and Charlene Shephard, and Richard and Patricia Robuck, thank you for your guidance and unending help.

To Jennifer Lyn King, my friend and critique partner, who manages to remind me again and again of the light and power in this process. For crossing oceans and states, and reading at double speed, I am so grateful.

To Kelly McMullen, who has inspired my interest in female archetypes, what it means to be a woman, the relationship of the sacred and the profane, and how my faith fits into my process, much peace, love, and gratitude to you, friend.

Finally, to my husband, Scott, and to my three sons: sitting at the table with you all each night in our home, watching you pursue your talents, sharing adventures with you, spreading out, and coming back together — my family, you are my greatest blessing. I love you.

SELECTED BIBLIOGRAPHY

In addition to the poetry of Edna St. Vincent Millay, I read many books, journals, and letters from and about my subject. My favorite biographies are Daniel Mark Epstein's *What Lips My Lips Have Kissed,* which reads like a love letter to Millay, and the incomparable Nancy Milford's *Savage Beauty.* The books listed below are a sampling of helpful sources about the period and the poet.

Barnet, Andrea. *All-Night Party: The Women of Bohemian Greenwich Village and Harlem, 1913–1930.* North Carolina: Algonquin Books of Chapel Hill, 2004.

Brittin, Norman A. *Edna St. Vincent Millay.* Revised edition. Boston: Twayne Publishers, 1982.

Epstein, Daniel Mark. *What Lips My Lips Have Kissed: The Loves and Love Poems of Edna St. Vincent Millay.* New York:

Henry Holt and Company, 2001.

Gurko, Miriam. *Restless Spirit: The Life of Edna St. Vincent Millay.* New York: Thomas Y. Crowell Company, 1962.

Hudovernik, Robert. *Jazz Age Beauties: The Lost Collection of Ziegfeld Photographer Alfred Cheney Johnston.* New York: Universe Publishing, 2006.

Leese, Elizabeth. *Costume Design in the Movies: An Illustrated Guide to the Work of 157 Great Designers.* New York: Dover Publications, Inc., 1991.

Milford, Nancy. *Savage Beauty: The Life of Edna St. Vincent Millay.* New York: Random House, 2001.

Olson, Stanley. *Elinor Wylie: A Biography.* New York: The Dial Press/ James Wade, 1979.

Stonehill, Judith. *Greenwich Village: A Guide to America's Legendary Left Bank.* New York: Universe Publishing, 2002.

Wilson, Edmund. *The Shores of Light: A Literary Chronicle of the Twenties and Thirties.* New York: Farrar, Straus and Young, Inc., 1952.

Wolczanski, Gail Blass. *Images of America: Around the Village of Chatham.* Charleston, SC: Arcadia Publishing, 2009.

■ ■ ■ ■

READERS GUIDE:
FALLEN BEAUTY

ERIKA ROBUCK

■ ■ ■ ■

A CONVERSATION WITH
ERIKA ROBUCK

Q. What inspired you to make Edna St. Vincent Millay the subject of your third literary-themed novel?

A. My studies of the Fitzgeralds for my novel *Call Me Zelda* led me to Millay. Two of F. Scott Fitzgerald's Princeton friends, Edmund "Bunny" Wilson and John Peale Bishop, worshipped Millay, and their adoration of her reminded me of my interest in her poetry, which I first read in college. Wilson's moving obituary for Millay in his essay collection *Shores of Light* inspired me to learn more about the poet who had such an "intoxicating effect on people." It didn't take long for Millay to cast her spell on me.

Q. A poet, a seamstress, and a sculptor — there's something poetic about that combination. How did you come up with it?

A. My visit to Millay's home Steepletop, a

seven-hundred-acre estate in the Berkshires, inspired the characters in my story. When I first saw photographs of the pastoral place, I imagined what an ideal retreat it must have been for Millay, where she could compose her poetry in peace. On my visit, however, I realized this was not necessarily so.

First, Steepletop is very remote. Traveling the winding mountain roads bordered with forests reminded me of the opening of Stephen King's *The Shining*. Once I arrived, I was struck by two things: First, it was almost blindingly bright, and, second, the terrible buzzing of bees could be heard everywhere. When I entered the house, the blank-eyed gaze of the large black bust of Sappho in Millay's parlor made me uncomfortable, and I was further disturbed to stand in the foyer at the bottom of the staircase, where Millay had fallen to her death.

When I walked upstairs into Millay's rooms, I was interested to see elaborate robes hanging in her bathroom, and to learn about her dramatic reading tour wardrobes. I was reminded of the poetry collection for which she won the Pulitzer, *The Harp-Weaver and Other Poems,* about an impoverished mother who magically weaves her son's fancy clothing on a harp until she dies.

All of these research ingredients blended in my imagination to form and connect my poet, seamstress, and sculptor.

Q. Millay's desire to plumb the heights and depths that life could offer, all in service to her poetry, makes her a fascinating figure. Why do you think we are drawn to her, and people like her? Do we secretly wish we had the courage to go where she dares to go? And as a writer yourself, how do you reconcile the need to feed your creative muse while remaining a responsible, "highly functioning" grown-up?

A. Women like Millay, who live so fiercely on the edge of what mainstream society might consider scandalous, are captivating in any time period. What I found most interesting about Millay and her husband was their belief that her experiences in life, love, lust, and pain were part of her vocation, and, therefore, worthy of being taken as far as she was willing to go. I'm sure we all have secret thoughts and fantasies that we either let loose or rein in, depending on how impulsive we are, how ingrained our moral beliefs are, or any number of other factors, but those who flout convention make fascinating characters.

So far my imagination has been able to

supply all of my edgy material, much to my husband's relief.

Q. *In the last few months, I've come across several mentions of Millay. Caroline Kennedy has quoted Millay's "First Fig" in interviews and suspense writer Sophie Hannah has called Millay one of her five favorite writers. Are we poised for a Millay renaissance?*

A. I'm intrigued by the idea of Millay's second renaissance, since it was her poem "Renascence," selected for an annual poetry anthology when she was just twenty years old, that initially made her a celebrity.

In Millay's own time, she sold out thousand-seat auditoriums on reading tours. Her adoring fans sent her endless correspondence about her poetry. Her collections were continuously being reprinted, and she was one of the first women to win the Pulitzer Prize. At her peak, Millay's writings made her approximately thirty thousand dollars a year, which would be nearly half a million dollars in the present day. Our time is rich with captivating women artists, musicians, and writers, and Millay is worthy to stand with the best of them.

I believe our culture is poised not only for a Millay renaissance, but also for a poetry renaissance. As our attention span constricts in response to the gadgets we use, poetry could supply a new consciousness with deep meaning in short form.

Q. *Through the character of Laura Kelley,* Fallen Beauty *explores what it meant to be a "fallen woman" in the 1930s, but in some ways, Edna St. Vincent Millay might also be considered a fallen woman. Would you share some of what you hoped to convey in this regard?*

A. I wanted to show how making judgments about people injects poison into communities, how frequently all is not what it seems, and how those who outspokenly oppose something that they see as corrosive are often battling aspects of the very behavior they denounce.

Through the women in particular in *Fallen Beauty,* I wanted to explore how we seek fulfillment, what it means to be an "ideal" woman (if there is such a thing), how our desires can either help to build us up or destroy us, and how we can remake our lives after we fall.

Q. *You mentioned once that car accidents were a hallmark of novels set in the twenties and thirties, which came as a surprise to me. Can you explain?*

A. The use of the automobile accident, or the vehicle as a symbol of violence for dramatic effect, is typical of works set in the twenties and thirties, when driving became more prevalent and cars were associated with certain freedoms. F. Scott Fitzgerald uses a car accident in *This Side of Paradise* and at the climax of *The Great Gatsby*. In *Appointment at Samarra* by John O'Hara, the car becomes a device for suicide. In 1936, Millay was in a car accident with Eugen in the driver's seat, in which she was flung out of the vehicle and into a ravine. Afterward, she suffered permanent problems with her back, which led her to abuse prescription drugs. A car accident seemed a fitting device for illustrating the trouble that becomes the catalyst for events in *Fallen Beauty.*

Q. Edna St. Vincent Millay seems to have been especially close to her mother. Can you tell us more about Edna's upbringing and family dynamics? Were her two sisters at all like her? And does she have any descendants through her sisters?

A. After her scandalous divorce from her

husband in 1900 for gambling, Cora Millay raised her three daughters alone, often leaving the girls for long periods to work as a practical nurse. Cora insisted on the education and betterment of her girls in spite of their poverty, and she was their greatest champion and supporter. They worshipped her, and Vincent was said to enjoy her times of illness because Cora would stay home to take care of her.

Vincent's sisters, Norma and Kathleen, were artists in their own rights. Norma was an actress in the theater and Kathleen was a writer, though she existed in Vincent's shadow. Neither had any children.

Biographers have noted the extreme closeness of the women, saying that they often lived and socialized together, wrote poetry for one another, and crafted strange, almost adoring letters to one another. I found Vincent's "love letters" to her mother both charming and unsettling.

Q. The three novels we've worked on together all explore the idea of redemption in one way or another. Is that a deliberate choice, or a theme that cropped up without your being aware of it?

A. I believe it was F. Scott Fitzgerald who said that writers have only one story to tell, so I suppose redemption is my story. My mission with Ernest Hemingway, Zelda Fitzgerald, and now Edna St. Vincent Millay is to show their humanity through their fascinating lives in order to honor them and remind readers of their work. I like to read novels that offer redemption in spite of hardship, so it's only natural that I employ similar themes in my own fiction.

Q. You've now explored in your novels Ernest Hemingway, Zelda Fitzgerald, and Edna St. Vincent Millay — all of whom were contemporaries of one another. From your current perspective, are there any commonalities you see in their lives and work, or any conclusions we can draw — however tentatively — about their relevance for our own time?

A. Commonalities I've discovered are the way they used real people in their fiction, often without regard for the feelings of those being exploited, though all three approached this differently. Hemingway fictionalized his experiences after he'd had them. Zelda wrote autobiographically, often exposing her own personality flaws and insecurities. Millay was in love with love more than she was with the people who received her brand of love, and she used those heightened emotions to inspire her poetry. In each instance, the writings seem corrosive to those involved, though the work is often brilliant.

As a writer, I'm interested in understanding the creative mind, and just what is necessary to make great art. I find that question relevant to any time. Stories are what help us make sense of and empathize with one another. Perhaps by studying the lives of others, we can learn from their mistakes. Millay often wrote about nature and the cycle of the seasons in her poetry, and she used nature's lessons to comfort and instruct herself in love. History has cycles, and examining the past helps us to anticipate the future.

Q. Are you ready to share the subject of your next novel?

A. The subject of my next novel is a very private gentleman from a long time ago who often felt isolated in spite of being surrounded by his loving family and accomplished contemporaries. I will not yet reveal his name, but I will say that through him, I will explore loneliness and, most certainly, redemption.

QUESTIONS FOR DISCUSSION

1. What was your overall reaction to reading *Fallen Beauty*?

2. How are both Edna St. Vincent Millay and Laura Kelley "fallen women"? How does each rebuild her life after her fall?

3. Discuss the changing dynamics between Laura and Edna over the course of the novel. How do they hurt and help each other? By the end, how would you define their relationship?

4. Discuss the many kinds of isolation in the novel. How much of it is self-imposed, and why do some characters choose isolation? How does community act to reinforce or counteract that isolation?

5. Laura is keeping her lover's identity secret. Discuss the secrets that other people

in town are keeping. Do Edna and Eugen keep any secrets?

6. Compare Laura's relationship with her unidentified lover and Edna's relationship with George Dillon.

7. What role does the statue of the Virgin play in the novel? Why do you think Erika Robuck included it?

8. Erika Robuck has said that *Fallen Beauty* is based on themes from Nathaniel Hawthorne's *The Scarlet Letter.* What do you think she means?

9. Talk about the various mothers in the book, and what we know about the choices they made. What kind of mother might Edna have made? What direction might Laura's life have taken if she wasn't a mother? Based on what the novel reveals about Cora, how do you think she helped shape Edna's life?

10. Do you think, like Edna, that artists should seek to live fully in order to have profound experiences to inspire their art? What price might an artist pay in doing so? What price does Millay pay? What about Laura?

11. Attitudes about out-of-wedlock births have changed dramatically since the 1930s, when this novel takes place. Do you have stories to share, perhaps from your own family, about women whose lives were affected by a pregnancy outside of marriage? How different is your own attitude to those held in the thirties?

12. At the end of the novel, Edna calls Laura a "cruel beauty." What do you think she means? How is Edna herself a cruel beauty?

13. What do you think you'll remember about this novel long after you finish reading it?

ABOUT THE AUTHOR

Erika Robuck is a contributor to the popular fiction blog Writer Unboxed, and she maintains her own blog, Muse. She is a member of the Hemingway Society, the Millay Society and the Historical Novel Society, and she lives in the Chesapeake Bay area with her husband and three sons. She is the author of *Receive Me Falling* and *Hemingway's Girl*.

The employees of Thorndike Press hope you have enjoyed this Large Print book. All our Thorndike, Wheeler, and Kennebec Large Print titles are designed for easy reading, and all our books are made to last. Other Thorndike Press Large Print books are available at your library, through selected bookstores, or directly from us.

For information about titles, please call:
  (800) 223-1244

or visit our Web site at:
  http://gale.cengage.com/thorndike

To share your comments, please write:
Publisher
Thorndike Press
10 Water St., Suite 310
Waterville, ME 04901